LEX

LEX

Reminiscences of a late 60's student

*Life at Washington and Lee University during
the late 1960s*

Andrew G. Hollinger

Writers Club Press
San Jose New York Lincoln Shanghai

Lex
Reminiscences of a late 60's student

Writers Club Press
an imprint of iUniverse, Inc.

For information address:
iUniverse, Inc.
5220 S. 16th St., Suite 200
Lincoln, NE 68512
www.iuniverse.com

Any resemblance to actual people and events is purely coincidental.
This is a work of fiction.

ISBN: 0-595-22236-6

Printed in the United States of America

*To **George Sherston;** a man who could never quite say "Good-bye to all that." and to **Lauren Schneider** who has, at last, taught me how to live "Good-bye to all that"*

Late Lament

Breathe deep the gathering gloom,
Watch lights fade from every room.
Bedsitter people look back and lament,
Another day's useless energy spent.
Impassioned lovers wrestle as one,
Lonely man cries for love and has none.

New mother picks up and suckles her son,
Senior citizens wish they were young.
Cold hearted orb that rules the night,
Removes the colours from our sight.
Red is grey and yellow white,
But we decide which is right.
And which is an illusion???

    —Graeme Edge

Preface

The reader is reminded that this "reminiscence" is a novel and, as such, is fiction. While the places and institutions are certainly real and much of the content was drawn from first person perception, the events and characters are entirely fictional. Any connection between the people and events described in this novel and actual people or events, no matter how plausible, are purely coincidental. As a "reminiscence" the scenes, mood, aura and vocabulary are presented in the author's view of the period's context with no effort made to make them more politically correct in terms of the social conventions, philosophies or policies of the institutions described (or society in general) at the time of publication.

This book is over 10 years old at publication. There have been at least three distinct versions. There are several manuscripts in circulation or in the possession of several people who have been kind enough to read it and provide me their thoughts. This last edition is the best and draws upon their suggestions and especially the editing of Lauren Schneider but, alas, has retained some of the errors, problems and clumsiness infused by me—for these, I apologize.

CHAPTER 1

*P*erhaps it is that we were the first TV generation, but I visualize almost every part of my life as scenes from a program. Not that I expect everything settled in 30 or 60 minutes, like TV; or to be wonderfully choreographed as in the movies, but I tend to edit out long evolutionary growth in favor of quick, graphic transition scenes, staged climaxes, and, of course, wonderfully intriguing and engaging openings, complete with soundtrack. Maybe the box's influence was too great—maybe not great enough; I don't know.

No director could have visualized a better opening than the reality of my first few days in Lexington. The photographic beauty was an added extra. Picture this; my entire family and I rolled into Lexington, Virginia September 1st, 1969. It was the second day of our trip south and for the last four hours we were enjoying the scenery of the wonderful Blue Ridge Mountains framing both sides of the Shenandoah Valley. The sun, the trees, the fields bordering the highway made for a perfect day. My father and I had been there almost a year before, during my college selection trip, so we had two days' familiarity with the town. Vague recollections were quickly reinforced as we turned off the interstate and entered what was legally a city but, in reality, was little more than a 250 year old village. From the east, the road into Lexington resembled any one of a thousand small southern towns. Lonely gas stations, a shabby cafe, and almost shack-like houses occupied the three blocks between the off ramp and the second most striking feature of the town.

Taking that third block's bend in the road brought you between the sand colored concrete buildings of Virginia Military Institute. Packed into several square blocks on the northeast edge of town, the hollow square barracks, classroom buildings, library, and faculty housing all looked alike, but out of place. Instead of a southern or medieval appearance, VMI had the color scheme and architecture like something out of the North African desert. Only the statue of Stonewall Jackson, the institute's patron saint, under the barrack's main arch and the confederate gray uniforms of the cadets on the parade grounds reminded you that you were in Virginia. There, somewhere around 2,500 young men carried on the tradition of THE SOUTHERN MILITARY SCHOOL (see movies Brother Rat and Mardi Gras) almost in complete opposition to the anti-military spirit of the times. But, it was absolutely picture-perfect and appeared to those outside to both know and enjoy its projected image. It was a West Point with charm. It was the school of Patton, and, more importantly, General of the Army, George Marshall—Architect of Victory and Savior of the Peace. It was a strong, old school having covered itself with glory during the unpleasantness between the states by not only sacrificing its engineering professor, Stonewall Jackson, to the Lost Cause but also by its student body losing a skirmish against Union Cavalry 35 miles up the road at New Market in 1864. The Union Cavalry had retaliated by burning the place to the ground. Being rebuilt in the early 1870s, it was, by far, the new school in town.

Lexington, with its barely 5000 inhabitants, (waiting another seven years for its first McDonalds) five traffic lights, six churches, and the seat of Rockbridge County will always be the one, true Shrine of the South. You see, it not only boasts of the final resting place of Stonewall Jackson but also his commander, General Robert E. Lee. After his defeat, Marse Robert had come to Lexington to head the other, older school. Starting in 1747 as Liberty Hall it had evolved to Washington College by Lee's tenure. But, wrapped around his grave had grown a small, patrician, and curiously outstanding college known as Washington and Lee University. It was there that I was going.

I had fallen in love with the place during my college trip. It looked like a college was supposed to look. All along the ridge at the top of a beautifully lawned hill were five Greek revival classroom buildings built in the 1830s. As if ordained by a set designer for a classic college movie, they were dressed in white pillars, red brick, and ivy—all shaded by huge, ancient hickory and oak trees. The back campus consisted of buildings added since the civil war and, though similar in nature and affect, could never compare in significance, charm, or the simple impact of the front campus. Those five buildings all faced the chapel, first Lee's office and then his grave. It also came to be the grave of his father and son. All; the chapel and the college, were dominated by a life size statue of the recumbent Lee behind the chapel's lectern. There, Lee was surrounded by the actual flags of Virginia's regiments loyal to him till Appomattox. It was almost pagan in its reverence to the leader of the Lost Cause, the paragon of southern virtue, the perfect gentleman, the true hero. God, it still sends shivers down my spine and brings tears to my eyes. This was what college was supposed to be; as I knew it had to be. Students in suits and ties (though we were to change all that), speaking to one another as they passed, going to and from their living arrangements in town to the "Hill" (meaning the campus), still practicing traditions dating from the institution's birth in the 1740s. Honor codes, fraternities, single sex; it reeked of a movie set. And, we were going in, just like the other 300 Freshman guys and their parents.

All of us unpacked with the help of our mothers, then hurriedly sent them off to one of the three motels in town to "freshen up." We dutifully waited and then attended them as they took us to out to one of the four respectable places for dinner—one last time. During that pause in our family identity, we became "college men" and went around our dorm floors to meet one another. W&L was a little unique in that we all had single rooms and were assisted in maintaining them by a "butler," one to every other floor (which was, even in those days, a bit anachronistic). We all recognized each other by condition rather than familiarity. We all looked almost identical: ears showing from new haircuts; new clothes too carefully worn and that outwardly robust; healthy appearance that comes from good living. All that would soon fade as the semester's life-styles became established. At dinner with our parents, and after in the dorms, we all radiated a delightful nervousness that exuded the desire to get started. Being at college in the late 60s was a new adventure, not only to us—but to the nation. Movies, Woodstock and <u>Life</u> magazine had shown us that, to some, there was adventure ahead. But, to most of us, those were images foreign to our experiences and expectations. We were good kids, had two parents, worked hard in high school, played sports and had bright futures. We were essentially the same as all the boys from decades past, but, what we did not know then (and do now) was that we were the last of a long line and the start of something not yet finished. But then, in our jeans and t-shirts, staying up late, talking and smoking, we were just new Freshmen, new to Lexington or, now what we learned to call it, "Lex." We were echoes and reflections of boys arriving since the 1870s.

I say the 1870s, but at least in American terms, the place had a history much older. There were the ruins of Liberty Hall about a quarter mile behind the present campus where the fiercely Presbyterian school had been organized in the 1740s. In reality it was just two three-story walls and half of one joining them together standing black and silent in a grove of oak trees. We would soon know that they were haunted. Because of this, they would be the objective of many a midnight walk, both with dates and without. This was the school that George Washington had seen before the French and Indian War. It was this school that had impressed him so much that in 1783 he gave, what was then, the largest gift ever given to a school. The trustees had named the school Washington College in his honor.

Much of the present campus had been built with the income from George Washington's gift and it was to this cluster of buildings that Lee, and his beloved horse Traveler, came after Appomattox. With the strength of his name and will, he had raised the money for much of the rest. One of his unique legacies was that his renown and character had—and continues today to attract a national student body. The campus he built, including the dorms, was still in use with only the barest of modernizations. Moreover, he set the standards, still in use today, for the academic intensity of the school and the behavior of its students. His concept of honesty, the virtue of liberal arts education, and his desire to bring many different types of Americans together, are still vibrant parts of the school.

The place reeked of that history. In those days of 1969, I swore I could feel the past seep into me and permeate everything I did. Boot scrapers protruded from the front campus building entrances. Most of the seats in class were wooden right-handed, row-chairs purchased en-masse during the 1870s in some "once in two life times" great deal. Even indoor plumbing had to be retro-fitted into the nooks and crannies of most of the front campus. Added to this was the character of the boys who came. Some were 3rd and 4th generation sons of southern industrial and judicial aristocratic alumni; some were the sons of families that were rich enough to desire the label of southern aristocrats; some wanted to assume the traditions or scholarship and some came just because it was the perfect place to avoid the draft. I came because I could not escape its aura and because no one else from my high school had ever gone there before.

Now, when I think back, I remember the second day, that first whole day on campus more clearly than all the rest that followed. I opened my first checking account, talked and tried to make friends with the boys on my hall and walked around to find my bearings so as to appear not-too-new at life in Lex. It was a short day, though. At four in the afternoon we would be bussed to an immediate two and a half day "camp" out at the Natural Bridge Motel—eleven miles away. The administration believed it would allow us to make friends in our own class before being devoured in the onslaught of fraternity rush. Rush itself consumed almost an entire week of constant activity. Only at the end of rush would classes and "real" or traditional college begin. All the logistical type activities, matriculation, registration and the photograph session for the Freshman face book were taken care of during the week of fraternity blitz.

No, that first day on campus, as a college student, minus parents and flush with the envisioned young adult freedom promised much. My next-door neighbor in the dorm was George. He was fat and from New Jersey. I could tell the minute he and I shook hands that morning he was destined to be one of the "out-crowd." He was already sweating and his new slacks were pressed. But, that early in the morning, he was all I could find to accompany me in exploration. By the time we walked the 20 yards or so (the army had not yet taught me to think in terms of meters) to breakfast, he was already out of breath. He talked constantly through the "Common's" breakfast line where we received our morning dollop of liquid eggs, my first grits of a lifetime, and coffee whose close proximity to motor oil would become as legendary as the gray mystery meat we would often have at dinner. He reported he was going to major in both pre-law and pre-med so he would be busy, much too busy for what he called "fraternity foolishness." I was already unimpressed and bored with his talk; and although I was not sure of what my major would be or what the hell a major really was, I already knew it would be tough enough not to have two.

I was in college because that was where boys of my socio-economic class and background went. Every boy in my high school went to college. Besides, there was a war on and college beat the draft hands down. The idea of trudging through the swamps of Viet Nam made the college decision very easy. More important, there were college girls to meet, to date, and to hopefully seduce. All together, there was a future to find. Half-way through the food I was already mentally tuning George out. I was not quite to the stage I would be in about a week, when I would be embarrassed of him and made efforts to avoid him, but I knew then, I would get there. However, he did want to take a walk around town and since that looked interesting; it became a perfect way to start not just "an" but "the" adventure.

After breakfast we walked out and off campus. The day was bright, sunny and warm. I tried to remember the street names as George and I walked that day in and about the town whose two traffic lights east-west and two north-south marked the boundaries of its world. Most of the shops seemed 19th Century and looked charming but dull. There were two movie theaters; one playing Disney pictures and one, for students, that showed posters promising lurid and exciting "skin flicks." Now, before you get the wrong idea, although we thought then that these movies were pretty hot, they rarely went beyond jiggling bare breasts and fat men, still clad in underwear, bouncing on them—barely today's cable. They were not the more lurid adult movies we were to find a couple years later in Roanoke.

There was the hotel "Robert E Lee" whose six stories was the single building of Lex's skyline. Two blocks down, just past the faintly pink Presbyterian Church there was the two-story Montgomery Ward store above which I was to live two years hence. There were several student cafes; the most promising named the "Liquid Lunch." A Chevrolet dealership, a drug store—complete with six stool soda fountain, two gas stations, the Kroger, the post office and the county courthouse buildings—all old, a bit shabby but new to me—were just awakening. The homes on the skirts of the business cluster were beautiful and quaint having deep lawns on narrow streets (they had not yet been transformed into one-way). In almost every block was a fraternity house, or some sort of student apartment, or just an obvious impact of the two schools' domination of the town. Most interesting to us, and we noticed it then, were the people. Between September and June the students took the place over and you didn't see too many townies on the street. They had already started disappearing.

This particular day was the traditional start of "Rush Prep." All the houses were being opened, cleaned and painted for the recruiting activities that would start later in the week. Upperclassmen were swarming everywhere. Joyous reunions, loud music and parties seemed to be going on in every block, even at 9 in the morning. They were everywhere, confident in their knowledge of the town and the system. Hair a bit more ragged, jeans truly worn, everything about them advertised they were not Freshmen to us on our walk. We were in awe.

What I remember most were the girls. They were imported from Randolph Macon Women's College in Lynchburg, Hollins in Roanoke, Sweet Briar in Amherst, Mary Baldwin in Staunton, a bunch of "lesser" schools like Madison and Bridgewater, and the already notorious Southern Seminary Junior College for Southern Women in nearby Buena Vista—already termed "BV." Steve, a dark haired and angular guy from the second floor of our dorm and self-proclaimed expert on everything feminine, had already set us straight. Sitting with us at breakfast, he told George and me all about the place. At least according to him, it seemed that most of them, the Semies, were horseback riding majors (Equestrian Arts). This activity made them so horny that they were likely to become nymphomaniacs. Steve reported this to us as if he were reading from Scientific American. Now, it is hard to believe he was serious or that he wasn't trying to put over some sort of complex joke on us, but he sat there, with a straight face, secure in his knowledge and that he was helping us out. He said that he knew this from good authority since he had gone to prep school in Staunton and his brother had graduated from W&L last year.

While he was telling us this I remember consciously observing both boys seated with me. George was visibly agitated to the point of eating his coffee cup. George bought Steve's report and his flustering made him seem incredibly immature. As much as I wanted to believe all this, and thought of it as vaguely shocking but very "adult," I resolved not to show any reaction. Second, Steve was the first boy I had ever met that appeared to have his hair styled. Not just cut, mind you, but styled, so that his madras shirt and black slacks would project a worldly and sophisticated aura, even at breakfast. This totally orchestrated and integrated appearance impressed and intimidated me. I was worried. If college girls expected or required this, I could never compete—at least not now. Just before we left, he stopped eating, leaned forward and started speaking to us in an especially earnest hush. He asked that if we were lucky enough to find a nympho, to let him know -as he would us—we could all have our fun and fulfill the girl as well without getting too many guys in the game. Steve was serious. I couldn't see any signs of humor or being "conned." George, on the other hand, was almost shaking, and beads of sweat started to trickle down his forehead. I may have been a kid from the suburbs (and a virgin at that) but I knew a line of bull when I heard one. However, the very idea of there being the slightest bit of truth to this ridiculous story excited me no end. It would be part of the free life, college of the sixties, images of free love, and the reason we were all trying to grow our hair as fast as we could.

I, however, was not out for a beautiful nympho. Well, not just a beautiful nympho, anyway. That was certainly part of it, but I was out for the whole scene. The jovial, adventurous and almost combat infantry intimacy of the fraternity was as big a part of the dream as the whore-angel who would become devoted to me during this four-year span. I wanted to be brilliantly engaged by wise professors and understand rather than memorize. I wanted friends to grow old with and with whom I would recall fabulous adventures that others around us would never believe. I had internalized all the parts of the dream that college was supposed to be. But, as we walked up and down the streets of Lex, I still could not help being fascinated by all the girls smiling, laughing going into and working around the fraternity houses.

These were the legendary "dates" helping fraternity boys with their chores. It was right out of the Ricky Nelson College episodes of <u>The Adventures of Ozzie and Harriet Nelson's</u> TV show. They, the girls, were dressed in everything between shorts and t-shirts to skirts and blouses, but all, compared to the high school girls I had known, were horribly adult. Being the twilight of the old era, I did not know then, but would a scant few weeks later, that they could not stay overnight except in "approved housing." All the girls' schools had regulations for visiting overnight, which were vengefully enforced. If the girl was not at the appropriate rooming house (an industry that abounded for decades only to die in one weekend after Kent State) for bed check at midnight, she found herself going home not to school, but to her parents. Birth Control was not only unavailable (except in the Texaco station in the men's room machine for a quarter a piece or at McCrum's drug store behind a counter guarded by a grey-haired 180 pound battle-axe of a woman who scared freshmen with a simple grimace), but also deemed to be unacceptable for the young ladies of these colleges. Girls found with diaphragms or rubbers, the pill not yet legal for underage, unmarried women—were also sent home.

Throughout our Freshman year we learned all sorts of rules like this. Girls were not to be in our dorm, or men in theirs, when we visited. We, and they, had to dress for dinner at our schools—meaning ties for us and dresses for them. They could only have a specified number of "weekends" in Lexington for each semester and even these were grade-dependent. On our side, we had the fraternity housemother (another casualty of Kent State) who would make sure that no girl gained access to the top, or sleeping, floor of the house. This was still the era of social rules as well. One couldn't call for a weekend date after Tuesday for fear of being turned down simply because you called too late. All this was unknown to me on our walk, but surmised from what the movies or TV had taught us. This was the new culture into which we were thrust, albeit for a very short time. It was just like joining a very old club. Because of these ancient rules, we also wanted to join the old tradition of breaking them—in all the prescribed manners. What we didn't know then was that we were the last initiates—the system would die before the year was out.

George and I returned in time for lunch and, after another round of hallway bull sessions, off we went into Freshman Camp. This was to be the first real event of the semester. The buses were rather quiet as I remember. We talked, but all but a few seemed rather subdued. There seemed to be a realization that "it" was going to start.

It was at Freshman Camp that I was to meet one of the most important boys of my years in Lex. That first evening, we were all supposed to go to a "camp fire" where we would sit and learn about campus organizations and the like. Some of the truly adventurous quietly, though making sure almost all the boys knew, sneaked out to look for booze, marijuana and / or girls. I think the reality of it was that they walked two or three miles in the dark and found a rural grocery that sold beer to underage students. These exploits, or rather the fantastic expansion of these exploits, dominated all the talk for the entire next day. But, that night at the fire, there was a question about a History Club. The author of the question was a tall, slender (no, not skinny, because even though I was about 6' and only 120 pounds, we were not skinny but slender!) boy with a radical Beatle style hair cut. It was dark enough that all I really got to see was his silhouette. Being a history buff myself, I quickly foraged through the crowd afterward and found him before the meeting broke up and we all sauntered off to our rooms in the motel.

He was Fran Campbell from Wyoming and, since his name was far off in the alphabet from mine, we were not even in the same block of rooms, even though we were five to a room. Finding a bench

and street light, Fran and I talked till well past midnight quietly testing each other about how much military detail we could muster in
the friendly give and take discussions about historical trivia. I did
reasonably well. Even though I was, and am, no slouch, his grasp of
things military was truly awesome. Our discussions quickly tired and
out-stripped the other boys who had stopped by our discussion
before drifting off, one by one. We never noticed them leaving and
wouldn't have thought of them as anything but so many casualties if
we did. He and I smoked endlessly and argued, joyously, the merits
of Confederate organization before Stonewall's death at Chancellors-
ville, the benefits of stirrups to the Franks at Tours, the effectiveness
of daylight precision bombing in WWII and the superiority of the
German 88 to any other artillery piece of the 1940s. We criticized the
great and defended the unpopular. Gladly, happily, we fell into what
lasted for all four years, a love on his part for all things German and,
on my part, of all things British. Neither admitting to the other that
anything German or British had much merit (depending on which
side we favored for the day) we would delight in these endless com-
parisons. Almost at dawn, out of each other's cigarettes I crept into
the stifling, almost claustrophobic room. Things got so busy that I
almost forgot Fran's name for a while and only got to know him
again after we found that we were part of the same fraternity.

For two days we endured Freshman Camp. It was much like basic
training was to be in the army. Everyone shed their pajamas for T-
shirts (though it would be another year till anyone had anything
written on them) and "U-trou," again mostly our family supplied
white briefs. We talked and a few bragged about the past. Soon we
got through all the standard questions with which we would again be
deluged during Rush. "Whereyafrom?" "Whatsportyaplay?" "What-
doya think of the new XXX album?" (The XXX could be Chicago or
BS&T for the trendy but not deviant; Crosby Stills & Nash for the
proto-woodstockites; Beatles for the traditional; Hendrix for the
heads; Joan Baez for the few politicos; and Its a Beautiful Day or

Moody Blues for those quietly looking for psychedelic adventurists.)
We were all careful to be just right among our new comrades. Farts
were passed silently, pimples were not picked in public and everybody smoked. We all were part of the "college kid" aura just waiting
to bust loose. We were finding those with whom we would share the
ensuing four years and their traumas. Two major memories stand
out. The first and almost un-thinkable now was that no one yet wore
jeans as constant attire or as a symbol of our newly subscribed "student-hood." Second, was the big scandal: we lost two boys the second
night in Camp to the drifting and mysterious rumors of being "discovered together." If I knew then what pot smelled like, I don't think
I would have found it there. We were all still too scared of the
"authorities." It was still too illegal to chance it that close to adults,
teachers and the like. At best violators would go to Viet Nam. More
to the point, there probably weren't but eight or ten of the boys who
had tried it, no less had some on their person. No, all that was to
come.

Freshman camp soon dissolved into Fraternity rush. For six solid
days the 300 of us visited and slowly tried to find our place in one of
18 established fraternities authorized by the school. Just like we were
led to believe, all the "houses" were there. The jocks; the Jews; the
rich; the face men (blonde and ruggedly handsome); the southern
anti-intellectual partiers, and the boys who were southern anti-intellectual partiers but not so good-looking and / or rich as to get in the
first one; the proto-hippies (though we did not think of them as
"heads" or "freaks" yet), the nerds, the northerners, Texans, Califor-
nians and several in-between were all represented and actively
choosing their newest members. Endlessly rehearsed Freshman
facades were quickly seen through or just dropped from exhaustion.

Each fraternity hosted "Open Houses" (two in the afternoon and
two in the evening) that the Freshmen could choose to attend. Later
in the week, each fraternity asked Freshmen whom they were
recruiting to "Rush Dates." "Have we gotchya comin back?" Later,

when I became an assistant rush chairman, I realized the strategy in all this, but then it was just a long, fuzzy blur. I met almost 700 new people. Each house talking about how diverse its membership was but, back in the dorms, those of us who were unfamiliar with the Greek alphabet could name each one by its unique brand of conformity. Each house tried to interest only the right group of pledges to continue its diverse yet precisely definable tradition. Beer, (only after the third day so as not to totally impede the frosh's judgment) cigarettes, talk of road trips, dance parties or "combos", winks about girls and even rumored fixed up liaisons with properly motivated Semies, filled our ears in order to convince us to join the "right house."

Usually it boiled down pretty quickly to one or two and then, thankfully, just to one. Almost all of us among the 300 found our place in the fraternity stratum of Washington and Lee. It was, pretty much, in the first two weeks that we were frozen for the ensuing four years. Those that did not—about 40 or so—were to be labeled Nufus (non-fraternity) and therefore banished by tradition to obscurity. Questioned the next morning, George said he would be too busy, but his face showed differently. I thanked God I was not in his shoes because, for all intents and purposes, it was then we lost George into the uncharted world of social oblivion. A casualty after two weeks in Lexington, he never recovered. I believe he transferred out at the end of Sophomore year, but don't know for sure.

Luckily, I had found my place among the living. It was one of the "northern-boys-whose-fathers-worked-for-a-living-and-were-only-middle-class" houses and thus not exactly on the top of the heap. No: it was, probably, only one or two from the bottom. Those houses consisted of the notorious or outrageous nerds and the funny looking "fish" and were thus in the social basement. I was glad to be where I was.

Ever since rush began in 1887, the LAST NIGHT OF RUSH celebration was the classic ending to this scripted by tradition opening scene. On paper, there were rush dates from 3:00 till 5:00, 5:30 till

7:30 and from 8:00 till 10:00. Since almost everyone was already pledged or designated, it was a drunk from 3 o'clock on. Rumors abound about this last party in all the houses. Though some houses tried to revive the tradition the next year, the happenings on Kent State, Viet Nam, DC and just the mood in general, forbid it. Most of all, I believe, it was a party that could not be topped. We were all in coats and ties for the beginning but I, for one, found myself in a strange pair of too-big jeans the next morning. Our House Mother, Mrs. Fazer, locked herself in her room around 8:00 P.M. to escape the frenzy. She claimed to remember very little of what happened. Our house, which had a hundred 8X10 window panes in kind of a picture window across the back of the second floor, lost seventeen of its windows that night, four of which were still out (though covered deftly by years and years of Saran-Wrap) when the house folded in 75.

There are stories from other houses of groups of Semies "gatoring" among the Freshmen. I can be positive that this did not happen to us. No, I accepted the bid on this last night of rush and joined the house. I drank too much beer with all the new brothers and tried hard to remember names and faces. It seems that as the night went on we were all wearing most of each can of beer. We joined arms and learned then sang the University song—the W&L Swing. We threw officers I did not know yet into the showers on the third floor. We rolled down the grassy hill behind our house to our softball field in an effort to throw up so that we could crawl back up and drink still more. We made passes at all the girls who seemed to disappear somewhere in the midst of the fray (probably with Mrs. Fazer). It was a movie scene sound tracked with Blood, Sweat and Tears, Rare Earth, Clapton and Chicago. Just before we left for the "quad" (the courtyard enclosed by the three wings of the Freshman "Old Dorm") I remember at least two or three inches of beer cascading down from the third floor, past our second floor vantage point, to the chapter and dining room level below. Arthur, a shadowy casualty of our first exams, was down there with several of the people whose age must have made them upperclassmen, catching the beer in a wash tub. This liquid was used as ammunition in milk pitchers by the Sopho-mores, who, though they lived on the third floor, were caught by us (the pledges and more upperclassmen) on the ground floor. We were keeping them down there with spraying beer cans. It became a mili-tary feat of daring for them. They braved our deluge to rush past us, up the stairs, only to be met by trash cans full of water, beer and who knows what, and forced back down. It was great! It never could be repeated. No one ever tried.

The battle was called a draw before we all set off, as tradition dic-tated, for the quad. There were close to 500 people enclosed by the U shaped Freshman dorm. Since the beginning of fraternities in the 1870s each house met there on the LAST NIGHT OF RUSH to estab-lish, re-establish or defend its moral dominance. While I never saw or heard of punches being thrown, there was plenty of pushing, shoving and yelling. "We're number one!!" was mingled with the Greek call letters or abbreviation of each group. "Beta, Beta, Beta"; "ZBT, ZBT, ZBT"; or as we would yell "Chi Alpha", all consuming to the yellers, yet absolutely meaningless to anyone more than 3 feet away. I don't remember the end of the party. Perhaps I wandered away, since it was the first time I had ever been drunk ,or at least that drunk. Maybe I passed out or half-way out and Mickey (the guy who would end up to be my best friend and mentor) put be in bed. I really don't know.

The next day I awoke at noon. Checking the card in my pocket I verified which house I had, in fact, joined and tried to get ready for the first day of classes the next day. It was a great beginning; just like the first, almost wordless minutes of a movie. The opening scene to all my hopes and dreams

CHAPTER 2

G oing to class or, going to school in general, was something natural to me and boys like me. Other than part time jobs in groceries, fast food restaurants, or the various family businesses, we had done nothing else since we were five. We were all professional students. To get here, or places like here, we had learned to earn good grades in all subjects—even those we didn't like. This is not to say we learned much. Most of us just practiced our craft of memorization for a test, psyching out the teacher, and learning what to produce for the desired grade as an almost unconscious part of our being. Some of us were unlucky enough to hit real obstacles. Mine was German. I had struggled with it throughout high school. It had kept me out of all sorts of honors, but now in college, I was sure that was past. What I was to find was that grades as I knew them were a thing of the past. Here, the sometimes mystically subjective "curve" was the almighty grade machine. In a class of fifteen there would be 2 A's, 3 B's and the rest C's or worse. It got worse in the advanced classes where they might number only six guys. While you had to be the best to get one of the high grades the converse was also true. You had to really suck to draw a D or F. That first year I was to get both, plus the unique distinction of getting an E.

Being a Freshman, we did not yet know who to pick for teachers or which courses were known to help one's GPA. Not that there were many such courses, since there were no sports scholarships; they weren't much needed. But, Art Appreciation (Look-at-the-pictures), Set Design (Hammers'n'Nails) and Music Appreciation (Drop-the-Needle) did wonders for lazy Upperclassmen's grades. No, freshmen were trapped firmly in the "core curriculum." But then, that was all we knew having graduated high school in the era before electives. We had all met with our advisor during rush and before matriculation. Mine was Dr. Oliver Bradley. He was the University Historian, about 90 years old, and the movie perfect picture of what a history professor should be.

I had received a letter from him that summer. It was full of pleasantries, wished me welcome to W&L, and asked me to see him at such and such a time and place that September. The letter itself, beyond the message, impressed me. It was even written on "Cosmos Club" stationery. I had, and have, no idea what kind of club it was in Baltimore, but the effect was electric. This was seemingly a scene right out of the movie <u>Mr. Chips</u>; leather chairs, books everywhere, old men arguing about forgotten facets of history; and only the British accent would be missing. The handwriting in a perfectly level, straight almost illegible scrawl completed the image. When I called on Dr. Bradley, after Freshman Camp, I was not let down. His office was on the top floor of Washington Hall, one of the five front, Colonnade, buildings. It was floor-to-ceiling books on all four walls including the space above the transom. There were two chairs, one for him behind the massive desk (whose heavy wood, dust and yellowing papers all looked as if from Lee's tenure) and one for me, considerably less comfortable, in front of it.

He stood up as I entered and reached over the desk to shake my hand. Taller than I had imagined, his soft southern drawl was too clear for his age. He had done his homework in that he knew not only my name and hometown, but also my high school record. I am not really sure, however, that he had given my Freshman year much thought. Not out of any laziness or lack of concern, but because, back then, there were few choices. English was a requirement, as was History. I could choose mathematics or Greek (some choice!), which science and which language I would take. Being no fool (or so I thought then) I took German, Calculus, and Chemistry—having taken them all in high school. (Yet, two of those three I would fail). Nevertheless, I was impressed. Dr. Bradley called me "Mister" and warned me about fraternities, life's priorities, women and not studying. The positive virtues of resolution and focus and purpose were outweighed by my graphic mental illusions of the dangers ahead. It was a fatherly chat, from a stern father to be sure, but a chat he said that he had been giving for more than 50 years here at the school. He related that he had several fathers and sons and was looking forward to his first third generation student soon. His eyes were focused on me and I felt I had now stepped into that line of endless students. I don't' remember the exact words of his speech—his soft, cool southern voice seemed more to project images than enunciate words and sentences. But, again, I was electrified. Such an explicit warning must mean that there was something to be aware of; there must be danger and adventure ahead. Perhaps I had been sheltered but I had never heard of anybody being warned about the dangers of "irresolute" life in high school.

The warning about women and a specific "sort" of women stirred me to a quick, surreptitious daydream about what they must be like. He told me that as a "W&L Man" I might be thought of as a prime target for a "scheming girl bent on an upward marriage." (Please!) He was adamant that I should "keep my wits about me." I should think of each girl as if my mother was meeting them and consider what my parents and pastor would think about her character and manner. He went on in that vain for a few minutes, his left hand softly tapping the open book on his desk and his right vaguely pointing toward me. By that time, of course, I wasn't listening to a word in terms of internalizing the message, but was totally engulfed in the concept. I mean, just thinking of some beautiful, passionate coed luring me to her bed, just to marry me made me shiver. Me! I know, now, that Dr. Bradley didn't have much to worry about. Not that I was something undesirable, but the last time he had been aware of the social aspect of dating at W&L was in the 1930s—and that was hazy at best. Girls, or as they were beginning to demand to be called, Women, regardless of their virginal status, were not exactly dying to get upward marriages any more or at least as blatantly. Well, all except Semies anyway. I knew, though, with my checkbook or that of my father's, I had little to worry about, even from them. Luckily, I was able to end my internal reverie as his speech was ending. He handed me my schedule, shook my hand and wished me luck. As we stood, he told me his door was always open and I should feel free to talk to him or ask his advice about any aspect of life at the University.

Once out of the building, I read my schedule. This was the first year in the school's history that there were no Saturday classes. This major reform was lost on us Freshmen no matter how many times the Uppers lectured us about it. I had no 8 o'clocks either and the only afternoon class was a Chem. lab. Comparing this around the dorm, I was incredibly happy, it was as good as a Freshman could get. At Washington and Lee, these were the days of limited cuts and tardy slips. This rule, another of the ones to be swept away with the Kent State murders, said that in all classes, for the entire semester, we were allowed only six "cuts" or unexcused absences. Two "tardies" were considered to be a "cut." It never bothered me. The ten minutes allotted between classes was plenty of time and I only had two classes back to back. The rule, however, was another of the regulations on the books for the sake of form. With only 15 students in the large classes and six or seven in the smaller ones, a professor would certainly notice the empty chair. With only a thousand students on campus, the chances were good he (and, back then, not only was the student body all male, but the faculty was as well) might run into you before your next scheduled session and ask you about it. It didn't take long for even the dimmest Freshman to understand the connection between a professor's opinion of your priorities regarding his class and your grade. It was never an issue, even the worst class there, excepting maybe Math, was worth the effort.

Most of the time, between classes, I would go back to the coffee shop, the "Co-op," and drink nickel-a-cup coffee with the frat brothers. There were, however, several tricks that we Freshmen had to learn. Usually it took the better part of two years for us to find the bathrooms in the Front Campus buildings. It was not an uncommon sight to see a boy flying back to the dorms desperately trying to reach relief before the unmentionable accident would overtake him. For some strange reason none of the rest rooms in the colonnade buildings were marked, labeled or mapped in any way. It was as if it was a well planned and long held conspiracy against Freshmen. They looked like broom closets. I don't remember anyone ever volunteering their whereabouts either. After I found them, I know I didn't. The search was often not worth the effort in that once you did find them; they were often not available. They were simply small rooms with a light bulb and a toilet. Not surprisingly though, the one under the main staircase below the Admissions and President's office was tiled and had a mirror. But, that was just part of the deal.

The back campus consisted of buildings whose furnishings and classroom configurations were similar to any other classroom I had experienced in high school. Much older and containing ashtrays of course, but they were still just the same classrooms in which I had spent all the previous years of my life. Math, History and English, during those years, were held, however, in the Colonnade buildings. These buildings were never designed for central heat and Virginia got cold in the winter. The classrooms within them were small, had 15 foot ceilings, old maps or pictures on the walls, and contained the infamous row seats. These benches were puritanical and devoid of any capability for comfort. John Knox would have been proud of their enforced posture. No matter how one would slouch, and we tried, there was no relief. They were constructed of slats of some ancient wood, probably oak, and had at least half a million coats of lacquer applied to them. One was more or less forced to sit straight up, with both feet on the floor. Worse for me, they were all right handed.

In every room I would take a middle row seat on the right side of the room. On my right I would lay however many layers of coats the room's temperature allowed me to discard, and my books. Classrooms often defied the season. In winter they could be hothouses while many times in the spring, the tall ceilings and thick walls kept it at icehouse temperatures. On my left, I would occupy the neighboring desk surface with my clipboard. Like every Freshman, I started bringing notebooks and all the course books to each class. By midterm it was just my clipboard and fountain pen. This fountain pen was my signature quirk. A ballpoint was merely a pencil with ink to me; a soulless technical innovation. I had to use a fountain pen. They had history and tradition and were *the* writing instruments of scholarship. Because of this, all my jackets had emergency ink cartridges in them. Since I was a college kid, I was smart enough to use washable ink to lessen the damage to my clothes, but several jackets had blue smudges giving testament to their use. What it also signified was that, as time went on, the clothes became the uniforms for class and were no longer special, even though they were suits. But, in the classroom, after settling my things, I would then scrounge around for one of the ashtrays. These were still the days where at least half the boys, if not more, smoked. During all four years, I can only remember one professor asking us not to smoke in class. The ashtrays were as eclectic as the maps or pictures on the wall. They probably out dated-all but the oldest initials carved in the chairs. Heavy glass, tin, some were even made of porcelain; we all had our favorites. I can't remember ever having to use any of those black plastic jobs that you saw in offices or restaurants a decade or so later.

So, I would sit there occupying at least three seats, smoking during lulls, hurriedly scribbling notes during the active portions of lectures. There was no attempt at multimedia or concern about accommodating a student's "learning style." Lecture was the overwhelming class format, even in the "labs." But, again, this was how I believed it should be—as it was in the movies. As a Freshman, I remember English and History seemed to be the only true college-esque subjects. All the others seemed to be just a continuation of high school. They were harder, more information was presented, higher expectations as to the expected student absorption, the teachers more dignified, but they were just high school in nature and presentation if not impact and scope.

My English teacher, or professor as I was beginning to call them, was out of the late sixties handbook for "relevant-and-concerned" intellectuals. Maybe I would have to add to that a healthy dose of academia "loony-toons" to get the precise portrait. He would always enter five minutes late, and, regardless of the weather, open the window in the front of the classroom. Not just a crack, he would strive to open it to its full measure. Somewhere in December one of us had the genius to nail it shut from the outside—our classroom thankfully being on the ground floor. He would always wear the same tweed coat, one of three flannel shirts, his singular greasy tie, and corduroy trousers. His black, unkempt hair was well over his collar and covered his eyes as he walked. We all thought him terribly outrageous. A visiting professor from up north somewhere, it's no wonder he only lasted one semester. We all called him "Dr. Dope." After opening the window, or trying in vain after the first week of December, he would turn to face us, check both jacket pockets, and then ask us for a cigarette. Tearing off the filter, he lit it (he always had his own matches), take two paces to the right, turn and pace back and forth while beginning to lecture. The room was only 15 feet wide. He never stopped pacing or talking, pausing only to request and receive more cigarettes. After 15 minutes the air was so thick with blue smoke that those three rows back couldn't see him, but I don't remember anyone complaining. Never faltering, his thought-stream would often wander but we were always fascinated by his various meanderings on English Theater. He would never refer to notes and would only stop at the bell, look up, stamp out his cigarette and say "thank you—next time" and leave.

When other students would hear our tales, they would never believe us. After the first several weeks we began to introduce new boys to prove our point. Lost in his smoky monologue he never seemed to notice. Only one or two at a time, so as not to become too obvious, but just about every class had a new kid who just had to see if it were all true. The course itself was fairly traditional. We read Shakespeare and some of the more modern playwrights. It was a survey that Cliff's Notes could easily carry one through. His lectures, though, were often bizarre in the extreme. I have never heard so much about the social relevance of King Lear in my life. To Dr. Dope it was as if the bard had foreseen our involvement in Viet Nam and the "Imperial Presidency." Luckily, his lectures were really stream-of-consciousness drivel and we were never tested on them. Between Cliff's and remembering to salt my test essays with several of his often-repeated phrases, it was one of my saving "B"s.

History, on the other hand, became a love experience starting with the first lecture. I had always liked and done well in Social Studies, but this was different. While we come from the generation whose high school's Social Studies was not watered down sociology, and was more history than anything else; it was still just Social Studies. This was History! I was lucky enough to get a gifted teacher in Dr. Taylor. This was his first year teaching and it showed. He cared more than the others and was passionate in his desire that we not merely memorize but also understand the issues and events involved. W&L had no graduate school and with its small classes, our professors were teachers first and scholars second. This point was often proved during vacation conversations with high school friends. Dr. Taylor and I were to become, in the ensuing years, good friends. With his enthusiasm for teaching and mine for absorption, it was a perfect match.

Curiously, I saw my relationship with Dr. Taylor and with some of those that followed, as being that of a friend and mentor, rather than merely a teacher. They would shape my mind and thus my life through our personal interactions and their expectations. Test essays were often annotated with not just red marks or slashes, but sentences and sometimes whole paragraphs squeezed between my written lines or in the margins. Rather than merely being "right" I was expected to communicate my understanding and some level of integrated knowledge. Realizing this, even in its first vague notions, Freshman year meant to me that "it", college, had started; that the comfortable childhood schooling had ended—everything within me became consumed by the University.

I actually looked forward to going his lectures. I would not only read the assignments, including the supplementary books, but also ask him for other material. I think my ardor blew him out a little. History was not just a story to me but an interactive legend between the past and me. Since it was simply a Freshman survey of European History before 1815, it was still general enough to have good guys and villains. Now, at this point, the good guys were always the "old school" or the British, or, more to the point; both. I would, as the years went by, become increasingly radical and support the revolutionary causes especially in Eastern Europe, but never against the British. It was in this class that my Anglophile tendencies were first fertilized. On my exam books and term papers I would always use the British spelling of labor and color. Dr. Taylor said, years later, that he never noticed: my spelling was so bad, that it just blended in.

As one might expect, I would talk a lot in class. Of course I would be conscious of the bell and not ask questions in the last five minutes and often would purposefully save some point of argumentation for the inevitable after-class discussion. Through these self-administered policies I aimed at escaping the censure of my less zealous classmates. I don't think I would have really cared if I hadn't. By the second month I knew History was why I had come to college. It seems strange to me now how intellectual passions were born then. I never really thought about how this would help me get a job. I never asked the question about what this had to do with anything in my life then or in the future. That was not the point. I was passionately involved with the History course and nothing else mattered—except the grade. While I would trudge through <u>King Lear</u>, Math, and Chemistry and absolutely die in the German, History would breeze by. Often I would read till two or three in the morning and not notice. I don't think I was conscious of this passion's hold on my life. It was beyond that. It is not that I would talk about it at the house, to my dates or even to my dinner crew, (well, not that much, anyway) but it was the high point of that first semester, and most of those following. History did not have to relate to reality; it was reality. The notebooks from this class, filled with the scribbled excitement from that fall of 1969, are all upstairs in a trunk—they're my history of my beginning.

Mid-terms came and I approached them with the same effort I had always given exams in high school. I would study my notes, cram with the textbooks and, in the end, merely try to get a good night's sleep. I knew I was in trouble in math and German but thought I was doing okay in English, History, and Chemistry. In my midterm grade print out (given to all Freshmen, their advisors, and parents) I got a 2.0. If only it could have been all C's. I had two "B"s, a "C "and two "D"s. The curious thing is that it didn't scare me in any way. There were no visions of swamps and black pajama clad "Charlies" firing AK47s at me. Today, I don't remember why I didn't understand the warning. It was like these grades didn't matter. I knew I would do okay in the end, I always did.

My parents, however, were quite concerned. I had been a good student in school—getting almost all A's. Seeing their copy of my grades, they worried about me living too wild a life at W&L to say the very least. It was inconceivable to them that I would get D's. Being good liberal parents however, they didn't get too mad or become overbearing (at least within my earshot). Since neither of them had ever been to college, I think they were a bit hesitant to criticize. But unknown to them at the time, and slowly becoming clear to me, was the simple fact that "parents" were no longer the central adults of my life. While they paid most of the bills, their words about having my "own life to live" came back to them before any harangue. To me, they were fast becoming phone calls once a week on Sunday. Besides, both of them were too glad to see me on Thanksgiving for my grades to be too big a problem.

Dr. Bradley, however, was a different matter. He dropped me a note asking to speak with me about my grades. I was nervous as hell for the entire day before our 4 o'clock appointment. In November, it gets dim around 4 o'clock in Lexington. He had the lights on in his office and he did not get up as I knocked and entered. He didn't even look up as I sat down. The stern, this time not pleasant, father started from the beginning. He asked if I studied enough and then told me that I did not. He asked me if I studied on weekends and then told me that I should try to put in at least five "good" hours on both Saturday and Sunday. He asked if I had a steady date and was pleased with my negative mumbled reply. He then looked at me for at least a full minute from his chair. Slowly he reached up and, using both hands, took off his glasses, placing them upside down on the blotter before him. Even though I knew it was for dramatic affect, the gesture had me totally cowed. In his silence that seemingly lasted forever, I sat in the shadows, listening to the clock in his office and the wind outside. Finally, he asked me if I was trying as hard as I could. The real answer was I didn't really know what trying was. I had never done anything but "A"'s by reading the text and listening in class. But, the answer I gave him was "I thought I was—but I guess…I would just have to try a lot harder." Luckily I was looking straight at him at the time. He retorted, "I hope so." and put his glasses back on.

I thought this would be the end and mentally prepared to leave. Instead, he seemed to breathe easier and began to speak to me in a lighter tone asking after my life in Lexington and the college. He seemed to enjoy telling me not only of how it was when he was a student here, and how it was when he began teaching, but also how it was in the 1870s or 40s or even how it was at the turn of the century—the 19th Century. He talked and, as I relaxed, I asked him questions. We went on like this till well past five. At the end he asked if I had purchased his new book on the college's history. I tried to decide whether to lie or tell the truth. I told the truth, or almost the truth. I told him I hadn't since "I was short of funds and with Christmas coming up and all…" He smiled, and reaching down to a box next to his desk pulled out a copy. He signed the title page and handed it to me saying "Merry Christmas—early." I put the book under my arm and left thanking him profusely. I remember thinking how lucky I was getting out of there alive. To this day, I don't know of what I was afraid before I talked to him. I guess I thought I would get yelled at or something. It was then I realized that Professors had replaced parents. After all, he was an adult. Vaguely I was aware he had the power to restrict me to campus, even to ask me to leave or cut my scholarship. I was just feeling lucky as I walked back to the dorm in the darkness. At the end of the Colonnade, I turned and looked through the pillars in the night. Each building had a large brass light over its door so the pillars were both white from the light and gray on the night's side. It was cold so I couldn't stand there and stare too long, but it was beautiful. It was the right scene; another movie-perfect scene.

I never saw Dr. Bradley again. He died just a few days after our last interview. I never had an advisor again. Whenever I needed a faculty signature I would use Dr. Taylor. I forget now if the school's registrar or soon to be installed, computer, even assigned me to anyone. It didn't matter. The school was small enough that no one got lost in the cracks; and no one could have filled his place in the picture, anyway.

I don't mean to present that I was blasé about my grade situation. But, in the grand scheme of things, a 2.0 at midterm wasn't too bad among my peers. Many of us were getting our first taste of college reality, versus our previous high school fantasies. I held a steady and certain faith that it would get better; that I would find my rhythm sooner or later and the grades would be okay. But there was more to it than just learning how to study and produce; other things occupied my mind. All their talk about "living too wild a life" was not true enough—at least for me. That first fall I was trying to fit myself into the "real" college dream: the house and girls; the important stuff.

I say "the house" meaning the local fraternity organization which had a living building off campus for at least 12—16 of its members. During the Freshman year, not living there, my only real contact was Wednesdays when we ate at the house and on Sundays, when we watched football or the movie. Being my "day off" I usually spent late Sunday afternoon and evening in the Chapter room with my "brothers." I would sit and talk, watch football and stay to see the Sunday night movie. For the most part, though, I still maintained the most contact with the boys I met in the dorms and at Freshman camp. On a higher, philosophical level there were few real friends among them. I am sure they too just seemed to congregate around the same table for dinner or lunch because it was convenient. As the year wore on, this would change in favor of our clustering around our fraternity pledge brothers; the intended social silos becoming hard and real. But, in that first few months, the transition had yet to occur. During this first fall, I experimented with the various campus activities, clubs, interest groups, whatever, hoping to find one to consume me, to engulf me, and carry me along for four years; just like in the movies. Nothing like that happened. The house became, in the end, the lone non-class, non-history focal point for college life.

The major activity of "pledging" (the process of becoming a full-fledged member in a fraternity) in our house seemed to consist of long lists to be memorized. We had to know all 35 or 40 of the upperclassmen's names, nicknames, hometowns, girl friends, exploits, and interests. That was hard enough since they had little use for us, and we them, except for the Sophomores. Less than most of the other pledges, I didn't get involved with them till later in the year. I would go to the house and do what I had to do. Every month the house would sponsor a house party, usually during some "official" college function like homecoming or a big game. For me, the house parties with the big dinners and the live band (Combos) became the center of my social life: music, drinking and girls. No one in our house went to football games or the like, since none of us were jocks. I think I went once that year because I couldn't think of anything else to occupy the time. On "off" weekends there would be apartment parties or road trips to neighboring girls' school functions. I tried to participate in these as much as I could.

"Participate" means date and date successfully. Even to this day it is hard to describe just what that means. I guess the most blatant meaning, back then, was to get laid. These were the days before Kent State when good girls still said "no" and birth control was limited to condoms; available only in the gas station lavatories; three for $.50. Ever-present in my mind was the thought that maybe, this girl would be the one. I was extremely embarrassed about my virginity and above all else Freshman year, I wanted to end it. I was too smart and too prideful (and frankly too scared out of my wits) to go to a brothel even if I had known where to find one. Lexington had none I am certain and these were the days before the massage parlors sprang up in Roanoke or Staunton. Besides, that would be cheating—it had to be a college girl. Just any girl would not do either. While it might satisfy me in my desire to be shed of this invisible badge of cowardice, a "one night stand" was not dating successfully. No, she had to be publicly enamored with me and find favor from the house. Most of the brothers dated steadily one or two main women. The girls, themselves, found tacit approval within the house. There were notable exceptions. "Oink-Oink Sue" was one.

I met her as a date of one of the Juniors and found her to be a nice, interesting girl if a little fat and simplistic. The Junior in the house was one of the hangers-on. (When I would be involved in rush, we would call them "filler-at-best." Not helping the house's reputation, but not hurting anything dramatically either.) Stan Fitz was really a good enough guy, but he would seriously date almost anything that moved and, of course, that could stand him. Now, I would say that his desire for acceptance was overwhelming and certainly clouded his judgment or taste. Then, it was better to date than not to date and it allowed him entrance to all sorts of house functions and discussions that being "dateless" would not; hence Stan dated "Oink-Oink." I'm not saying that he didn't like her; I think he did. It's just that he couldn't admit it among the brothers. But, he was getting laid. She dated Fitz for almost the entire year but was only (and barely) tolerated, not liked or considered part of the house. This would not be "successful" dating. Perhaps one aspect of the problem was that she was a Semie. There was never any status given to Semies. On the other side of the spectrum was "Marsha the Machine Woman."

MTMW dated Steve Kirk, a seemingly always drunk Senior whose major claim to fame was that he had played hockey in high school. He was somewhat short, but incredibly powerful. Topping the image was his receding hairline and missing teeth. To most of us, in private of course, he acted as if his head had stopped one too many pucks. He was always doing something manly and rough or dangerous. He was consistently excessive. MTMW was a cute Sophomore at Mary Baldwin. For most of that year, from the time she stepped in the house on a Friday evening till she left on Sunday, she would stay in

Steve's room. Kirk was one of the few Uppers who lived in the house since the third floor was reserved for Sophomores. He had a small room across from the stairwell on the main floor. It and another room just like it, shared a private bath. On MTMW weekends Steve would come out for meals and take two plates back to the room. Sometime on Sunday we would hear the shower, then 30 or so minutes later Steve would drive her back to Staunton. Most of us had only fleeting glimpses of her in the several months she and Steve were dating. Steve would return from Baldwin, collapse in a Chapter room chair and soon fall asleep. He didn't need to brag or even say a word. The walls, not to mention the floors and ceilings were incredibly thin. Reality probably surpassed even my imagination. No, this was not successful dating either, though Steve didn't care.

To date successfully the girl had to be pretty (of course), bright, well liked, party well, get along with the other dates, and be able to play both sides of the authority game. She had to be able to please Mrs. Fazer, our house mother, and the parents if she happened to be around on Parent's Weekend, but also be willing to break the rules and sneak upstairs or into the dorm to make love. There was one more thing—she had to like you and show it. When I try, now, to remember the brothers who dated successfully, or rather their dates, it strikes me that they were the type we ended up marrying the first time. In the old days there were stages of dating: going steady, being pinned, giving a lavaliere or various other substitutions for engagement. Veemies still did it and it was rumored that Semies were impressed by it; but normal people, by this late in the 60s, simply rejected these rituals. By the third date, the relationship was considered "serious" and people would take notice. If a girl lasted a semester she began to be OTG (One of The Guys).

It took all of about two weekends for me to realize this. I would ask one of the brothers on Monday if he could get me a date for the weekend or just Saturday or whatever. He would then call his steady girl and ask her to get dates for all the Freshman or Sophomore boys who had asked him. I guessed that this was a tradition at W&L as old as the telephone. When I was a Junior, and dating Beth, I would tell her I needed seven dates and one could be a Sophomore. Then, I would list the guys who had asked me and she would think of somebody with whom she could match them. The two major qualifications were school year and height (both for the obvious reasons). The established date would then go down her hall asking girls if they wanted to go to Lexington or the Chi Alpha house for the weekend. The responsible brother would drive either his, or a borrowed car, to the school and pick up the girls.

The waiting boys would be in the living room at the fraternity house dressed, fidgety and talking usually about nothing at all—very nervously. This wait could be the most harrowing time of one's college life. It was common to find ten or so Freshman or Sophomores (by the time you were a Junior you were expected to find your own dates or, at least, not wait for them in the living room) bouncing around the living room, smoking endlessly, lost in nervous expectation. All one could think of was the chance at bliss or the agony of an entire weekend of hell. When it was my turn to be the upperclassman getting dates, the car rides from Macon were often quiet beyond politeness for the same reasons. Blind dating was not just a custom at W&L—it was a necessity.

Usually, it seldom worked out to be either end of the dream spectrum. Usually one got a "reasonable" date and had a "reasonable" time. I kept hoping that this would be the one girl I had been waiting for—the one meant for me or at least the one I dreamed was meant for me. Instead, I got to meet a bunch of nice, young, middle-to-upper class girls who ranged from pretty to almost ugly and from average intelligence to exceptionally smart. Looking back from today, it seems obvious that it would be that way, but then one could always dream. It never, well—almost never, became a scene suitable for the movies. It was as it was destined to be—two young, stressed, hormonal strangers trying to get to know each other, if, indeed either wanted to get to know the other. The first ten seconds, were crucial. Your life depended on that first impression; the first reflection of the possible dream. Eye contact was essential. For, in that first ten seconds, you could tell if she were disappointed and she, if she were watching, could tell the same about you. If either reaction were negative, both would quickly resign themselves to being "polite" or at least only on the surface, "interested." A mere gleam of interest however, would trigger each, in his or her own way, to start working for towards magic. Regardless, one had the date for the weekend and one had to make the best of it.

One could not "dump on" a girl or embarrass her or do anything really gross or disgusting. Not that any fraternity code of honor, or Lee's premise of gentlemanly conduct kept us in line; it was pure self-interest and survival. W&L had a thousand students and 18 fraternities. There were lots of girl's schools around for us to date; the usuals—Sweetbriar, Hollins, Randolf Macon Women's College, Madison and Mary Baldwin and there were the minors: Bridgewater, Sem, and Roanoke College. There were always Home-town-honeys and a few from colleges far-afield like Mary Washington. For that pool of girls, we had what we considered dating competition from UVa in Charlottesville, and, though vastly devalued, VMI, the boys at Bridgewater, Madison, Davidson, and Roanoke College. Thus, apriori, we considered ourselves top-shelf—our game to lose. Most of these girl's schools were as small, if not smaller than W&L. A trashed date could end that fraternity's dating career at a dorm within a school or maybe the entire school if the incident became scandalous enough. "Suitcase schools" (where the girls packed their suitcases each weekend) were like that. Plus, since dates came from other dates, each fraternity had contacts in only so many dorms of only so many schools. A foolish Freshman could end several romances all at once. So, even if the date did not enter the blissful dream category, one usually went through the motions of having a good time. It was good training for future life—both for marriage and business.

Because there were so many reasons not to trash a date, those who did it successfully, were considered demi-gods. Legends grew up about these men of fearless courage and extremely sick senses of humor. As a Freshman, we learned within our first two weeks of Bart of the ATO house. The ATOs were a house comprised of Southern rich boys who were so cool that they could defy all forms of rational social conduct. Girls were supposedly warned never to step foot in their house from the first day of their college career. Examples are many, but as a starter, they consistently mooned the Veemie Church Parade as the cadets marched by the ATO house on their way to the Episcopal Church (Robert E Lee Memorial). Now, with a few more years of maturity behind me, I wonder if any of this was true—but I believed it then. Bart was their leader. Legend had it that he once urinated in his own beer bottle in front of his date, then drank the "beer." It was said that he had photographed his drunken date swinging from a chandelier and sent them to her anonymously with postmarks from all over the United States. My favorite legend was that he convinced two Semies to make love to each other for his amusement and had filmed the whole thing. All the boys at school considered Bart a celebrity—if not a god—or at least the Freshmen did. It's so strange to see his picture in alumni magazines as a bank president today.

Our fraternity's champion was Dimitri Kaminski, though as he was my classmate, we didn't know it at the time. He was classically Polish. Short, blonde, stocky and round faced, his smile was disarming and his wit electrifying. He knew five languages when he came to school and had incredible powers of memory. Phenomenally successful with women, Dimitri became our "True Teen Idol" and was often called "TTI." Dimitri was known to get drunk and sing the <u>International</u> in Italian (though no one could ever tell if he actually had all the words right) while dancing on the bar in his jockey short underwear. He had pants made with the crotch cut out so he could flash people. He once put a Rock Cornish Hen in Mrs. Fazer's bed and turned the electric blanket on high. He was his best when debasing his dates, especially the Semies.

The first escapade that made legend status was about the time he had a beautiful little Semie upstairs in the bedroom of a brother's apartment near the end of our Freshman year. Five other brothers and I were in the living room with our dates, drinking, talking and listening to music. It was Saturday afternoon so there was nothing heavy going on at all. Suddenly, there was a peel of hysterical, high pitched, classically insane laughter from the bedroom in question. A naked Semie ran, almost fell down the stairs, ripped a curtain from the window, and scrambled out of the apartment. We were never to see her again. Nobody said anything, we were too shocked. One of the other dates, also a Semie, followed her, but the rest of us were truly awe-struck. In the few seconds that we had seen her naked, we had seen a large red smear all over her breasts and stomach. Had the True Teen Idol gone too far and tried to cleave the girl asunder in some fit of passion? We were a little scared to go up and see Dimitri. We didn't have to. He came down the stairs, naked, with a jar of strawberry jam and a hard-on glistening with the red goop. As he told the story, the Semie had enjoyed the first part, but when he reached for the Peanut Butter, she freaked out and left. No one knows the real story. It was a good laugh and it made Dimitri an immortal of house legend.

But, all this was ahead of us then. I dated every weekend that I could that first fall. I did okay in that my dates were nice enough and I got to meet a lot of interesting people, but no dream girl. One date had enough mutual attraction for us to spend the better part of an evening making out in my dorm room. It was what we now think of as "High School", but for me then it was big-time sex. We would kiss and pet, and when I figured she was passionately turned on enough to be distracted, I would disrobe one additional layer of clothing. After about two hours and a thousand standard and mother-inspired "Nos" we ended up with her in her underwear, sans bra, and me in my jeans without my shirt. That was as far as it went. I was pretty proud of myself in that I had only known her for a day and had gotten farther than I had figured. I asked her back for the next weekend hoping to complete the scene for, as everybody knows, you start from where you left off. There was never any thought of back sliding when it came to sex and dating. But, on Monday she said no and on Thursday I received the promised letter of explanation. It seemed she had a hometown honey (HTH) whom she loved and it would never work between us with her mind on him. It would not be fair to me if when we were making love, she thought of him. My luck. I really didn't care. She could think of anybody or thing she wanted to—if it meant I was going to get laid.

That disappointment was only just the start. The last thing that any party needed, during any era, was unescorted males and Freshman stags are the worst. However, it was acceptable if you came over to the apartment or the house, had one beer and left. It usually helped fill the apartment with people and thus, the party spirit. Those with dates that were not going well would and did welcome the company. One could also get to see some of the blind dates so, if the original pairing didn't go well, one could call them up for the next weekend. All this provided the necessary base experience for one's eventual graduation from blind dating. Sometimes unexpected girls came along so they could be picked up. No one actually explained all this, but after a few weeks, we all just knew it.

That weekend not only had I gotten that letter, but also my midterm grades. I guess I felt that I should do something to make me feel better. I thought that it was more or less expected of me to get drunk or something. The movies had prepared me that much for adult life. I had received the proper motivation; it was up to me to provide the proper scene. I was not then, or am I now, a heavy or even a moderate drinker. As fraternity or college standards go; I was an alcohol whimp. A beer and a half back then, and now, will make me feel the alcohol enough to buzz the airfield. Three beers and I am three sheets to the wind, gone and on the verge of passing out. A whole six and I passed out a beer ago—and I've never made all six. The party that Friday was at the "Spook House." It was one of the apartments handed down for generations through the fraternity and it happened to be next to the Lexington Cemetery. Two brothers had the entire one story house and its basement. It was a great place to party.

I dropped over around 8:00 to have my one beer and look over all the dates hoping to find one free. There were about 10 or 15 couples sitting, drinking, or downstairs dancing. I was one of about a half-dozen stags; in other words, it was a fairly typical apartment party. I talked to a couple of the upperclassmen with whom I had made friends and with a couple of my pledge brothers. Most of them seemed to be having, or hoping to have, a good time with their dates so I heeded the polite facial expressions asking me to leave. Having made the entire circuit, I went down stairs to watch the couples dance and listen to the music. I could then, and still do now, make one can of beer last a long time.

Lots of Motown and Credence—danceable stuff greeted me as I sat on the stairs just behind a girl. She seemed about 5'2" and weighed probably 100 pounds soaking wet, but she had a figure for which I would gladly die. When she noticed me and turned to say "hi" her black turtleneck could not hide (and why would she?) a body I had seen only in my dreams. Her face was okay and the rest of her was all attached appropriately, but I didn't get that far, then. She seemed perfect. I was incensed; drawn; truly, mentally and physically, aroused. The longed for and promised "college seduction scene" was finally starting to take place. I sat down and lit a cigarette. She continued looking at me while asking me for one as well. Her face was round and heavily made up, but beautifully framed by her short dark hair. Being the days when most girls wore skirts on dates, she was wearing a short, dark kilt type (as I could see the pin in the side) and the thigh that showed beneath it. She smiled. An angel! I was hoping this gift from heaven was an unattached, acrobatic, double-jointed and highly aroused angel. She said "Hi" and with an exaggerated handshake, introduced herself as "Christy." I answered and asked where she went to school? "Sem" and what year she was? "Freshman…you?" I answered her and tried to think of something interesting to say all the while looking for her attachment, her date, who ever he was, to be returning. I really, though I tried for months afterward, can't remember what I said next. Whatever it was, it must have been good enough for she smiled and patted the stair next to her thus asking me to move down. Even with the music blaring, I worried that she could hear my heart race, see the sweat forming under my hair, and notice my uncomfortable trouser configuration.

She smiled again, and my hopes and dreams soared to unparalleled heights. We shared her beer and she had another while we did the college thing—talked of the music, college and the war. It had been almost 25 minutes and still no date! Suddenly she turned and kissed me. Not a peck, but a long, soulful, torturously passionate, devouring kiss. Taking me by surprise, I just about exploded in my pants. This was beginning to be too good to be true! My mind raced—where was her date? A second kiss and I decided I didn't care and went for the third and a caress. It seemed like a teenage record length of time before we came up for air. The shadow looming over us indicated her date was back. With my luck it was Steve Kirk. I should have known. I knew what to expect. Steve had played hockey in High School, he was one of three guys in the house most people would consider "big." He was known to be a mean drunk and liked the reputation.

He picked me up with one hand and threw me up the stairs. I rolled, no, crashed through the, partially opened door. While I was saying an assortment of curses and ouches, I, thankfully, did not cry or scream, though my mind was blinded by sheer panic and an intense desire to leave (no matter how it might have looked). I did not even consider fighting for my Semie conquest—not against Kirk. While I thrashed around trying to get my feet under me, he bounded up the stairs grabbing me again by my collar in the process. As my eyes focused I noticed that he was laughing. I hoped he was in a good mood. He hung me out with one hand and watched my feet try to touch the ground, actually trying to run the hell away. Since he was holding me with his left hand he reared back with his right. I knew then that he was not in a good mood. I envisioned thousands of parental dollars of orthodontics being destroyed and yelled at him "Not in the mouth!" He burst out laughing. Pausing, he laughed again. Taking one step, he opened the outside door and threw me into the yard. As I rolled in the lawn I could hear his loud, obnoxious laugh. I was desperately trying to think of what to do to avoid the inevitable beating. I scrambled very quickly to the sidewalk before turning to decide in which direction it would be best to run. He was not following me. Thank God! He simply turned and went down the stairs to the basement. I stood there trying to breath normally, keep my heart from a frenzied race and figure out if I had wet myself. Mickey had walked out on the porch and looked at me seeming to find out if I were okay. I did not know him well then and only noticed him in passing as I was busy brushing myself off and trying to settle down. He must have surmised that I was okay, took a pull at his beer and returned inside to his date. No one inside was particularly aroused or upset by this behavior. Kirk was Kirk, and Freshmen that sniffed around dates in general, his dates in particular, had this coming. I am sure, and was assured later by those present, that I had escaped with a very light sentence.

I decided I was going to be okay as I brushed off my clothes further and lit a cigarette. As I put my lighter away I noticed Christy coming through the door with her coat on. Walking with that mad, purposeful gait that girls do when they are angry. She came up and asked me if I were okay. She didn't exactly embrace me, but she did reach out and hold my arm. Now, this was the time for quick thinking, or better yet, deciding. It was true that I was on the threshold of a dream come true. This could work out to be something great or at least noteworthy. Nothing like this ever happened to me. But, rationally, it would take Kirk about 30 seconds to come out that door, now completely enraged, and do his usual animalistic thing by beating me to a pulp. Sex or Safety? Passion won. I grabbed her arm and walked with her, more accurately dragged her, down the street, ducking through the ally two houses down by the Montgomery Ward and then toward the dorm. I didn't hear any commotion, so I thought I was safe, I didn't stop to check. I—we would figure out what to do about Steve Kirk if and when it came to that. For now, I had my angel who had been so passionately aroused by me that she was leaving her rightful date.

She came well equipped. She had two beers hidden in the pockets of her Navy Pea Coat. She drank both as we walked to the dorm. I had an occasional swallow, but did not want alcohol diminishing my amorous powers or tactical thought stream. I just knew that this was going to be my night. Every ten feet or so I would stop her, look into her eyes, tell her she was beautiful (or some such thing) and kiss her. By the time we got to the dorm she was almost drunk and I was ecstatic. We had to sneak in through my window, which was not too much of a hassle as I had a ground floor dorm room.

Once inside, I turned on my tape deck, took off our coats and threw them on the chair. From the chair to her in one fluid (or seemed so then) motion, I immediately began kissing her passionately and moving her toward the bed. We paused while she finished the last of the beer. She began to return my passion with incredible zeal. From trying to engineer the opportunity, now I began to consider just how I wanted this to happen, for I finally, finally knew it was going to happen!

My mind raced with calculations about when to make this move or that. I started taking off her shirt and ended up assisting her in removing her bra without any delay or diversionary kissing. I sat back to worship at the sight of her huge breasts. I was astonished because she kept right on undressing. She took off her pants and

underwear and began to take off my trousers while I struggled with
my shirt. Naked, I lay on her, savoring the feel of our bodies. It was
dark so I didn't get to see or inspect all that I wanted to, but I got to
see enough. Besides, I was busy. I desperately tried to remember all
that I had heard, been told, read, or imagined about being a good
lover. I moved slowly and purposefully, fully expecting her to awake
from her alcohol clouded passion and start crying, screaming or
something to keep me from my goal. However, it all went well -she
was really into it. After sufficient kisses, caresses, murmurs and whispers; it was time to enter her.

She put her hand in the way. "I can't."

"What?"

"I can't, I just don't want to—that's all."

"What about...us?" I tried to sound soft, loving and passionate,
emphasizing the part I thought would be significant to her—the "us"
rather than the desperate boy I really was.

She continued to say "no" and refused my advances. After about
the third series of attempts, she pushed me over and turned to her
side and said "Here, let me take care of you." As she said it, she sort
of sat up and leaned down and proceeded to do something which
previously I had only dreamt about. Well, I have always been a boy
who would rather get half of something for sure rather than risk all,
to end up with nothing. Besides, she might be sobering up soon. By
that time, I was so worked up that the entire physical interaction
took about three minutes. It was a good three minutes, mind you,
but three minutes all the same. "Afterwards," as we shared a cigarette.
(aren't you supposed to?) I, at least, was lost in my dreams.

She interrupted the passionate thought stream by asking me for a
beer. When I said that I didn't have any, she sat up, shook her head
and groaned. She glanced at me quickly, smiled theatrically, and
started looking around the way girls do when they are looking for
their underwear; want to find it fast; yet not look desperate. I put
both hands on her shoulders, pulled her back gently, began nibbling

on her ear, and whispered for her to stay. Turning, she kissed me on the nose and told me that she would "love to" but it was against the rules for her even to be there. "Besides," she "had to get back to Sem." I dressed and went down to the phone at the end of the hall to call a taxi.

As we waited outside, I tried to kiss her. She would have none of it. I asked her when I could see her again. She didn't answer. As the taxi approached, I turned her to face me, and asked her why we couldn't see each other again. She looked up and with a sad, almost painful expression, told me that what we had done was "nice, but really very stupid." Sometimes she did things like this and it wasn't very "healthy" for her. For the first time I imagined then that this sort of thing had happened before. That, in itself, didn't bother me. I never thought that I might be the first (though that would have been romantic), but I worried that everyone was probably not as reasonable as me about it. I looked in her eyes trying to be loving and sympathetic. She continued to say that she thought that she could like me, but would be too embarrassed to try now. With that, she kissed me on the nose, smiled, patted my forehead and stepped in the taxi. It was the end of the scene. I was puzzled and a disappointed. I went back to the dorm to go to sleep. The room still smelled of our sex. I became happy—I was almost a non-virgin. This episode had been incredible. This was the way it was all supposed to happen. Now I had to figure out how to handle Steve.

To my relief, Steve Kirk never brought up what had happened. It was one of my life's anticlimaxes that never bothered me. I guess that he was too embarrassed about losing a date to a Freshman to make any sort of stink about it. He may have been a bit proud of me; who knows? Instinctively I knew that my dental health depended on my silence. I called her once or twice before Christmas, but every time she couldn't come to the phone.

Though that situation offered great promise, it faded as other problems or situations became paramount. My future as a student became the highest priority. Strangely, it was the draft that brought much of it into focus. I spent the afternoon of my 18th birthday filling out draft forms in the Lexington Post Office. It made me think about the war in a new light. It was now my war. It was personal, no longer an intellectual abstraction or the subject of an interesting conversation. I would have to decide to go, resist, or just try to avoid the decision as best I could. The latter, the best of the three, would require me to make a better showing at being a student. In those days Draft Boards had the right to take those boys who were failing, but still registered in college if no others were available. More than that, it made me realize that I was no longer the passenger of events, dutifully following the lead of others, like a child. Now, I was responsible for what I thought, became, or did, like an adult. I wasn't old enough to drink or vote, but could easily die for my country. After I filled out the form, the school sent a notification of my full time status to my draft board back home. I would get my 2-S providing me safety till graduation—almost.

I came from a high school in which every male graduate went to college. It was not that all of us were that smart, but nobody wanted to get drafted. This was all well and fine, but that draft board, and those like it, still had their quotas to fill. Around that time there were two competing theories about how to make the draft fairer and let those boards make their quota. One was that those holding 2-S deferments would be called after all the 1-As in inverse order of GPA. The second was the lottery where each boy's birthday would be chosen and given a number. Those numbers would be called in order and anyone with a 1-A would be drafted—no excuses or deferments.

The lottery won of course. That November we spent an anxious night, like all the boys across the nation, listening to the radio waiting for our birthday to be called. Early in the evening there were screams and groans of real agony from various rooms in the dorm. Later, there seemed to be a grimness settling down over the entire school. I walked to the library on that clear, cold November night.

There was no one there. The draft was more important than studying. Returning by way of pledge brothers' rooms we all compared luck. My number was somewhere in the middle. If I could keep my 2-S, I should be OK. I remember reading at the time that if they could not get enough from the 1-A population the 2-Ss would be revoked again, by inverse grade order. That had me worried. My current 2.0 was not too good a bet. I registered for R.O.T.C. on the spot. Better an officer than a private and at least I would get to finish college—if I could stay in school. Now the war was not an intellectual pastime or delayed decision, it was a sure thing, unless by some miracle it ended before I got out of college.

This action proved to be one of the better decisions in my life. My semester final exams pulled my grades down rather than up. I ended up with an "F" in German, an "E" in Math (that is an "F" if I failed the next semester or a "D" if I passed), a "C" in Chemistry and "B"s for English and History. That was a 1.6 or a D+. If I had not been in R.O.T.C., I probably would have been called.

Christmas vacation was no fun at all. I got lectures from my parents that ranged from angry polemics to sad, guilt ridden sob sessions. Mine had been the honored luxury of going away to college—an exclusive, private school at that. I was urged to look at state schools that were easier and cheaper. I must have been asked, "What's wrong?" 47 times an hour. My mother asked me if I was on drugs. My father asked me if I spent too much time with girls (I should be so lucky). My brother, the genius, enjoyed all this immensely and publicly "advised and helped" me with my study habits. My sister just giggled. It was this vacation that I found true regard and affection for the only member of the family who did not bitch at me—the dog. I received about 25 letters from the appropriate people at school telling me to meet with them upon my return, that I was on "Academic Probation," that my student loans were in jeopardy, and all sorts of dire disasters were imminent. After all this I was sort of glad that Bradley had passed away. I would not have wanted to disappoint him. I was urged to study, reappraise, buckle down, push my nose into some mythical grindstone, keep my pecker in my pants, and just plain produce the good grades I had received in high school and of which they all knew I was capable.

There was good news in this. First, because of the war, the school was hesitant to throw anyone out without at least another semester's chance. Expelled from school would place you in Viet Nam by Easter. I knew this. Second, it gave me an excuse to spend a lot of time with one of my friends from high school who had just accomplished much the same feat at his school. We drank beer, talked tall stories, listened to loud music, lied about girls, and looked forward to our return to home—that is to school.

Even after only three and a half months, the change had been made. "Home" was school; we visited the houses of our parents. College was our home for the first time that January and, in many ways, it would always be home. While we still called the place where our mothers lived "home" out of politeness; school was our real home. Being a student now meant more than being some idle rich boy waiting to join the labor market. It became more than just education or even going to classes. As I remember it now, we did not even talk about it helping us to get some future job. Most of us, at least then, knew what our job was going to be after school—we would all end up working for Sam, Uncle. Being a student took on almost a caste status. We were our own social layer complete with various statuses, rituals, rules and dogma. That spring the usual school versus school type thing started to fade as a new universal "student-hood" emerged. Individually, school was where we were becoming ourselves, or at least trying. I, however, had to put my identity crises on hold for a while and decide just how I was going to stay in Lexington. Another semester like the first and I would be wearing green for sure. With Bradley gone, and I knew that I couldn't have asked him anyway, I had to go to someone who could help me figure all this out; maybe Dr. Taylor.

Between all the appointed meetings my previous semester's disaster had for which I had been pre-scheduled, I scheduled one with Dr. Taylor. Scheduled in those days meant asking if he'd be in his office that afternoon at about 2. I remember it clearly. Though I did not know it then, or think it then, I was probably the first student to ask to talk to him about matters of grave importance. He was wearing his gray tweed jacket that looked like it had belonged to his father and his usual knit Rooster (they were square at the bottom) tie. Dr. Taylor was maybe seven or eight years older than me at the time. While he was still an adult by vocational status and marriage (to a beautiful woman), his never-needing-to-be-shaved face made him seem more like one of us. Being in the same boat now, I think that he probably felt closer to us than some of his faculty colleagues. His hair was shorter than ours, but he let if fall down in front to give him a slight 60s flair. That gray jacket seemed to help him, and me, be sure of which side of the desk we were supposed to sit. He was tall, slender and had a gleam in his eyes that shone with pure sincerity. He was into being a professor and, more than that, a History Professor at a good school. Like us, sometimes he would get so worked up in lectures that he would lose his train of thought and start sputtering. He would look around, smile self-consciously, and just start telling the story where he had left off. He never quite added the sound effects to battle scenes as Campbell and I would privately, but I think he wanted to.

His office was little more than a closet lined with books, next door to the one which had been Bradley's. It was just wide enough for a chair to be pulled back comfortably from a small desk. Another chair was placed along side it. There was a typewriter precariously balanced on the window sill, pipes, ashtrays everywhere and millions of books. Inside each book had to be at least five 3X5 cards and probably two or three folded sheets of paper. Exam books and term papers were given the prize location of the second chair so that when I came in, he had to stand up and put them somewhere. This action took several moments because there was simply no place to put them. He almost sat down with the two-foot thick pile of papers and exams in his lap. Having decided that this would not do, he balanced them carefully on top of his old typewriter. This added an element of tension or entertainment to the meeting. I was never quite sure when a gesture or even the wind from the cracked window might produce a avalanche of sliding exams, papers and perhaps, the typewriter itself.

We shook hands and he looked at me for a moment before asking me in his best, serious, professorial and sincere voice about what was wrong. I told him straight out that I needed to pass this next semester and showed him my grades. I told him I didn't want to wear green at all. He looked at them for what seemed like a long time and finally looked up, seeming to be quite shocked. He said that he had thought me one of his best students and hadn't thought I would have trouble in any subject. After taking about three minutes lighting his pipe, he told me with a chuckle that it "must be that hard Freshman life" or some-such thing. Thank God he did not ask me about how hard I worked, or how long I studied or any of that crap. He pulled out the catalog and looked through it carefully without telling me what he was looking for. Finally, he told me that I should probably forget the math for the time being. If they changed the core curriculum as the faculty was discussing, I would not have to take it anyway. I would have to gut it through with the German since it was required for the History Major. He told me to keep the Chemistry, English and History of course, but I should take Sociology.

I had never even thought that I could drop a subject like math. It was like when you're a kid and you're allowed to stay up past 9:30 for the first time. Ever since Sputnik, we had been brainwashed to think of math as being the foundation of our national freedom, our future and the bedrock of democracy. To drop math was an act of rebellion as much as burning your draft card. But, there was little room for philosophic debate; my "F" had been a real one—a 50 and was a gift at that. It was strange, but as I bid adieu to mathematics for the last time in my life I asked him "What the hell is Sociology?" He laughed; really laughed, right out loud. Not in a way to embarrass me, but just because he thought that sociology, and my question, was funny. "Organized common sense, mostly...Just think your way through and you'll do fine." Math was out and Sociology or "Sosh" was in. That was that. He wrote up a bunch of cards, I signed them, he signed them (I had to remind him to add R.O.T.C.), and he wished me luck. When he said that I should come by again, I had the distinct feeling that he meant it, not just being the usual adult way of saying good-bye.

Second semester Freshman are probably the most obnoxious students in existence. They are probably even worse than Sophomores who have a universal reputation of being insufferable. Though we still lived within the traditions of the campus, more and more of us were becoming what Life magazine would call "Students" with the capitol S. We were relevant; we were concerned. We used phrases like "far out," "outtasight," "man" and "heavy" as they were seemingly required in every other sentence. Our language became quite colorful in many more ancient and traditional ways as well. Mustaches were sprouting from some very unlikely lips. Side burns were below the ear and very few ever got a hair cut after Christmas vacation. Our rooms seemed to change or evolve toward this new consciousness, as well. This would come in fits and starts, maybe a little at a time to be followed by some tidal wave of fad. Instead of pictures of girls, we had Conan the Barbarian posters in "day-glow." Almost everyone had some sort of peace sign somewhere among his personal paraphernalia. Phosphorescent mobiles of planets were hung in front of black lights. Deep, hidden securely from any rumored, fabled, but always feared impending FBI search were beginning to be bongs, water pipes, cigarette papers and baggies full of marijuana; "grass."

While this was not universal, it was considered normal, usual and definitely okay. Only the real right-winger, straight-arrow or Republican Hitler-Jungend Americans ever got upset at people for smoking pot or doing what the late 70's began to call "recreational drugs." Even the Young Republicans, at least on our campus, used pot—though never in mixed political company. No one, that I knew anyway, used or knew anybody who used anything that required a needle, and cocaine was almost unheard of then—besides being too expensive. Many boys considered it more polite to smoke pot than drinking beer. It, or the social customs required while consuming it, certainly bothered fewer people than beer. That's how student's felt, but the law saw it differently. These were the days when Marijuana—what we called "dope," was especially illegal. If you were caught with a seed we were sure that we would go to federal prison for 20 years. I remember going down the hall for something one night in January. I knocked on the door and waited. I knocked again. From within I heard "Oh shit!" and much banging, coughing, and the sounds of stuff being shoved in the closet. When they finally opened the door I was grinning ear to ear. They were white with fear then with rage when they saw it was only me. Paranoia was the rule of the day. Fear may have been omnipresent, but it never stopped anybody. After February I could spot the smell of someone smoking a joint a long way off.

I don't know why I didn't start smoking dope then. Perhaps I had some deep seated moral problem with "drugs," but I think not. I just didn't smoke dope and didn't even drink that much that semester. I spent most of my time studying during the week and trying to get laid on the weekend. Dope was still so secretive that few did it openly or with dates that were known only a short time. Strange, but dope was a thing you did among your friends and not in a "party" setting. Parties still revolved around dancing and beer. My luck in dating seemed to be going from bad to worse. The first few blind dates I got that winter just didn't seem to work out at all.

Spring comes early in the Blue Ridge—about the last week of March. That first smell of Spring brought back golden memories of baseball games while still in grammar school and the knowledge that the world was about to burst forth in beauty. Those early, sunny days set me off with high spirits and optimistic energy no matter what the dating or grades situation. I got out of bed one morning, walked to breakfast and knew instantly it was spring. Snow never stays too long in Lexington, so winter is merely a particularly long series of dismal, gray and damp days. Spring is something else. All at once the household gardens all around Lex explode with both intentional and wild flowers alike, the trees with leaves and even the sky seems to deepen its blue. From the town you can see the surrounding mountains explode with life and color.

In Lexington, we students came alive along with the flowers. All of a sudden there were games of catch in the quad before dinner. The fraternities had music blasting from each open window in the afternoons as students sunbathed on the side lawns. Even though spring was a sign that exams were not far ahead, there were almost universal smiles on the boys' faces. Our hearts and minds, though, renewed their focus down the road for romance and adventure.

Mickey was a Sophomore. He was a big, burly guy that was not fat, but large. He wasn't solid or muscular or anything; but definitely not fat. Standing at least 6'3" he commanded immediate respect, but most often he would act as if he should almost apologize for his stature. From behind his wire rims you could see by his eyes that he was one of those gentle, good-natured giants. That spring was the last time in the three years I knew him that anyone could see his ears. Already, his brownish, red hair had reached his collar (it would go farther) and his sideburns were an inch below his ear. The spring of '70 saw his first mustache, too. He was a religion major who had started the last year as pre-med. Religion was a good major at W&L. It was tough enough to establish respect; relevant enough to be popular; could lead to a draft deferment; and did not demand Christianity or any formal belief system of its registrants. Mickey held his own in dating and in grades, but his major achievement, and how I met him was he was the house's third best Bridge player. I became its forth.

Most any night our house would have one or two brothers in the TV room, a group playing our pinball game "Helen" (who gave five balls for a quarter)—yelling at their failures and cheering their wins. The Sophomores, who were the only ones who actually slept at the house, lived on the third floor and would be upstairs studying or shooting the bull. That year, as in as many years as one could remember before, but only one to follow, there would also be a Bridge game. The Bridge game was to become another victim of the yet-to-come revolution. Bridge was as much a part of college as classes, grades, girls and pot. It was a set of lessons in life itself. Our Bridge Game was where Mrs. Fazer reigned as mightily as any monarch in their court.

Mrs. Fazer always sat in the same ladder-backed cane chair, back to the window, facing the door—so that she could say "hi" to the brother who came in (or as we all knew, to make sure no one's date could sneak upstairs) during every game. The game was held in the living room that was both convenient for Mrs. Fazer's access to her apartment at one end and the entrance to the stairway leading up or down for the brothers at the other. Besides, Bridge was a living room event and demanded as formal an environment as we could muster..

Mrs. Fazer was a slender, brown haired woman in her early 60's or so—it was hard to tell exactly what age she was. I never learned details about her past. She had been a widow for some 15 years and seemed to enjoy her role as House Mother; living along side the 15 or so Sophomores upstairs and the 30 other brothers who did everything but sleep there, comprising the fraternity. When she would have a few too many drinks she would say things she shouldn't have, but never to the point of scandal (no matter how hard we tried). Mrs. Fazer's official tasks were to manage our two servants, run the kitchen, and provide the boys with a motherly and mature influence. However; her real success lay in her precarious blend of personality, actions and her abilities of balancing between the brothers and the outside, adult world. She was not at all too vigilant as the guardian of the University's rules in the fraternity house and thus kept us in her camp, but she also provided the parents some smiling reassurance of our decency and civility. By playing, teaching and coaching Bridge to perfection, she was able to serve student, parent and school—all three masters, well. In the two years I knew her, though many complained that she was intolerant of the new student ways, no one ever slandered her the way most boys do old ladies. In her own way, I and most in our house, thought she was pretty cool.

The Bridge Game would usually start at about 4:00 P.M. when most brothers came back to the house from the hill. Their destinations were only slightly different. They watched the "Stupid Movie" (which was the Roanoke station's <u>Dialing for Dollars</u> program), stood around the pin-ball machine to play or cheer or, gathered in the living room around the Bridge Game. It would last several hours past dinner or, on weekends, when we had enough players for substitutes, throughout both days. While Fazer was good; Dalton was better. Dalton was a Junior that year and the oldest son from a Virginia farming family. A wrestler (one of our few jocks) proudly bearing a 2.0, he was a true card wizard. Fazer and Dalton had played together for almost 3 years when I met them and they, as a team, were incredible, invincible and in all manners Olympian. She would smoke and utter monosyllables and he would just talk about nothing at all, but always smile. Together, they would win. There were four or five other Junior and Sophomore players including Mickey that made up the opponents. Though the opposition varied, the results never did—winning a rubber against those two was a matter about which one bragged.

In our class there were two who tried to join the group; Dimitri and I. Dimitri could play very well for short periods of time, but after about an hour he usually became too distracted—today we'd call it ADD. He would get bored and start playing what he'd call

"Bakunin Bridge," which we were to discover was anarchist bidding and playing methodology named after the founder of international anarchism. First, he would start to mutter in Polish or Italian almost under his breath. After some defeat or some stupid comment from the gallery, he would start to bid in German. We would learn over the year that this was the sign for the other players to demand his ejection. Hand after hand would be overbid and underplayed with increasingly brilliant conversational wit. It was like having Oscar Wilde sitting next to you. If no one rescued the game from him, Mrs. Fazer would excuse herself in desperation and the game would end. Strangely, no one ever got pissed at Dimitri for this; insanity, after all is a great defense and all would be forgiven to his charming blonde smile.

No, Mickey and I, after my initial foray into the game, would be the ones to challenge the pair three or four times a week. I would leave early for studying, but that still gave us three or four hours, with a brief pause for dinner, of masochistic Bridge. I had learned to play with my mother, brother and sister. It was rough company. My family, I was to learn, were all bloodthirsty players. That stood me well for even though I was not that good, and a little rusty, I survived the first few and thus crucial games at the house. Sometime in late November I meekly sat in for a player who left to relieve several beers. I did okay enough to become a sought after replacement, even if in last resort, for departing players. By spring I was one of the boys regularly called to the table. By the next year, I had one of the seats.

Our card table was one of the few good pieces of furniture the house owned. Along with the never played piano—donated by some long lost alumni; and the great books collection—eventually hollowed out to stash dope; the card table was one of the few civilizing influences in our house. It was oak and had a green cloth cover over the top. I am sure that it once had been felt, but it was still green where it was not burned by loose cigarettes. It could hold all the players, their ashtrays, drinks, extra cards, and the score pad without looking cluttered. We would sit around it, oblivious to the entire outside world, smoke, talk and play. It was not its size or location, but the passion and intensity of the game that made it into an arena.

There was seldom any real table talk about the game among experienced players. Kirk claimed that he had danced nude around the room during a game and Fazer didn't notice—but no one really believed him. I, and probably most of the house cognizant of the game, would probably think it to be possible. We learned that dates could make it upstairs if they didn't slam the door and disturb the bidding. The conversation ranged around light politics, light girls, light gossip and plans for the next weekend's date. With Fazer there, one had to keep it light besides, anything that took one's mind off what was a central definition of one's worth as a human being could lead to disaster. The conversation was only a cover, anyway, trying to shield from the outside world the concentration, effort, focus and incredible passion being consumed in the attempt to stay respectable in the face of heavy fire. This was no game; it was not for fun; it was for real.

It was the first time I took the chair opposite Mickey that the miracle happened. As usual, he made some mocking sarcastic slur about me being a Freshman and how he should get a handicap, though we all knew that it was in fun, and threatened my life if we should lose; which we all assumed we would. An empty threat, for it was inevitable that we would be humiliated. Fazer and Dalton never lost. It might get close but in the end, the double line would show them ahead. One's only hope lie in Dalton leaving for enough hands to put together a rubber or in him getting bored and switching chairs. When that happened everyone scrambled for the empty. By dinnertime we had gone down two straight rubbers and each had humiliated ourselves with a blatant misplay. Dalton would smile widely and, in an almost kind manner, explain to the offender that he "really didn't mean to do that," since we "knew that the correct play was" such and such. Mrs. Fazer would reach across during the next play and pat our wrist or something to show motherly concern while our pride sank through the chair. The grandstand would not be so kind.

The other upperclassman who lived on the first floor across from Steve Kirk was Bob Canard. I never saw Bob play bridge. But, he would always watch and lead the other two or three spectators in the room in long analytical discourses after a hand about our mistakes. Not being mentioned by him in one of these was a badge of honor that few new players ever earned. The grandstand was a "before dinner" phenomenon. Bob would disappear after dinner to study or to find a date, so the game could continue in a more traditional setting and with increasing intensity.

Whether it was the poor pot roast, the 12th cup of coffee, or the 20th cigarette; I don't know, but Mickey and I were hot that night. We still lost, but our score above the line was better than theirs, and the rubbers were close. Everything was clicking except they would get marginally better cards when it mattered. At eleven we were still going at it and did not let Dalton or Fazer leave the table when they complained about being tired. That rubber had been going on for hours with us vulnerable and thousands upon thousands above the line. Voices were sharp, words were quick. Secondary conversation died. Eyes darted back and forth as much from excitement as from caffeine and nicotine. Mickey and I were playing well enough to drive them into desperation bids which we were, for once, smart enough not to follow. Somewhere around midnight we sent a brother to the hotel Robert E Lee (the only place in town open that late) for cigarettes. Slowly a crowd gathered and watched, hushed through respect for the spectacle being played before them, from the feeling that something monumental was happening. Now, I know that Dalton and Fazer had more pressure than we, the underdogs, but then, I felt that my entire future, at least in the house, was on the line. Finally, about 1 or so in the morning, we put together the second game. We finally had made one of the small slams we bid. I had played the hand and Mickey smoked three cigarettes while I did it. We had won a rubber! They were gracious as they left. We just sat there as the collection of brothers talked loudly about the adventure, recalling all the salient points and the major facets of the marathon game. Half an hour later, Mickey and I just sat there and looked at each other. We smiled, shook hands, and stood up. Each of us knew then that, going forward, there was a special bond between us. Victories make the bonds of brotherhood last well past graduation.

We never boasted of it, but from then on, we became Bridge partners and, more important, friends. Not that we did everything together, though I would have liked that. Mickey was one of the most popular boys and involved in many things with the multiple factions of the house. He had a regard for me that other boys didn't. On my part, I would be a friend to him while others became disciples. Mickey had a way about him that brought follower-type of boys around him and as such, he became the house's "Peer Group Leader." While I never joined the "Peer Group" fully, I could spend time with Mickey and not "follow him around" as some of the others did. While I was not aware of all this yet; it just felt good to have made what looked like one of those special friends the college experience was supposed to provide.

That game had been on a Thursday. Mickey asked if I wanted to go up the road to the Madison Mixer the next night. Of course, I said yes. Spring mixers were a tradition. The Madison ones were the most famous. By spring, the optimistic enthusiasm for blind dating had worn off for almost the entire unattached college population of the valley. March saw almost every girl's school having a mixer, to which our house went. I guess it had a lot to do with Madison being predominantly a state teacher's college. It was thought that there would be more good-looking, unattached girls actually attending the mixer there than anywhere else. They didn't seem to need the personal introductions the old social mores expected and some of the socially haughty demanded. Madison was also the biggest school in the area with about 5,000 students so maybe that had something to do with it, as well. More often than not, one could go and come back with several phone numbers or a date for the coming weekend's combo.

It was a 60-mile road trip up Route 81 to Harrisonburg. Madison's "old" campus was a collection of nondescript gray stone of buildings. Recently, the school had expanded so, on the periphery, here and there, were equally nondescript red brick buildings. Neither the school nor the architecture had much in the way of traditional Virginia College class. It was simply a "state school"—one similar to those spread across the nation. But, being the only such school in the valley, or at least accessible to us, it had its own unique character. Technically, it was co-ed, but in truth there were maybe fifty guys there since it had only admitted males for the past two years. It was pretty much still a women's teacher's college. The mixer in March was always in the student union. I went a total of four times, it was always the same.

Mickey and I drove up in his "Super-Bee" cruising around 75—80 mph. We talked of classes, teachers, grades, the house and the war. It was unusual in that it seemed not to be a rehash of magazine articles or schoolboy gossip. It certainly did not consist of world-class wit or deep wisdom, but it was a genuine conversation that was rare to those times. The talk was thoughtful and revealed real opinions on real issues. Both of us were listening and reacting to each other—both of us taking the words seriously, but not so much so as to become embroiled in argument.

When I think of those road trips now, I often wonder how we stayed alive or have any hearing left at all. While I did not often drink more than one beer, Mickey would often do the other five. Music was a necessity and it would often be at a deafening level. Even today I have retained the skill to carry on a discussion when others find the deafening music drowning them out.

Stan Fitz was in the back with two other brothers. Stan had a habit of trying to take part in the conversation going on in the front seat from the back. It would often end up with a series of "What?"s that would be tactfully, though sometimes graphically ignored. Most of what Stan said was for emphasis anyway—he was a kind of "color" man of the bull session. He was one of those guys who only said stuff that amplified the point of the previous sentence made by another boy. By the time I knew him as a Senior he could make a paragraph of re-hash based on a single sentence spoken by another. Though the road-trip up was like many of the others we would take over four years, this mixer was to produce for Stan the love of his life. He would date her off and on for the rest of that year and the whole of the next: Fearless Fosdick.

Fearless was the last in Fitz's long line of nicknamed dates and she was truly his best. She was from someplace in Pennsylvania about which no one had ever heard. She was a math major with the fashion and grace normally attributed to that line of academic endeavor. She had all the appropriate parts that girls are supposed to have, but they didn't seem to quite fit correctly on her body. Her nickname came from a large, protruding jaw much like the Al Capp character out of Li'l Abner. It's not that she was ugly, just strangely configured. The reason I don't know her real name now, is that I was the one who coined the nick name on the ride home. It fit so well that, almost from the beginning, even other dates in the house referred to her as "Fearless." Never in public of course, the nickname was so perfect everyone referring to her constantly had to check their natural instinct to use it in place of her name. But, Stan and Fearless were naturals for each other. Drawn by some invisible force, it was fate that they met early. By the third dance of the evening, you could tell at once that they were in love.

After a quick swish of mouthwash (always kept in the Super Bee's trunk for such occasions) supposedly masking the odor of beer and cigarettes, we paid our $1 to get in. Immediately, we started circulating, separately, in search of good-looking girls. Mixers were different from the high school dances I had attended. In high school both the boys and girls would stand around in clique clumps, face inward and talk about the other groups. Occasionally one boy would venture out to ask some girl to dance. This would continue till only the "Unmovables" would remain clumped on opposite sides of the gym for the remainder of the night. In college it was different. Girls would stand and watch the band in ones and twos. Boys would circulate, like hungry sharks, trying to get a good, yet unobtrusive, look at each girl. Once a suitable target had been found, we would stand strategically, off to the side, but in front of our intended prey waiting for the beginning of a song. At that moment you could turn, make eye contact and ask the girl to dance. There was danger of course that some other male had marked your target but stayed just out of your line of sight—only to confront the girl with two simultaneous requests—but this seldom happened. Very few requests were turned down, but very few lasted for a second dance. More often than not, at the end of the music, her eyes would immediately start looking around, as would yours, and both would know that the process was starting again. If she looked at you and made conversation, you might have found yourself a date. Finding her agreeable for a slow song, spaced strategically every six or seven songs in a set, meant that you had indeed, the beginnings of a mutual relationship and the dating rituals would begin.

Fitz had met Fearless on the second dance and by the first break they were making out in the corner. He later swore, though we didn't believe him, that he nailed her in the bushes during the second break. Most of us didn't care, we just threatened, joking of course, to turn him into the ASPCA. Mickey, Campbell and I ranged around probably dancing every other dance. Timing is crucial at a mixer. If you are there too early only the real loser girls show up at the beginning and one would lose heart. Too late and any reasonable girls would be already taken. If the ratio of girls to boys is even close to one-to-one it got much too competitive and most of the girls would start leaving, making it even worse. The first half hour of the event, much like the first ten seconds of a blind date, usually spelled the fate of the evening. If all of our group were bored we would go find a store to buy some beer with Mickey's fake ID, try to remember some girl we could call at that, or a close-by school, or just drive home. It was never majority rule; it was driver rule. When the driver decided to go, you may try to persuade him differently, but he was, in the end, the Starship Captain.

That night, each of us had a pretty good time. We each had talked to several possibilities and were dancing a lot. Those of us alone during the slow song would gather to check in and compare notes and attitudes. By the second break, though, we were ready to leave, having at least one name and number to show for our efforts. We couldn't find Fitz. Though we joked among ourselves about leaving him, it was universally considered "bad show" to maroon a brother. He was nowhere to be found in the Union. We stationed ourselves at strategic points so that we could quickly find him upon his return. This took the better part of an hour because one or another of us would see some girl and go after her. We had to regroup constantly to try and keep our plan together. When we finally found him with his shirt buttoned wrong and smiling all too profusely, we told him that we were leaving. Mickey gave him ten minutes to be at the car. It took him fifteen and even then he took five minutes kissing Fearless "good-bye" all over the trunk. Stan was showing off. We let him. Even Stan needed to be a stud once during his tenure in Lex.

Besides road-trips and mixers, Freshman Spring was also the time when pledges became full members of the house. Ours was the last class destined to be the traditional fraternity pledges as shown in the movies: with duties, humiliations and such. Our pledge master was a Senior of impeccable reputation; James Buccanon. James was never Jim, not to us or anyone else in the house. James would do everything well enough to be cool, but not too good to attract any sort of self-infatuation stigma. He drank but was not a drunk; smoked a little pot but was not a head; in fact, he did just about everything that anyone expected a college kid to do, but in a moderate and, most of all, cool way. His only fault was an ego that made him believe we saw all this as his natural state and not the character that spent time constructing this image for us to appraise. It wasn't so much a façade, but a personality he assumed as one would dress oneself with tailor-made clothes. Whatever the faults, it worked. It was his destiny to date beautiful, smart girls, rumored to say "yes" in an appropriately short—but respectable—length of time, get good grades, and be universally well liked. He did all this without any apparent personal effort and a nonchalant ease that bothered most of us when we were not in awe of him.

That spring he held weekly pledge meetings each Wednesday, after dinner. During the one just before initiation, he got off on some tangent about sex and dating. His talking about birth control to a bunch of freshmen, who were close enough to real sex every weekend, but, more likely than not, were going without, was taking his life in his hands. James did just that. No one actually said that they were upset or blown-out by his talk—but it appeared we all were. On the walk home to the hill, a plot was hatched, springing almost spontaneously from each of our minds. It evolved with each interaction, cascading one-way and then another. By the time we reached the dorms all the plans were made and we each knew our roles. We didn't talk about it much at breakfast but kind of silently enjoyed the fermenting composite will our pledge class was assuming.

The next night, at dark, we all met as agreed, in the quad. Almost without conversation we walked the four blocks, invaded his apartment and captured James. He was sitting at the kitchen table when we entered, front and back simultaneously and grabbed him. Quickly the ten of us stripped him naked, carried him upstairs (with only a knocked down wall hanging to show the struggle) and tied him, spread-eagle, to his bed. First, we bathed his penis in indelible black ink. Then, flipping him over, each of us wrote some epitaph on his butt in magic marker. James would have to explain a lot to his date the next night. She was a beautiful rich girl from Sweet Briar (James was the only one in the house cool enough to date that school); the one he used as the example in his birth control speech. We left him there like that to be found by his roommates, confident that the brothers could not take revenge on all of us. Jubilantly we went back to our dorms, joyous in our victorious, witty and soon-to-be-legend adventure.

Few of us locked our doors in the dorms with the honor code and all. It was a testament to that code that we didn't, but that night we should have. Each of us was dragged bodily by five or six of the brothers to waiting cars and quickly whisked off to be deposited in the living room of the house. We were wearing only what we had worn to bed plus a jacket one of the brothers grabbed from our closets. I was one of the first captured and was in my U-trou. By ones and twos I saw the rest of my pledge brothers dragged in and thrown on a couch or chair. The whole process probably took the better part of an hour. Our nervousness increased with the glowering upperclassmen maintaining our ordered silence. When completely assembled, we were blindfolded again and hustled back into waiting cars. Again in silence, we were driven around for what seemed like hours. One by one we were deposited alone, almost naked, on a dark, country road. By the time I was able to get my hands loose and the blindfold off, there were only fading taillights to be seen.

While the days were warm in March, the nights were cold, making us most uncomfortable. Once left, we quickly undid our blindfolds and by listening to the screeching tires from other drop-offs, found that most of us were within a mile of each other. After a half hour of calling, whistling or just plain yelling, we were together again. Now we were a group of half naked boys trotting (to keep warm) in an unknown direction down a back road in rural Virginia looking for anything that would tell us where we were. The time we had spent in the car provided possible solutions that were fantastic if not frightening. We could have been in West Virginia or Harrisonburg or

Roanoke. Our imaginations were running rampant with imagined fears. Added to our apprehension was the ages old fable that should a W&L student spend the night in jail, he would be asked to leave school. Pride and this fear mandated that we not be caught. The cold sharpened our senses, but we knew that we were at the beginning of a true adventure. This was as it should be; just like the movies said it would be.

What we did not know was that most of the town's folk for miles around Lexington were accustomed to such pranks and looked at escapades such as these as traditional rites of spring. Probably since just after the Civil War such events had been taking place in the Valley. We were scared, not of being lost or hurt, but being found in our naked state and not being able to pull off some imaginative, daring and altogether ingenious recovery. We couldn't exactly hitchhike back. Any car might be a cop and we knew that we would be arrested with a call to the dean (if we were lucky) as our punishment. The whole school would know that we were whimps or worse, losers to our house's upperclassmen. One of our number called a halt. We had been trotting for about half an hour and seemed to be getting nowhere. We were miserable without cigarettes or shoes. Everyone had some sort of an idea. Campbell wanted to climb a tree to see some stray light from civilization. I wanted to keep moving in the direction I thought was east because I had seen out of the corner of my blindfold, the car heading west. Someone else won the argument by starting to jog again to keep warm. After an additional half an hour we found ourselves in the resort village of Natural Bridge: home of Freshman Camp and about eleven miles from Lex.

Eleven miles is a long way to walk in the cold when one is naked and barefoot. Besides, the longer we stayed on the road the higher the chance of being stopped by a cop. Huddled behind some store we came up with an idea that quickly won over the pack. One of us had found a dime in his jacket's pocket. We could call Cal who not only was a pledge brother, but a townie living at home and thus saved from this assault. Now all we had to do was find a phone. As luck would have it, there was no roadside pay phone in Natural Bridge. The whole town was several streets of homes, a gas station, two shops and one large resort type motel. We decided against the private homes. There was no telling when one would happen on a judge or something. Everything else was closed.

Luckily the gas station was one of the old fashioned types with a house right behind it. We figured that it had to be the attendant's living quarters. Campbell said that those guys were usually assistant policemen or something worse, real rednecks. Necessity voted him down. One of us, I think it was Greg whom we would later call "Sun King," went to the door and started knocking. While he would later become our leader, he was not selected for any particular reason besides having the longest jacket. At first he tapped politely, but this didn't work. Then he started really banging. A dog's bark exploded from inside the house and we started to find cover. Lights started at the second story rear and progressed quickly through the house. The door opened with an old man wearing trousers held on with a single button and a rifle. We froze. Greg froze. Through a thick stream of cussing we could see him open the door. We were still out of sight and Greg stood there, naked from the mid-thigh down, motionless. The man finally realized that he was still holding the gun, put it down, and invited Greg in. Greg looked over his shoulder as if to say to us that he was doing that for us, and entered.

Greg was in there a good 15 minutes before he came out to get us. We were concerned, to say the least, but too frightened to storm the house. After Greg called for us, the man and his wife, who had come down to investigate the commotion, enjoyed the sight of the ten of us straggling in from our hiding places; each trying not to look too ridiculous. She scolded us about what our parents must think while giving us hot chocolate to help shake off the cold. It's strange, but as I now remember it, none of us asked the man to share the cigarettes he was smoking, though we all wanted one badly. I guess it still felt strange for us to be smoking in front of adults.

Cal arrived and, after two trips, left us at the dorm to spend the night recounting the adventure. By morning every detail had been described, completely analyzed and, of course, extremely exaggerated. We were too excited to sleep. Everyone had something to say and in the spirit of universal adventure, no one was left the goat. The most popular pronouncement came from Greg who remarked that he was extremely glad that Dimitri had behaved himself (more than usual) and had not sexually abused the man's dog. The dog was probably glad as well.

We decided that night that James was not to be let off. There was never any breakfast at the house on Saturday morning. It was traditional, however, for all the brothers and their dates to eat lunch together and plan the evening's events. James could not miss this meal without a severe loss of face. Though usually few Freshmen went; we all decided to go. The dining room consisted of five long tables each easily seating ten apiece—though on weekends we often had to squeeze more in. We planned to place ourselves so that James could not sit without most of us being able to look at him. We would say nothing, of course, but just look at him and then her—the silence and the smiles should be enough to set James or, better yet, his date to saying something or doing something that would generate laughter.

He came early and, with his date, took corner seats at one of the far tables. We had already seated ourselves so that he could not take any chair facing a wall without sitting right next to us or splitting himself from his date. The plan worked. She soon realized that every eye was on her and had been since her entrance to the room. Her smile, then laugh, then hurried exit were the fitting results of such an adventure. James was too cool to tell anyone the specifics to her reaction to his body's new artwork. We all wondered if she found the changes, one in particular, refreshing, exciting, or repulsive.

This was the last spring spent the way it had been spent by W&L boys since the advent of automobiles. Like Pledge Class activities and antics, April saw the traditional panty raids on the area girls' schools. The first was aimed at Sem. Every house sent a contingent to storm the school. I remember being at the back edge and watching a group of about 200 surging toward the dorms, another said to be the same size approached from the rear. Some said that they got in. We, or at least the group I was with, did not. Their campus cop ran us off and fired his gun over our heads. It made for many tales of excitement and valor. Smaller sorties later in the week were made to Mary Baldwin and Randolph Macon. I got up a downspout at Macon. That could have been my chance for glory if once up there, I could have figured out how to get in without breaking a window. I was not so afraid of falling or getting hurt as I was afraid to actually damage anything. To my dismay, none of the girls would open them so I just shimmied down. My heroics were lost to everyone but myself.

There were house parties and I used my Madison numbers to no great avail. We played baseball before dinner when we were not playing Bridge. We had almost an entire month before exams, the weather was warm and most of us just enjoyed being at school. One day blended into another. Now, looking back, I know we were doing what we were supposed to do, what all had done before us. Nobody could see that it was all to die in May. I never realized it before, but even real life has lulls before its storms. That April was one of them. Dating, where many, unfortunately not I, were getting laid for the first time, studying, intramurals, just floating with the enjoyable tide seemed to occupy the entire month.

CHAPTER 3

Now, with years of historical training to help my understanding, I realize that revolutions do not happen in a single day. That is not how it seemed in May of 1970. This was a month that seemed to smash into my life and then hurry away—leaving dents, scratches, deposits and some memories that would color my life forever. Though not important now, for those of use that were living through it, one might compare it to April 1776 or November 1917. I could only watch with a certain nervous wonder as the world in which I had grown up suddenly changed and mutated before my eyes. Politics, styles, morals, life, and college—all the rules changed—obviously the work of sudden, significant historical forces. In reality, its full impact lasted till the end of my college years and its significance gradually petered out several years after that in our generation's renewed lust for jobs, family, success and wealth. Because of May 1970, I was certain I was living through an "important time;" a time that would stand out in significance from all previous ages. I did not realize, then, that this was to be like all other revolutions; destined to be swallowed up by its aftermath, evolving into something quite different, almost antithetical to its initial events.

"Kent State" was all we ever had to call it. We all knew the term did not simply name the Ohio State University in Kent, Ohio. It was the murders there of students by National Guard troops struggling to contain a fairly typical and one of the myriad of anti-war demonstrations then occurring across the nation. That the whole thing was a bloody mistake and that the killed students were passersby and not demonstrators made it all the more significant. It was them (the establishment, the military, and our parents) versus us (freedom loving, anti-racist, love-peace-Woodstock youth) made universal by the over-powering onslaught of the media blitz that followed the killings and our campus led reactions. It was the spark that set that particular Spring aflame and it ended the way springs would forever be spent on colleges—especially those like W&L. To anyone in college at the time it was the end of the innocence for student youth. Rationally, we know that it was a culmination of events and a decade's evolution of political attitudes chiefly those of American Youth. That single event seemed like an earthquake, striking un-forewarned into our college life, followed by aftershocks and tremors that rocked us throughout the following years. There was no middle ground anymore. One was young and a student or someone totally out of touch with our reality. It seems strange with all this build-up that I can't remember the exact date of the massacre. But, after all these years I can clearly recall that evening.

The day itself was nothing special—exam nerves starting, dates being planned, baseball or lacrosse in the quad, and a dismal dinner at the Freshman-dining hall just like every other day. After dinner I, as usual, went back to the room to study. I had taken to the habit of studying in my room rather than the library as it was quieter and offered fewer social interaction distractions. I don't know if it was more efficient however; for after a couple of hours at the desk, I would retreat to read on the bed. There, the notorious Rack Monster would grab me after 20 minutes or so and I would doze only to wake with a start and begin the whole process over again. Between rotations, I would wander down the hall to talk and smoke a cigarette with one of the other boys. They were acquaintances, not friends, but we all had similar routines. This would go on till about midnight or 1 o'clock when, one by one, the lights on the hall would be put out and doors closed as we went to sleep. I remember how lonely one felt when, during some all-nighter, you would walk out of the room for a break only to find that you were the only one still up.

That particular night I remember someone crashing through the hall door and running down to the other end. The boy who lived there was one of those wire-rimmed-glasses type of boy, who studied a lot and was intellectually intense about almost everything. He was pleasant enough, quiet, but serious about politics and the scholarly effort of being a student. Because of this, and his consistency in this, we thought Jerry not only mature, but wise. Normally, he would study; door closed, and only come out as a late night observer to one of our study break bull sessions. Any entry he would make in these discussions seemed to be well thought-out and reasoned to the degree that we could never seem to find fault in any assertion. For a generation that defined itself as questioning everything, it is amazing to me, today, that we never asked for verbal footnotes from anyone the group thought of as "wise" or even "smart."

The invading student banged on his door and called his name again and again. Rising to the alarm, several of us went out into the hall, but remained standing in our doors so as not to intrude, but examining the disturbance closely nonetheless. Jerry finally opened his door and the other kid started yelling that the army was killing students. We all ran down, each exclaiming associated "What?!" and other interjections trying to join the ensuing conversation.

The messenger excitedly told how he had watched Walter after dinner and seen a group of soldiers firing into a bunch of students; slaughtering them. We all asked him to slow down, catch his breath and retell the story. Though, in each iteration, it consistently gained intensity we began to get the sense that "it" had finally happened. "They" had declared war. The confrontation and violence foretold by the music had arrived. Never did we think that the protesters had carried guns, attacked or even threatened the army in any way.

Intrinsically, we knew that the military had finally played their trump card—their ownership of the bullets. Deep within us, no matter what shade of political conviction, we knew all along that it would come to this. It had to. How else could the destiny of the 60s be achieved? We all wondered what we should do, what would happen next, if this was the beginning of the end for the nation, for the war, or maybe, the birth pangs of a new society. Jerry was the only one among us not to ask questions; not to get excited or generally lose himself in his own day-dream political vision. He walked over to his short-wave and tuned in the BBC but there was nothing about it (yet) and then to a Washington, D.C. station which did have some details. Immediately we quieted down, but continued to theorize and comment in whispers. This was all very momentous to us, and we wanted to look and act especially serious and significant. We knew that this was part of our generation's special mission; our chance to change the nation and thus the world. Cigarettes were lit and studies forgotten. This was important stuff—not like mere final exams.

We were, indeed, a special generation, a different youth (something each person then alive knew to be true—then). To be sure, in all ages past, youth grumbled, protested, and rebelled against their powerful adult masters. But, for us, we knew we were different. We, the last of the post WWII baby boomers, were different in that we were the children of the world's most total victory—military, economic, cultural and philosophical—and thus a chosen group. To the generation that began to come of political, social, and intellectual age of awareness in the late 1960s, all advantages had been bequeathed as a matter of birthright. We were the sons and daughters of the most powerful nation on earth. Not only our parents, schools, newspapers, but the TV (the miraculous box of truth) convinced us it was so. The optimism, idealism and invincibility, grown out of our parents' experience in World War II and the explosion of abundance in the 50s, had been sown within us from the beginning. We believed it all. Why shouldn't we? We could accomplish anything and everything. The dogma found fertile ground. There was nothing to show us or teach us any different, for, unlike those born just before us but after WWII, we were also the children of a new geographical and social institution—Suburbia.

The white flight was yet to come; but the postwar housing boom, driven by the GI bill, VHA mortgage program, and the establishment of home-mortgage-only "Thrifts" financial institutions, made rootless communities out of what had been, until recently, pastures. These communities were the breeding grounds of not only the late post-war baby boom (us) but also the idealistic optimism upon which we fed. Even the experiences of our communities reflected this boundless, enthusiastic expansion. Our education was solidly, if not fanatically, pro-American and thus we were totally enculturated us with the tenets of the American Dream. More important, these communities teamed with the educational institutions to instill a gospel like quality to the success stories. The elements of free enterprise, equal opportunity, the documented fairness of our society, wisdom of a democratic government and the ever-continuing upward spiral of the standard of living provided to us by business and technology gave us the boundless energy and fanatic faith of those who knew their manifest destiny. There were chinks in our armor—McCarthy and Sputnik had seen to that—but nothing as of yet to shake our belief we could fix the problems and bring the dream of the ages to pass. There was nothing in our experience to deny any of this or even shake our confidence in any part of it in those of us who found ourselves at the threshold of adulthood. Today all of this seems incredibly idealistic to a point of gullibility or simplicity—but then it was an almost unquestioned part of our foundation as a "generation."

Being at college, we knew we were privileged—being at a good school like W&L, we also knew we were the elite. Far from discouraging us, it placed us in all the better position from which to lead. To most, including me, it was just an undercurrent of faith—much like the almost unconscious religiousness we had even though we scorned church. Now, I understand we were a small sliver of society, but from the inside, our sense that this was universal seemed natural.

Many of us had never seen Negroes in anything close to our living, working or socializing proximity. Beyond that, we had never seen or experienced, first hand, poor people. Everyone we knew had two parents, a father with a good job, a mother who saw to it that our needs were met, along with new cars every other year and the like. The economic differences were not measured in the absence of any of these things but in the level of their accumulation. None of us had ever lacked anything substantial only the amount of advantages or "things" we enjoyed. As little boys we had learned that we could be anything we wanted to be, and we believed not only that, but the tenet that anyone else could, too. The only thing that showed us anything different from our snug, secure, prosperous world of perfection was the TV. But, far from being a problem—the TV simply gave us our list of objectives. It was on TV that we learned what needed to be fixed—what changes our generation would make.

No other force could have propagandized a generation of people so thoroughly. I am talking beyond the stereotypic views of America it presented. Lives shown by <u>Donna Reed</u>, <u>My Three Sons</u>, <u>Leave it to Beaver</u>, and all the rest had enormous impact. Though I never knew anyone whose life was exactly like those TV families, there were few that looked fundamentally too much different from the outside. Years of programming had set us up for the fall. This fall was to be different from all the previous generations' disenchantments. Our youthful disillusionment with society was experienced remotely through the TV; in total personal and intellectual safety. We were insulated from the consequences by an immeasurable distance between where the danger was and our living rooms. Beginning in the 60s, the news programs, special reports, and the like, began to examine the problems of our society. Programs exposing slums, graft, dishonesty and racism began to appear on the same medium and packaged in the same slick manner as that of our chief support mechanisms. All were explained and resolved in 30 minutes (or if it were a huge problem—maybe an hour) minus the commercials.

If the problems shown on <u>Father Knows Best</u> seemed to be simplistic, black or white matters of judgment; so did the situations shown on the news. To us, we could not see how good people could tolerate such things as slums or racism. We sincerely knew and believed that the color of a person's skin had no bearing on his worth. It was part of a universal youth creed. Like religious tolerance, it was accepted unconsciously by almost all young people or, at least, the young people we knew at college. We honestly believed that all Americans thought as we had been taught. We asked our parents how these problems could exist and were given excuses that failed to satisfy us as real answers. Science and concerned, focused thought had conquered all our problems and foes before; why not now? Confused, we began to question more and more about our society and its ruling elites, if not their underlying philosophies. What we found, if we could have seen it clearly, was surely not all bad, especially in respect to the rest of the world. On a relative scale, it was actually very good, perhaps the best. But, because it was not perfect we were crushed; and totally disillusioned.

As we began, in our church groups, scout troops, school organizations to try to learn more about our society and get involved, we were met with stiffening adult resistance. Those of us, who did not get involved, watched the resistance on our TV sets. Because freedom and equality were so basic to our view of the nation, the Civil Rights movement took on special meaning to us. We would have to mount a crusade to dispel this blot on our nation's record. It was up to us to fix the problem that had existed longer than our nation. Starting with "those people" far away, the unrest spread in both location and intensity so that no community could consider itself untouched. TV saw to that. From Gov. Wallace to Martin Luther King, we saw everything in minute detail in flickering black and white. From marches on TV to <u>The Autobiography of Malcolm X</u> taught in our high schools, the fight became our fight, at least intellectually in the safety of our detached communities. Not that everyone was close to being personally committed; fewer actually acted to help the oppressed—but everyone was touched. TV made sure the sight of tanks in Detroit's streets became central in our generational memory. I remember the smell of smoke and the nightly fear caused from watching our own city's riot in 67. We saw the ruins as we went downtown to church that summer. It was, however, the last year our family would go to that church.

The war captured our attention directly versus the rather intellectual, spectator draw of Civil Rights. We were involved. We hoped not to be committed. I don't remember a time in my life without war. We were children of the great, heroic and utterly victorious crusade against all that was wrong. World War II had captivated our parent's lives and, having done this, shed its glimmer on us as well. By age six, we all knew just what our Fathers had done in the war. Those of us with "Combat Dads" felt especially proud. Many fathers did brag, mine did not, but they didn't have to. TV continually sang their song. This, along with WW II's exceptionally light casualty figures, seemed to spread an invulnerable halo around our wars and our soldiers. None of us knew anyone who had died or even knew of anyone who had relatives who had died in a war. How could we? They didn't live in the suburbs and our grandparents sure didn't talk about their lost sons. Korea stayed forgotten and was all too minimal in its population penetration to tarnish the universal WW II glow.

As boys of all ages do, we became absorbed in the gadgetry of the war. After all, we were told that WW II had been won, as the next one would be, by a combination of American fighting spirit, superior morals, and undoubtedly the world's best technology. By fourth grade many of us could not only spout baseball statistics, but also the characteristic functions and features of each plane in the US Air Force. I could, for that matter, provide additional if not exhaustive detail on the Luftwaffe and the Royal Air Force during WWII. John

Wayne went beyond being a movie star and became, in our minds, the archetype of how an American soldier should behave. Years later, in the army, I saw countless soldiers playing out their own roles in <u>Sands of Iwo Jima</u>. Before I served, I hoped, unconsciously, that I could, too. War was a somewhat sacred duty that an "all knowing" and "always right" government called you to do. We were taught by our mothers that you never threw the first punch and that "violence never solves anything"; but somehow this didn't count on a national scale. We knew that we would have our own war to win. Vietnam started out for all the right reasons, against all the right foes or so our government said.

By the time the Civil Rights problems got through with our faith in society; our War never had a chance for unquestioning, even moderately faithful support. As soon as one got even the least bit below any of the bombastic reasons the government used to cover our involvement; the contradictions and, thus, the disillusionments began. Even the most right-wing students could only say that the government must know something that they are not telling us about why we were there. In almost every discussion, conservatives were forced into an "Our country right or wrong" type of defensive reply. To us, the Reds had always been in China, Eastern Europe, and Cuba. We had all gone through "A-bomb Drills" in the schools' Fallout Shelters and nothing ever happened. Were we to believe that once Saigon fell, the reds would be in San Francisco? If we were there to support the Vietnamese people, why did those monks set themselves ablaze as we had seen on TV? But this, like the Civil Rights drama, was remote—the crucial aspect bringing the war home to us was the draft.

Each of us had to make a decision. Being a student could delay it, but we all knew that we would, someday, face Uncle Sam and the wearing of the green. Were we to die in the cause of a lie? Only a small minority of students were truly radical in the SDS (Students for a Democratic Society which is still on the FBI subversive organizations list) sense of the word. Most of us had liberal tendencies in terms of human rights, the environment, government programs and we all believed in Superman's virtues: "Truth, Justice, and the American Way." Most of us however, never did anything about it, except talk. Many didn't bother with that. But all of us knew that the draft for the Viet Nam war was wrong, horribly wrong. Nobody could see themselves dying in an Asian swamp for some silly CIA sponsored dictator.

As we clustered around the radio that night and hurriedly digested and commented upon each news report, someone shouted to the entire hall that there was a "student meeting" in the Freshman dining hall that night at 8:30. No one knew any details. No one seemed to know who had called it or what it was to accomplish. But, we knew without saying it that it was now "our time." Shortly thereafter we started flowing out into the hallways, into the stairwells, then into the quad. It was a warm, clear night so it was easy to talk in ever enlarging circles. As groups would grow, multiple conversations would begin within them and, in turn, start their own circles. The library emptied as did most of the fraternity houses so that shortly before 8:00 almost all the students were out on the front lawn.

Rumors started to spread about the Virginia National Guard being activated in or around Lexington. The VMI cadets were said to be in the process of being armed. One of the Kent State student leaders was said to be en-route to the University of Virginia in Charlottesville (U.Va.) for a massive rally at dawn. Several carloads of boys set out to join it. We heard that the President of the college had called and asked the town police, all six, to stay off campus out of the fear of starting violence. After each rumor was enunciated, a ripple of excitement ran through the crowd—we were all warning ourselves to stay cool and think our way through what was undoubtedly the dawn of the new revolution. All argued about which side was right, and if the chips came down, would we fight or not, and for whom. There was an elemental practice and belief in grass-roots democracy—as it should be in the "new society." All opinions garnered respect, and could be voiced; after all isn't that what our martyrs had died for? Some, however, were more popular than others. Everything was done in absolute seriousness. I don't remember a single laugh or joke though now it seems to be a scene from a bad "Youth" movie. Then, we thought, no—we knew, it was real.

Somewhere just after 8:00 P.M. people started filing into the dining hall. There was probably close to 700 or 800 people in it, milling around, smoking and arguing. The room began to get very full, very warm and very tense. I remember what I had seen in movies about "crowds" and what I learned in history about the power of the "mob." I was living it now. Angry, concerned, serious (and if the truth be known also scared and confused) young men were waiting for a leader. Since no one knew who had called the meeting, if anyone had, there was no acknowledged leader. To this day I don't know if anyone planned what happened or even wanted it to happen the way it did.

I was one of the last to go in. I ended up at the far edge of the orchestra stage that spanned the width of the dining hall's rear. It was about fifteen feet deep and was set about ten feet above the floor. Behind a white wooden railing, it formed a natural and large podium. It quickly became the functional front of the hall and center of attraction. All I could see were heads, shoulders and faces of the crowd. As the room got smokier, sounds started rippling across it, someone started clapping their hands and, in this action, the room unified itself. The president of the student body appeared and fought his way to the center of the stage.

Though everyone continued talking and clapping, all eyes were on him. He held up his hands for silence and, remarkably, the clapping stopped. It was, after all, a polite gentlemanly mob. He spoke in a loud, clear voice using short sentences. Unfortunately, he was noticeably ad-libbing and not very dramatic. Five to ten minutes into his "speech" he called for calm, and reason. He paused, seemed to gain confidence in his power over the crowd and did the cardinal sin by asking everyone to go home to wait for the "true effect of the day's events to become clearer." "Boo"s immediately filled the room. He stood rigidly still and watched the crowd impeach him. Antiwar slogans and insults to Nixon were yelled in unison as if our student body president had been part of the federal administration or an adult or something. All of a sudden his well-known association with the campus's largest group, the Young Republicans, became evident. Someone pronounced this and made himself heard. The president's face seemed to panic. Looking quickly from side to side, he held up his hands again, with the probable intention of explaining his words, but was ignored. His time had passed and he found himself in Trotsky's dustbin of history.

At that moment a young man, with long (a year later it would be considered conservative) curly dark hair tied in place by a red bandanna stood on a chair on our stage. He held up his fists the same way our president had held up his open hands for silence. The chants slowly died. The floor became his as he also ad-libbed. His "speech" was a prolific collection of antiwar slogans and short paragraphs about the evils of the war, racism, the draft, and adult society in general. He was frequently interrupted by shouts of "Right-ON!" and applause, all punctuated with clenched fist salutes. The speaker was gaining self-assurance as the crowd was gaining enthusiasm. I began to see for myself how the power of the crowd and its leader could take form. Our student body was, in my mind, becoming a mob. I was getting scared. I think that this leader was too.

He continued to speak for an additional 45 minutes and when he finally stepped down from his chair, not with any ending but with simply nothing more to say, he received thunderous applause and vocal acclaim; he had become "Our Leader." The hall was with him though he had not actually suggested anything for it to do. After a moment or two in which he was undoubtedly proud of himself, he quickly looked around for someone to take his place on the speaker's chair. There may have been no other reason but to get himself out of the hot seat of limelight. Another student stood up and raised a cheer by boisterously putting his red bandanna on. His speech was shorter but repeated, what needed no clarification, what the students saw wrong with the government, the war, why their resistance was justifiable and why the society (and its ruling class) who had spawned all these evils must be changed. The hall was becoming frantic in its support. He seemed to be getting increasingly worried since he didn't know what to say next. The pauses between paragraphs became longer and longer. Fortunately the crowd's yells and voiced slogans did not diminish so there were no apparent gaps implying a need for action.

Sooner or later I figured that someone would actually talk about doing something and that worried me no end. I could see an angry mob, rampaging through the campus, looting and burning in a fit of ugly terror. I began reacting to what I thought was the more reasonable enunciations by yelling "Right ON!" myself and saluting them with my raised fist. Maybe I could help keep the more moderate speakers in control. It was my duty to support the moderates against the Jacobin left. By now there were speakers from the floor being recognized by Our Leader. He began to act like the unofficial moderator of our meeting, and was becoming the acknowledged leader of the students assembled. Our Leader must have been a Senior, for though I had seen him on campus, I never knew his name and never saw him after that spring. I watched him gain confidence and slowly flex the power of an orator. I began to compare him to Trotsky. I envisioned how it must have been in the Petrograd Soviet during the winter of 1905 or 1917. Maybe I was watching the birth of a new Trotsky. The major difference was that Leon Davidovich knew what he wanted to do and why, this kid was as much a victim of events as the crowd.

By 11:00 P.M. Our Leader, the crowd and I were in a feverish, frenzied pitch and emotionally exhausted from the evening's ordeal.

Our Leader began to speak again standing atop his authoritarian chair. This time he made a motion (I guess the idea that Robert's Rules of Order gave legitimacy to almost any meeting was another one of our generation's philosophical mainstays) that we appoint "Marshals" to keep order and protect the campus. All in favor cheered "Right ON" (which must have suggested unanimous consent) and he called for volunteers to meet him afterward. Next, he made a motion that he confer with a student delegation and call on the University President the next day. Then, he would ask him what position the University was going to take. There was thunderous applause, mine included. My visions of an ugly mob dissolved as I realized just what revolutionary actions had been decided upon. Thus; the meeting broke up as we began to walk slowly outside. Nobody went back to the dorm but continued to mill around the quad.

By the end of the hour there were "Marshals" wearing red armbands patrolling the campus. Walking in pairs and relieved regularly throughout the night, they were very serious about their revolutionary duty. We all obeyed their challenges and instructions. It was late, so many drifted back to smaller groups in the dorm. Almost everybody listened to the radio or tried to find a TV set to get the news. We were sure that we would find the nation on fire. The media news told us we were right.

Attendance was light for the following morning's classes. I had to attend since I had German first thing. I could let nothing get in the way of my attempt to pass that crucial course. To go to class I had to cross a picket line of a dozen students wearing T-shirts emblazoned with stenciled red fists over their suits. By Ten O'clock posters were everywhere saying that the University President would address the student body the next afternoon on the front lawn. No one went to classes the rest of the day.

I went to the house and found the Bridge game in session; nothing got in the way of Bridge. We played all afternoon, but our hearts were not in the cards. Mrs. Fazer couldn't see what all the fuss was about. She thought that the killings were a horrible mistake, but the students were going too far. Mickey was very upset at the violent nature of things. I feared a civil war. I don't know if any of us really thought that we would all grab guns and fight it out in the streets—but, we talked as if that were going to happen and we were concerned that it might. Many of us talked about which side we would be on. Surprisingly many would be on the side of the adults or "Law and Order." While things may be bad and the war wrong; they were not willing to fight the government. They were determined to pursue legal, peaceful means for their vision of change. Many of the more radical students were going to DC to join the masses of students forming there to protest. By evening we heard that the faculty had met and voted to continue school without interruption or change. This incensed us no end. There had been talk of a nationwide "moratorium" of college classes and exams (and most importantly grades which precluded anyone losing their 2S classification) while the students did their political duty. We all talked about our options and acted defiant, but almost all secretly continued to study. Better a passing student than a failing draftee.

The President of the University's speech on the following day was full of concern and sympathy. While his audience was polite and still respectful of his position, there were more than a few that were sullenly angry at his membership in the "establishment." He called for "reason and action" and was cheered. He deplored the deplorable, asked for reasonable reason, and called for visible vigilance and all sorts of things to defuse student emotions. It worked. He said that school would continue but all who applied for an "incomplete" because of involvement in some political activity would get his approval—providing the grade was made up before the beginning of the fall semester. He continued by saying that a committee made up of students, faculty and himself would consider what the university could do in the present circumstances; again, a good move. He told us all that the institution was named after men who had defied what many would have then called "the establishment" and had become great in their doing so. He challenged us to emulate their motives, their reason, and their sobriety. Most popular of all, he proposed a joint committee to look into changing some of the more moribund social rules that would report back before the school year end. Classes would resume the next day. The "Marshals" didn't come around that night, or ever again.

About 20% of the students took "Incompletes," some of them undoubtedly for political reasons. Two or three of the brothers left for Washington to work for peace. They returned before the end of the year complete with multiple adventures to relate which became colorful additions to house legend. I stayed on to pass and because I was not particularly committed to the student rebellion, I could not break with my family history or heritage by leaving school for Washington, D.C. or anywhere else. My R.O.T.C. professors were quick to point out that any such activity would endanger our continued presence in the program. The campus mood quieted a bit but remained tense. I did feel that we were now in a "them and us" situation and although many of us would not break in any formal way, we had left "the establishment" spiritually.

The rules simply fell away. It was so close to the end of school that we all but ignored the rules about social behavior or dating, anyway. Our school and those around us tried to set up interim codes but they fell quickly in the few weeks remaining to the 69—70 school year. We had a couple of weeks before exams so it was not yet time to start cramming. We reverted to the traditional spring ventures of girl chasing and partying albeit with a new sense of freedom bordering on reckless abandon.

Greg had been steadily dating Victoria, a girl at Randolph Macon Women's College in Lynchburg. It was her birthday and he invited us all to a party being organized in the Pines Cabins on their campus. Fifty miles down twisting, mountainous U.S. Route 501, "Randy

Mac" was a relic of the late 19th Century. Set up as a female companion school to Randolph Macon College (an all male institution) else-
where in Virginia, it had developed into a small, liberal arts school of
reasonably good repute. It was no "Vassar of the south" nor was it
"Sem;" it was somewhere in the middle and considered, by them and
us, a good school. The 900 or so girls attending were not typically as
rich as the girls from Sweet Briar or as intellectual as those from Hollins, but were a good cross section of smart girls from upper-middle
class to wealthy families. For generations these girls had married into
the economically progressive professional families of the middle
south. Thus, they were, and had been, prime targets for our fraternity's dating efforts.

On the edge of Lynchburg, right on 501, Randy Mac was surrounded by an eight foot high stone wall. Inside, the educational
enclave exuded a mixture of charm and respectability. The whole
campus was of Victorian brown brick with white painted trim,
shaded by many old, tall trees. Throughout the campus were benches
near clumps of these trees as if the girls were expected to sit and
absorb the serenity of the campus. There were four or five classroom
buildings standing in front of four dorms; Main, Wright, West, and
Bell.

Each dormitory was in a consistent, if not memorable, architecture of a vertical design of five or six stories. The upper floors consisted of two rows of good-sized rooms housing one or two girls a
piece with a shower at one end of each hall. The first floor however;
consisted of "dating parlors" and a large reception room. These
rooms were, before the revolution, the only ones in which males
were allowed. Each contained a record player or television supposedly to provide entertainment. I never saw either used. Except for the
reception room, which was totally open, the furnishings seemed to
be an odd assortment of chairs and couches each carefully chosen
precisely so that two people could do nothing more than sit. The
parlors were not, of course, lockable but fortunately each room had a

chair that could be quickly and silently placed to prevent a sudden and unwanted opening. Somehow, I knew, that for generations these rooms had "made do" for personal indoor privacy in a pinch—over the ensuing years they would for me as well. Over the years I spent there, I would often wonder while sitting in a parlor, what stories the room could tell.

There were two architectural claims-to-fame on the campus. The underground library was the first. It had been built that way so as not to disturb the setting of the surrounding buildings. The second was the newest building on campus, the chapel. It was one of those ecumenical buildings having little in common with most churches but housing a truly magnificent organ and some beautiful stained glass windows. It sat at one end of a heavily wooded ravine called the "Dell." In the "Dell" were small cabins (collectively called "the Pines") that once had been sorority lodges but where now available for girls to "sign out" for various social functions. These cabins consisted of one long room with chairs, couches, and a fireplace in front of a kitchenette and a bathroom—everything one could ask for in which to party since they also had electrical outlets and a refrigerator. In the old days there had been many rules governing behavior while in the "Pines." Now, since the revolution mere weeks previous, it was gradually evolving toward a free zone. There would be no hassle for any activity providing there was no undue noise and everyone left by 3:00 in the morning. It wasn't quite there yet (we'd have to wait till next year for this level of freedom) but it was becoming close. Privacy was assured since neither of the two campus' security cars could approach without their headlights giving ample warning to the inhabitants to recover respectability or their clothes. No one had ever heard of one of the guards approaching on foot. Greg had orchestrated Vicki's birthday bash in one of these.

At least four cars full of W&L boys came to the party. Some were outsiders dating one or another of Vicky's friends, but most were from our house. Even in those days, fraternities did not tend to mix into each other's social events—in Lex or not. While this party was returning to a kind of blind dating for most of us, it was with a new freedom caused by the political events of the spring. This was a new experience for me; with no bars there was never a real "pick up" mentality or practice at W&L. Only the occasional practice of enticing stray dates, parties such as this or the spring mixers made you into a hunter-gatherer of girls. Greg had done no more planning past the basic numbers. If everything worked out, there would be approximately the same number of girls as boys.

Beer and music soon filled the cabin with a cluster of people in the "living room" and couples slowly pairing off to dance or talk. I sat with Campbell talking politics and general philosophy with three girls; two Maconites and one visiting friend from "up north." Apart from the general group; we formed a boy—girl circle in one corner of the floor. Now that I remember what we said and how we said it, I think that we were both after the same girl. She was beautiful. Tall, long straight hair, a pretty face—all of which dimmed in respect that Campbell and I both suspected that she wore no bra. Her breasts were not large but since nipples were rarely seen—or at least as clearly—in those days, even the hint of their appearance instantly intrigued us. The first time she moved, both of us instantly caught that noticeable sway. Campbell and I knew, or maybe better stated—assumed, that girls who did not wear bras were making both a political and social statement. We knew what that statement was and each wanted to be part of it that night.

We were trying to be "cool" though, and did not try any frontal assaults. Since she wore no bra, both of us knew she had to be too socially aware and experienced for anything blatant to have a snowball's chance of working. Both of us must have come to the conclusion that the first boy to pounce would be instantly rebuffed and thus drive her into the clutches of the other. So we spent time talking to the two other girls while constantly steering the conversation back towards her. Maybe she spotted the tactic, for she would have none of us. Why she didn't leave our circle is beyond me. Maybe she really was bored or secretly stoned, or both. Her only replies to our most engaging of intellectual conversations were monosyllables. In passing, almost unintentionally, therefore, we got to know the other girls reasonably well.

Sitting closest to me, and thus at least nominally mine was Pam, a Freshman from Cornell. The revolution had closed her school and she had come down to visit her friend Beth, now occupying the floor next to Campbell. After exams they would both fly to Europe where their fathers were both stationed in the same U.S. multinational company. It's hard to describe now just how embarrassed they were about their fathers' stature in that company. Their rank made them a part of the "them" world. They were apologetic about being such blatant and affluent symbols of the establishment. Macon was like that—the guilt would have been completely overlooked at Sweet Briar or analyzed and completely hidden at Hollins. Sem, well, Sem didn't count.

Pam was dressed in a stripped, long sleeve shirt buttoning down the front and a pair of bell-bottomed blue jeans with the fly buttons showing. Her black hair was rolled or ironed straight (during the evening, curls and waves began to appear as the room and activities grew warmer.) I guess that she was 5'3" or 4" tall and probably weighed somewhere around 110 pounds with a nice figure. I remember thinking that she wasn't the best looking girl in the room, nor the worst, but just on the down side of very pretty. It pleased me that she seemed to be warming to my conversation. She was trying to decide whether to major in Political Science or Philosophy and liked Bob Dylan and Joan Baez. Skipping from one subject to the next became increasingly easy and slowly our conversation seemed to drown out the rest of the room.

Campbell and Beth wandered off to the dance floor and the bra-less girl, probably bored by the slackening of our flanking efforts, had moved over to upperclassmen. I remember distinctly noticing all this and not caring. Pam and I danced, drank and smoked. After the second slow dance I continued to hold her hand. That was always the first move. During the third, I held her very close indicating my rising interest and, at the end, kissed her. She kissed back. This was going great. I was both happy and nervous. It was time for precise tactics.

The lights had long since gone out in our cabin. The only light was coming from the kitchen, where those who had either not found dates or those whose dates were evolving more slowly, were standing around drinking beer and talking. The living room was completely occupied by dancers and couples talking softly, closely—around the edges and in the corners. Luckily we had another slow song almost immediately and I could swear she was pressing into me as much as I, her. At the end of the song instead of kissing her as she expected, I just looked at her with my best "deep and brooding" stare. We had just continued to dance slowly in circles after the song was over. I figured this would suggest a spontaneous feeling that "all that existed was me and her." Either she was thinking the same thing or my gesture worked. Once our eyes met I knew that it was time to leave the confines of the cabin.

I took her hand and we walked, scooping up our beers as we left, out of the cabin, down the path to the edge of the Dell. The trees contained the music well, for after a couple of yards down the path, the night became quiet enough for us to be conscious of even the smallest sounds from each other or the campus around us. Near the chapel there was a small amphitheater resembling something one would imagine finding in Greece. Rows of stone seats were sculpted into the grassy hill. There were already lovers making-out on most of the rows oblivious to the outstanding acoustics which made their murmurs and mutterings public. Looking at each other and giggling, we quickly moved along the edge of the trees till we got to the back wall of the chapel.

There, I stopped to look through the stained glass but more as an excuse to kiss. During each ensuing embrace the passion with which I held her steadily increased. Finally, I turned her around in my arms so that my head was on her shoulder and arms crossed in front. With this position I figured I could tell just how interested she was. From there, I could kiss and whisper. She could get out or walk easily away to break the mood, or to increase our passion she would have to consciously make an effort to kiss me. She gave me her sign with a sigh. As she turned to kiss me, I slowly moved my hand up in a more ardent caress. Lightly, tentatively at first, I soon grew bolder with her absence of objection. Not only did she not seem to mind, but seemed to be really getting into it. I was ecstatic. This was going better than I ever imagined it could. My strategy had worked as I, or better yet, we were in a good tactical position. I had to be careful now in order not to snatch defeat from the jaws of victory. As our making-out increased in tempo I knew that it was time for the final assault.

But not there; as it was too open. I was not going to get disturbed or, worse, worry about being disturbed as that might distract me from the matters at hand and dampen my performance. I needed all the concentration I could muster, not only to accomplish the goal, but to do it in a respectable, not nervous or hurried, (no matter how close to reality it was) manner. I spotted a small clump of birches about 50 feet the other side of the chapel by the hockey field. Quickly, I determined that the location offered suitable cover and several avenues of easy escape should they become needed. I gave her another of my "romantic and sober" looks and took her hand. Neither of us spoke. We walked quietly and slowly, almost deliberately. The silence and her following was the answer to my question. I knew it was.

As we sat down between the trees I unbuttoned her shirt and tried to look experienced as I fumbled in my attempts to unsnap her bra with one hand. Later in college, that particular maneuver would become second nature, but then, it was a feat of incredible concentration and physical dexterity interspaced among frequent, passionate kisses. I figured it would show that I had the requisite experience. She undid my shirt and our chests met. It was heaven in that the warmth of our closeness was incredible. But I needed to do something farther. As I kissed and nuzzled, I slowly undid her trousers. Surprisingly, she actually helped me pull them off her legs. This was beyond compliance and bordered on outright enthusiastic teamwork. She grabbed my belt buckle and opened it. Stopping, she leaned back on her elbows to watch me take off my trousers. Her gaze was serious and soft; I think she was not as much judging my physique as much my ardor. I tried not to rush but one foot would not come free. After what seemed like fifteen minutes, but barely a third of that many seconds, it came free and we were naked, against each other once more.

Fingers and kisses explored each other's bodies. I was trying to make this experience last forever while I tried to figure out just when was the appropriate time to complete the act. I was trying not to appear to be too anxious, but I didn't want to take too long. Each passing moment gave a new chance for a stray student or security guard to break the spell. Finally, she whispered in my ear that she was on the pill. Relieved, I took my cue. I had often wondered if I would have to decline German verbs or mentally recite multiplication tables in order to contain myself while waiting for her climax. To my immense relief I found that passion did not drag me into anything premature or unduly foolish. I was so absorbed in the momentous historical awareness of this new threshold of my life that distraction wasn't necessary. I had almost forgotten to notice the sense of pleasure. Every movement, feeling, thought, taste and smell recorded themselves indelibly in my memory for future consideration and analysis. As we progressed I concentrated on doing the things that seemed to please her, believing that I would be the easy one to satisfy. It was nothing like the movies or books. It was much quieter, more subdued but also warmer. Her passion grew steadily thereby feeding my confidence and ardor in proportion. By her moans I gathered that it was about time for me also to finish. Now I could lose my self-consciousness within her arms and body. I did. As we relaxed, I continued to look down at her with my "soft and sensuous" look while on the inside I was smiling to beat the Cheshire Cat. I wanted to tell her in some way but decided against it; no telling what it would her reaction might be—maybe she knew, anyway.

Internally, there were brass bands playing and fireworks announcing my entrance into manhood. On the outside I was soft and romantic leaning down every so often to kiss her nose and nuzzle softly. She smiled, kissed me again, and squeezed me from the inside. We giggled. After a while she asked me for a cigarette. The trick was to reach my shirt and trousers without withdrawing from her. I found a crushed pack in my shirt and matches in my pants. There was no way we could smoke one cigarette without changing our position. The sensation of leaving her was almost as sensuous as that of entrance. Arm in arm, we shared the one that remained, though it was bent and mangled. I did not think that we were finished, nor did I want to be, but she reminded me that we should go back to the party and rejoin our friends. We helped each other dress with all the necessary playful reactions to each other's underwear and the hiding of socks. Finally we stood up, brushed ourselves off, took leaves from our hair, kissed and slowly made our way back to the cabin.

No one had missed us. I looked at Campbell, who should have known by my expression that all had changed. He didn't seem to react, but later said that my "shit-eating-glow" had attested to some sort of altered state or, at least, a healthy dose of radiation poisoning. I was trying not to smile. It wouldn't be cool to smile. I wanted to shout and yell that I was one of the guys now and a member of the club. Almost as soon as we entered, Pam left for the bathroom, leaving me time to ponder two thoughts: is that all there is to this stuff (?) and how do I get her outside again—tonight.

Maybe it was my first case of post-coital depression, but I had thought there would be more of a spiritual or emotional reaction from my date. I had not yet read <u>For Whom the Bell Tolls</u> so I wasn't looking for the "earth to move." I enjoyed our session well enough, but I would have wanted to relax fully and take more time. Something more important to the whole experience seemed missing or wrong. I had expected her to be more demonstratively in love with me afterward. This was supposed to be a bonding process in which she would proclaim herself to be mine. Unconsciously, I guess, I was expecting some great love being born, through this scene, which would sweep her, and I, off our respective feet. Rationally of course, I expected none of this. I was still having trouble remembering her last name; but I knew there was supposed to be more. Again the movies; it wasn't like the movies. Upon her return and renewed smile, I decided that I was thinking too much and decided to continue having a good time and enjoy my victory over purity.

We continued to dance, talk and generally enjoy the party. She stayed close, acted interested, and held my hand constantly the entire night. That seemed to help keep all the analysis in the background. Campbell had returned with Beth. His date did not let us out of her sight for the rest of the night. She looked at me strangely after her first joint trip to the bathroom with Pam. I think she was trying to be protective, maybe just inquisitive. This was a reaction prone to Freshmen; for by the time they were Seniors, girls would no longer protect friends from their lovers. Her intense, but not angry, glare made me feel proud. The night had gone well.

On the way back to Lex, Mickey and I talked in the front seat of his car. It was the shotgun's duty and main objective to keep the driver awake. The other three passengers soon fell fast asleep (passed out?) in the back. He had a good time, met a cute girl and was returning with a name and number. So our first topic of conversation was the girls at the party. One by one we went through each with judgments—back and forth—about their looks, acts and words. I think that guys, in general or maybe fraternity guys specifi-cally got a bad reputation in those days without merit when it comes to talking about one's dates. We never got down to any details that weren't obvious in the first place. We tended to talk about a girl's looks or her perceived intelligence with plenty of scenarios to illus-trate our points but we never talked graphic sex or really personal stuff. Every once in a while one of the guys would brag, but that was universally considered bad show and looked down upon. Frankly, as the years went by, I found that girls specify a lot more of the sexual details and activities than do guys. That night was no exception as Mickey and I went through every girl we knew or met at the party. When I talked about Pam and my desire to see her again, he looked at me and smiled. Maybe I was transparent, I don't know, but I was trying to be almost nonchalant in my attitude towards her. Overall it had been a good show and we were well pleased.

It was times such as this that I began to absorb the essence of col-lege. Mickey, lit only by his cigarette and the glow of the dash, slouched behind the wheel, talking and listening to the radio stations drift in and out, made me feel that not only friendships, but futures were being formed. He would feign cynicism in many of his opening comments but he would soon soften and show softer emotions in the stories that followed. No matter how contrary my opinion would be, he would probe it gently so that our conversation would continue in earnest rather than dissolve into argument or confrontation.

After we talked about women, of course the war came up. We were trying to find meaning or as we called it then, "truth," in both the domestic and foreign news. Different theories emerged from our conversations about the motives and strategies of all the parties. We were constantly pointing out to each other how different things were now from our parents or even the immediately previous generation of only a few years back. Soon we drifted into Bridge and music; sub-jects which could effortlessly carry us the hour ride home. Over the years, 501 began to drive itself—the car knew the way home from Macon with only Deep Purple, Moody Blues or Santana to help.

Upon entering Lex, the back seat woke up and demanded a truck-stop run. Mickey, Starship Captain, made the decision in a flash; always being up for such a run. Out we went to the old "Lee-Hi" Truck-stop on Route 11. With the completion of Route 81 that coming summer, a newer, fancier and generally cleaner "White's" truck-stop would open in Raphine which would gain our late night or early morning allegiance. But, in the spring of 1970, for the last time, this little run down concrete block building was all we had past 10:00 in the evening.

In ensuing years we would feel safe only in larger and larger groups in such "non-student" environments, but this place had been a traditional student hangout for forty years—maybe longer. The waitresses were fat and surly. They were as much a part of the draw as was the never-explored menu. The only two items I ever saw consumed were the grilled cheese sandwich (with pickle) and the "Breakfast Special." For two dollars you could get a couple of greasy eggs, coffee, toast and a show of truckers, "rubes" and "townies." It was the type of place that had machines for tiger striped condoms in the men's room and toilets that would never flush. Half the tables were filled with guys from the college recovering from various social events, the few other customers were almost invisible townies who had already surrendered control of the room. We all ate and joked around. Half the fun of the place was the stuff they had to sell at the check-out area. It ranged from religious relics and icons to truckers accessories and low class tit-mags. Dimitri once bought a log-slice-plaque of John Kennedy and Jesus which had a clock between pictures of the two men. It would remind us in the years ahead of this road trip, the old truck-stop, and our first year at school. I had my own reasons this last trip to the Lee-Hi was significant; I was still in a thoughtful daze about the night's adventure into manhood.

The next morning, after brunch at the house, I called Macon to try to find Pam. I called Beth who lived on the same floor of West as Vicki to see if she could be found. Few girls had their own phones in those days. Calling the main number could cost you fifteen minutes of long distance time. Some Freshman at the desk would try to look up the requested girl in a directory and invariably cut you off while trying to switch you. Once you got to the floor some girl supposedly had phone duty and if she happened to hear the phone (few girls ever answered when not on duty), she would, if you were lucky, find your person before you went too far into debt to Ma Bell. Out of necessity, we kept these calls short which was easy because no one discussed personal subjects with each party in the middle of some communal hall. It would be Junior year, in my apartment, before I would have my own phone and about that year when Macon girls would be able to get their own phones.

When Pam finally came to the phone she sounded happy enough to hear from me. As I asked the inevitable question, she informed me that Beth had planned most of that day. The next week was out of the question since she had to finish several projects and papers. My exams started the following week and she was leaving the country in the middle of it, anyway. I don't know if she was lying, but she told me all this in such a way as I believed her—but then, I wanted to. She volunteered her address in Europe and asked me for mine in New York. She promised to write and meet during Thanksgiving vacation next year as I did not live far from Cornell. There was not much more to say other than goodbye. While I envisioned a mail relationship for a moment or two, I knew that I would never see her again. It upset me from the standpoint of a missed romance; however, the time together was significant. She would always be special to me. I carefully saved my grass stained underwear for years only to lose them in one of my moves, well after college. Pam and I traded two maybe three letters that summer slowly drifting into the bland newsiness that signals the end of a close relationship.

I worked hard during my exams. I was rewarded by yet another F in German, (my professor said it was, however, close this time) three "B"s (English, Soc and History); an "A" in R.O.T.C. and a "C" in Chemistry. It gave me a 2.3, or a C+. To me it was an uncompromised victory. I had met the enemy and though I had not yet won, I had kept grades from getting me kicked out of college. I had survived to be a Sophomore.

My parents came down to pick me up two days after exams ended. Those two days were almost nonstop partying. Since all the girls had left except for a few Seniors staying on to meet parents and such; it was a stag affair. We retold all the stories of our first year. We had entered house legend. Soon there would be new Freshmen to hear of our exploits, three short months and there would be new adventures to chronicle. We all moved our stuff to the house in anticipation of September. We couldn't wait. All that was left to do was party, get our hair cut, and wait for our parents.

Leaving Lex, I answered my parent's questions about grades and why I seemed a little green around the gills. I couldn't wait to get back and start where I left off. I would conquer German, find romance and adventure, and grow to understand more of what I had started. It was just like a movie. I just thought of Pam, and found the courage to smoke in front of my parents. I hoped the summer would go by quickly and be profitable. It definitely would be no vacation.

CHAPTER 4

$\mathcal{M}$y Freshman summer was really quite uneventful. I was lucky enough to land a good factory job which paid better than most of my peer's student-level summer jobs. With a shift bonus and no bosses around, I opted to work nights. Graveyard shift people live in their own world. From 12 midnight till 8 in the morning we worked at the various machines under the supervision of a lone foreman. Not that he really watched, for he mostly slept and slept soundly with the knowledge that we were doing "just fine." The two team leaders had everything organized and the whole crew worked smoothly once we students settled down and learned the routine. We rotated work positions so that not only no one would get too bored, but also so that everyone got to take double the normal breaks. I took in the whole experience as a live Sociology lab.

I originally thought that the "workers" would resent us. They had worked for years in that department while, after a few weeks, we were almost as adept as they in the various processes and skills needed to get everything done. Moreover, this was merely a profitable pastime for us; while this was the mainstay of their lives. I detected no antagonism at all connected with these factors of our two groups' relationship. There was very little thought given to us as interlopers or upper-class-rich kids. We came in to handle the summer load and allow them to take their vacations, and thus were a kind of fringe benefit. Since our jobs usually lasted for three years worth of summers and they almost never changed, the guys got to know some of us pretty well.

Originally, I thought that our politics might offend them. Surprisingly, there were few who goaded us into political arguments. Those that did, were usually the workers who themselves were not liked or respected by the regular crew. Few cared what we thought about the war, Nixon or anything philosophical. What I found was that each had their own all-consuming life outside of work and that occupied their thoughts. On breaks or at lunch we played Euchre and talked whatever hobby dominated their real life. Some were avid fisherman, boaters, hunters, softball players, football fans and the like. Several played the market with surprising sophistication. A few were into women, pornography, or just drank all the time. So it probably didn't matter what you, as a college kid, felt about the war, but it probably did matter if you had an opinion on changes to the Fish and Game Regulations for New York State. It was sociology in the raw. Not abstract models to be studied, but men with real lives and dreams—growing and evolving according to their plan or slowly dissolving before us. None were into their work as a career, only as a way to pay the bills and buy the toys essential to their real existence.

In a way, I did learn a lot. It was interesting to see people who had not bought into the process, but were just trying to make do and gain the desired material aspects of life. To them and quickly to us; work, the jobs, positions, processes, schedules and rules were all a game. Strategies, motivations or personal commitments were all just Business Administration mumbo jumbo. Set up the rules, schedule and the pay plan and then get out of the way. It all boiled down to the money and the least effort to get the most of it. They knew that the rules were stacked against them, however; with thought, luck, and enough ingenuity one could get by. Every victory over the system, the bosses or society in general was avidly cheered by one's shift mates. To be sure it was a nonunion shop, and the income of these "workers" was solidly middle class, but everybody knew who the bosses were and upon which side of the "us and them" equation one belonged.

When given the choice, I tended to work at a machine in one of the smaller rooms separated from the main bay by a hallway. Working alone, I could set my own pace, think, dream of Pam and just generally glide through the night. One of the repair mechanics, who would come up to fix the monster, would often pass the time by stopping by my station between his calls. Fred had been working in the factory for almost 25 years. He had come to the factory in 1946 right after the war and was still there. Sometimes, when he was especially thoughtful, he would recount how the factory had changed, evolved before his eyes. In the midst of this technological history he would relate how his family had evolved as well. His view of time was more family than work, though. I think he enjoyed our sessions. I would ask leading questions knowing that his answers could span several hours. Family or factory stories would keep me entertained and awake without having to resort to too much caffeine.

He played the game, too, by asking me questions on philosophy and politics. Fred would not so much argue as question. His quiet, soft spoken questions were either to point out some apparent weakness or to find humor in my passionate zeal, ambiguity or just youthful myopia. I could tell that he had me by the way he would start to smile about half way through my answer. Suddenly there would be teeth under his moustache and a twinkle in his eyes and I would know that I had risen to the bait.

With the crew, I learned a great deal about fishing, hunting, boats and the like. It fit well into my liberal arts education. With Fred, I learned about, or at least his views on being a grandfather, father and husband. I learned how to react when he showed me a picture of his wife and daughters. She was as old as my mom. What should I say? His daughters were grown, married and had kids of their own. I actually saw pictures of grand-cherubs and was vocally appreciative.

It meant something to him that I look and smile; so I did. This friendship was perhaps the first where I was consciously adult or at least tried to be. Fred may have seen a son in me, but maybe just a work mate who shared enjoyable conversations and both of us knew it was a great way to waste time. I wasn't just a kid—or simply a student—but a co-worker and, hopefully, a friend.

Between discourses, and his efforts at fixing my machine when it frequently came out of adjustment, we would redesign my position's whole process. By the middle of the summer I started jotting down our ideas. After I wrote them up, I asked Fred to sign the suggestion form with me. He declined saying that I was the one with the ideas, he had just helped me think them through. Surprisingly, I received over $500 for my redesign. Fred refused to share my money. Nonetheless, he seemed proud of me and our work. I told Fred to take his wife to one of the nicer restaurants on me. When he still refused, I bought a gift certificate to the place which only he could redeem. I was glad when he was finally forced to go.

He would ask me what I wanted to do with my life or just simply after college. I told him I didn't know, but I wanted to do more than simply make money. I told Fred that I wanted to DO something, make a mark, pass the world along a little better than I found it. He would sigh and wish me well. When I left that fall, I gave him a pipe; he gave me a silver Parker fountain pen. I would use this same pen for every exam till the end of graduate school. I have still it today.

Socially, the summer was a bust. A beer after work with the guys is fine, but at about 8:15 in the morning it was not quite what it could be. By July, Pam's letters were as personal as old newspaper articles. Not that I had any grand illusions that it would turn out differently, but I had always retained a bit of romantic hope. Working nights and saving for school restricted most of my activities, especially partying. I was left with one friend from High School who also worked graveyard. Dave and I would get together to drink a couple of beers on our day off. We would go to his house, listen to loud music in the garage, and talk over the woes of the world and just "veg out." It was there, in one of these bull sessions, I finally learned how to smoke pot.

Marijuana was, in those days, one of the forbidden subjects even among close friends. Parents simply did not understand; very few people did. Legal action for even small amounts was swift and harsh. Rumor had it that it was the fastest way to find one's self in the army. Worse, the criminal record would stay forever and there might even be jail. With all the prison hysteria about what happened to young males in jail, we all would rather die than be sent to one of those places. The biggest hesitation came in simply broaching the subject. One risked a lot. You didn't just ask if the other guy smoked pot. He might say no and think you a druggie. Deep in our minds, it was still "drugs" and closely linked to some sort or personal decrepitness. While we might do most anything to rebel or show our disagreement with the establishment, dope was different. It was big time—you were betting your future. Even if you did find a kindred spirit, knowing from whom to buy it or where to find it was another problem. It wasn't something to take lightly or discuss with just anyone. There was always the lingering suspicion or paranoia that the wrong person might find out and, therefore, might be willing to tip off the police or FBI. We still believed they'd care; come and get us—if for no other reason but to fill a quota—and ruin our futures.

Near the end of the summer, while in Dave's garage, his older brother came in and talked for a couple of minutes. He acted somewhat funny and laughed or, better stated, giggled at almost everything we said. At the same instant, Dave and I could smell why; both of us had been around enough of it in college to recognize the aroma. We were very intrigued; maybe this would help cure the lingering social death we experienced during the summer's time off. I don't think that Dave was any more experienced than I. We both just looked at each other, sort of giggled ourselves and then at him. The silence became unbearable. Finally Dave's brother asked us if we wanted to get high. Nervously, with wide smiles, we both whispered "yes."

We rolled up an old throw rug and used it to block the crack above the door jam which led to the house. We turned the exhaust fan from low to high but turned the music's volume from high to low. We needed to hear any intruders coming before they surprised us and disaster might strike. This was all done almost without commentary and accomplished in less than five minutes. We may not have talked about it or actually done it, but its funny we didn't have to think too hard to react positively and effectively to the invitation. Huddled in a circle, he brought the "joint" out for us to examine. It was a thin, yellow cigarette of about 3 inches in length with the ends hand twisted. We had both known people who had done grass in school but here it was in our hands. I was nervous as hell, but anxious to try it. After lighting it and taking a long "toke" Dave's brother explained to both of us the theory and practice of how to properly smoke a joint. He would watch and coach as both of us were concentrating on doing it correctly and not looking too foolish doing it. The objective seemed to be the immediate and total inhalation of all smoke from the cigarette and an ability to hold the joint without burning one's fingers as it got short and became a "roach." Any stray smoke was immediately sniffed up by one of the other guys. After about 3 minutes, in which we had stopped twice to listen for our very real fear of approaching parents, the joint was reduced to a "roach." The finishing touch was that our roach was expertly roasted with a pair of needle nose pliers.

At first, I didn't think that much had happened to me or my perceptions. Then I tried to stand up. Everything was different—it had all changed. After both of us were standing, Dave and I started to giggle. Everything was funny, too. We got thirsty; we had the munchies; we thought in grand terms but couldn't remember half the proper nouns we tried to use. The music could not be loud enough for our taste but was always too loud for our paranoia about

Dave's parents. After about a half hour, we decided to go for a walk and let the garage air out. It was a beautiful, starry night. Somehow everything was beautiful, symmetrical and in total harmony. We stopped and stared at the sky for a century that lasted five minutes and in that space of time smoked two cigarettes a piece. The stars seemed to move into some sort of ultra 3-D environment. In many ways it seemed as if it were the first time we saw them. My conscious appreciation for things beautiful dates from this night. We would say deep and meaningful truths, only to totally forget them after several minutes. It was a happy, innocent stone. Like the experience with Pam, I felt as if this were another of those important episodes needed in maturing and becoming a man.

It is strange that we didn't do that again that summer. It would be several years till I would feel comfortable using marijuana as a recreational drug in any planned or regular manner. I think that I didn't want or like my consciousness clouded. Perhaps I didn't want to feel as if I was not in total control. Maybe it scared me that I could have as negative a time as the previous experience was positive. It was something that I was glad I tried but did not feel was part of my life. Not like sex was, in any case.

Although Pam had left me wanting for true sexual gratification, she had given me my start. It was no longer trying to start a sex life, but trying to continue, refine and make it more frequent. I knew it would all be easier now. I looked forward to school, knowing that this year I would be able to be more adult about it all. I still wanted some level of emotional love with sex. Not that I would pass anything up, mind you, but if I had the choice, it would be preferable to be "in love." Greg and Vicky were in love—though they'd never talk about it that way—and I was jealous of their relationship. What I saw with them was the way it was supposed to be. Like them, I wanted that quiet assurance that the other person in the pair wanted, needed and liked being there—without thought or effort—just like in the movies.

The best aspect of the coming year was that I would not be Freshman. This new status would give me more opportunity to explore and indulge in the various aspects of college life. Also, this was to be "our" year at the house. It was a fraternity rule that all Sophomores must live in the fraternity house, proper. We had all picked rooms and roommates on system of GPA preference. The highest got to pick first—both rooms and roommates. So the highest six got the rooms, and then simply picked roommates. While it might have been contentious, and I guess one might expect some sort of hassle, there really wasn't. The resulting pairs didn't seem to be best friends, or really have any sort of underlying plan. It was almost as if they were totally random.

Randy West and I became roommates after the choice session held at the end of our Freshman year. My grades were such that it was he doing the picking. Randy was a serious student who was going to major in Political Science. Campbell said that he must have been born 40 years old since he already drank a specific brand of Scotch and smoked a pipe. Nobody our age drank Scotch nor smoked a pipe. Randy never wore jeans; wore loafers a lot; was a Young Republican; was in the R.O.T.C. band; liked to talk about Robert Taft and would squint through his glasses when he got excited. Today it would be called "diversity" while back then; we just knew our house had some "odd" people in it. Randy was perfect for our house and actually made a good roommate for me and the way we worked out schedules and modes of life. Over the summer through exchanged letters, we decided that we would paint our room a kind of tan and our curtains and bedspreads would be made out of army camouflage parachutes purchased at the surplus store. This would be original and we thought, quite attractive in a weird sort of way. We were both looking forward to moving in and fixing up our room.

The relationship with one's roommate could determine what the rest of the house heard or felt about you. I never found out just why Randy picked me. We hadn't been friends other than to say hello during our Freshman year. I don't think that any of the pairs of guys were great friends that year. As it turned out, our best friends were in other rooms. Like the army or boarding school or camp cabins, there was no hiding anything from the roomie. They tended to know you at your most private; your best and worst. Trust really didn't apply—we were one and together—besides after a few weeks one usually had enough dirt on each other to keep private things private. Roommates were important to setting the tone for the year—it was a back-drop to how a year would progress. The relationship could also determine your social life. Working out "who gets the room?" question could make being alone with one's date convenient or contrived. Before we left Freshman year, Randy and I worked out how we would trade off, who got top bunk, and study versus stereo rules—all the important stuff.

The Sophomore September was the last time my parents took me to school. When we got to the house; it took about an hour for my Dad and me to unpack my stuff from the car. There were already two or three guys there also in the process of moving in and getting their rooms ready. Maybe it was a hold-over from our more polite upbringing but each was extremely obvious in their attempt to act properly polite when around my parents. They and the house in general, however, already smelled of beer. My parents met Campbell, who was going to room with Greg just the next room down the hall from me, as we were carrying in the last boxes. He was in the process of ripping unwanted bookshelves out of his wall with the help of a hatchet. My father just winced while my mother meekly asked me if I thought that he knew what he was doing. After my last box was in the room, both parents quickly decided to go to the motel to clean up and rest and would drop by to take me to dinner "later." I couldn't wait to open the beer I had seen in the upstairs refrigerator and get to talk to the guys. Campbell, Greg, myself and one or two others took a break and joyously started telling stories, some of which I am sure were true, about the summer, and sharing our plans for decorating our rooms and our views of the fall term ahead.

I was barely ready for dinner on time and not much had been done on my room in the mean time. During desert my mother announced that she thought that it would be best if they left early the next morning rather than stay to help paint and clean as they had originally planned. I was extremely relieved—it might have a disaster of untold proportions. While I tried to look as if I could deal with my disappointment as she told me, I was internally elated. She said she hadn't expected our house to look or smell the way it did. All she could say is that it was obvious that Mrs. Fazer, due to arrive in a couple of days, did not get up to our floor at all and we should try to keep the place a bit cleaner as she wasn't sure the place wouldn't affect our health. She wasn't really mad or anything, just distressed. I was glad they decided to go back early. I didn't want them around the house to restrict me or any of the other guys. I was also secretly worried that several of the guys wouldn't be as restrained as I thought they should. That night, no one got much sleep. Most of us worked long hours to get our room just the way we wanted it and took frequent and long breaks while doing so.

Though Randy was not yet there, I proceeded to arrange the room as he and I has scoped out over the summer via letter. It's not as if there were many choices about room design and furniture place-ment. At best, the rooms were eight feet by twelve feet and in that space we had to find room for two dressers, two desks, two chairs and two beds. Our bunk beds were along one wall and the tape deck on one dresser facing the bed so that it would be heard best from the bed. One of the dressers was stuffed in the closet and the two desks took up the remaining wall space. I made some decisions on the fly. The bookshelves that Campbell ripped out of his room were attached over the dresser in ours and, after classes started, were always overloaded with books and stuff. Sometimes I would wonder how the laws of physics were defied the entire year as the shelves stayed up without true molly-bolts and only a small piece of a stud with two screws in it. When Randy came the next day, he brought with him the envy of the house; a window air-conditioner. It was old, and would frequently spit ice, but it kept our room cooler than any other place in the house. Our room quickly became the place for bull sessions in the fall and spring when Virginia's weather became hot. It was also great for dating as we had a built-in excuse for not only going to our rooms with our dates, but also closing the door—often the first and foremost hurdle. We were also lucky in that only one pane of our two windows was missing and thus required the traditional plastic-film covering.

Soon all the Sophomores arrived and, after several beers and more stories both new and the repeated and exaggerated, we all started to work on the rooms in earnest. The hall began to take shape. Since the house was 20 years old, there were at least 20 layers of cheap paint on every wall. It was an obligation to paint one's room. We had a tan room. There was one day-glow orange and one painted as a checker board. One had both mattresses on the floor, discarding the bed frames and, arranged road signs from different towns all over the walls and ceiling. One brother's mom stayed all one day and painted his egg-shell with light blue curtains and matching bedspreads. Believe it or not, it stayed that way till about half way through Rush—we thought it rather "camp." Someone, however used some spray paint to christen his walls with "Jets" and "Sharks" graffiti both showing his distain for such a pristine and traditional room but also his cultural muscle-power in the process.

We all thought Campbell's room was the best. He painted the ceiling blue with large white stars, the walls in red and white stripes; he had outdoor turf carpet on the floor. Trusty hatchet swinging, he destroyed the bunk beds and put his bed on stacked concrete blocks so that it formed a sort of bridge as it spanned his desk. Both of the dressers were shoved into the closet. What remained of Greg's bed, Campbell had shortened it with his hatchet, stayed on the floor. We shuddered to think of what would happen the first time Campbell tried to get a girl in his precariously balanced contraption. He did though, and it only fell once while occupied. He said its insecurity was part of the allure. Perhaps it was; he had a very good year in that respect. The hall was a masterpiece when finished. It was anarchy and yet traditional. Each boy had a dresser, bed and desk and each worked—sort of. What more could our mothers ask?

The Juniors and Seniors controlled rush and were busy assigning tasks to everyone available. On the third day, we shampooed the rugs, painted the living room, re-saran-wrapped the broken windows and did the yard work. Our class gifts to the house were the stalls in the upstairs bathroom. Up until that year, the Sophomore hall bathroom had two toilets sitting side by side right out in the open facing the sinks and next to the shower room. The original equipment urinal had died countless years before and had been modified to embarrass the unknowing. Its drain pipe, which normally would have gone into the wall, was turned 180 degrees and would splash your pants and shoes. Only strangers or Freshmen fell for that; and then only once. There were three sinks and a four nozzle shower room (that vented into the attic—much to our luggage's demise) and those two naked johns. Somehow this was beyond the pale for us in our middle-class innocence and our post adolescent sense of propriety. Nobody really planned the stalls or figured out whose idea it was or started out to be. Two guys just went down to the hardware store and bought the stuff and, well, just constructed them. The walls were one sheet wide and tall—with the luxurious addition of doors. Several of the brothers thought that we were getting too civilized but we didn't—and we lived there.

With the Sophomore hall done and the house clean, most the jobs requiring completion before the start of rush were had been accomplished in record time and with at least passable attention to quality. To signify this event Dalton brought and ceremoniously hung, a sign on our hall door reading "Swine Exhibitors Only." It hung there as long as our house survived and we considered it a great honor from an important upperclassman. We had worked fast and with Dalton's sign we knew there was nothing, officially, further required from us. In the few remaining days before rush most people simply partied as more upperclassmen arrived. The day after the sign was hung Greg mentioned that Vicki was moving into West dorm at Macon that day and wanted to know if any of us wanted to help him move her stuff. The idea caught on like wildfire. Why help only Vicki? Why not cruise and prospect the incoming girls under the cover of helping them to move in? It was either Campbell, Cal (who had demanded from his parents the right to live in the house even though he was a townie) or his roommate Doug who first termed it "Freshman Hunting Season" or, as it became known in future years: FHS.

From the first ideas enunciation, the drive that year down 501 and in a hundred bull sessions over the years, the theoretical aspects of FHS were quickly and exhaustively elaborated upon. It was thought to be a superlative way to get the jump on all the other houses on campus and, as with all such concepts, had many different strategies, analysis options and, frankly, tactical applications when discussed in a detached (if not inebriated) manner. But, in practice, it was simple in the extreme. We would go down to Macon and simply hang around the parking lots helping girls move in on the day Freshmen were to arrive. In those days before security concerns, it was really very easy to show up, and identify one's self as from W&L and appear (at least) willing to do some work. That's all it took—in three years of FHS, we were never challenged by any school authorities. Who was going to stop you? Since the girls' fathers would be relegated most of the work, they could hardly refuse. The two man Randy Mac's campus security would be too busy just trying to survive the day to investigate or run us off.

With this one simple FHS activity, we could pick out the best looking Freshman girls, (not to mention upperclassmen moving in as well) know names and numbers before the great blind dating game began! We would be able to get dates for this coming week-end—fully a week before the usual opening day. This would be a great advantage during rush. A house full of good looking Freshman girls would surely attract pledges—not to mention entertain we Sophomores when the Rushees were gone. All of us were convinced that this could be the decisive factor in starting a great dating year. Details and implementation ideas were fleshed out as a group while we shaved and brushed our teeth—even put on ties to complete our W&L image for the Freshman parents. We knew that we had to at least look clean cut even if our objectives were not.

Three cars with twelve brothers descended on Macon arriving about one in the afternoon. Greg had to help and, worse, stay with Vicki, but the rest of us quickly scarfed up girls arriving in the parking lot closest to West. The girls were excited, the fathers grateful; while the mothers, on the other hand, were concerned. This attitude was the result of good judgment because we were, in reality, up to no good. Each scenario was its own story; it's amazing what one learns while carrying in boxes or the obligatory trunk. We kept names and numbers in one spiral notebook kept in the backseat of Greg's car, along with notes about what each looked like and all the differentiating aspects of the girl one could remember. Usually two brothers would help one girl so we had at least two opinions. At the beginning we refused all offers of food or drinks. There was too much important work to do. After several hours, however, and at least 20 girls, the brothers started drifting off, not only to the other dorms, but to the cokes and lemonades promised by the families. Campbell had seen Beth. He did not get to stop and talk because he was on the tail end of a steamer trunk with some sweating, overweight father trying to finish the job for another girl. He lit out with that family (she was, after all, blonde, curvaceous and cute) for a cold drink and I found myself alone with some Freshman girl named Marion from New Jersey, her younger sister, Mom and Dad.

She was embarrassed because her mom kept trying to get some significant conversation out of me as I came in and out of the room unloading boxes, bags and stuff. It wasn't like I was being interrogated, but just questioned carefully and closely. Marion was fairly good looking, the mother nervous, the younger sister acted bratty, and the father just dead tired. While philosophically it was very similar to my own arrival the year before it seemed much different. Girls brought much more, it seemed, to school than guys and everything weighed more. I swore that most of what Marion had brought was either bricks, concrete tiles or body building weights.

It was about 4:30 in the afternoon when I decided that I was tired and this was the last girl, at least for me. There were no brothers left in the parking lot so I did this one alone. Most of them had wandered away to revisit the cute or just to pass the time with their last load before we were all to regroup at 6:00. When the mom asked if they could buy me a soda, I decided that I would relent and said "yes" as I dropped the last box and collapsed on the floor of Marion's 5th level room. Mom and the two girls looked puzzled at my directions to Macon's student union, the "Skeller," to get the drinks. Since it was simply a couple of renovated rooms in the basement of Main hall, therefore not designed as a central meeting place, the directions were, indeed, complex. I ended up drawing a map. I knew it would take a while which was what I needed for my purposes.

As soon as the girls left, Marion's dad and I lit cigarettes and I sat back against the wall and looked at the ceiling. We were too tired for small talk and I was glad, never knowing what I should say to the father of a girl after which I am (or would be soon) lusting. For a few minutes we simply caught our breath, enjoyed not climbing stairs and smoked. When he spoke, he came right to the point. "What kind of girls go here?" I answered that I didn't know what to say. Dad looked at me hard, not mean, but hard. He asked "I mean are they all rich snobs, are they all book worms, are they easy dates or what?" He was nervous and asked the question in hopes of an easy answer. I was nervous not knowing how to answer. I could tell that more than likely, similar to my dad, he had gone to college after serving in WWII—which made it entirely different—and that the girl who was to live in this room was his first to leave. He had probably had very little involvement in picking this school. By being one of the guys with me, and perhaps catching me off guard; he was hoping to get the inside story. He was hoping I would make the next few months of his solitary thoughts less painful.

I took another drag on my cigarette realizing that I could answer anything I wanted as long as I was subtle. Whatever I would say would stick. I could give him nightmares for a month or I could put him at ease—but didn't know what would do which. I whimped out and tried to tell the truth but not so much of the truth as it would scare him. I think it was the first time I spoke to an adult as another adult—not at work, but just out in life. I told him that most the girls at Macon were middle class or probably upper-middle class. There were a few rich kids but not as many as the other schools in the Valley. I went on to say that our house liked Macon because most of us were reasonably serious students and from middle class homes and liked the girls we found here. To ease his mind about college's rumored universally wanton sex, I decided not to tell him about the pines or the parties therein, but told him about last year's rules making it seem as if she wouldn't be allowed to go wild. I didn't play this up much. To make it believable, I acted as if I was somewhat discouraged by the rules. Not too thick or anything, but just enough to make him feel good. I told him about our house mother, the honor code and how hard we worked. By the end of our little talk, he was noticeably more at ease. His wife, though, arriving just as my series of replies was ending, wanted me to start over at the beginning as soon as she gave me my Dr. Pepper.

Here I was, not yet nineteen and much too tall for my weight. I was just a little dirty and had been sweating for about four straight hours. I had shaved, not that I couldn't get away with not shaving for a couple of days, but my hair was all askew and my tie was filthy and loosened halfway down my sweat stained shirt. I was sitting against the wall so that my bells rode up enough to show that I wore no socks with my Pumas (in those days, that in itself was revolutionary). My hands were draped over my knees as I smoked a cigarette using her daughter's trash can as an ashtray. Hence, I was not in my best form for my first college Mom. When the father didn't move as she entered, neither did I. She sat down on the bed with her daughters taking the chair by the desk and the younger one actually sitting on the desk, all three facing me. Seeing I was the total and undivided center of attention, I figured it was my cue to leave. Just as I was butting out my smoke in the trash can, her mother placed her hands on her lap, looked me straight in the eye and said "…Now tell me…yes, tell me about you." I froze. My mother had taught me enough not ignore her—but what was I going to say?

This was a first for me. My previous exchanges with date's mothers had been back in High School and were short pleasantries before we left or immediately after we returned from my dates. I never had to speak with one for more than a few moments. These exchanges could hardly be called conversations. I mean it was hardly talking or anything; it was more a series of formalized questions and responses. Like saying "Hi…how are you?" "I am fine, and you?" They were uttered without thought and were only significant if absent. And besides, these people knew my parents or at least of them and we all had access to previous interactions sometimes ranging back to fourth grade. Now I was trapped between the proverbial rock and a hard-place. Anything I said that would charm Mom or make her feel better would destroy any chance I had with Freshman Marion. If I didn't do well with the daughter I would be the subject of several rounds of derision among the girls on that hall. You could bet that I or my answers here would be talked about that night both among Freshmen and Upperclassmen alike. The next day, what was said on the hall, would make its way through the dorm and then the school.

Macon might be lost to me for the year. The setting offered little hope of anything positive, so the best to work for was a draw. Macon seemed to consistently draw me into scenes that required precise tactics. I began to think of trying Hollins next as I was at a loss for words. I drank from the Dr. Pepper to give me time to think.

I told her that I was from upstate New York and a Sophomore at W&L. I was a history major and our fraternity came down on this day to help out the girls here at Randolph Macon Women's College. My delivery was staccato and sounded a bit (!?) nervous, but I think most of it got out with some sense of sincerity. I told her that we considered this dorm a "sister" house to our fraternity (a nice touch I would remember to pass on to the others during the ride back) since several of the boys dated here. I hoped to leave it at that. I stood up and lit another cigarette thinking that it might give me some cover so I could leave while I was ahead.

Mom, however, was too fast for me. She nodded to all of this, but went on with her questions. She also asked what I "thought of Randolph Macon College for Women." I began to get the idea that this was not Mom's choice for a school either. I couldn't tell if she were using me as an argument for or against Randy Mac. Marion, sitting silently, trying to become as invisible as I, went absolutely white. I think that she was planning some sort of jungle torture for her mom by the look in her eyes. Her dad just smiled, got up and told everyone that he was going to the car for something. I felt that he was leaving me to my dire fate; he, at least, could leave. For a moment, I tried to think of something I needed from his car, or Greg's car, or any car; but couldn't. The brat loved every minute of my torture and Marion's torment. I started slowly by saying I didn't know what she meant but "I, for one, kinda like Macon. The girls weren't really snobs or egg-heads but seemed to be smart girls you can talk to." Mom's expression was neutral and Marion's seemed to be softening. So far, so good; I was alive and could see the light of the open door—but I wasn't out of it yet. I tried to put on as "serious and philosophical" look as I could under the circumstances. "They—Randy Mac girls—are popular at our house because they weren't into the silly games of college life." I tried to leave it at that and looked quickly for any indication that I could physically leave. I even turned to move, but Mom held me fast with her friendly gaze.

"What silly games are those?"

(Why did I say such a thing?) Now, I think, I went white along with Marion who had renewed her horror at her Mother's question. The only person with any color was the 13 year old brat sitting on the desk. There was no escape, I was one of the 80 as the Red Barron did a barrel roll over my smoking Sopwith Camel which was failing to respond to my stick and pedals. I was crashing and burning with the best. Somehow I stammered out some words that seemed to make some sense. "I don't know, I guess, people trying to be things they aren't…" I let the sentence drift into silence rather than properly end it trying to give me some drastically needed thinking time. I continued the "philosophical" look. "These times bring out some silly things in people…socially, I mean…" I was desperately hoping for someone to jump in and save me. A baseball through the window, a bomb falling, some brother walking down the hall, anything to save my butt from this insidious Mom. This rest break was increasing my sweat problem; my deodorant was failing me.

"What do the girls do for social occasions here?"

At this the brat sputtered into uncontrollable laughter and Marion dissolved, melted and looked as if she just hoped to die—ending up with eyes glued the floor. Dad walked in as she was finishing the sentence, wearing the same smile as when he left. He knew when his wife was on a roll and he could (or would) do nothing to help me. Mom, on the other hand, seemed to be oblivious to the pain in either Marion or me. In her own way I think she was trying to be "with it" and friendly, inquisitive, not intentionally antagonistic, and was trying hard to be conversationally interesting in the process. I couldn't detect any malice at all. Perhaps she was just unaware of what she was doing to me, not mention to Marion. Didn't she know that she shouldn't ask those questions of a stranger; especially one who was in the process of lusting after her daughter; or at least seeing if he wanted to? Didn't she realize that there was no way out for me to be both exciting to the Freshman and respectable enough for her? She had me. I was playing for my life. The girl would never tell the whole story but she might repeat some of what I said to someone who might know me. This could be the making of a great first week legend. All schools had them. I could be the butt of a legend telling of a "crash and burn" before school even began. What a laugh. Being a boy scout did not help you get good dates—only dates with good girls—and that was not the purpose of FHS.

I leaned against the dresser so that I could look out the window, hoping to see one of the brothers that I would immediately need to rejoin. No such luck. "Well, if we come here we usually go to a movie or some campus function. You know…concerts in the chapel or lectures. Sometimes we just go down to the 'Skeller' and listen to some of the students play guitar and sing." I was making this up as I went along. I had dated here only a few times and we either spent time in the Pines or had gone up the Blue Ridge Parkway to drink beer and walk under the stars (a polite euphemism). How was I going to tell Mom that? "Mostly, the dates here are just…really…kinda…informal…because…usually…we go back to Lex." I was in the process of biting off my tongue in punishment for adding the last part of the sentence. It left begging the same question about the fraternity and what we did there. Mom just continued looking, smiling at me. If she didn't know that she was torturing me like a cat with a cornered mouse, she was out-to-lunch as far as young people go. What was I going to do? Mumble, groan, head for the bathroom? The window offered no escape. "In Lex—ington, we usually have a dance at the fraternity house or go to some sporting event." I had never gone to a college football, basketball or baseball game in my life; nobody in our house did. It was a tradition, at least then, at W&L to leave the games to the jocks and guys who had boring dates. I finished my sentence looking out the window. There was going to be absolutely no eye contact allowing her any continuation of this line of questioning.

I didn't want the next question which was to "tell me about your fraternity" or anything like that. It could all become twisted and get back to humiliate me. Suddenly, my tactical sense returned and I decided the offensive offered fewer risks. I asked Marion what she was going to take that semester. If that answer didn't last long enough to rescue me, the brat was going to be questioned about High School and her college plans. I would never again allow Mom the conversational initiative. You can't win a battle fending off attacks, sooner or later you have to launch one yourself.

It worked. Marion lightened up and said that she didn't know. She would take English, French, History, Biology and Calculus. She then asked me what I had taken as a Freshman. This interchange started the necessary cover of conversation till I spotted Campbell sauntering across the front lawn. I yelled through the window, waved and excused myself from the room after hurriedly shaking hands with Mom and Dad. Marion walked me out with the smiling approval of Mom, the brat and Dad. They all seemed to be busy brushing themselves off getting ready to leave themselves. Marion left her parents in the room and walked me down the stairs alone. I was impressed and a bit surprised that she made the effort. Maybe I had done better than I thought. I made a production of getting her last name and I told her the phone number for her all as she didn't know it yet. I finally got a good look at her and realized that she was really rather pretty. She smiled at me. I suddenly wanted to kiss her goodbye; like it had been a date or something. I knew I had earned it and I think she wanted me to, but the brat ran up and yelled out "so long" breaking the spell. I resolved to follow this one up. I was more relieved than anything else.

The hall never looked so good; the stairway glorious and the front door the Promised Land. I figured I hadn't said anything stupid enough to get me into too much trouble so the afternoon could be qualified as a success. As we reassembled, I found that almost every-one had similar close-calls, but, in general the exercise had been suc-cessful and fun.

Back in Lex, there was little time for anything but the final touches on our Rush work till the weekend. We had the first house meeting of the year that night and agreed that all brothers would report for work at ten sharp; under penalty of fines or working the DNABs (do not ask back). Rush was thus a full-time, all consuming, endeavor; at least till two or three in the afternoon, though we were supposed to work clear through till dinner. We would finish lunch at about one and work one more job till a Bridge game would unexpectedly break out; a baseball would demand to be thrown around the back yard; or brothers just disappear on some unaccountably urgent errand to one of the apartments. By dinner time, the two Rush Chairman would usually be pissed at several or all of the brothers and usually each other. After dinner it was Bridge or tunes or TV allowing all the goodwill to regenerate. We had done a good job, though. All the downstairs had been repainted including, much to her delight, Mrs Fazer's apartment. All of the glass in her rooms was still intact as were most of the windows across the back of the living room. We had only one upperclassman living on the main floor so the other room was turned into a lounge.

This room, the "study lounge," was another of our collective Sophomore brain-children. We got three fitted brown sheets, put them on three old mattresses and piled them, like a couch along one of the walls in the room. The old easy chairs were put in a corner around some forgotten braided rug. The room was then painted tan with a navy blue ceiling. On the walls we put various rock posters and album covers. The coup'de grace however, were the small day-glow stars painted randomly on the ceiling and the two florescent solar system mobiles in the corners. To set everything off, we had a tape deck (willed to the house by a brother past-due on his bills) and a black-light. This was to be the answer to our dating problems. The new university rules specified that no girl could spend the night in a fraternity house. Further, no girl could be on the Sophomore sleeping floor except on weekends, when they had to be out by 3:00AM. This room would be our spare for week-nights or when the roomie had your room. We even had a spare desk shoved in the closet so that we could pull it out and call it a study on Parent's Weekend. It proved to be a good draw for Rush. We acted like it had always been there and was constantly in use.

Rush started that Saturday. The entire weekend would be filled by "Open Houses" in the afternoon and evening, while the more important Rush Dates would start the following Monday. School stuff would also start that week with matriculation and the like, fighting with Rush for our and the Freshmen's attention. The first day of classes began the week after that. Rush—beginning School—It was going to be hectic but it was extremely important, too. A house's future depended on how many and of what quality Freshmen pledged. It could set an optimistic or pessimistic tone for the whole year. It was the type of joint enterprise which fused or destroyed a fraternity. Thus, Rush was the central event in a house's life, a kind of anthropological procreation. It seemed to me, then, to be organized with military precision, Machiavellian political skill, and with a cunning, ruthless type of salesmanship that I was not to see again till well into my business career. Later, when I found out the actual facts; that it ran mostly on momentum, tradition, lore and un-thought-through decisions made it all the more amazing.

Tradition was the major ruling feature in organizing and executing Rush. Technically, Rush started the last two weeks of the previous year. Our house would elect two Rush chairmen, one rising Senior and one rising Junior to coordinate the house's efforts and activities. Their first task was to design and write our full page entry to the Freshman Rush Handbook to be delivered to incoming Freshmen at Freshman Camp. This was usually a couple of pictures showing brothers participating in sporting events or at a party attacked by a beautiful, if half-naked, girl, and always followed by a copy of the composite house picture (a collection of wallet-sized formal portraits of all the brothers). This was captioned by some sort of write-up extolling the virtues of the house's scholarship, leadership and all around great-place-to-be-ness. Our Sophomore year, our first year of Rush, our house's entry was totally revolutionary.

Our two Rush Chairmen had scoured their text books for pictures of historical figures and had written a thoroughly funny description of our house. It told of our field trips to Lake Lexington and our yacht (showing a picture of the Britannia). There was a picture of Versailles captioned as our house; A Playboy Bunny for our house-mother, Albert Einstein for our tutor and the like. It was tremendous in our eyes and we wondered if it would make it through the administrations censorship. While all the other houses had stuck to the traditional format, ours was a breath of fresh air. Maybe it was Kent State or the new rules or the fact that this year's freshmen didn't have hair as short as we had when we arrived, but it worked.

The day before Rush began, was also the day the Freshmen got back from Freshman Camp. All the houses sat behind card tables lined up in the Quad. There, they waited for the Freshmen to sign up for Open Houses, Rush Dates or parties. Other than the tables, there was supposed to be no other contact—a rule frequently bent by "friends" of previous relationships, guys from the same schools or the like. There were 12 open houses and 16 fraternities so by definition there would be four losers for each Freshman. Obviously, it was to a house's advantage to be in the first 12, but tradition fixed table order as being alphabetical—using the Greek alphabet. We had been, since time began, number 13, our lucky number. The handbook spread worked and we filled up our open houses quickly. That night, the "Rushees" the Rush chairmen and a few picked assistants matched the sign up list against their pictures in the Freshman face book. Brothers, mostly Sophomores, were assigned to pick them up for each appointed function. Each driver would be given a 3X5 card with the Freshman's picture and dorm room number on it. At the Intrafraternity Council official's whistle all the fraternity members would race up into the dorm, get their assigned targets, and escort their charges to the respective houses. It was a lot like the beginning of some sort of race. There was never any real explanation of why all the hurry, except the fact that it had always been that way.

Once at the house, the frosh would be given a soft drink and casually interviewed by several brothers trying to pick out some identifiable interest or trait that could be quickly matched to one of the brothers "Whereyafrom?" "Whatsportyaplay?" "Whatmusicdoyalike?" "Whatchyagonnamajorin?" All were questioned until some facet about the boy popped into the escorting brother's mind which would give him an idea of who within the house would make a good or suitable match for the prospect. The escort would then take the frosh to that brother and quickly write down on the 3X5 card any thoughts that he might have. If, at any time, the interviewing brother thought that this kid was a complete disaster, not even "filler-at-best", the boy would be guided to the DNAB corner. There, some brother undergoing some dire punishment tried to keep the one or two fish occupied while the real rush was gong on around them.

The rush-able Freshman would be guided through as many brothers as possible by their match-mate till an hour elapsed. Then, the original escort would try to bring the frosh back for a Rush Date later in the week, peeking at the other houses already on the Freshman's card. We would try to cause the Freshman to cancel some other house as a defensive ploy. Often we would try to fill up their Rush Card (much like a 19th Century lady's dance card) to corner their attention. As soon as they signed up, they would be driven, often at breakneck speed, back to the dorms. Getting a frosh back late could cost the house $50.00. Since there were only 15 minutes between open houses, the next wave of cards were slipped to the drivers as they left. By about the third open house this process all started to become clockwork.

Between events the house would be quickly straightened and brothers would collapse to have a cigarette or talk to their or someone else's date. Dates were strictly controlled during Rush. There had to be enough of them to provide the proper sexual allure, but not too many to distract the brothers or the Freshman from the matters at hand. It was considered very bad show to spend time with your date during the actual Rush process. Girls, who were trusted by the house, would "train" girls who were new to the process. Blind dating was never allowed, there being no place to hide the disasters. I was lucky enough to have Marion down from Macon, since Vicki had met and liked her. That entire Saturday, though, I hardly even talked to her. I didn't mind, I was working on important stuff and really enjoyed being in the thick of the action. She looked happy enough being a hostess and shown off to the Freshman. I was proud.

Saturday went well. We had plenty of "signees" and I only had to work the DNAB corner once and then only to spell a brother who looked like he was coming apart with frustration. I was not being punished or anything, it was just that I was a Sophomore and they needed someone to do it. I didn't feel slighted, though I probably should have. I was not what you would call a leadership type in the house, but then none of the sophomores were, with the possible exception of Greg. I cajoled Campbell to join me and we had fun talking above and around our three captive fish. It turned out to be as fun as the actual process since we got to project all sorts of fantasy interests, exploits and advice. While you couldn't trash DNABs (because like dates, trashing them could hurt your reputation) you could have fun and be ridiculous.

The last open house ended at 9:30 P.M. I thought that at least then I would get to spend some time with Marion. But, before anyone did anything or went anywhere there was a mandatory meeting downstairs in the dining room. The Rush Chairmen sat at the head table with the brothers seated around the three remaining tables placed perpendicular to it. Each table was supplied a face book to remind the brothers about each Freshman. One by one, each boy was debated in detail. Everyone who had talked to the frosh would give some sort of comment. The frosh would then be matched with an escort and two or three brothers assigned to talk to him during the upcoming Rush Date. This took forever but the debates lessened to a few comments per prospect as the night went on.

It was two in the morning when the meeting broke. The dates had left at around eleven. This year they were not required to sleep at approved housing, but groups from each school were staying at different brothers' apartments. Mine, Vicki and some of the other Macon FHS contacts were at Mickey's apartment over the Montgomery Ward catalog store on Main Street about four blocks away. We rode with Mickey to his apartment to see our dates. Five of us tiptoed up to the door and Mickey knocked. Slowly, the door opened with Vicki, their self-appointed leader, telling us that everyone was asleep. Her hair was down and she wore a long sleep-shirt. Standing at the only partially opened door she was the picture of modesty except for the way the sleep-shirt seemed to amplify rather than disguise what we knew was beneath. All of us instantly noticed and tried not to stare. Mickey quietly slipped in the door that didn't seem to open wide enough for half of him. Greg made the next move to join Vicki and was met with an outstretched hand and a kiss on the nose. "We're all real tired, we'll see you in the morning…bye." Click and the door was closed for the night..

Greg seemed to lose two inches in height as he exhaled. He at least thought that HE would get to spend the night with her. This struck us as funny, very funny. We all talked about the various social forces at work in the situation on our walk back to the house. All agreed that nothing brings out morals like a bunch of girls who knew each other only slightly. It would take a lot more time or somebody within the group to make the first move before they would "publicly" sleep with their dates—the 50s were still with us even though it was already the 70s. While most of the freshmen girls sleeping there that night were probably not virgins, (or at least so we hoped) and they thought of Vicki as an experienced, worldly Sophomore, blatant unmarried or casual sex was still too daring for public knowledge among one's peers, certainly amongst from first week Freshman. We felt let-down for our first dates of the year thus we decided that Greg owed us breakfast at the new truck-stop to alleviate his guilt. His anguished reply was that he had a sure thing while the rest of us probably wouldn't have got anything at all; knowing us, he was sure of it. By the time we got to the house we had him convinced that the least he could do was drive.

It was lunchtime on Sunday before we got to see our dates again. Campbell and I were up by nine but we waited for Greg before walking over to the apartment. Greg, never one to miss any sleep, didn't finish his shower and pull on pants till almost eleven; even though we did our best to first wake then hurry him. We didn't make it up the narrow stairs to Mickey's door till it was almost time to go back for lunch. We found the apartment in constant motion. The stereo was playing loudly and there were at least two hair dryers going competing with it for background music. Everyone there already had coffee and we certainly needed some, so we helped ourselves to the murky brew. Mickey was sitting, unshaven in jeans and a t-shirt, staring out the window with a cigarette and a cup of no longer hot coffee in his hand. He stated that, except for the bodily necessities, which he had to forcefully demand, he hadn't been allowed into the bathroom yet. The apartment certainly looked like five girls were visiting. There were open suitcases everywhere with all sorts of clothing and hair stuff (curlers, dryers, etc.) spread all over the bar that separated the galley kitchen from the apartment's sleeping areas. Every girl was borrowing something from one another. The front room was where most of them had spent the night and it was here that we tried to talk to our dates. Mickey's roommate, Stan Fritz (adopted by

Mickey out of a sort of big brotherly good will move) spent the night in his cubicle but, being dateless (he was not allowed to bring Fearless to Rush), was more or less tactfully ignored by all. Small talk was impossible, since they were all trying to put the finishing touches on their Rush appearance and this, being their first dating weekend of their college career, were also more than a bit nervous. I felt their excitement and was glad. After much furor, we finally left for lunch in a Noah's parade—two by two; Mickey staying back to shower, shave and dress in relative peace.

Everyone was there, but this was the quietest I had ever seen the house with girls in it. No one really talked at all. It was like we were saving it up for the Open Houses where we had to talk. The two Rush Chairmen came last into the room. I had a sudden urge to stand when they passed me. They were deadly serious and talking between themselves while occasionally barking an idea or order to one of the brothers. No one bitched at them or gave them a hard time; they were in command. At 1 P.M. they told us to get it started. That's all they had to say. "Get it started." We picked up our cards and started the process over again—by now we were all pros.

It was less exciting than Saturday, but we were better at our job. If anyone had asked us, then, if we wanted to be salesmen we would have told them they were crazy, yet that is exactly what we were doing. We smiled, got excited, laughed, joked and got each Freshman to bare himself to whatever degree we wanted. I did not even appreciate how good we were at this, then. Even the girls seemed to get into the competitive spirit of the events. There was competition between the houses for success in Rush and between ourselves for the plum assignments. It was a true event, a long hectic one, but an event all the same.

It being Sunday, after the last open house, several brothers were nominated to drive the dates back. Stan was one, and we Sophomores all realized why which brothers were nominated as drivers—their opinion during the ensuing meeting was valued less—internally each breathed a sigh as we were not asked to drive. As before, each frosh was discussed, though with much less enthusiasm, even from the beginning. There were more snide comments and sarcastic remarks. The Rush Chairmen, however, would just stop and look at us, like our High School teachers had when waiting for us children to quiet down. We would, and they'd continue trying to get things done and done well.

Each weekday would have three Rush Dates with Friday being the last night. During the week, everyone also matriculated and bought books for their classes. In our mind, however, these schoolish activities were only to pass the time till 2:30 rolled around and the Rush Dates began. Each was two hours long and, this time, beer was permitted—if not mandated (I guess Virginia thought it was 3.2 percent alcohol beer then legal for 18 year olds). This was when the real work began. This was where the freshmen, the houses which rushed them and we the people whose futures were already interwoven with the houses would have their futures decided upon.

Like before, each cluster of brothers assigned to a Freshman would talk and try to get to know their targets. All the while brothers would subtly talk about how the frosh's interests could and would be met by joining our house. No bids could be given without a vote but even from the start enough hints would be given to keep Freshman interested. We would attempt to find out what other house was interested and subtly disparage them till we felt our points were made. Not that we would out-and-out say negative things, but just point out that they were all jocks or something so that a Freshman in which we were interested would think twice. After all, if the IFC caught a house disparaging another, it would fine your house $50.00. No one was ever fined. Somewhere along in the process one of the Juniors or Seniors would agree to sponsor a frosh at the "ball session" (the vote on membership) following the last rush date of the evening thus beginning the political process of selling him within the house. Beer was strictly rationed to the bothers so that no one would get overly drunk. Several always seemed to get more than they should have, but that just meant that they would not get to vote on new pledges. It was 11:00 P.M. by the time we started the "ball session."

Supposedly, any one brother could "black-ball" or deny entry of any Freshman to becoming a Pledge. In reality, the factional leaders of the house, still just hazily recognized by my Sophomore eyes would provide the deciding opinions. There was a subtle give and take process between the more popular brothers and the following factions within the house. Since there was no outright majority, each faction would form coalitions to get or reject certain prospects. Brothers like Stan knew not to say anything and Sophomores were never supposed to say more than descriptions. Not that any of these rules were written down, it was tradition, and as such, it was so passed on to each ensuing class. Usually, if any two of what I came to see as the four house leaders wanted to wait, we would wait; bid, we would bid. Likewise; if two were in any way negative, that person would be DNABed. Often, as a compromise, the frosh would be guided by the doubting leaders during their next rush date. We all looked for affinity in interests and social class. Our house was probably recognized as being in the "lower tier" since all our fathers worked for a living, though some made more money than others. None of us were renowned campus leaders, notorious face-men, or jocks and none of the pledges we got were either. While none of us consciously tried to get pledges just like us, it always worked out that way. By Friday, we had done very well with 12 confirmed and 2 considering. It was a success. There was much cause to celebrate.

We all, especially the Sophomores, looked forward to a repeat of the previous year's Last Night of Rush. At the start of the last Rush Date everybody made a concerted effort to get rowdy as well as drunk. Vicki led the Macon dates out on cue and Mrs. Fazer disappeared. But, the spirit of the previous years just wasn't there. A beer fight did not catch on and no one tried to evict us from the upstairs hall. We all seemed happy and jubilant enough—Rush had been a success—but nothing seemed to catch. When we marched down to the quad there were only small groups from other houses gathering also trying to recreate the magic. Nothing seemed to work. After about a half hour of yelling, all of us just started wandering away, not happy, exhausted drunk as before, but just tired drunk. We knew then, though we didn't know why, that the coming year would be different.

I don't know why it ended. Maybe it was that every house had a Combo the next night and there were a lot of dates in town. Perhaps it was part of the innocence lost the previous year over Kent State. Several of the houses, however, had disastrous Rushes. They were the ones that would fold by the middle of the year—again we didn't know it then, but suspected it. For the first time in memory only 75% of the Freshmen joined houses. No, it was definitely not the same. These freshmen seemed different and in many ways not only were they different, but saw the times different as well. They would never wear suits to class or join R.O.T.C. to avoid the draft. They did not have archaic rules not only to memorize but also to live by and were already experienced in rebellion against established authority. Though, in reality, a year younger, they were in many ways, older and more seasoned than us. They had already turned the corner while in High School. This was not all apparent, then, as we stumbled home, but would become obvious as the year progressed. The upper classmen were silent—we were just disappointed.

Saturday was the first extended period of time we had found to spend with our dates. There was a Combo Party at the house where a band would come and play after dinner. Everyone had dates and finally we would get to be with them. Randy was an exception. He had no date for the weekend but, with Stan, went up to Madison for its opening mixer in hopes of finding one. Stan, of course, would bring Fearless back.

That gave me sole possession of the room to be alone with Marion. She had come up on Friday night to help with Rush. She seemed to be withstanding Rush and our house's character rather well. Though new to it all, she seemed to thrive in the chaotic social environment. She seemed friendly and happy among Vicki and the other Macon girls and was continually adequately responsive and attentive to me. Though it was our second date (entire weekend dates being long times in terms of college romances), it was the first time we would really spend time together. Moreover, it was the first time we could be alone—really alone with privacy and everything. I picked her up at Mickey's before lunch, a little later than the others so that we would have to walk back to the house by ourselves and therefore could talk—finally.

I held her hand and tried to make small talk. She had started classes, which carried us for a while, but I was interested in what she thought of the house, the guys and me. She was not too communicative on those subjects. As I pushed, I began to get the idea that she thought Rush a bit juvenile, almost to the point of being stupid. She did however, like several of the freshmen very well. The process was all a "game" in her words and my comment to her mother came ringing back to me. She wasn't mad or anything, but just a little disappointed that the experience was so "phony." That upset me because I was in love with the whole experience of Rush. Rush was part of the way college was supposed to be. Yeah, it looked childish and, on close critical examination, it was phony, but it was an important ritual for the house to survive. That was the most important thing and we all had our parts to play. I passed it off to being tired and she being a little mad at being ignored. She had, after all, been put on display for a bunch of silly Freshmen (though they were not as silly as we had been), ignored, and had spent her second Friday in a row,(and the second of her college careers in a small apartment sleeping on the floor with a bunch of other girls. What a way to start!

Lunch passed well enough and afterwards we went for a walk through the town and campus. It was quiet and beautiful. The trees and lawns were lush while the sun blazed in a cloudless sky. Luck was with us as it wasn't even too hot. We walked out past the hill (the nickname for the front campus since time in memorial), the football field,—all the way to ruins of the original school, Liberty Hall. I stood there, looking at the ruins, alone with her, her hand in mine. I just squeezed a bit and brought her close. It was the romantic gesture in the romantic setting for which I was looking. It was time to begin.

I turned her to kiss me. She kissed back, but it was one of those singular type kisses which mean "I'm having a good time. I seem to like you, but don't push it." I was too inexperienced to know what she had said with that kiss, so I tried again. She responded with a kiss that started enjoyably but ended quickly, showing that she was not in any sort of passionate mood. I finally took the hint. We walked a bit as I pondered strategy and found ourselves sitting under the nearby trees on the edge of what was known then as White's farm.

I put her hand in my lap in an effort to establish some pictur-esque, romantic setting to my intended passion. I ran my finger-tips through her hair as she closed her eyes. I wanted her to sigh, but since none was forthcoming, I just started to talk. It was a languid, monotonal type of speech that I thought especially romantic. I spoke about how beautiful the trees and hills were. I didn't know that I really felt this way about this setting till years later, but then, I just thought it would start her thoughts running on a more sensual plane. I talked about the ruins. I wondered aloud what stories they could tell. What were the stories of the boys who had lived there 200 year before? What did they do? What were their lives like? These questions or daydreams were real enough to me, but hardly what one might think was "dating" conversation—but at least it wasn't phony.

Marion would respond by glancing at me through a couple of words, and then close her eyes again. I couldn't tell if she were drift-ing in some comfortable fantasy or just bored. I was trying my best to be soft and romantic, almost poetic. I was silent for a while. I put my hand on her chest while I stroked her hair as a diversion. Without even blinking, or any noticeable reaction, she put her hand on mine, not softly as a caress, but around my wrist. That communication I had no trouble interpreting—I knew what she was saying. I watched for her smile but there was none. She didn't even open her eyes. Nothing was working. Since this was getting me nowhere fast, I just sat there silently with her, hand in hand. Getting up after a respectable length of time (so the failure wouldn't be too apparent) and, with a kiss to the forehead, we started walking back. She made small talk about her family and about the classes she was taking without prompting from me. This was a good sign, but I was a little disheartened and while listening tried to figure out if I was failing to win her or had just used mistaken tactics. The rest of the afternoon was spent in a haze. Before dinner she asked if she could lie down for a while as the last night had been a long one. I gladly traded her nap in my room for the Bridge game starting up. I felt good having a date and having her do regular type things. It was like she was comfortable and part of the whole environment. It was almost adult.

Dinner came and went. It was the first time that the entire house, new freshmen included, had gathered for the new school year. There were joyous faces of expectant guys, concerned faces of those whose blind dates did not seem to be measuring up and lonely ones of those who did not have dates at all. Marion and I, Campbell and his date all sat at Mickey's table. Mickey lorded over it like a gentle giant sitting at the head in the captain's chair. Like the father figure he quickly assumed, he directed the conversation. All the girls were from Randy Mac. so the stories, comments and house legends were all about that school. It was all great fun and the time went quickly. Afterward, we all retired, with five or six other couples, to Mickey's apartment for the pre-combo party.

These affairs quickly became loud cocktail parties. In the safe confines of student apartments, the state's liquor laws were totally ignored. In fact, during my entire career at W&L I don't remember worrying about the drinking age except for the fact we couldn't buy it—legally. We would drink, listen to music and talk. It was like a warm up. The objective was to pass the time till 9:00 when the band would start. If it were a big party, it could be more fun than the combo. This one was big for the apartment. There were Freshman attending so appropriate house legends had to be told and still more adventures recounted. Enough conversational variation seemed to spring up so that the dates could be included and weren't reduced to listening to us tell the same stories they had heard in abundance for two weekends in a row. I felt great since several of the stories had me playing a part. It was a good party. Marion, as most of the dates, said little but would comment back and forth to the other dates during conversational pauses. It seemed only girls who where OTG (one of the guys) would actually join in. Vicki was one of them. Now, I realized that we looked at her as a kind of peer, not merely a sex-object or a "date." Around the central discussion, little circles would form talking quietly among themselves about more normal topics. In these, dates would get to know each other. It was a two-fold existence that of the group as a whole, and you and your date in particular.

Nine o'clock hit and we all walked over to the house in the warm night air. The first set is always the longest and we danced till thirsty. Then, we would quickly get a drink from our BYOB bar and go back to the dance floor. After a while you got good at dancing without spilling the drink in your hand. Dateless brothers ringed the dance floor watching and listening to the band. One of the measures of a good Combo was the absence of these watchers or at least too many of them. Marion and I danced most every dance. Once or twice she would see one of the freshmen she had met during rush and want a dance with him. I didn't mind, I was waiting for the first break.

Somewhere around 10:00 I kissed her during a slow song and she kissed back. I made sure to keep dancing a bit after the song was over. It was time to go back to work. During the next break we refreshed our drinks and went upstairs to my room. As we passed by Greg and Campbell's room Vicki dashed quickly from their door, the two steps to the bathroom, clad only in a sheet. She never saw us but we did her. I hoped that it would put Marion in the mood. The Moody Blues on the tape deck completed the scene and we settled down in my bed to do some "serious listening." According to plan, within two songs we were doing some serious necking.

Slowly, I made progress. My shirt was open and hers was off. The bra had been easy but she didn't sit up to take it off as I would have hoped. It had been easy enough with only minor and short bursts of resistance quickly overcome with bouts of sincere passion. I was working on her pants when she stopped in mid kiss. I looked over and softly moved a stray strand of hair from her face with my finger looking serious and remaining silent. For long moments I just looked at her and she at me. I leaned down to kiss her (thereby reassuring her) and to, hopefully, restart the intended action. She kissed and then pulled away, looking seriously at me and saying "You know, of course that I am not going to make love." Her voice was all too calm and quiet for my liking. I tried to kiss her without answering. She moved back an inch, looked at me intently and continued. "I don't want to make love tonight." Her gaze remained as intense, but she just stopped there waiting for a reaction. She was not mad or angry; she was being simply declarative, firm, open—and not phony. She seemed to be asking me to argue with her. She, not to mention the closeness, demanded an answer.

I stopped moving, continued the gaze and smiled. Actually, I was thinking fast, trying desperately to come up with something that would not only agree with what she was saying but also put her mind (more important—her guilt or morals) at ease so that we could continue and get on to the business of making love. "I never thought we would." Smooth, quiet words followed by a light kiss. "We shouldn't worry about things…we should just follow our own lead…get pleasure from each other and enjoy the evening." I was trying to make my voice as quiet and as like a lullaby as I could and thought I did pretty well. This was to be the philosophical voice of sensual pleasure, rocking her into a defenseless, trusting mood. I stopped working on her belt and caressed her lightly, to give the impression of the thoughtlessness of soft sensual pleasure.

She kissed me again and caressed my chest. "I just don't want to make love yet. You understand…don't you?" I kissed my reply. I did understand—didn't agree—but did understand. Now was the time to either go for "plan B" of interesting, less invasive, varieties of sex or keep on going for the kill. I chose to keep going. I did, however, realize that for the time being, I could go no farther in my undressing efforts so we just played around. She seemed to relax within her defined range of activity so we did have some serious teenage fun. The band started up again which signaled the end of the session; there being no excuse to stay when the band was playing danceable music.

I lit a cigarette as we lay silently together before getting dressed, chest to chest. She seemed to be lost in thought. With the cigarette in my hand, I brushed the hair from her face, kissing her lightly. "What's up lady?"

"Why are we here?…I mean, why are you and I playing like this? What do you think of me?" Pushing my hand from her breast, she got up on one elbow. "…Really what do you think…of me…not just my body, but me?" Her voice was not angry as much as strident—maybe scared. (It is surprising to me, now, that this sort of comment could be made—in all sincerity—by anyone. I mean, I was a Sophomore, she was a Freshman, we had just spent half an hour kissing, caressing, and playing half naked and there was the expectation that this would be somehow meaningful in terms of life's grand adventure. But it was—meaningful—in the sense that it was the sex game as we both knew it and meaningful in that both of us were, indeed, looking for love or, if not love, looking for what college was supposed to be—what the movies said it should be.) I tried to figure out if she were angry, just trying to proclaim some sort of statement of personal politics or was really asking some sort of philosophical question. I concluded that this was the attack of the Freshman jitters. Maybe the drinks were wearing off. Perhaps some warning from Mom was suddenly recalled and flashed through her mind. Yes, I had probably got closer to my goal than I realized. Not any mad passionate loss of control, but probably just a thought running through her mind asking if now was the time to lose the virginity (how quaint that we, back then, but less so after, always thought freshmen girls were virgins unless proved otherwise) in which she, and her mother, has set such store. If not that, then perhaps she knew she wanted to be in love and suddenly realized she wasn't. I don't know now, nor did I then.

She was beginning to look hurt and confused. I felt miserable. There was no way out. I explained that I liked her and found her enjoyable and liked what she talked about and all the other things that one is required to say to a girl to make her believe its not just her body. It was a longish speech, reasonably well crafted but I don't know if she bought it all. She rolled over me and found her bra on the floor on top of her shirt. I watched her putting it on. It struck me that it was probably the first time she had ever put it on in front of a man (or boy) in bed. Oh, to be sure she had probably done stuff in cars and on couches and all—but this was a bed and not only a bed, but a college bed. These were the media advertised home of "Free Love." She turned around to fasten the snap.

Never have a mirror available to your date. As she buttoned her shirt, she reached into her purse to grab her brush and stepped up to the mirror. I thought that she was quite lovely. Eyes darkened with smudged eye liner, hair all messed up, lips slightly swollen and puffy; she looked like the gorgeous girl she was and that she had been making love. She met her eyes in the mirror and started brushing her hair with brutal silent strokes. I knew that there was going to be no more fun, at least in bed, that night.

We made it down for the second song. The dance was great. We sat the second break out downstairs as Campbell borrowed my room. He noted that we were lingering with several other couples and asked discreetly if he could borrow it. I said yes and in a flash he and his date disappeared. I warned him, however, about messing up my sheets so he probably used the floor. I consoled myself in that Marion and I were probably doing okay, just encountering a temporary, minor set back. We were one of the 10 or so couples who lasted the entire third set. I was hoping to reestablish the more promising mood. While the band was breaking up and loading their truck, I walked her out on the back lawn to look at the stars. A few kisses into this and I could tell that we were not going anywhere. She had checked out. I walked her back to Mickey's apartment in almost silence. It was about 2:00 in the morning when we reached Mickey's door; purposely left unlocked for the returning girls. We tip-toed in and heard him with his date in his sleeping area. He wasn't trying to be rude or anything, but there were no walls only several bookcases and a curtain separating his sleeping from his living space. Two of the front room girls were already in and sleeping. Marion turned, said good night and kissed me goodbye. It was all one gesture. All in all, it had not been what I had hoped, but not a total failure; I kind of liked her and the dance was fun.

I got back to the house and walked through the rubble of drunken Freshman in the living room and up the stairs to our hall. Somehow the hall light cover was missing leaving only a bare florescent bulb. One felt it was later than it was; with everything in that surreal glare and sharp shadows cast by the harsh light. Campbell and his date were just leaving my room. I said nothing as I passed, but noticed that his date was braless. He would pay if my sheets were slimy. In the room, I dropped trou and tore my shirt off while switching on the tape for one last cigarette. Randy walked in sniffing noticeably and asked if I had a good time. I guess the room smelled of more than my cigarettes. "Not me, man…Campbell just left with his date."

He smiled and quickly threw his clothes on his desk chair, checked his sheets then jumped into his upper bunk. The year had started.

Sunday was lunch and a quick goodbye to a waiting car driving the Macon crew back to Lynchburg. This was the last Sunday free of homework, reading or preparation for the ensuing week's classes and we spent it watching football and telling fraternity stories to the Freshmen. Brothers would join the crew as their dates departed or they returned from taking them back. By 6:00 almost the whole house was there so we ordered half a dozen pizzas and watched the movie. Monday would be classes and teachers. School would start and we would begin to try to learn (or at least memorize) what we needed to in order to get the grades we wanted. It was like what one would feel years later going back to work from vacation.

We weren't in awe of college anymore. It was more our definition—what we were in life, our station. Being a student was an occupation like any other. This year, however, was to be different. We didn't know it then, but things had changed. Almost by pre-arrangement no one wore suits anymore. Half of us still wore our coats and ties, but not suits. The hair started the year out as long by previous year's standards and would go longer. Many of us were beginning to find out that the social environment had changed as well. Greg said that the girls at Macon even had a birth control—other than abstinence—lecture presented during orientation. Last year, no Macon girl could get a prescription from the school infirmary, this year they were available on demand—without parental consent. That perked our interest; we all knew, then, it was going to be a good fall.

CHAPTER 5

*D*uring the week, I always had breakfast. It was the best meal of the day. At the house, or in later years from my apartment, I would shower, dress and hit the dining room as early as possible. Sammy, our butler, would bring me a mug of coffee and his wife Gladys, our cook, would call out asking what I wanted for breakfast. Her voice was always the same; it was a warm, almost sensual way to begin a weekday morning. This ritual was to become one of my most dreamed about memories of W&L.

Now, there are at least two important points about Gladys and Sammy that should be explained. The first is that they were seemingly right out of the script of old, bad movies. Gladys was about 6 feet tall and weighed a good 240 pounds. She was a solid, large, round woman that always wore a smile. After a year or so of knowing her, one knew that she seldom talked directly to you when she was mad, but would talk to herself when she was angry and wanted you to listen to what she had to say. At first sight she reminded you of the Aunt Jamima label before the Civil Rights movement made their trademark less stereotypic; right down to the bandanna. If she liked you, it was easy to tell. She would laugh and talk to you the minute she saw you. If she didn't like you, you were ignored for everything but the most blatant request. She never asked about classes or school things, but always about family, health and girl friends. She was constantly harassing Sammy who at 5'5" and 140 pounds was her exact opposite. Sammy behaved and looked exactly as one imagined the characters of Amos 'n Andy would. Laughing, stories and jokes were his way of letting you know he liked you. He'd never answer Gladys when she harangued him; merely not hear her. From the outside, or our side at least, they were a happy couple. Now, I still remember Sammy's cigar. Gladys only let Sammy have one cigar a day. By noon it would be chewed to such a pulp, that it was absolutely disgusting to anyone who might spy it balanced in his personal kitchen ash tray. But, it was his cigar and since he only got one a day, he was going to enjoy it as much as he could.

Sammy would clean our rooms and the house while Gladys cooked all three meals. In reality, Sammy was always joking and telling us his tall stories while rearranging the dust on our living floor (how clean does it have to be to get our approval) and doing a fair job on the floors Fazer could inspect. Gladys, a barely passable cook, became our mother, meeting our dates, consoling our troubles and giving general approval to "her boys." When either spoke, it was in a thick Virginia mountain, black dialect that was almost impenetrable to Freshmen, barely understandable to second semester Sophomores and finally deciphered by Juniors. It was not uncommon for underclassmen to hear Gladys or Sammy talking to them, smile and look pleadingly to a Junior for help.

The second facet that should be explained was that for the first and probably only time in my life, I, and most of the other guys in our fraternity anyways, had servants. Sammy would clean up your room, hang up your clothes (first emptying your pockets on your desk) and make your bed. He would straighten the room and even neatly put your shoes together. Nobody dared to ask him to polish their shoes for we were scared he might actually do it. It was like a super-mom without the bitching. Gladys would cook your breakfast to order and bring it out to you at the table. Sammy would get the coffee and even mix the cream and sugar. It was great. To us in 1970, it was also embarrassing. Few of us had ever had servants in our previous lives and we kept treating them like family. I think that Gladys and Sammy understood, but when their teenage son came in from time to time, he radiated an intense sense of spite, almost hatred, toward us. We all knew exactly what he was feeling so we tried to avoid him during his occasional visits. Gladys was our cook and Sammy our butler, but they were his Mom and Dad. Deep down all of us felt guilty and even when we thought we were being generous with their Christmas tips, it didn't make up for it. Many of us even had trouble tipping them at Christmas. You don't tip family. We compensated for our guilt by loving them in our rich college boy sort of way. There were several of us who made it into their family circle and we appreciated that—and them—probably more than we did our biological parents.

What Gladys felt about our dates was much more important than what Fazer did. As they got to know me Sophomore year, she and Sammie would comment about the girls as if they were my parents. If my date was there, Sammy would sneak out to the dining room and sweep the floor around her, pretending not to look. Returning, he would let the swinging door shut and laughing, start to tell me, with sharp jabs to the ribs, how lucky I was going to be that weekend. Gladys would frown, throw something in the sink, place her hands on her hips and tell him to hush as I would only date "nice" girls. If I dated her more than three weeks in a row, Gladys would start to ask family type questions. When we would break up she would snarl about how "that woman had missed a mighty good boy." They were always "girls" when we were dating but "women" when we broke up. Her concern, though, made me feel good. Thinking about it now, makes all this seem hard to believe. It's almost out of a Thirties movie or something—but it was real—a family away from home. It wasn't for everyone but only the ones who would sit and talk while she made dinner or take the time to listen to Sammy's stories.

But, in the morning, I would sit down, grab the Washington Post's first section (the Sports would already be gone, though—even then—I couldn't have cared less) and Gladys would bring me my pancakes and grits. She hated grits. Every morning she would say something that by Junior year I understood to be "How can you eat that stuff...I swear that you should know better coming from up north like you do." Everyday the same, some days I would have bacon or sausage or ask her to kill two eggs, but always I would have my grits. By the end of my years in Lexington, I would do it only to test her reaction. She never failed me.

Finishing, I would smoke a cigarette and read the editorials. If I was alone, Sammy would sweep up in front of me, stop, and rest on his broom. This would mean that there was a story about to begin. Sometimes he would talk about being a wild youth in the 30s; racing down mountain roads to dance with girls at church socials. Sometimes he would get serious and talk about being a combat engineer in World War II; and the adventures he had outsmarting his white officers or the army establishment. Sometimes he would tell some house adventure about brothers who had graduated a decade ago. Sophomore year these stories were tough to endure since they were practically unintelligible. But, as the years went by, I began to get an insight into what it must have been like for him growing up. Somehow I knew, that he knew, that his destiny was to be here, sweeping up for white boys. He never seemed bitter or even angry—at least to me. His sense of cheerful fate and the kind of subtle tales of racism's oppression were educational to me. I would always listen. He never asked for anything or made a play for more money. I think he just thought of himself as a part of the house not just an employee of it.

Gladys would give him about ten minutes for him to tell his story. Almost as if she were timing it, she would yell at him to move his butt and finish. What she wanted was for him to finish the work early enough for her to take a couple of hours off in the afternoon to visit her lady friends. Sammy would then take this time to walk over to the one black cafe, drink his one allowed beer, and finally smoke that soggy cigar. He would look at Gladys in mock anger, wave her off, behind the cover of closed kitchen doors, and dutifully restart his work. This was the signal for me to start off on my mile hike to the hill. In the nice weather, I would cut through fraternity back yards and through the middle of town. In the bad weather I took the front sidewalk.

The sidewalk route took you past the post office (always checked at least twice a day) and over Lexington's famed bridge-over-nothing. Actually, there was a large gully along the south edge of town. The bridge spanned it nicely and kept the road flat, but we all saw it as an Army Corps of Engineers wet dream. In those days we were always blaming the Corps for any stupid act of civilization; be it paved, bridged, dammed, or filled. Now there's a parking lot there and even some stores and such—then it was just a gully with some run-down shacks that maybe people lived in. The walk would take about fifteen or twenty minutes before one found oneself at the hill, in the co-op or class.

Sophomore year I had a great class schedule. Again no 8:00s and only one afternoon class on Tuesday and Thursday. I always had time to have a cup of coffee (at the new, inflationary, price of a dime a cup) and a cigarette at the house table. This year we didn't play pinball as much since we had Helen at the house. However, there was still a discussion rotating through the brothers going to and coming from class that would endure till lunch.

I was religious about attending class. I never cut. It may have been an off-shoot from my strict upbringing, but I think that it had to do with the way I blatantly loved my classes; even German. German this year came no easier, but I memorized better and thus started to become borderline passable. History, Philosophy, and Religion were my favorites. Each revolved around intellectual exercises and was presented in a form that I considered fun. I had Taylor for the history class so that was great, my Religion teacher, though, was a good lecturer, and a better wit. Further, I actually found my Philosophy class useful for how I was living college.

I expected philosophy to be led by a wise old man, dressed in tweed, who would help us ponder questions like "Why is there air?" Instead we had a vibrant "young" professor who was storming his early 40s like it was a beach and he a marine. His voice boomed as he strode through the classroom with alarming force and speed. He made a point to kick out guys coming to class unprepared. "Did you read this chapter?" he would ask a boy stuck on a question. If you said no, he would simply say "Please leave!" and you would go. If you said yes, and had only skimmed it, (remembering that we did not lie cheat or steal) he would turn the hour into an ego roasting session. In the middle of some discussion or lecture, he would turn to you, from any spot in the room, and ask another question about the assignment. Later, when I visited his office, I found framed pictures of Korean War vintage Panther jets, an aircraft carrier, and a mounted Navy Flying Cross. Some philosopher; we loved it, of course.

We quickly bored of the memorized equations that were required as a foundation or introduction during the first few weeks. We had to identify the basic concepts of Voltaire, Berkeley, Kant, Hegel, and all the standard great theories of knowledge. It began like any other "Intro" course (maybe because it was, of course, an intro course), though the traditional quickly ended. Dr. Jackton took these foundations and allowed us to build our own ideas on problems with which we were currently dealing. We would argue questions such as: "How do you know something is right?" "Can some action of man's be right?" "Are there universal rights and wrongs?" "Can killing be justified?" "What was the philosophical justification of war?"—those sorts of things. This was heavy stuff to us Freshmen and Sophomores. It was the kind of stuff, however, that one talked about during our bull sessions or maybe with dates. With the war or government killing us, these were topics we actively considered and tried to fathom. We were encouraged to bring in our own thoughts, but Dr. Jackton and the class scrutinized them in terms of the greats. He would stop and call across the class to some boy and tell him that "You are Hegel. Tell me about Mr. X's statement." By semester break he had dispensed with the rows of chairs and desks, so the 15 of us sat in a large semicircle without desks. There was no hiding; there was no holding out. We worked hard because, as in all the other classes, there would only be 1 or 2 "A"s, 3 or 4 "B"s and the rest would get "C"s or worse if they deserved them.

Sometimes it got downright blood-thirsty in the room. Heaven help the guy who could not think fast or talk convincingly enough to get at least a couple of the others on his side. Dr. Jackton summarily dealt with the wallflowers. He also made sure that the same guys did not "win" all the time. Not only did we begin to realize the nature of a coherent philosophy and a convincing way to express it, but also the psychology (Dr. Jackton called it "mental philosophy") of vocabulary. We could start to read, dissect, and anticipate an argument based on the verbiage used. (I know that I was not alone finding this incredibly useful on dates during the ensuing years!) No one gave any quarter, though Jackton always rescued a dying boy before any true damage was done.

For me, if all philosophy had been like this, I would have majored in it. It was reading, writing and arguing at its best. Unfortunately, only history always encompassed those tenets of the liberal arts as completely or as well. This semester I had British history with Dr. Taylor. He started us out reading Kipling's <u>Puck of Pook's Hill</u>. Like the children in the great book, we became filled with the character and nature of the enchanted island's history. As a dedicated and longtime (still to this day) Anglophile, I was in heaven. A Tory by heart, I would even defend a Wig, Germanic-British king against the perennial frog financed Jacobites. Taylor made History become a story with facts—movies of the mind. One forgot that this was supposed to prepare you for a job—hell I had Viet Nam didn't I—but became engrossed in it like a good book or a great move. The bell would ring for class to end and though three quarters of the class would leave three or four of us would remain with Taylor to finish the argument or to ask a final question. Reluctantly we'd know that class was indeed over and it was time to retreat to the co-op or to lunch or the house.

It is not that these thoughts consumed us all the time. As soon as we would file into the classroom the transition began and after about 10 minutes the small group of "histories" would be totally immersed within that world. The questions at hand were important, vital, as if they affected us that very day. Campbell was a member of that select group. Alone, we would often talk as if the War of Austrian Succession was a question of contemporary politics. Sometimes these discussions slipped out in front of non-historites but usually they were reserved for when we were in class or alone together. It wasn't the same as being one of today's nerds; it was just an incredible immersion level. Part of the glory of being at an all male school is that this level of involvement wasn't just for outcastes—many of the most popular guys would succumb to this level of enthusiasm—it wasn't as if it were in front of dates or anything. Boys could still be boys.

It was a classic, dual existence. In class, or when studying, the subject would consume our consciousness. We would joke about it; talk about it, live it with a kind of mental empathy. When not in class, or in public, it was a kind of hidden secret, not to be discussed with strangers. How could they understand an emotional outburst or extreme opinion about Robert Walpole or Bonnie Prince Charlie? How could they consider you normal when you would know the caliber and weight of the Brown Bess and could recite the dates of origin and original Colonels for Britain's first 30 infantry and cavalry regiments? How could normal people understand that it would bother you if you were wrong; even when other people wouldn't know you were wrong? It was like being boys at one moment, in secret, and trying to be men the next, for the outside world on the weekends.

After the last class of the day I would go back to the house for lunch. Lunch at the house probably lasted a good two hours. While the food started at noon, we would eat, and then retire to the chapter room with its TV for Jeopardy at one. Twenty to thirty guys sitting around watching other people answer trivia questions became a house ritual. We had our own heroes among ourselves that could conquer almost any question in one or another topic. There would be an intense loss of face if they missed too many questions in their strong suit. I did reasonably well on history, but was never considered one of the Gods. We would rush to answer the question before the contestant thus showing our superiority. Once in a while someone would start thinking that they were better than the contestants, but a howl would go up about TV cameras and pressure. Once we even sat in front of the offender, staring at him to simulate what it must be like. After Jeopardy there was Hollywood Squares which would occupy people as they began to get it together to go study or go back to the hill for an afternoon class.

Two days a week I had German in the afternoon and on Wednesday I had R.O.T.C. drill. German was an incredible chore for me. I could not get into it like the other subjects at all. It was work; no torture really. I must have had a mental block against the subject. I would churn away at the homework reading assignments and try to do well in the class. Usually they consisted of reading selections from German classic short stories or novels. The instructor would give a short, ten minute lecture on German culture, then ask us to start translating from the appropriate German text. Several weeks into the class I happened on a tremendous idea. Why not translate word for word, writing each in the margin between the lines. This started a notable improvement in my class performance till the Professor caught on. Soon after, I got the idea to go to the library and get the English version to give the illusion that I understood the nature of the text with only a few marginal guides. Even I was amazed at how much better I did after that. Once a section was read, then understood, I could go back and make the sentences almost make sense. I was going to pass it that year and once I did, I resolved never to look back.

R.O.T.C. was another thing entirely. After Kent State, R.O.T.C. on our campus never recovered. With the draft lottery any guy with a three digit number immediately dropped out and most above the high 80s did so as well. Nobody joined that didn't have to because of their number or need the money to stay in school. Often guys would not want to be seen in their R.O.T.C. uniform and would take great lengths to hide it. I, on the other hand, joined the Ranger unit. While the faculty of the R.O.T.C. unit thought that these were the elite; we thought of it more simply: "as long as we were going to be in the army, we might as well do military things." While the ordinary clowns were marching and learning the rifle drill, we were learning how to repel, patrol, fire different weapons, and do all sorts of neat stuff. We did one overnight every semester and practiced night tactics. It was really just one step above the playing "army" we did as kids. The best thing was that the uniform was fatigues, berets and boots. We didn't have to look foolish walking around in stupid "Class A"s with the funny hat and skinny tie.

On the two afternoons I didn't have class; I usually read or did light studying. Once the semester got into full swing, there were papers to research, write and type. Basically, from 1:30 to 4:00 I did student work reasonably diligently. That is, when I didn't fall asleep while trying to study with the tape deck going.

During the good weather, we would start to gather for a baseball game in the back yard around 4:00pm. We had a huge back yard whose deep left field, unfortunately, was a faculty housing apartment building. We would never have enough guys for a real infield so we would play "pitcher's glove" instead of having a first baseman and outlaw right field entirely. Whether, in the fall or spring, more often than not you could find eight to ten of us in the back yard playing ball. If it rained or we didn't feel particularly athletic a Bridge game would be started or we just watched the 4:00 <u>Dialing for Dollars</u> stupid movie. There would always be several guys grouped around Helen trying to beat some astronomical score. (Helen proved to be a financial gold mine for the house.) The juke box would be programmed to play the same songs every night by the same guys. I had my four tunes that I liked and so did four or five others. This would go on till one or another of the brothers would go berserk and beg the house treasurer to give him enough money to buy a bunch of new 45s so that there would be at least a change in the play list.

At 5:30 I would go to work in the kitchen as part of my job as kitchen steward. This "job" would pay for my date's meals and would allow me to talk to Gladys and Sammy in depth. I would chop ice, mash the potatoes, set the tables, or do whatever needed doing for the half an hour before dinner at 6:00. Then the bell would ring and Mrs. Fazer would come down to take her seat at the head of the head table. Next to her would be the president and his friends. It wasn't any honor to be at the head table except on good meal nights. Then, the best food would find its way there. By the second or third week we all had our usual seats and there would be very little change during the rest of the year. From time to time someone would get pissed and move to an open seat or if a brother missed several meals someone might take his seat causing a general reshuffle. For the most part, however, it was just like home with everyone having their own, if not assigned, seat. Grace would be said and we would all sit and begin passing the food. Kitchen steward was a good job for food. I would always put the meat in front of my place. Therefore, I could always get a decent piece of whatever we had.

Gladys was not an original or, in truth, a very good cook. She had been with the house for probably ten or fifteen years so no one ever asked why she was our cook. She was honest, and loving—and, most importantly, our Gladys. Firing her to get someone more skilled would be tantamount to firing Mom. Sammy would actually wait tables in a white, starched serving coat. We all took this for granted, but visitors from other colleges were astounded at how much opulence we were accustomed to. Meals do not last long in a male society. After about fifteen or twenty minutes, max., most of the brothers were in the Chapter Room watching Walter.

I can still remember watching Walter explain the truth to us. He was our Prophet; our Voice of God; our one source with indisputable integrity. I had been watching him since the days of the Twentieth Century program rehashing the history of World War II; as my father would say "with the original cast." He headed the whole CBS family with sons Roger Mudd, Harry Reasoner, Dan Rather and all the rest. About this time a couple of daughters started to show up but we all knew that this was really for EEO reasons. We never watched any news except CBS. It was not only part of our family but part of our expected existence. Even when the Redskins would be winning, or some other facet of our lives seemed to take precedence over all the rest; Walter would simply give casualty figures and those little flags would appear on the screen. That brought, at least for a moment, everything—our being students and safe with those of our generation not as lucky as to be smart or rich and in Viet Nam—back into focus. Nobody believed the figure under the North Vietnamese flag or the Viet Cong banner since they were D.O.D. propaganda, but as the toll under the US flag rose, we all knew it was a machine coming for us and our kind. Walter never said anything but read the numbers, we all knew what he was saying and believed.

After dinner (the term dinner included both eating and Walter) the bottom of the house would empty. There might be a Bridge game for a while, but most of the upperclassmen would retire to their apartments, the Sophomores to their rooms or the remainder of both would head to the library. I never studied in the library. There were too many people there. I would get distracted and go browse the magazines or the stacks and lose all sorts of valuable time. My preference for studying in the room worked out well since Randy was a library person. The house would stay quiet from 7:00 till midnight except for the 9:00 cigarette break. At nine those of us left on the hall would usually pile into Cal and Dan's room where Dan would be studying and bother him for about ten minutes. It is curious that we never planned it but one or another of us would always walk into his room and put on a Sam & Dave or James Brown record and just start talking. It didn't matter what he was doing. We would write graffiti on his bed slats, smoke cigarettes—which always bothered him, or just generally give him a hard time. I can't remember why he was singled out for this honor, but it just seemed natural, just and right.

Dan was a short, party maniac from Boston. He was to become, by the end of the year, the leader of the "Earls" which had something to do with the song <u>Duke of Earl</u>. Not being an ordained member, this is all hypothesis and thus, we can never know for certain. The history majors in the house tried to explain to him that there was never a title called Duke of Earl but that didn't matter to Dan. The song was as close to history as he got. Dan was never accused of being the smartest member of the house, but, then again, he didn't need to be. After college he was going to work for his Dad's manufacturing business no matter what his grades were.

Dan and his "Earls" were into traditional partying. They would drink nothing but Budweiser Beer and never used any other variety of drugs. Official "Earl" music was Motown or "Soul" to the extent that it was the only type allowed at "Earl" events. Whether a record was or was not suitable for "Earl" events was solely up to Dan. "Earls" always wore hats even though nobody in our day and age wore hats when we could avoid it. Dan and his following would date girls whose ambition was to be housewives and mothers or just liked to "party hardy." They did, however dance well, typically look good (in a big, busty, heavy makeup sort of way) and were fanatically loyal to their "Earlish" men. Far from being Politically Correct (in today's terms), Campbell and I saw them as hilarious or somewhat foolish. Perhaps we were a tad bit jealous about the loyalty of their women. The "Earl Dates" were the type Campbell and I would talk Hegel with when their dates were off getting beer or some other "Earlish" thing, thus providing us much entertainment—at least upon later analysis. Both of us hoped that they would think Hegel dirty or weird or something and then ask Dan who he was. Dan, who was smart enough to know that Hegel was somebody real but not know which century, country or voaction, would then have to stammer through some sort of explanation understandable to an Equestrian Arts major from Sem. We were forever doing stuff like this to him. This would piss him off for the rest of the night and delight us no end. Study breaks were a good time to ask him about such exploits.

The "Earl" movement within the house was an evolutionary one that grew not only on its own accord but also in direct response to the growth of the "Peer Group." The "Peer Group" were the house heads, or as they called themselves at the time; freaks. They were the druggies. As the "Earls" grew to include the house alcoholic, the Peer Group encompassed the few brothers who went too far with the drug culture. But, unlike the "Earls," where loud boisterous behavior was required, the "Peer Group," under the titular leadership of Mickey, would sit and smoke pot at one of the apartments on week-ends when there were no dates and passively listen to loud, heavy music. Again, like the "Earls," these groups were hazy at best at the beginning of the year but crystal clear by the end of Sophomore spring. Dimitri simply dubbed the "Earls"—"JCY" (Juice Crazed Youth) and the "Peer Group"—"DCY" (Drug Crazed Youth). This seemed to categorize the situation for most of us in the middle very well. The names caught on to the point where we'd use them in polite conversation and then be stuck to explain the terms without self incrimination. While we might roar with laughter and get no end of pleasure in asserting to Dan that James Brown was gay; to the "Peer Group" we would ask if they were having trouble with the

"Freak Environment Test" consisting of finding your feet. The majority of us were in the label-less middle and on partying terms with both.

Dan, however, was just too easy to harass. The 9:00 breaks were only a beginning. Every Wednesday he and his "Earl" buddies would go down the road to Mary Baldwin or Sem to party in student lounges, dance clubs or just mess around. While we might have a midweek road trip once in a while, Dan was regular. We began to sabotage his room for his drunken return. Short sheets, no mattress, or even a booby trapped door firing a flash gun all found their way to Dan's Wednesday Night Return. We all pitied Cal for having to live through his reaction every week, but since he joined in the fun, (though Dan never realized it) we got to hear just how good or successful we had been.

When Dan would get his date in the room for a marathon session (we all knew when Dan was getting laid because he would put the <u>Four Tops Greatest Hits</u> on repeat), Cal would be found wandering from room to room in his jockey shorts trying to find a place to sleep and muttering obscenities. Sooner or later a group of Sophomores outside his door would start singing along with the record. Dan would come out naked, wrapped in a towel or something; sputtering mad. Everyone would scatter behind locked or barricaded doors. The time Dan used to chase us, allowed Cal to return to his room and jump in the top bunk, pulling the covers over his head. Dan would then be forced to continue with "company" or find a new place to plank his date. In the beginning of the year, Dan would usually hustle his date out to his car to finish the evening ala teenager. By the end of the year, however, he seemed to relent and continue, often with audible arguments from his date, with Cal in the upper bunk.

The real study break, however, was at midnight. This was officially dubbed the "Witching Hour." For this hour—and this hour only—there were no rules governing behavior, noise or maturity. The hall had a ribbed rubber mat running its entire length. Campbell started the first week running down the mat with a floor sweeper. The noise it made was incredibly loud and bothersome. Some say that Fazer, when she first heard it on the floor below, jumped out of her seat and had to get a drink to calm her nerves. From that moment, for the entire hour starting at midnight, anything went. Everybody put on their stereo, not especially loud, but playing different music and people went from room to room enforcing a no study rule. Several of the brothers would practice hockey slap shots in the hall, trying to hit one of the no passing signs covering a hole (made by hockey pucks) at each end. Campbell sometimes would throw his hatchet at his door—which was cheap so the edge of the blade would suddenly appear out in the hall. There was always something crazy going on. One of the guys started giving Tarot Card readings. If Dan were gone, we would form a congress and legislatively decide what his Return Fate should be. Each suggestion had to be philosophically defended at great length and appropriate flourish. It was Sophomores only. If upperclassmen came up, we would all quietly go back to whatever we had been doing and ignore the intruder. The upper would get the hint and leave. I think we all were a bit embarrassed more than exclusive. A couple of the more serious guys would take showers since they could not study. One night, we lifted the vent (the shower vented directly to the attic) and poured cold water on them for their unsociability. As they raced out to get us we took pictures. It was a joyous time. No paper, no test cram, nothing was more important than this period of absolute childishness. By 1 A.M. all would be quiet with me usually in bed.

Dan was not the only one to have Wednesday night road trips. He was only more consistent about them than the rest of us. If we had steady girl friends, Wednesdays would be the night that you would go to a different school. Greg, who always was dating Vicki on the weekends, had several friends at different schools for Wednesday night exploits. It could be the way you would break out of a bad run of blind date luck. If one school had dumped you, it was a way of breaking into another. Mostly, road trips were all guy, adolescent fun. Mickey and I, along with several others, made several to the Roanoke Skin Flicks that year. These were not the triple X, hydraulic splatter films of today. Back then, if you saw a decent looking girl with no shirt on, it could be considered a skin flick. It was a different era; like considering freshmen girls virgins; these skin flicks were tame enough to be shown on Cable TV today. Roanoke was an hour's drive, even at Mickey's breakneck speeds, to get there. That gave everyone their chance to drink as many beers as they could hold. The movie cost a dollar or $1.25 if you wanted to sit in the balcony. We always took the balcony roost. From there we could make noises and running commentary on the flick while looking around for Roanoke College girls there on a dare. We had heard that they did this and though we never found any evidence, we were always vigilant. From the theater we would go to the local Taco Hut, Lexington having none, and scarf down a dozen or so tacos apiece. We could be home before the Witching Hour and have some new adventure to relate about watching fat men in underwear simulate intercourse with ugly, chubby girls wearing no shirts to relate.

The Skin Flick trips did end, though. What turned out to be the last time Dimitri went with us wearing his flashing pants. Nobody noticed the special pants when he got into the car. These were brown corduroys with the crotch cut out. We should have known that the evening was headed for no good, disaster, jail or the world of legend; right then. I got the bright idea to take a squeeze bottle of mayonnaise in the theater with us to annoy the other voyeurs. We had noticed that there were a lot of guys there who were really into the flicks. From time to time we would spot someone with a newspaper on their lap or their jacket covering some very suspicious hand movement. Crude jokes and boisterously audible comments would follow. I brought the mayonnaise and several spoons to provide, what seemed to me to be, the next logical step.

Half way through the first flick, during a particularly heavy scene where two topless heroines made love to some greasy guy in his underwear—the normal "climax" of the movie—I passed out the spoons. On each spoon I put a little mayonnaise. I demonstrated my idea by using the spoon to propel the substance at one of the voyeurs below. I missed but the splatter hit the back of another guy's head. He put his hand back and brought white lumpy goo back on his fingers. I am sure that he almost fainted. By the time he would turn around, look back or even up, we were "just sitting there." The voyeur was always too embarrassed (simply being in the theater in the first place) to make a scene or complain. One by one we would try our skill to hit some unsuspecting voyeur. We were able to do this for almost an hour before one voyeur's reaction brought us to gales of laughter and thus to our ruin.

I think it was Dimitri's turn (it was always Dimitri's turn) and he hit the back of one guy's head who was sitting alone way up front. We all snickered our congratulations. The target reached and brought the substance back on his fingers. Every one of us was watching him intently to get his reaction. Later, when we all compared notes, we all confirmed that no one noticed him smelling it or anything. Instead he just looked at it for a moment, played with it in fingers, then popped it all into his mouth. That was too much to believe. None of us could resist getting vocal about that. Later, I often thought that we were lucky nobody went over the edge of the balcony in our laughter. Needless to say, we were asked to leave by the short, old owner and his two muscle-bound bouncers.

At the Taco Hut, the five of us piled into the place talking, joking and laughing, much out of place in the quiet, fluorescent almost surrealistic plastic interior. Each of us eventually ordered with much comment and confusion. Getting our food, we went to a side table and ate while whispering comments and jokes about our adventure in the skin flick. Every once in a while, the attendants would be startled by a loud laugh leading the others into a roar till, self conscious, we would be quiet again. Dimitri was in rare form. Not only was he being obscene with his burrito but he had a way with words and facial expressions that would reduce even the most stoic person to fits of laughter. He was describing the actions of our Mayonnaise attack in terms of French existential literature full of illusions of Sartre and Camus. We thought that the night's adventures had ended, but in came a full troop of Girl Scouts with two housewives as escorts. The veins began to bulge on Dimitri's neck.

You could tell that they were not at all happy that we were there. We were college boys, giggling and probably smelled of cigarettes, beer and pot. Our jokes became more hushed and the women tried hard to ignore us and to keep the girls occupied so as not to notice us. They couldn't do it. We would catch a couple of them staring at our long hair, jeans, and general studentness. Dimitri started to talk about the girls. He made some crude insinuations about what the girls did as a troop. He started describing the requirements for several inappropriate merit badges and the like. He, and our reactions to him were getting out of hand. Thankfully, even if we did have to stuff several tacos into our mouths at once, we were ready to go.

As we were cleaning up, Dimitri started walking toward the front counter under the guise of taking some trash to the container. The path crossed by the end of their table. At almost the same moment of our demise, Mickey remembered what pants he had on. He went white all of a sudden and asked me (because I was nearest) to "C'mon we gotta get him outta here before we get arrested." Too late. He just stood there about five feet from the end of the table and let his coat fall open. One of the youngest girls, near the far end, saw it first and started to point and giggle (serves him right). The escorts looked up and for a moment were frozen in astonishment or something close. In that single, silent moment Mickey and I caught either arm on the run and started dragging the protesting Dimitri toward the door. Campbell hit the door first as he dashed past and let it swing open for us. The housewives started screaming and we saw the counter girl frantically dialing the telephone. Dimitri was crying out his innocence, his love for the scouts and insistence that this was an educational exercise while Mickey fumbled for the keys and finally opened the door. We threw Dimitri in the back seat while we all piled in as best we could. In twenty seconds we were out of the parking lot and on the highway.

We all cursed Dimitri and worried aloud about the cops. We turned often and went toward the opposite end of town. A quick council of war determined that it was safest taking the long, back way home; through Lynchburg. All, except Dimitri, who was busy expounding his constitutional rights to erotic free expression, wondered if the counter girl had gotten our license number and were busy dreaming up excuses or alibis if they had. As long as we had Dimitri and those damn brown cords we knew we were sunk if stopped. That thought came aloud from someone in the back seat. Although we wondered aloud if we should just drop him, we could never sacrifice our TTI (True Teen Idol) to the Virginia State Police no matter how crude he had been.

Somewhere on the south edge of Roanoke, while stopped at a light, Dimitri rolled down the window and threw a spoonful of mayonnaise on the window of the car next to us. As luck would have it, the car was full of Townie males. Antagonistic to college kids by nature, we thought nothing of their yelling and furor. We thought that they were just being obnoxious as usual since we did not know of Dimitri's dirty deed. Dimitri gave his high pitched laugh and explained why the "indigenous fauna" were so mad. Just as Mickey looked over to them, they pulled a shot gun out and pointed it at our car. "Holy Shit" was Mickey's only reaction as we bolted the red and started screaming down the highway to escape. They were right on our tail for almost twenty miles. Finally we were ahead enough to drive the car into a side yard and hid ourselves behind a garage till the townies cleared. It was disastrous to their lawn, but it was them or us. Now we had to avoid two groups on the way back; cops and townies.

Back in Lex at 3:00 in the morning, we were too beat to do a truck-stop run. No one was willing to trust Dimitri in the restaurant anyway. We were lucky to be alive, him especially. But, we had a tremendous adventure that would live in several scarcely recognizable house legends for years to come.

The other major legend beginning that fall was about Campbell's Raisin Bran. For Fran, and for all of us to a lesser extent, that fall was a magic time. The previous spring's revolution had changed the social setting, the mores and our social life a great deal. Basically, from a position of formal regulations governing all types of social (dating) behavior, there were no rules left. Girls still couldn't spend the night in the house. The IFC (Inter Fraternity Council) threw a sop to the administration with their "no overnights rule" which, when enumerated, meant that dates had to be out of the house by 3:00 A.M. and had to stay out for at least two hours. In other words, somewhere around 1 or 2 on Friday or Saturday nights we would get together with our dates and hit the truck-stop for a late night snack. Girl's schools did not require registered housing anymore so they all started to spend the weekends at the apartments.

More important, the pill became readily and universally available for the first time. This changed everything. Without the fear of pregnancy, girls burst out of their parent provided dam in a great deluge of sensuality. This was helped by the prevailing mood of youth—parents and the establishment had brought us Viet Nam, unsafe autos, all sorts of outdated rules regulations and the like. Rules were out; freedom was in. Coupled with the just beginning Fem-lib movement where "rules for girls were not the rules for women"—it was a great time to be dating. All sorts of girls were saying yes who had never dreamed of saying it the year before. There was more opportunity, less fear, and a great deal more sex expected from dating as the student Revolution hit its peak, spawning free love as one of its most renowned hallmarks. This was not to say that it was one long sex-orgy (in our dreams, maybe) but the games of dating, relationships and sex became much more one of personal decisions, desires and fun versus what we had grown up with during the 50s and early 60s.

Those of us without the usual draws; looks, money, sports or a fancy car, still had to rely on our wits. Many of us had good luck ties, u-trou or whatever; Campbell had his Raisin Bran. The first Wednesday of the year Campbell brought a box of Raisin Bran to the table and ate it rather than the provided meal. No big deal. When he continued this till Friday, everybody had to know why. He even did it in front of his dates. By the second week, he finally told us that it was a secret weapon giving him mystical powers over women which, in every case, got him laid. He said that as long as he ate only Raisin Bran for dinner he would never miss. It worked for seven straight weeks with seven different girls. Fran wouldn't brag or tell us any details, he never needed to. Greg, his roommate, would relate how this or that girl had reacted to Campbell's shaky, elevated bed. We would also check back through which ever girl had got Campbell the date. It got kind of spooky. Finally Campbell broke down and ate regular food. Either his desire for normal food won out or Vicki's threats of exposing the source of his unnatural power to all his dates, before they ate dinner, did the trick. Campbell, always a man of few words, never told the story. He didn't have to; it had already become a matter of house legend.

With this dawning of our Shenandoah Age of Aquarius, most of us settled into efforts of intellectual endeavor in class and a search for romance (or sex anyway) on the social front. On the outside everything was fairly traditional. We still had combos and apartment parties; there were mixers before games; road-trips to the various girls' schools; as had our forbearers before us. There were pot parties in several apartments on the week nights or dateless weekends, but, except for a couple here and there getting stoned, it was still low key.

Most of us Sophomores were still looking for a major girl friend while dabbling in the free love movement to kill time. Even in this age of free love, we were really still looking for the girl of our dreams, the steady date and, even though we didn't think of it at the time, the future wife.

I knew that my relationship with Marion wouldn't go anywhere and we decided to be "just friends." That phrase, then, and now, meant that we agreed that the romance was going nowhere so why bother—a kind of mutual dump. Vicky, though to her credit, had to hear this from me which freed her to get Marion some other date in the house. So, it was no big deal that Marion started dating one of our pledges, Jimmy, a guy with money, looks and, believe it or not, a sailboat, here at school. He surprised most of us by saying yes to our bid since he seemed to fit better in one of the other, more socially prominent houses. The fact that he was seriously crazy helped him fit comfortably in with us. I drifted back into blind dating till I met Becky.

Becky was tall, blond and, to my eyes, incredibly beautiful. She had long straight hair, a beautifully proportioned body and legs that seemed to go on forever. Her eyes were blue and she had the best Nordic complexion, I had seen in my life. She dressed simply; button down blue oxford shirt and those skin-tight gray cord bells I grew to love. She was perfect. I spotted her as a blind date of one of our Freshmen who seemed to be in the process of passing out in the down-stairs bathroom while his two pledge brothers, their dates and Becky waited around the corner in the living room. Even as a Freshman I would have never done something that stupid.

It was a Friday, and he and his two companions had consumed too much beer in the car on the way back from Madison. He had beer with dinner, and never made it to the apartment party being held at the Spook House. She was sitting in the living room with the two other couples waiting for her date to come back from the bathroom. I, sadly dateless due to a blind-date mix-up at Macon, just walked into the living room after almost being bowled over by the errant pledge on his way to the bathroom and asked one of the Freshman guys what was wrong. As he told the story, I got a close look at Becky. Instantly amazed and enamored by her beauty, I went into tactical mode and went around the corner into the second floor bathroom intent on both throwing the guy in the shower (and stealing his pants) or out the window. I didn't have to do either as he was out cold; lying in his own vomit. Quickly, I went through his pockets for wallet and keys. Finding them, I put him in the shower but left the water off and used his jacket (I couldn't find anything else and it served him right for trashing the house) to clean up the barf. Someone else could sober him up. Someone else would have to, because I would, by then, be off taking care of his neglected date. Upon reflection, I impressed myself by my own quick thinking.

On my way back through the living room I dropped his wallet off in Fazer's good hands—this would keep him from going too far till sober, but kept the keys to the car he was driving. Since he, and probably his two friends as well, were much too drunk to drive, I would gallantly offer to drive the girls back to school after the party. Neither he nor his friends were in any shape to mind and I was too busy trying to understand my seemingly incredible luck. At my suggestion, the six of us left quickly. There was certainly no sense hanging around waiting for him to sober up, or allow someone else a chance at stealing this angel from me. Those who hesitate are lost and those who wait for others not to hesitate are foolish. As we walked out of the house, it suddenly struck Becky that she was now in the company of another guy, in all intents and purposes she had a new date. She had been snaked! I nonchalantly put my arm through hers and started to ask her all the blind date questions. I simply did not let embarrassing questions arise. Half way to the Spook House party, we stopped, said the obvious to each other, introduced ourselves formally and laughed at the situation. She really laughed. It was beautiful; it was relaxed; it was working. I was nervous; things like this didn't happen to me. But, through luck, fate or whatever, this was happening and it was a great beginning. I prayed my tactical sense would continue to operate flawlessly.

The rest of the night we danced and talked. It was free and easy; since I had no expectations, everything positive was a bonus. It seemed that she liked to listen to some of our stories, liked the same music as me and so on. For a date that was never supposed to be, this was becoming fantastic. At the end of one of the slow songs, I kissed her and she kissed me back, afterward pulling her head back and smiling—a good sign for sure. It was like the smile was happening to both of us. I reasoned that this emotion was too good to rush. The big objective at that point was to get most of her time in the near future secured to me, thus having the freedom to follow up and investigate further. I had the dream of a major romance in the making. Since she had agreed to a Friday night only date with the drunken Freshman, she had to get back. The other two girls decided to stay the weekend and places were found for them with the other dates staying over in the Spook House. My star must have been busy that night as I would get to drive Becky home alone.

In the car, we listened to WABC from New York City wafting in and out over long distance AM radio and just talked about general stuff. Neither she nor I seemed to need to talk, but wanted to. It was an hour to Harrisonburg, so we had the time to get to know one another fairly well. She was going to be an English major, a teacher after; was from Culpepper, Virginia; and had never dated seriously before. I vocally discounted this. "You're too beautiful not to have been a HSQ" (High School Queen)! She denied her evident looks, explained that her family was quite poor and she had been busy working in a stationary store in order to go to college. She hadn't had a lot of time to go out during High School. Besides, she continued, she didn't like all the "jock phonies" that she seemed to attract in that small town. Internally, I was ecstatic. There would be no trouble fitting into her expectations of a good date. I told her about Fred, my job and my family. I told her that I, too, was the first person in my family to go to college. She snuggled closer. The star continued shining; it was still working.

The goodbye kisses in the car were straight out of High School. After about twenty minutes and my furtive, glancing caresses, I suggested that she go in. What a stroke of genius! She was not expecting me to suggest ending the session and said so. What is more, she said she wanted to stay a bit longer! The caresses were not as furtive as before. Ten more minutes went by and the car windows became completely fogged. So was I, but I tried not to show it. She told me that she needed to study on Saturday, but if I wanted to come up.....I quickly pounced on the hint and agreed that I would be up by 2:00; we would study till 5:00; and drive like hell to be able to make dinner at the house by 6:00. There would be some sort of party after that. I didn't know how I was going to get there, having no car, or way to get her back on Sunday; but it was a chance too good to pass up. I was happily planning the Significant College Romance all the way back to Lex.

When I got back to the house, our passed-out pledge was still lying in the second floor shower so I turned on the water in the shower him. As he sputtered awake I gave him his keys, told him who had his wallet and that he was an asshole. Randy was already in bed, but we talked a bit before going to sleep. He was going up to Madison the next day with Stan, perhaps I could convince Stan to change his plans to fit my schedule, as he didn't mind. Crushing out my last cigarette in the bedside ashtray, I drifted off to sleep knowing that I could pull the deal off. Stan was always reachable by flattery, attention, and by appearing to be his all around good buddy. At lunch I approached him and ate with him pumping him for information about his weekend plans. I tried to act like I was just being friendly rather than blatantly pumping him for a favor. Slowly, I convinced him that he could have a great time by conforming to my proposed schedule. The only catch would be that he and Fearless (along with

Randy and his date) would study with Becky and me for the afternoon and ride with us both times. I had no idea how Becky would
react to Stan or Fearless. However, better there with Stan and Fearless than not there at all. Off we went in his beat up red Renault. We
talked about almost everything under the sun on the way up. Stan
really wasn't such a bad guy when you got him alone. He almost
seemed to have his own, distinct, personality. After that ride, I rather
liked Stan and thought of him as not such a wastrel after all.

It seemed that Becky knew Fearless, and the four of us, Randy and
his date had wandered off from the beginning, started studying in
the Madison College library. After twenty minutes or so, Stan and
Fearless took a break, going back to Fearless' room for her cigarettes.
Both of us knew what that meant. We looked up as they muttered
their excuse, smiled then giggled a bit and went back to studying. At
least she did. Trying not to stare, I just kept thinking of her and wondering why I was so lucky to be in the process of falling in love with
such a beautiful girl, more important, one who seemed to be going
through the reciprocal process with me. She put her hand out over
the table while reading; I reached out and held it, trying to appear
casual. It must have looked funny, but for half an hour we held hands
across a library table. I did get some work done, and from the looks
at her progress we probably were both just going through the
motions. She did have some sort of book report to finish and I did
the proof reading for her. It seemed very strange to read something
written with green ink having lots of loops in the letters and the "i"s
dotted with little circles.

I kept on thinking if she were the Significant College Romance I
had been waiting for. How would she look in twenty years? What
would she be like in the morning? Could she cook? How long would
all this last, maybe forever? I knew that all this was too fast for pru-
dent tactics; not to mention my own sensibility. It was always better
to let the girl verbalize every level of commitment first. It was real
hard to keep my tactical mind in proper control with my emotional

mind going crazy on the inside. I resolved, however, to play it cool and win. I started to pack up early, before Stan and Fearless were back. Becky looked at her watch, smiled and gathered her things, too. On the steps outside, I pulled her to me and told her that I had not done this today, while kissing her. I was trying to be my best "happy-go-lucky in love—casually enjoying being together with a beautiful girl" person. She kissed back. Even though it was daylight the star was still shining. Was it me, my tactics, or just lucky hormones? It was the tremendous transition scene from all the movies of which I had dreamed of happening to me.

The rest of that weekend went well as did the next five or six. In our house, if someone dated the same girl for three consecutive weekends it was considered serious, for five or six it was a major romance. Becky and I had become a house couple. I enjoyed the feeling and status of being considered a couple by the house. The other steady dates got to know her and Vicki (our class' ruling date) seemed to like her as well. We exchanged pictures for our respective room's desks and even went out to dinner on a real traditional date once. It was cool.

Sexually things were going within expectations. In the privacy of my room we had made out naked by the third date. In that heated session she told me that she wanted to stay a virgin till she decided on marriage. She was willing to do anything (and everything) else but wanted to be "able to look her father in the face." In those days, this sort of thing still made sense—it wasn't all foolishness; good girls wanted to be good girls. I was so much in love (though we both avoided that word) that I agreed. So we would indulge in all sorts of alternative orgasmic activity while avoiding actual intercourse. It didn't seem to matter to me since everybody assumed that we were making love. When I didn't have the room, I would stay with her in the front room of Mickey's apartment where our sounds would mix with the two other couples' lovemaking. During the later breaks in Combo parties, we would retire up to the room to indulge just like everyone else who had steady dates. We were a regular couple in the Avoid-The-Curfew Truck-stop runs. I was happy enough in the sexual arrangement even though I did want her to make the ultimate commitment. Not that I wanted to marry—well at least not then—but I did want the prize all the same.

Thanksgiving came and, in reward for my passing grades, the parents let me drive one of their cars back to Lex and keep it till Christmas. I picked Becky up at her parent's house on the return trip from Thanksgiving. Eating dinner with her family was a real experience. The father said little and just looked at me, while the mother tried to make conversation and act cheerful and pleasant. I don't think that they totally approved of me. A history major from a working class family; in R.O.T.C. with an unpopular war continuing to kill young men; no to mention the fact that I was at least thirty pounds (maybe forty) shy of my height—no, I probably wouldn't have approved of me either. Reading their minds, I saw that they didn't want all their hard work going down the drain in the first college romance. I didn't know what I was going to do after school, other than the Army anyway. Maybe they were not ready to see their daughter in the company of a guy they didn't know. Becky's 16 year old sister, on the other hand, was excited and kept asking me about the fraternity house and all the things we did. To the High School Sophomore even my sanitized (for my protection) tales must have sounded extremely grown up. Her brother, a Senior with no prospects of college, I am sure thought that I was a whimp. Thankfully, at her suggestion, almost immediately after dinner we left for Harrisonburg.

At first, in the car, all was quiet. Finally, I asked her how I did. She just looked at me and tried to explain her parents. I got the idea that she was trying to make excuses. I reached over and took her hand telling her to hush. She looked at me a bit confused and I told her that I had been nervous because I wanted them to like me. I told her that I had never cared about parents before, but this was different. My heart was pounding as I struggled to make full effect from the timing. After that tactical pause, I turned my eyes from the road to her's and told her "What they think really matters to me...you see...I love their daughter."

In my mind, I had just dropped the Atom Bomb. I had never actually told a girl that I loved her before. I expected some physical reaction of overwhelming happiness from Becky (just like on Love, American Style). She was supposed to say that she did too, laugh, then snuggle close and kiss me. Instead, she just stared at me with a blank expression, her finger playing with the ends of her hair. It seemed like half an hour. I had already broken my promise to myself by telling her how I felt before she declared herself to me. I knew I had taken a tactical risk with that declaration. I now had to muster all my willpower not to commit tactical suicide by speaking out next. Finally, after what seemed like hours, she started to talk.

She asked me why I had said that. I responded by saying it was the way I felt. Her lack of reinforcement was taking years off my life and I was rapidly trying to think of how to recover as much as I could from this evident tactical blunder. She interrupted these frenzied thoughts when she started to speak in her low, most serious, voice. It was a voice I hadn't heard often, and then only when she was being really serious. What she had to say was presented in a halting, almost staccato manner. She was trying to choose her words carefully (always a bad sign) and trying hard to think and speak very clearly (a worse sign). Becky told me that she had known of my feelings for a long time and she thought she felt the same way. I squeezed her hand. It was that she was not prepared for all this yet. It was all so overwhelming. She wanted to finish college. She had never considered being serious with anyone for years to come. Her father had given her a speech with a similar message upon hearing of my planned dinner. She said she didn't care what he said, but I knew that not to be entirely true. Everything she said made sense except that is not how I felt and she said she felt the same way, but didn't want to. It was confusing that she knew what she thought she felt, but since she had always thought this type of relationship would come much later, simply dismissed it. She was happy I felt that way about her and hoped I would understand that she felt that way too, but was not so excited about it. Saying those words meant much to her and she knew, she said she had always known, that they would change her life. She was just starting out and she was sure she didn't want to get that involved. It would take her six years to be the kind of teacher she wanted to be and this level of love might change her plans. Back then, all this made sense, but did hurt. Finally, she started to smile again. Quickly, she added that she was involved with me and liked that level of involvement but "saying it out loud" made it all so real and serious. I was being told something there, and it didn't take a genius to understand the less said about this the better.

I couldn't decide whether this was a mere tactical set-back or a dramatic and strategic disaster. I cursed my hormones. I told her I understood and held her hand in silence. After a few moments, I squeezed her hand and asked her if we "were going to go on in silence, or what?" She smiled, kissed me on the cheek, and snuggled close even though the Mustang had bucket seats. At the first stop light, I turned her head towards me and told her that "I do love you, you know that?" and kissed her. She said that she did know that and she loved me, too and kissed me back. I asked her to say it again only smile this time. It was supposed to be a happy statement. She looked at me for a moment, exhaled, relaxed, smiled, and kissed me hard.

I had survived, but all this did not bode well for the future. Further, it was not the way I had expected it to all to go—that was not a speech from the movies. Our next few dates were almost frantic. The sex was "prove you care" sex, and though unsaid, the motivation was from both parties. If pressed, I would have described it as such then; even though I hoped it was a new found passion caused by our mutual, emotional revelations. Our night time walks, which had been our special time together, became more silent. Being December, we had to bundle up to enjoy them, but the night's cold seemed to be finding its way into our hearts through the coats. Whenever we talked about anything other than trivialities there was an intense seriousness creeping in. Her exams ended before mine started. We studied together and actually studied. I called her after every day of exams. Things were starting to perk up. I told myself that the shock of our admission was wearing off. The night before she went home I gave her my first serious Christmas gift to a girl. It was a white porcelain rose.

White was becoming my trademark color. I wore white trousers a lot and I liked white ties. I even became a Yorkist, deserting my previous Lancastrian leanings, during our history unit on the Wars of the Roses. White was the color of birches, my favorite tree and the color of Julie Christie's turtleneck in Dr. Zhivago. I envied Tony Curtis' wardrobe in The Great Race. Besides, everybody knew white was what the good guys wore. I must have gone through about two pair of white pants that semester because any stain made the pair unusable. The house noticed, but even the shit they gave me made me feel good—everybody needed a trademark—Fran had his Raisin Bran and I my white pants. I wrapped the gift in silver paper and tied it in gold, white and scarlet hair ribbons. I couldn't wait to give it to her. She made me open mine first. It was book on Wellington. I loved it, not because of the book but because she used the word love in the inscription. She spotted the ribbons and saved them, putting the white one in her hair. The rose got the appropriate "ooh"s and "ah"s from her and the girls she knew who passed us on the steps of her dorm.

Sneaking past the student sentinel, we made our way to her room. Men were allowed in the dorms, but you had to sign in and keep the door open. If you didn't sign in, the monitor wouldn't check for the door or know when to ask you to leave. Finally, something happened the way it was supposed to. We got to her room, we shed our coats and she guided me to her bed. Putting the rose down, we started to make love, or what we called among ourselves making love. I remember remarking to myself that it had lost its frantic passion and was almost silent in its emotional intensity. Perhaps she had seen the same movies, but it was beautiful. When she was finished she crawled up and told me that she was happy to love me. I started to talk in a happy, no genuinely excited, manner about how I felt, but she put her finger on my lips and just drifted off to sleep. Even I knew when to be quiet—sometimes. It seemed as if we had weathered the storm and the relationship was becoming the one I wanted again. Some time way too late, we both awoke to sneak out. It was the first, and though I didn't know it then, the last night ever spent in a Madison dorm.

My exams did not go as well. I bombed the German test and put myself into probable failure. Everything else went good but I didn't kill any of them. I only got one "A", in British History, of course. I went home with the best marks I had ever got in college but an "E" in German. "E" was a hybrid grade. If I passed the next semester it would become a "D" if not, an "F".

Most of Christmas was spent thinking about Becky, getting stoned with Dave, and trying to decide next semester's courses. My big present that year was the car for the next semester or till Easter Break; anyway. I was glad for it made things easier for me to maintain the relationship with Becky rather than being dependent on Stan or someone else. Maybe Mom and Dad knew that, though I had not told them to what level our relationship had grown. They still asked a lot of questions about her. My parents didn't center on the normal stuff like her family, career, religion or things like that at all. My mother would ask what books she read and what her philosophy of education was (since she was going to be a teacher). Neither ever asked to see her picture or what she looked like. They didn't even ask what her father did. They were interested more in what her thoughts were about more significant subjects. When I would reach an impasse, I just made stuff up to fit the picture of her I had given them. Dave and I would agree time and time again that this was weird. But then, retelling any conversation with your folks while you're listening to Santana stoned out of your mind is weird, as well.

The post Christmas meal with Becky's folks was easier. Both her parents were easier on me than on the previous visit. I tried to discern if Becky had told them anything about our relationship. Her dad consciously tried to get me into a conversation about football and hunting. I tried to maintain it with some semblance of interest. Her mom even asked me if I wanted a drink. Noticing that Dad had a beer I said that it was fine. Becky almost fell off her chair since she had bought some of my favorite Gin. The sister was strangely quiet and just looked at me. I gathered that there had been some heavy discussions between the sisters. Her brother talked about the Army, which was his career choice made of necessity since he had been, for some reason, rejected by both Air Force and Navy. I just looked at Becky and glowed with the realization that every time I looked at her she would blush and smile. Stars were again in the sky as things were starting to go right after all. We didn't talk much on the ride back. There had been a snowfall in the past few days and the mountains were spectacular as we crossed them. It reminded me of <u>Dr. Zhivago</u>. I started for the first time to relax in the assurance of her love. I wanted to tell her so, but bit my tongue. Best be not too hasty. The last time we were in this mountain pass things almost went in the toilet. Maybe it was the mountain.

In her dorm we settled down to some serious sex. After, during cigarettes, we just snuggled. I asked her if she was more secure in our feelings. She got up on one elbow and traced some design on my chest with her finger. She said no, but she wasn't going to let it bother her anymore. She looked at me suddenly, seriously and said that she wanted to date others. I will never understand women's thought or thinking process. Christ! Here I was, naked in her dorm room after a mutually devouring event that could have added a second story on most buildings, and here she was talking about going out with other guys. The way she looked, this could mean serious competition. I asked her why. She said she needed to. She was "at last—at ease" with her feelings about me, but she wanted to be sure. She wanted her confidence to be strengthened and assured. I was, after all, "the first serious romance of her life." She laughed; kissed me and told me not to worry there was no one else. Bullshit. This sounded like the result of another parental talk. I was worried and I knew, with her looks and manner, I had good cause to be.

I told her that I never wanted nor would I ever keep her against her will, would not stand in the way and all that agreement crap you're supposed to say if you're liberal, modern or actually believe in that stuff. I did think then, and do now, if you try to hold a girl against her will, she'll eventually break the rope. I did ask her why she picked that moment to tell me (significantly not saying "ask me"). She said that she had never been as sure of her love as right then and it seemed to be the best time to tell me. Great timing (!)—so much for the security of our feelings. I couldn't help but wonder if this wasn't a nice way of saying goodbye in advance?

It was the third weekend in January before she said she was busy, so I knew it was then. With little warning I was dateless for the weekend, which, in itself raised a few eyebrows. I went up to the Zone the following Wednesday and she kissed me before I had a chance to say "hi." She, however, became "busy" more and more Wednesday nights from then on. Our sex got more frantic again and she seemed to be rather evasive about her feelings and there was never any mention even close to the "L" word. It was going down the drain and I knew it. I had never been in love before so, likewise, I never had fallen out of it before. Just how does someone start taking the hint and giving up hope? I was determined to leave this relationship tugging, kicking and screaming if there was any chance of it living up to my expectations of what I wanted in a Significant College Romance. She was careful to be cheerful and attentive, but she increasingly missed "I love you" opportunities. Valentine's Day passed and our date was probably the most torrid in our history. We had made love, actual intercourse. I think that she, not to mention I, imagined it would change things dramatically. It didn't. Curiously, neither of us spent much time examining why she had changed her mind. She said she wanted to be closer to me when I asked during the moment. Since I knew that things were drifting (though I felt powerless to change them) I did not bring up what that act was supposed to mean. Though to me, and for me, I hoped that it meant what it had once meant to her. I didn't want to focus or vocalize, fearing what might be said. It never came up again.

It was the night of the February Combo, after the band had taken their second break, and we had just made love for maybe the forth or fifth time since her change of decision. That night, I couldn't hold back anymore; it seemed so empty; like we were playing our own self-scripted parts. I wanted so much, but always came away empty from her eyes. I lit her cigarette and asked her if "it was as over as it seemed?"

She looked at me, startled, but exhaled and said "yes." She started to cry. I put my arm around her to comfort her, but secretly to provide me support. I knew it was what I was supposed to do, but had no idea of what was supposed to come next. She told me that it—us—was over but she really had wanted to love me. She cried that there was nobody else that even came close to meaning as much to her as I did, but…This time it was me who put my finger to her lips and kissed her forehead. In those days, love and sex were supposed to mean something, something significant, something beyond definition for which we were all looking. Both of us knew, if not when I asked the question, but now half way into our cigarette that, what ever it was, would never be found between us. Movies cut away and switch scenes; real life doesn't have that advantage. We sat and said nothing. It would have been perfect if we made love just once more, but I was too young then to believe that to be a serious possibility. We finished the cigarette and I drove her home.

The only thing of substance she said on the way to Harrisonburg was that she did "want to love me." She had met some Madison basketball player who was kind of interesting and not at all serious; not in terms of personality or relationship. She wasn't dropping me for him, but she had enjoyed her date with him too much to continue being that entangled with me. I couldn't help asking myself what the difference was. There was nothing to break up over, but she knew there was no going backwards—you can't just date once you've been in love—what would be the point? Those damn jocks. I could picture him as he talked about some game, amidst all his friends, swilling beer. I wanted to believe that he was the muscle bound dud of my stereotypes; but he probably wasn't. She said that she had a lot to do and live before she settled down. "We" had just come too early in her life. She wanted to continue being friends. These words probably came right out of her father's or mother's mouth; but I know she believed them, as well.

Whenever they start talking about "staying friends" you know that you are lunchmeat. When the friend talk starts you know that it is over and there is no recourse. Nothing can put it back together, why prolong it or torture ourselves (me anyway)? Friends are the people to whom they talk about the people they love. Friends are the people they smile at, pat on the arm as they wobble down the hall into someone else's bedroom. Friends are people their boyfriends aren't worried about. I had wanted it to work, to last, but it didn't. She had tried, too, or at least I think so. I didn't fault her. I probably knew that it was going to happen all along. She was just too damn beautiful, pleasant, sensitive and intelligent. I told her that it was okay, and that I understood (what else does one say?) and that it was, probably, all for the best.

The kiss at the door was a long one. For my part it could have been a peck on the cheek, but she was full of passion. She might have actually believed that we would be friends, that I'd be there when she was "ready" or some such stuff. It was still good-bye. I did not turn, though I really wanted to, on my walk back to the car to see if she were still looking or not. Hell, I had said "I love you first"—let her look at my back all the way to the car. On the road back to Lex I thought about the Significant College Romance and how it ended. I didn't feel any emotional loss. The end had been protracted and expected, though no one at the house more than suspected I it was happening. I felt as if I had been bested by the situation and by other players in the game. She had no other choice. It was not sad—just shitty. I got back to the house at three. Campbell was just leaving with his date to make a truck-stop run. He started to ask Becky and me along till he noticed that she was missing. He just stopped and sent his date ahead to the car. His face straightened from its former groggy jumble and looked hard at me. "Is this significant?"

I told him that "we, or better stated, she was history." Although he started to ask if I was okay; I cut him off and said that I was fine, just tired, and he should go find his date. He just stood there and looked at me. I told him that I was "fine, really," and I was going to bed. I wasn't lying but worked sort of hard to look as if I were. He looked one more time, patted me on the shoulder and went off down the stairs after his date. Randy was already in, alone, and asleep. The only notice he made was to ask if I were alone. He did not react to the quiet, quite conscious intensity of my answer.

The next morning is when everyone in the house noticed. Almost everybody just either ignored me or at least my aloneness so the day passed without incident and therefore was in that sense, okay. I think that the guys were trying not to call attention to my missing partner. I was glad that I didn't have to explain. These things happened all the time. A close friend or two would know the story and disseminate what was proper for house consumption. Besides having to look hurt or be hurt or to be nonchalant about it, either one, was too much work. I was weary from the whole thing.

Before Greg drove Vicki back to Macon, she stopped up to my room evidently to talk. I was reading, actually studying at my desk.

When she came in I pulled my chair back and motioned for her to sit on the bed. She asked the normal questions about if I were okay, was there any chance at reconciliation, and was there anything she could do? She was being the mother-hen we all had kind of expected her to be. I told her that all was finished, gone, but it was for the best. It had been fun, but was now over. "I would just have to try to find someone as good if not better." It was the quiet, softly sad, romantic me speaking, looking not too hurt, but damaged. Hell, what I really wanted to do was cry that Becky was so beautiful and that she was smart and kind and sexy and great to talk to and why couldn't it have worked out; but knew I couldn't do that. Vicki looked at me in a kind of maternal way and asked me why it had ended. All I could say was that I guessed that I was not her type of man and didn't fit her dreams and stuff like that. She took my hand and just looked at me almost mournfully. Quickly, I erased out of my head the erotic fantasy of how this could be turned into a sex session. Vicki was one hell of a sexy woman, but Greg was a brother and more popular and politically powerful than me. It would have been very foolish. Vicki's concern and affection could be more valuable than any sex would ever be. It was the end my first Significant College Romance. I would just have to start over.

CHAPTER 6

*M*arch was always miserable in Lexington and that particular year it seemed worse. The University had switched to a trimester form of curriculum which made the terms twelve, twelve, six. Not only would this give the political events of each spring a less dramatic effect on a student's academic record, but it also provided the necessary short term for those interesting and innovative educational projects so much in fashion then. March, then, was the last month of the second twelve week trimester. This meant there were exams for which to study and papers that required writing. There had never been a time when exams were fun; but papers were getting to be interesting—a kind of intellectual journey, the end of which you didn't necessarily know. March was also a windy, cold and just generally messy month in the Virginia mountains. The trees were still bare and the ground showed all the muddy scars and refuse left-over from winter. It's rainy and not yet warm; the skies stay pretty grey all the time with an almost universal cloud cover. Those four weeks, coming before an always spectacular spring in April, never brought anything good. It was just the gloomy prelude to something everyone looked forward. This seemed to get everyone a bit depressed.

Such it was that Sophomore March with Becky gone and nowhere for me to go. It seemed to me that all the good dates were already attached. It was right in the middle of everyone's post Christmas romances. There was too much work that I should have done, so I couldn't justify (even to myself) any Wednesday night road trips. I would date on the weekends but no one seemed able to get me anyone decent. It got real depressing, real fast. To top things off, Randy got elected to some office in Young Republicans, so his life was obnoxiously buoyant.

He seemed to be motivated and, worse, excited about being a Hitler-Jungend, Young Republican. I often imagined him and his kind dressed in brown shirts, Sam Browne Belts and lederhosen. On top of it all, this was their big year to Re-elect the President; much to our general disgust. In my mind this should have been illegal for anyone under twenty-one. Not only to vote Republican in the secret sanctity of a voting booth, but to actually profess it out loud should have been out of the question. Not that most of us thought we had any real alternative. Even the politicos like myself couldn't seem to find the hoped for leadership among the Democratic candidates of the day. Politics was a constant topic of conversation on the student level, though curiously, it was never important enough for a decent argument—at least in our house. The only real disputes were about global topics, the war, poverty, things far from any direct impact on our lives—except through the fading specter of the draft. Party politics was too mundane, we were too wise and cynical to care much. Besides, we all knew the only safe course was to throw the bums out and they're all bums. It didn't matter much anyway, since the voting age was still twenty one, only the house Seniors, and only a few of them, could actually vote.

The only bright side was my classes. German, studied under the "new" method, seemed to be finally yielding a passing grade. It was still borderline, but on the black side of the line for the first time in college. It wasn't much, but my German professor almost beamed at my "C" grade on tests. He became excited, almost started grinning, and shook my hand and everything, when I scored a "C+" on one.

There was an unspoken deal between us: I put in the work and per-formance—he would give me any benefit of the doubt to pass. If that happened we both knew that I would never grace the German class-rooms again—a kind of win / win deal. I would get excited late at night, just before sleep, when I would think of never having to take German again.

Papers before word processing were a major production. First, I would sketch out an idea, nothing fancy, but a general subject to write about. Next, was the card catalog search. Each book would be read and notes taken, one to a card, on 3X5 cards. I would then orga-nize the cards in the order about which they would be written in the paper. While the final process of writing, revising, and typing the paper took the longest, and had the highest cost (since I didn't type well) it was the easiest. The paragraphs seemed to glide from the cards onto the paper. I would gather the various viewpoints and weave a new version of some subject. Now, I wonder how Dr. Taylor and all the rest ever made it through all the rehashes of various his-torical episodes. To me, and we historites, it was the joy of exploring a subject in depth and then showing it off. To them, I am sure, it must have been exceptionally boring. Papers were almost automatic symbols of authority among our peers. In some argument the state-ment, by someone, that he had done a paper on it, gave an added, authoritative weight to his argument. It was the first stage in our increasing scholasticism reached immediately before actual oral footnoting; which would come later. We were undergraduate stu-dents and not bibliophile graduates yet.

March also saddened me because English history was winding down. It was then we were covering World War One. The First World War dimmed the generally exuberant, or at least mostly glorious, story of Great Britain. It really marked the end of the "Great" in Great Britain. 1918 was not only the end of the hegemony of the British Empire, but the end of the exclusively humanistic world—one that seemed particularly English. World War One was the right of passage from the human era to the technological one. Before 1916 and the Somme, or maybe Ypres, everything centered on human ideas, accomplishments, and labor. In the era just preceding 1914, the Europeans were expanding the achievements of human reason past the trite nationalistic boarders and were trying to become truly cosmopolitan or international. Even Marxism saw as its central facet, the value of human labor on an international and timeless scale. Somewhere in the famous fields of Flanders not only did the flower of British poetry die, or become forever disillusioned, but so did the essentially and exclusively human dream. The Somme, Ypres and all the rest proved beyond all human reason, the power of machines over men. It was the dawn of our technological society and to me, then, it seemed that we had lost something in the process.

These thoughts would often burden me on my rainy walks back to the house for lunch. It was a strange time for me; getting teary-eyed over Passendale and yet indignant over Viet Nam and Nixon. As these thoughts and emotions would strike me, I became morose and depressed. It would take years to lose the negative intellectual realizations born from this personal historical awakening. Although they did not haunt me throughout every day, their effects would continue to touch me from time to time after that spring. It was a sense that we were playing with a different deck of cards, a less personal and romantic one. The inter-war era and even parts of World War Two were full of birth pangs from the "new" forces unleashed in the trenches or in the dying gasps of the past. It took Korea, the Atomic Cold War, and (of course) Vietnam to bring us to the full realization that our society was not human based at all, but rather technology based on a global level. Taken in this light, even Lexington's bridge over nothing, which usually amused or even cheered me, became increasingly meaningless and gloomy.

Computers were just starting to make their impact felt across a wide band of the business world. Gadgetry was everywhere. There were many new things; not just entertainment toys, but new tools, changing things faster and more significantly than ever before. It started to dawn on me that it was a totally different time now than before. All my courses started to blend together. Years later, I thought of this as my intellectual awakening or birth. Maybe it was just my adolescence starting to fade but yet totally out of the picture. I started to actually care about a personal philosophy of reality (whatever that meant), what it meant to learn something and things like that. I began to try to understand music and art rather than just enjoy some of it. I started to spend a lot of time just thinking.

That rainy March those thoughts came to the forefront of my mind. It was a time when I would sit at my desk and look through the dirty windows (never cleaned in several decades to my knowledge) across the street to the opposite fraternity house. I would smoke my cigarette and wonder why all the romantic realities had to die before I had a chance to savor them. What it would take years to convince me; was that the good old times were not as good, nor was the new technological society as overpowering as our Sociology professors liked to make-out. After all, gangs of half starved and ill equipped romantic revolutionaries dressed in black pajamas were fighting the most technologically advanced army of all time and winning at that moment. They fought for the simple dream of freedom. But, I didn't see any of that then.

The papers were written and the tests taken. Religion, Political Science, History and German were all passed. I got the best grades yet with an average of 3.00! My German professor invited me, and one or two others, to his house for dinner. The final toast was to the end of my German career. The other guys around the table looked at me strangely, but I just smiled and raised the "Amen" to the toast. He had kept his end of the bargain and I would keep mine.

Those grades marked the end of my marginal record as a student. Something happened that March and I became one of the leaders, secure that I would not only be one of the best in each class (not just history) but also that I would get the "A" or at worst case, one of the

"B"s in every class I attained. It happened without my noticing. I don't know what I did differently, but school and all things scholastic came easier. I began to take exams, not let the exams take me. I started reading the assignments not trying to memorize them, but reading for real comprehension. I looked at assignments not exactly with relish, but not as nasty chores—they had become the reason I was in Lexington, the reason I was attending W&L. Surprisingly, I really wanted to learn whatever was intended. It was like all the pieces of knowledge were starting to fit into place. I was not a favorite of all the teachers, but I got along well with most of them. Mostly, I just started to know things, not just learn them. It was as if I was learning how to think all over again. Maybe it was that being a college kid was finally sinking in; not just the veneer of my personality, but to its core. Grades ceased to be a concern to me; course selection was. Something that had lasted since kindergarten—the "whadjya get" syndrome of grade worry—simply vanished. When I look back at this now, it should have scared the hell out of me, but it didn't—it was just the next logical step in being a college student at the time.

To celebrate my grades, the parents let me take the car back from Spring Break once again. They had survived with one car for most of the year so it didn't seem to matter much; though my brother and sister let me know how much they had sacrificed during my absence. Actually, I think they were quite content to see me go off to college by myself. The last time they saw the house they were none too impressed. What they heard of college did not lead them to want to know much more; first hand at any rate. The drive to Lex, down Route 15 to Interstate 81 ending at the house is exactly 501 miles long. It took about 10 hours, more or less. I would stop at the same restaurants every trip and mentally note any changes along the way. Going home was always a chore. The drive back to Lex was fun. These were the days before CDs or even car tape players; we were stuck with AM radio. I didn't mind. I would day dream about what was in store. I would plan romantic conquests, great grades and embellish on already renowned adventures. The best part of the whole day was crossing the Virginia state border. I would roll down the window and breathe deeply, emphatically and yell "home." The radio would be blaring and the Mustang would be cruising at about 80. It was a burst of bravado amidst a fairly circumspect life.

I was not exactly a house leader. I was always a bit careful about who I was around and what I said. Mickey and Campbell were probably the only ones with whom I was, in any blatant sense of the word, genuine. I was no "Earl", certainly not part of the "Peer Group" and I had no recognized date any longer to confer status upon me. I was simply one of the gang; a member of the large central, but undefined group. I was not excluded, but not exactly sought after for any functions or adventures, either. From my vantage point of outside the crowd, I saw things that others often missed. I could easily analyze people or situations, but I was not the center or leader as I had always hoped to be. When I did venture out, I usually did okay, but such circumstances were far and few between. The brothers, not to mention myself, did not trust me at the helm. I was a good enough follower and as one brother said to me as I tried to help him get to his bed so that he could sleep off his drunk: "You're okay, for an asshole…but just remember…everybody's an asshole to somebody…and everyone is an asshole sometimes…just never be an asshole to everyone all the time." Those words of wisdom helped me get through many evenings over the next few years; maybe the following few decades.

Spring was also a time for laughter. W&L started to come alive socially, but VMI and Sem went all out. Spring was the time for VMI to have their Ring Dance which put all Semies into a terminal fit of Ring Fever. From our vantage point at W&L and around Lexington, which we felt we owned, we would watch the nonsense with a sense of moral and intellectual superiority that would end in derisive laughter at their bizarre mating habits. Two places the Revolution failed to conquer, heck failed to even dent, was VMI and Sem. They were solidly in the pre-Revolution camp from social mores to rules to traditions. Both VMI and W&L are co-ed now and Sem died because of it and the changing of women's self perception; but then, on the cusp of all the changes, it was a lot of fun to watch.

The Ring Dance was the formal ball where the VMI Junior class, or rising Seniors, would be given their class rings. This was a big moment in the life of every Veemie. The VMI class ring was not only a symbol of their right of passage from the ranks of the underclassmen, but also a huge slab of metal and stone; their tangible symbol of survival. It rivaled West Point's in sheer mass and all the cadets would wear it forever. Now I know that W&Ls ring is not small either, but to this day I can spot a Veemie yards away—if not for the posture and glare (always mad for not having the fun we had), it would be the ring. The dance, however, was the ritual whereby they gained the right to wear this badge of their regained humanity. To mark the occasion every cadet got a date while parents and alumni flocked to Lexington to join in the festivities.

This was the night where many of them would lose their virginity to likewise virgin Semies, who had been frolicking at W&L for the year, but now would kill for an invitation to the dance. These "Virgins" a mere few weeks before had been hardy partiers at W&L and heavily partaking in the Free Love era. The Veemie would then make an honest woman of the girl who had surrendered her virtue to such an ardent conqueror and get engaged. Once accomplished there were obligatory pictures next to the sacred "Cadet Arch" at VMI and under the Rose Arbor on Sem's campus. This, of course, was done in full dress uniform and formal gown. It was like Pictures with Santa at Sears in December only the ages of the children were different.

We would make almost any excuse to drive or walk through VMI during this weekend just to see all the romantic excitement. With all the parents and alumni we figured it was like Salmon returning to spawn, or the prom night episode on <u>Ozzie and Harriet</u>. To us, as worldly sophisticates, this was all childish romanticism. When we would see Semies or occasionally girls from other schools join in this "rock hunt," or "ring fever"; we would laugh and speculate just how important it must be to the weak of mind to find a husband before graduation. While we had our share of June weddings at W&L, there was certainly no mass rush to the alter. In fact, the further we went into the "Student Movement" the fewer and fewer couples even bothered to get married, pinned or show any outward, formal, sign of a certifiable relationship. It was still too radical to live together openly, but more and more couples were finding ways to hide this truth from their non-accepting parents.

Romance was in the air, in our food, sunshine, the white flowers from the dogwoods and the leaves sprouting from the trees. Lex was like that in the spring. Those of us stuck without dates felt very out of place. It was hard to find good dates during spring. Lone males were also out of place in most of the spring's activities. Groups of couples would trade winter's apartment parties for sitting under the stars on the Blue Ridge Parkway or simply picnics way up in the mountains. We didn't need imaginations to know what these activities degenerated into, but those of us who were alone could only look on and wish.

I didn't give up, though. Sure, I'd felt sorry for myself a lot, but I would try to date on Wednesday nights and at least one night on the weekend. I had a string of losing propositions. Some of the girls were not the best looking or maybe a bit dull, but I would suffer through and try to have a good time. Trashing a date could lead to banishment from a girl's school campus and would, at the least, mean that the girl who got you the date, would do so no more. For some reason nothing clicked. Luckily Mickey was between romances also. Mickey and I would bum around together and talk, listen to music or just talk to other guys dates till that, too, became a bother to the other brothers. We would both know exactly the moment we were expected to leave and it would mean that we would be totally free, and alone by 9:00 in the evening on a weekend. Sometimes we would go to a girl's school to study. What we meant by this phrase was to hang out in the Library and try to pick up the girls who were in the library because they, too, had no dates. It was a good bet that they were between romances as well and we could survey the field before we would start speaking to them. Often we would just go to the VMI main gate and pick up their dates as they walked back to their rooming houses. VMI regulations specified that the Cadets had to be on post, alone, at 11:00 P.M. . so waiting to pick up their dates at 11:15 while the dates walked back was fairly interesting and easy. This, too got old fast.

Somewhere in late April, Mickey, myself and Campbell were spending a Wednesday night with Helen. Mickey was a god at pinball and could play for hours on a single quarter. I was mediocre with a tendency for a hugely successful ball followed by 4 disasters while Campbell would play well, but always tilt the machine as he tried to muscle his way through a tight spot. Usually this activity could occupy us for hours, but that night we could not find our rhythm. Campbell, who was then dating a beautiful, if overly endowed, girl from Macon suggested that we go up to Mary Baldwin to see if we could embarrass some of the "Earl" dates into fixing us up. If nothing else we would play mind games with them which usually provided us with great fun.

Off we went in Mickey's Super Bee, the 8-track blaring and two cold sixes in the back seat. Somewhere along the way we decided that the chapter room needed a new sign. Our chapter room, on the same level as the dining room, had a TV and a bar. Over the bar was a sign, borrowed—not stolen—in ages past, that read "Beaver Hunting Permitted." We all thought this was tremendously funny since the sign, itself, was totally authentic. Why none of us considered stealing signs as a violation of the honor code, I don't know. To us they were borrowed—eventually the state, institution or whomever would get them back. The school certainly did and when a batch of signs would disappear from the local Virginia highways, a notice would be sent to all the fraternity houses reminding them of the seriousness of the offense and directions on how and where one could deposit them in a "no questions asked" environment. Our house used them to cover the holes in the walls and for hockey puck targets; Fran would often throw his hatchet at them during witching hour.

As we pulled into Mary Baldwin we saw a sign that was made for the Chapter room. It came upon us as a stroke from heaven, all at once; together we knew it had to be ours. Believing that less is more, it read simply "Mary Baldwin College for Women" but as it was so finely painted on a large wooden background, it immediately stole our imagination. To this day I don't know why it was so special or important, but on that night, it was the sign of a lifetime. We had to have it even though it was mounted on the side of a truck parked in front of the main dorm. The three of us quickly agreed that the "Earl" dating effort could wait as we planned our attack.

The truck was parked in front of a small hill which was the lawn before a row of dorms. The dorms were all in modern, fake Greek revival and well lighted. Being 10:00 P.M. on a Wednesday night, however, meant that there were very few passers by. We had two options for our adventure. We could take the socket set and have two guys jump out of the car as it parked next to the truck, quickly disengage the sign, and hop back in; or park the car somewhere and sneak down and get it. We decided on the later. Parking the car next to the truck was the fastest and offered a good cover, but any cop seeing us could get the license number and we would be cooked. So, we circled the block and parked behind the row of dorms.

The three of us walked between two buildings and surveyed the parked truck. Campbell stood watch on the top of the hill while Mickey and I would work on the sign fifteen or so feet away on the curb. We left precise, if swiftly given, instructions for him to cough if anyone, anyone should approach. Mickey and I worked feverishly at the sign. The socket set quickly gave me my two bolts and I passed the tool to him. I held the sign as he worked on his. When he got the top one free the sign (it had to weigh 50 pounds) creaked loudly as my end headed for my feet. Mickey swore and started to work on the last nut. We heard a quick cough and looked up. There, by the hood of the truck stood not a campus fuzz but a Virginia State Trooper. He smiled and started to say something when the last nut broke and the sign fell making a loud crash. The noise not only startled the cop, but also gave us the chance to melt out of our fear inspired freeze and beat it around the truck. Luckily the cop ran to our side rather than the other. This gave us about a six yard lead as he started yelling at us to stop. I know now that "stop" is an invisible word when you're that scared. We never heard it, or at least I didn't. I just knew I couldn't get caught.

To this day, I don't know why we didn't stop as we should have. Maybe it was the sight of Campbell's slender form scampering away about 20 yards in front of us that kept us going. Why should he go free and not us? The cop stumbled on the steps that we frantically bounded up, giving us an additional 25 feet of lead. The lawn was a good 25 yards deep. When I heard the cop swear as he stumbled, I looked back, but kept moving, and then, looking ahead I noticed that Campbell had totally disappeared. One safe, now Mickey and I were on our own. There was no planning between us. I believe it is part of why one believes in God—that sense of communication beyond words, of a shared decision or knowledge of what has to be done. No words were needed between us; we had only one choice and both of us hit the front door of the dorm at the same time. By hit, I mean hit—we crashed into and bounced back. Being a large, heavy fire door—not to mention it opened outward, we never had a chance of going through it. We simply bashed into it and on our rebound pulled it open toward us and swung ourselves through.

We started yelling "Fire Drill," "Panty Raid," "Narcs" "Help" and frankly a lot of things I don't remember now, as we flew up the formal stairs two steps at a time. Racing down the length of the first floor, we started banging on all the doors and yelling "Rape." By the time the cop was half way up the stairs the hall was crowded with girls trying to figure out what was happening. We, on the other hand, made it up one more flight and down the hall before the congestion hit its maximum state. The dorm was entirely embroiled with loud shrieks, milling girls and one totally enmeshed cop. Quickly, we opened the hall window and hopped on the fire escape (thank God there was one—but we would have used a gutter or even jumped). As we went down a flight and peered through the window, we saw the cop trying to swim up through the crowd of screaming, half-dressed girls clogging the hall. When we hit the ground we dove into the bushes and crawled along the hedgerow for 50 feet before we ran back to the car. We never looked back. We didn't get the sign either, although, all the way home we verbalized how we should have—the coast being clear at that point. Campbell acted as if he had saved us with his cough; we, however, knew that it was an act of divine salvation we were continuing to be students versus long-term guests of the State of Virginia.

That weekend was when I met Beth again during a Library Prowling Session. The short semester was when one would take six hours (or two courses) that were usually very intense. That year, I took a course in the Social Responsibility of the Scientist and a history class on the Spanish Civil War. As I look back now, I see that it was the apogee of my intellectual idealism. The Social Responsibility course was full of applied philosophy such as whether it was moral for people to discover and develop things that went boom or disintegrated entire cities. The Spanish Civil War was the story of the last gasp of the romantic, human era; full of ardent Anarchists, fervent Socialists of five or six different flavors, international communists and a hated, treacherous, fascist foe. I was in my element. I loved each session.

What is more, it was the perfect set up for LPS (Library Prowling Sessions). You could cruise the library of any girl's school and easily engage almost any girl in an interesting and leading conversation. It was considered cheating, though we all did it, to hit on the girls who worked there. The methodology was simple. At first we would split up to find work tables occupied by beautiful girls seated alone. After this would fail—we found few beautiful girls at study tables—we ratcheted our expectations down to reasonable. A quick glance at the books around them could easily give you an idea whether you could launch a conversation. Seating yourself you would say "hi" and ask if you could sit. This would give you focused recognition (even if only for a moment) and a good look at her face. If all this went well you would have to work for at least an hour so not to indicate the actual objectives involved—besides, one actually did need to study.

During the hour you would roam the stacks, card catalog and the magazine room looking for material to take back and read, along with appraising the other girls in the library. If the girl at your table was still the best bet, you would return and read for at least twenty minutes. This established your credibility. It would be easy to look up after the proper time lapse and feign weariness. She would invariably look up at your noise and would usually smile. As soon as they did that you knew it was time to ask "What are ya studyin for?" in a whisper. From there you could usually start a reasonable conversation. If the girl answered two leading questions, we never failed. Since we were supposed to be silent you would ask if there was a place to go where you could buy her some tea. It had to be tea; somehow guys who drank tea could never be pick-up scalawags. You would mention, though, that you could only spare twenty minutes. This was a safety valve if it didn't seem to be working (or she already was embroiled in a romance) or good cover to one's real intentions. As you would walk her to the student union or wherever, you would engagingly draw her into some topical discussion. With my course load, it was easy. From there, phone numbers were easy to get. Friday nights were the best time to do this as it gave you a Saturday to immediately exploit if (when) you were successful.

I sat that Friday, in Macon's underground library at the table of a young, beautiful blonde. From her books, she had to be a Freshman and from her glasses and no make-up I knew that the night was intended to study. Girls who looked that good didn't do this unless they had a recent romantic disaster. Maybe my star had come again, as it seemed to be just my chance. When I got back from my rounds, she was gone, but there was a new pile of books in their place. I waited to find out if I should move or not.

I looked up from my book to a pleasant and inquiring "Hi" and to my surprise I saw Beth (Campbell's old date from that night in the Pines) moving over to sit on my side of the table. This could have been tricky for me. The last time I saw her, Campbell had almost ignored her during FHS and, afterwards, there had been no contact. She could have interpreted it as a year of the cold shoulder certainly from Fran, but also from me. Braving the circumstance, we whispered small talk for a few questions until somebody's "shh" drove us to the "Skeller" to drink some appropriate tea.

Beth was an excessively normal girl. She was probably 5'6" or 7," slender, with brown eyes and long, straight brown hair. While she was not a knockout, she was certainly well within the "pretty" category. It was hard to say where she was from since she was a travel-the-world corporate brat. I already knew that she lived in Europe, but soon found out that she had lived in Columbia (South America), North Carolina and New York City. For all that moving she was just a normal, middle class girl, not the least bit cosmopolitan or "rich." On the way to the "Skeller," I found that she had dated U.Va. (University of Virginia) since the beginning of the year, but was not, presently, dating anybody. She said that she had liked the guys from our house she'd met and, since she knew Vicki (who lived on the floor below her), she had kept up on most of the house gossip. She, of course, asked me the same and I said that I had been busy at Madison (true enough), but now was just lost in my studies (more true than I wanted it to be). Beth had decided to be a history major and asked me about my classes while she chose her tea. I, of course, chose English Breakfast.

The last thing I remember was that she was straining the bag with her spoon (as she soon taught me to do) just before I started in talking about the Spanish Civil War. You might have called her a good listener but, in reality, she had no choice. I discussed; no, better stated, lectured or dreamed out loud about the Spanish Civil War for close to an hour without a break. There were dramatic gestures, soulful pauses, but I was never once really conscious of how she was taking all of this. I described how this had been the last romantic effort of humanism—a true people's revolution springing from the individual's basic philosophic belief in Socialism (all six flavors) or Anarchism. Back tracking, I described, in parenthetical phrases, how the central government of Spain could not bring the country together from all its terribly disjointed parts. I talked about 1936 in terms that would have gotten me arrested in the 50s. With a hushed passion, I told her about the slow, but overpowering creep of the "respectability parties," notably the Communists (and how could the Communists be respectable in anything but a Stalinist's utopia), which strangled the people's will to win and the reason to fight.

That was where I paused; mostly because that is where I was in the course. Beth had finished her tea and I had not touched mine. I felt horrible. Here I was, with a nice girl, who could be interested and interesting but was blowing it by allowing my childish enthusiasm for a long past, and almost forgotten, war show through. I should have been talking and interacting about her—something strategic, or maybe just interactive. Perhaps I did show some level of concern, for, as I lit a cigarette which provided me time to recover, she reached out her hand and touched mine. Smiling, she told me how wonderful that class must be. She continued by telling me that what I had said was interesting and that I made it all alive for her. I laughed. "You don't think I'm crazy then?"

She laughed in response and said "No, but we have to get back to the library before it closes." I quickly drank my cold tea and walked her back. We made it to our books and back to the check-out desk just in time. I had five or six books I wanted, but the clerk informed me that visiting students were permitted only two at a time. Beth just took the others and used her card saying "You'll get them back to me in time." This was great. I couldn't remember a time when I felt so good with a girl or about my chances with her. Even more so since I was not trying to be "tactical" at all throughout the evening. Without knowing it, I was being myself; whatever that was. Then, I thought that I had found a girl who was interested in History, not just as a story, but as a movement of truth and knowledge. I should have realized that she probably just liked to hear me talk and enjoyed my stories. In a world of conversations that were usually about sports, weather or gossip, sometimes even history can be an interesting change. We dumped my books off at the car where Mickey was waiting with a girl he had found. I walked Beth to her dorm and while pausing at the door asked her if she could come down to Lex tomorrow. She said "yes" and I got her phone number so that we could coordinate. I walked back to the car happy that things were looking up for me and resolved not to let my mental picture of she and Campbell ruin what could be and what was truly a beautiful beginning.

Back at the car, I found Mickey already making-out with his new girl. I was envious, but not too envious, as I had achieved something good that night, as well, at least for me. Mickey saw me approach and told me that this new girl, Sharon, was coming back and why didn't I ask the girl I was with; as she could stay in the front room of his apartment. This presented a problem that required quick consideration. If I went back, I would tip my hand and look incredibly anxious. This was hardly good strategy for the growing or encouragement of a romance. But, on the other hand, it sounded like a good idea that might lead to better things. I bit. I walked till out of Mickey's sight, and then ran to West Dorm.

I reached the reception desk at West, just as the girls were changing vigils and the dating parlors were being closed for the night. I rang her number, no answer. The girl told me that I would have to leave. I kept on hanging on the phone, hoping someone would answer it and wondering where she had gone so soon. The receptionist was decidedly pissed and, grabbing the receiver out of my hand, hung it up for me. A girl brushed by me on her way up the stairs. I called to her to find Beth and to ask her to come down here quickly. She agreed, but the receptionist was winning her war to eject me so I had no time. Just as I was being backed out of the front door, Beth came running down, caught the door from the reception girl and stuck her head out.

"What's the matter?"

I quickly explained Mickey's idea and said that it would make the logistics much easier, but I would understand if…She smiled, asked for five minutes, and let the door slam. She looked at me through the window, smiled, pointed to her watch and took off up the stairs. I was in heaven. There was joy in her face and she looked as if she really wanted to spend time with me. Maybe I would even get lucky. I sat down on the last step to smoke a cigarette and think. This was going to be interesting; another Macon tactically sensitive situation—what else was new.

About ten minutes later (not five and I was checking), she hit the door carrying a large tote bag and quickly walked past me as I stood up to face her. I asked her to slow down; that is, when I finally caught up to her. She apologized saying that she didn't like to be late. She had started out of her room several times only to remember something she had forgotten and had to return. By the time she reached the front door not only had she remembered several more items, but she was so frazzled that she figured that she should just get out the door. I stopped her, and kept her hand. As she turned towards me, I said "slow down…it's all going to be fun" trying to look calm and collected along with fun and romantic. (Try planning that look.) The movement of her body was calculated to make her spin into me, and as she did, I kissed her.

First kisses were always the most important. It would establish a precedent, a mood, and tell me more than anything else about how a girl was thinking and feeling at the time. I was always nervous during a first kiss and this was no exception. It was somewhere between a passionate kiss and a swift peck; but it was supposed to be like that. This kiss was supposed to be singular, merely a gesture to slow her down and an attempt at establishing a level of intimacy that could be capitalized upon back at Mickey's. Since we knew each other, though only slightly, it wasn't as if we were just meeting—and we had been talking, or at least one of us had, for over an hour. In college terms, we were well into a relationship.

The ride back was uneventful, but full of conversation. Sharon and Beth knew each other slightly and we all made student small-talk on the hour ride through the mountains along 501 back to Lex. During the ride, Beth reached over and started sharing my cigarette with me. To me, this was a very sensuous gesture and I began to get the idea that we would sleep together. From the looks of things when I got back to the car, the first time, Mickey was probably counting on that with his date. With two girls, however, it is harder to accomplish than with just one. It is hard to get past the point of saying "good night." Both girls tend to be embarrassed or something when together, and it usually means that anything interesting just won't happen. It takes a lot of knowledge or friendship for girls to sleep with their dates, in those days, in a nonchalant manner. No, what needs to happen is one girl disappear, or be waylaid on the way back from the bathroom. That way the separation was not so blatant. There was an air of uncertainty that was necessary. There was never a blatantly open or casual attitude about sex as the press made out—at least among our house or the girls I dated.

Coming into Lex, I invented a reason for me to have to stop at the house. I had to drop off all these books and get a new pack of cigarettes. Mickey, always thankful of me not bumming probably did not suspect, but Beth reached over and tapped my jacket pocket. She felt the pack there and looked at me with a smile that said "What are you doing?" The evening was going so good that she quietly and willingly followed along. Once at the house I dropped off my books and did get a new pack of cigarettes while Beth waited downstairs. Luckily Randy was asleep, alone, so I could get in and out quickly. Rejoining her I told her that I was "enjoying myself and wanted walk with her and enjoy the night." I was trying to mask my tactical concentration with a veneer of "happy-romantic-go-lucky." This way we could walk to Mickey's apartment, allow him time alone with Sharon to develop whatever was going to happen there and I would have a chance with Beth.

I carried her bag in one hand and held her hand with the other. Her hair shone in the spring moonlight. I also watched her body's movements in the soft light as we walked. It was not that she was spectacular or flashy; merely beautiful. I remember that walk as incredibly charged with eroticism, though, then, I thought it was romance. We walked along and did nothing but smile with her eyes sparkling. Her teeth shone; everything about her seemed to glow. On the bridge over nothing I started kissing her again, and she kissed back. Finally coming up for air, I asked her why she seemed so happy. She just looked at me. I took this as a good sign. I asked her if she was really interested in the Spanish Civil War or did she merely want to avoid studying so desperately. She said that she loved history and that I got into it more than anyone else she knew. That made her pause for a moment and she kissed me once again. She looked at me straight in the eyes so that I knew something important was coming. She slowly told me that nothing ever happened between she and Campbell. Relieved, I told her that I didn't know what she was talking about. She said it all over again so I was now supposed to know exactly what she meant. I told her that I appreciated her concern, but her past was none of my business. It's funny now, but in ways we were still very "Victorian" and were almost intrinsically wired with underlying convictions, especially about sex. It did matter that she didn't sleep with Campbell both to her and to me. By saying this now, in the open without my question, she opened the door for us with no hesitations or furtive conversations with Campbell about the issue. It didn't even matter if it were the truth; once said, I would never check and Campbell was too good a friend to expose her if it were a lie.

I thought it a great signal to be making statements about a "past" on the first date. Maybe her friend Pam had exaggerated some part of her story last year; or to my horror as the thought hit me, maybe some part of me. We finally got to the apartment. The door was open but nobody was in the front room. Just as I had surmised and hoped, this ruse had given Mickey time to start the ball (so to speak) rolling with his date in his bed so as not to have us or they act as a wet blanket. For my part, the subtle noises were a great aphrodisiac. We found a sleeping bag on the couch and the stereo on loud enough to provide at least a veil if not total protection to the privacy of all concerned.

Though the scene reeked of being a setup, both of us chose to ignore the obvious. We settled down and smoked a cigarette and started making-out. Half way out of her clothes she told me in soft whispers delivered directly to my ear that she was having fun, and enjoying herself, but she didn't want to worry about having to say "no." I told her that there was an easy way out of that problem. She grabbed me and swung me down to the floor, kissing me, laughing. She said she realized THAT way. What she wanted was for me to not try, and she could then feel comfortable continuing. I looked at her and kissed her and asked her why. She said that it was none of my business with a kiss and a nuzzle. I told her that any reason was fine, I wanted her, but could understand and all that liberal stuff. A bird in the hand....

Two albums later, I was trying to find my pants. Beth was not the most experienced person I had ever met, but she was taking all sorts of records for enthusiasm, desire, endurance, and learning speed. I was happy—satiated, and content—happy. We had not actually had intercourse; yes, even in sex, a promise is a promise. Somewhere in the middle of alternative orgasms (this was becoming common enough for me to start naming these experiences AO), I found the reason for her limitations. She was no virgin, but some negative experience had caused her "not to want to be that involved again so soon." Somehow I seem to attract them. Again, the appearances and the actual experiences were enough to cover my disappointment. I found my pants and got a cigarette. She shared this one also. I asked her if I should get dressed and go. She said that I "could if I wanted to, but since it was already close to four in the morning you might as well stay." For the first time in my life I slept the whole night through with a woman. It was another of those little rites of passage that one expects to find amazing, but finds strangely quiet and uneventful. Since we were on the floor and I kept on losing my half of the sleeping bag we had unzipped and spread over us; it was not the most comfortable experience even though it was, and is today, one of the most memorable.

I had always dreamed of awakening to my lover, dressed in one of my shirts, pecking my cheek. She would kiss me fully with the turn of my head and hand me a cup of coffee. At least let me wake up to more love-making. This would have made the dream complete—a scene directly from <u>Barefoot in the Park</u>. What actually happened was that I needed to visit the bathroom. I grabbed my jeans and wandered, as quietly as possible (even after tripping on one of Mickey's shoes) around the bar, through the kitchen (separated by ten feet of floor and a bookcase from Mickey's bed) to the bath room. Sharon was already in there so I just filled the coffee pot on the stove and started heating the water. I knew Stan and Fearless were up since I could hear their loud antics in his room at the far end of the apartment. After the water began to boil, there was no noise from inside the bathroom so I knocked on the door. Sharon yelped and came out hurriedly. I excused myself and shot into the room just in time. Upon coming out, Sharon was there wearing a huge t-shirt, smoking a cigarette and handing me my coffee. She whispered that she must have fallen asleep on the john and went back into Mickey's area. With my coffee, I went back to the front room.

One should always judge women by what they look like sleeping the morning sun on the morning after the first night together. If not her appearance, then your attitude will make her beautiful. Beth looked concerned yet happy. It was a sort of seriousness in her sleep expression that gave me that feeling. The way her hair was spread out and her body, lazily spread beneath the sleeping bag made the intense expression a happy appearance. I knew I was getting romantically involved already. To luck out and get this far on the first date is one thing—to actually be falling in love is another. I knew that unless I kept my tactical cool, I would screw this one up, as I had with Becky. I went back and searched for tea bags. I found them after about a ten minute, far from silent, search through Stan and Mickey's one cupboard, and returned to the living room. She had just awakened and was in the process of looking for something to cover her body. She was naked, on her hands and knees, looking for something just as I came in. It is funny watching a naked girl trying to find her clothes because she is nervous about her nakedness. They can't use a hand or anything to cover themselves and besides, after what we went through last night, it would be ridiculous. Nevertheless, most girls are always nervous about their nakedness in the morning's light in front of a new lover. A shirt is usually enough but it has to be long enough to give her the idea that it covers her strategically. She noticed I had returned and this made her search more important yet she couldn't get frantic (though she wanted to) after our last night's interaction. I didn't want to let her know I was enjoying the show too much so I took my toe and flipped her my shirt. "Will this do?"

She answered yes, but only used it till she found her top and jeans. She took her tea with a "thank you," no kiss, and a fifteen minute trip to the bathroom—so much for my first romantic <u>Barefoot in the Park</u> morning. Upon her return, she looked composed, more relaxed and offered me another cup of coffee. Later, I was to learn that no life existed till she had brushed her teeth, then I was worried about rejection. We sat and talked quietly while the others in the apartment joined us piecemeal till all six were ready for a breakfast truck-stop run there being no breakfast at the house on Saturday.

The rest of the day was spent in typical date mode. We walked around Lex before lunch and studied after. She had brought some books and needed to read. Since I was not a library person, I asked her if she wanted to grab our reading and sit out near the ruins. While I needed to study, this would give me ample time to keep the proper level of intimacy established, as well as a chance to enjoy having a date again. Everybody at lunch, Campbell included, was happy that I had found someone and even Vicki made a big deal about Beth sitting with she and Greg. Randy told me that he was on his way to Madison and would be back. This was his way of telling me that the arrangement about him getting the room that night was still in force. I didn't care; I knew that I could still use the front room at Mickey's.

We stuck to reading for the first half hour or so. I tried to always maintain some contact, no matter how casual. She asked me what I was reading and I started talking again. I got lost a lot in my talks back then. They started as stories, but because I would add underlying ideas and thoughts, they became much more than that. As I got older, I grew better at noticing when my audience's attention was growing thin. Then, my sense of this was not as well honed, so I often over-did it. Beth was easy though. She seemed to enjoy these talks, lectures or audible dreams; which ever of these they were. She would interject from time to time, but mostly, she would seem to drift with my words. As time went on, I found that this was different from most dates she had experienced, and she was enjoying the change. That day I talked about my Social Responsibility of the Scientist course. I was full of optimism and idealism while she would always bring me back to a more defendable reality. Before we knew it, it was 4:00 and time to head back to the house to help Sammy and Gladys with dinner. I hadn't kissed her all afternoon, maybe that was the right tactical move. She grabbed for my hand as we walked back to the house.

When we entered the house and Sammy saw I was with a date, he was beside himself. Beth went into the chapter room to watch TV or something and, as soon as she was out of the room, Sammy jabbed me in the ribs. He was full of questions about "where'd she come from?" phrased about five different ways. He knew that I was dateless last night but had not slept in my bed. Sammy continued his teasing when Gladys walked in and told him to hush. He just waited till she turned her back and jabbed me once again. Wincing in pain, I tried to explain. He laughed and left to finish setting the tables. I chopped ice and answered Gladys' more polite questions. At dinner, Beth told me that our butler had cleaned the ashtrays in the chapter room three times and asked if we were brutes to our employees. I filled her in on the whole thing in an apologetic manner, thinking she would be upset or think us foolish. She didn't; she thought it was cute. She made a point to stay late after everyone else had left, wait till Sammy was in the room, and kiss my ear. She dragged me out and said good-bye to him on her way past. I don't know if Sammy has yet forgotten her smile to him as she said it.

The apartment party at the Spook House was good and we danced and drank. I watched Mickey and Stan. I wanted to give them about a half hour head-start till Beth and I would go back to Mickey's apartment. It was important to be the last couple in since we were staying closest to the door. Stan was easy. Anytime after 9:30 you could see him start to act like he wanted to leave. Fearless would have to hold him physically at the party. While I was never that blatant, I knew exactly how he felt. At least no one could complain that Stan was being duplicitous since he never hid what he was thinking from his date. Mickey and Sharon were different as they were having a great time. I don't think I had ever seen him into the music or dancing so much, before or after. I had a funny feeling that they had snuck off to smoke a joint by their grins, but I don't think so. They were too active to be very stoned. Sharon, a good foot shorter and probably 90 pounds lighter seemed to delight in her "Bear." The nickname stuck, though, and forever after he was "Bear." He looked the part with shoulder length hair framed by mutton chop sideburns and a full, old west mustache. Usually nicknames pronounced by a girl would not gain acceptance by the house. This, however, was too fitting to be rejected on sexist grounds. Beth and I danced and talked as we got to know each other. As we did, both became easier for us. Randy and his date, Helen, seemed to cling to us, though, and neither were my favorite people at a party. She was looking away when I said to Beth "Did I introduce you to Helen?"

"You mean the pinball machine?"

I burst out laughing. I couldn't help it. Helen, who looked like serious stuff for Randy, looked upset as if Beth were mocking her. She was about 5"4' and maybe a 120-5 lbs with black curly hair. She looked heavily Italian. The rhinestones on her glasses, though, showed me more than her looks ever could. I knew that this girl was into something which would paralyze Randy. After I explained about our pinball machine's name and confirmed it with a passing brother, she started a noticeably fake social smile and forgave us our faux pas. The four of us had to talk for a while—there was no way out. I don't know if Beth knew then that I wanted out or if she was having too much fun watching my pain, but we were stuck. Through the ensuing conversation I found Helen's raison-d'etre and why I knew, even then, that Randy had met his match. She was a fellow fascist; being the secretary of the Madison Young Republicans and was the female co-president of the campus Committee to Reelect the President. Randy was history, down the tubes, had bought the farm or purchased the ranch (depending on where you're from). Now, he was just smiling, drinking his Scotch and smoking his pipe, but he might as well have proposed. It was a match made in heaven.

Unfortunately, we couldn't seem to lose them. Beth was no longer enjoying my pain from our conversation with the fascist duo. Even when we would go off to dance, they would be right there when we finished. I even claimed to be a Commie ACLU member hoping that it would infuriate her into leaving us alone. Alas; it didn't. It was like arguing scripture with a Jehovah's Witness. Nothing seemed to be able to save us. If Bear finally did leave, we might never be able to break free. My one chance was that Randy wanted the room that night and maybe his hormones would kick in and he would drag her away. But that might not work either since I seriously didn't know if the Young Fascist League had some sort of rule about pre-marital sex like some of the church groups. Somewhere in a conversation concerning "how Robert Taft was the essence of the true conservative nature of the American people," Beth left for the bathroom and asked Helen if she wanted to go. Helen nodded and off they went. I have never been able to understand that facet of female behavior. It was an apartment bathroom so there wasn't enough room for both to be in there at the same time. Since we were at the Spook House, I knew that the toilet worked and that there was probably nothing too gross in there, but it seemed to take them forever. Upon their return, Helen led Randy away to refresh their drinks.

We ducked out the other door, hand in hand, laughing. Nestling, hiding behind a twin headstone, I kissed her and asked her how she had rid us of Helen and Randy. She smiled and told me that she didn't like to think this way about people, but she thought that we had only one chance. While in the bathroom, she had simply asked Helen all sorts of questions about Randy. Beth had told Helen that she was here on her first date and that Randy looked like someone she "should get to know." Helen was all smiles of course, but Beth would bet that Helen would get Randy away from her as fast as possible. That had given us our chance. I praised her for her wisdom, her sacrificed honor; and asked her if it were true in mock anger. We continued sitting there and just talked while smoking a cigarette together. We looked at the shapes around us, at the sky and we described the pictures we imagined in the shadows. I was trying to have our time together lose its planned or controlled nature. Although I, too, would drift with the conversation, Beth was becoming important enough for me to keep my wits about me, but it was natural and comfortable enough not to spend too much time worrying about it.

Maybe it was spring in Lexington; maybe it was her softly moving body against mine; maybe it was the Moody Blues' Nights in White Satin wafting out from the party; but I knew that I was falling in love. When she would look at me, I would try not to show it, but I knew I was. We would look at each other say something passing or just fragments and kiss passionately again. I was beginning to think about serious sex here in the graveyard, but at the first button she took hold of my hand. "You can wait, why not just enjoy ourselves here?" It was not mean or even angry, almost resigned. I swung my arm around her and let her head rest on my shoulder. I said something about being so moved or some crap like that and just settled down to bide my time. The music changed to the Four Tops so I knew the "Earls" must have showed up. This would not only give us a show for a while but would drive Mickey—now the "Bear"—and Sharon back to their apartment. I urged her up with an exaggerated groan and led her back into the Spook House.

The "Earls" had indeed arrived and were doing an "Earl Line" with their dates, which, I guess, was a too much Budweiser version of a conga line. It drunkenly weaved its way throughout the apartment. Beth, who had never seen an "Earl" in full flower, gasped in mock horror at their stampede through the party. What had been chaos, now was total mayhem and anarchy. They were there with t-shirts (white, with no lettering—the uniform of those who rejected the new slogan laden T-shirts) and beers. Their dates, complete with mini-skirts and full makeup lined up behind their respective heroes. They weaved back and forth while singing, off key, the words to the songs. Those of us who would not be drawn into their frenzy saw this as funny. Beth seemed to be upset rather than amused. I looked at her, took the hint and we went for a walk.

It seemed that her last romance was with some partying athlete at U.Va. and that was very close to what his scene had been. It was not that she longed for it back; to the contrary, what she saw in the Spook House convinced her that sort of lifestyle was stupid. To me, now, it is amazing this was all so serious then; but it was. It was like a major choice of life to us or at least her, then. I walked in silence (never attack an old boyfriend while he is down). She was visibly upset and asked for one of my cigarettes. We both smoked. She stopped and swung in front of me. Looking up she said that I was different, so different, and that fact was why she was having such a great time with me this weekend. She never wanted to go back to the old way of life again. I kissed her as she did me and we walked on. Now, I was thinking and a bit upset. Whenever they are rebelling against something and that is the reason for you, there is certain to be trouble ahead. The "difference" would give this weekend a glow but maybe not the next. Was this a rejection of the guy or just the way he partied; for a future between us it would have to be both. What about our own partying especially since next weekend's Last Combo of the Year, would probably, hopefully, get pretty wild. I knew all this mattered much too much to me and that I was falling in love too soon. This would call for careful footwork and a better, more thought-out psychological offensive. We were up to the Colonnade before she stopped me from thinking. She stopped, and since our arms were linked, so did I. She looked at me like she wanted to be kissed. I did and she kissed back passionately. She was supposed to say that she wanted to be here because of me and "lets go back to Mickey's." What she did say was that she was cold and we should go back to Mickey's—at least so that she could get a sweater; good enough.

The Bear had beaten us back. He and Sharon were sitting and talking in the living room. It seems that Stan and Fearless were taking a bath together and the living room was the safest place to be; perhaps the only safe place in the apartment. One could only imagine the horror if they popped out naked or us being close enough to the bathroom to hear what was actually going on. More, they could get from the bathroom to Stan's room unseen if we stayed in the living room. This was all that we could ask. Bear put on a Moody Blues album, turned on the black light, and turned off all the other lights. The four of us quietly talked amongst ourselves. By the gong, it turned into a High School make-out party. At the end of the album, there were no clothes off, but there had been plenty of soft moans to signify that things were getting heavy. Mickey asked Sharon to help him pick out some tunes and they both disappeared towards the turn table and tape deck in his bed area. Soon, John Barleycorn came out although they didn't. We smiled and started to make-out in earnest. She was naked and I in my shorts when Stan cleared his throat and announced that the bathroom was free. Beth yelped and dove under the sleeping bag. I got up and used the bathroom bringing back some cheap champagne I found in their refrigerator. There she was, waiting for me with the sleeping bag up to her nose as I handed her a glass. This was more like Barefoot in the Park and I loved it.

I got under the sleeping bag and she slipped my shorts off (a great sign). After a sip of our drink, I had only brought one glass and the bottle (the better to control the glass), we restarted our activities. Somewhere in there she pulled me up to her so that we were face to face. She kissed and gazed back at me softly, silently. "You know you're special don't you?" Her words more enunciated by her lips than the sounds coming from them.

"No...I mean yes...I mean I hope so"

"You are" she said and smiled. "Ya know I won't say no tonight" Smiling, I was released from last night's promise as I ended her words with a kiss.

This was great. Here she was offering herself to me. Maybe I was doing really great. However, as I nuzzled her chin a tremendous strategic coup occurred to me in a flash. I would say "no." This would not only blow her out, but should draw an indelible line between the old date and me. This momentary loss of screwing should pay itself back many-fold. "How 'bout we have a replay of last night?"

"What?!"

"Look, you know that I think that you're sexy as hell." I caressed her for added punctuation. "But, the way you talked tonight and last night, well, I...I don't want you to think of me...I guess...that way.... I want things to slow down a bit so I know...that you are comfortable with all that's happinin...You're so special too...to me...I just don't want to upset what we have..." I was my best slow and earnestly-romantic-sensitive ever; a great delivery. I ended with a long and passionate kiss. I wanted to be inside her more than anything else in my life, but I figured this move would shake her up enough to really focus on me not simply as a comparison to him. If and when I won, we could go crazy. This was no Freshman virgin, but again, I wanted and needed to be unique and maybe this would make me such. Not that what we did wasn't crazy. It cracks me up to think that most girls thought screwing was more important or intimate than the other stuff we did. I thought that I had made a great move. Judging from her passion that night, I did.

Sunday was a slow moving day. I awoke first, as usual, and sauntered into the kitchen area to make some coffee. I was joined by Sharon and soon after Fearless came through to take her shower. I got along with Sharon; she was a down to earth type person. Not quite a hippy but probably as close as Randy Mac got that year. She was an Ancient Languages major and was very "into" things like art and music. She would stand, leaning against the bar and talk quietly to me as if my opinion mattered. Everyone else started dragging themselves into the kitchen. I started the coffee for all of us then began with breakfast. I could not, and still can't, do eggs so that anyone would eat them. Grits, toast, even bacon I would gladly cook, but my eggs were, and still are, a disaster. Beth was the grumpiest person of the group till she spent her required 15 minutes in the bathroom.

The dishes got done by the crew that did not cook. I sat in the living room's window with my feet dangling out on Main Street enjoying the spring morning air. It was the kind of day Lexington was famous for; bright, sunny with a hint of a breeze. Sociologically, Sunday is great since in those days, the whole town goes to one of the four churches all within one or two blocks of the apartment. I saw Dr. Taylor going to church with his beautiful wife and boys. Calling out, I waved and he waved back from across the street. Just then Beth decided to give me my good morning kiss. I think Dr. Taylor enjoyed the sight of a girl leaning into the window frame to give a smiling kiss; at least he smiled as if he did. We all studied or talked between rereading the pages in our books till lunch at the house and the ride back to Lynchburg.

In Lynchburg, at Macon, I got some time with Beth all to myself. I wanted to consolidate the gains of the weekend. We finally talked through all her classes till it was time for me to lead into the heavy subject of where we were between ourselves. We both knew it was time and we both knew it was my job to bring it up. I started by saying that I never talked like this "on the first date or even this early in the relationship, but after considering what Friday night and Saturday were like—I just wanted to know what you thought." I was in my soft-serious voice right now; trying hard as hell to be romantically sincere. She was silent for a moment then reached over to take my hand. She absent-mindedly ran her thumb over the top of my hand (a good sign). She started speaking while looking at the floor. She started to say that Friday was about being lonely and Pam had liked me (she smiled) and that had made her feel good. Saturday was fun for her. She said what I said that Saturday night had made her feel so safe and secure around me. I interrupted by asking "how 'bout special?"

Beth, looked through her bangs and smiled; "Special…for sure …" She thought I was interesting and she, after a long pause, said she was interested. I couldn't believe that she would say all that. I was expecting something like, "I had a good time." and I get some soul searching judgments—in my favor yet! My heart went soaring within my body while my body did its best not to show it. Tactically, I should be calm, cool and collected right now. I should smile and take her into my arms, carry her to the bed, profess and then act my love within her body. She, of course, would wilt right after her climax and cry with joy of her love for me. Right! Well, though I knew it wouldn't be all that perfect I decided to try. So we started the scene anyway. I smiled and carried her to the bed. It wasn't the smoothest move invented, since she weighed just 30 pounds less than I. On the bed I started making love to her and when I finally got her past the "Not here" stage (we didn't know where her roommate was) there was a knock on the door. Mickey said that he was leaving in ten minutes. Just my luck.

The week went by quickly, maybe because I was so excited about the coming weekend. Not only was this the Last Combo of the Year, but also I would get the room both nights. Randy was up at Madison for some Young Fascist Bund war rally or something and was completely out of the picture. I was anxious to test Beth's commitment to me and our relationship. This was an important weekend as the year was winding down to a close. The weekend after this was the week before her finals, and mine were two weeks after that. There was little time for anything to happen that didn't happen this weekend. She was going to Europe the end of the week I was taking exams. If I were going to capitalize on the relationship or tie it together for the summer, it would have to be this weekend. Also, my anxiety was caused by my lingering fear that she would suddenly wake up and decide I was not her style after all. Maybe the jock from U.Va. would call and proclaim that most sincere and successful of all male lines: "Oh Baby". She had a lot of weekends invested in him. She had made love to him and not me; that seemed to count for a lot with girls.

Friday, I drove down to get the girls; Vicki, Sharon and Beth. Driving through the twisting roads and lush, green mountain sides, bathed in sunshine was extremely enjoyable and led to prolific daydreams when you could momentarily relax between curves on 501. I had the window down and could smell the excitement as I motored onto the campus. They were all ready and piled into the car. Though Beth sat up front with me, she might have well sat in the back. There was a three way conversation between them all concerning grades, tests, and gossip about people I didn't know. Half way, Beth noticed my subtle frown and reached over to touch my hands with hers. While she continued the conversation towards the rear, she just held her hand there. The gesture was exactly what I had needed and would have been the one I would want had I chosen it. In her own way she was anticipating my fantasies. I could imagine what that night had in store.

Dinner, the apartment party, a walk through town all took place as they should. However enjoyable, I saw these as merely the prelude to the main, passionate, event. It wasn't like it would be the first time, but it would be the first time with a girl who I was sure liked me beyond ordinary. Me; just as I was, history crazed and all. I was sure she thought of me—as I saw me—and her positiveness, even given a week of possible reflection and analysis, made me even happier. Though she did not say it (neither did I), I was sure she loved me; she just had to. It was in her face and in mine, the way we talked and walked and laughed as fresh and free as that spring day in Lex. It was perfect.

When we finally got to my room, I kissed her quickly then put on my Moody Blues tape. There would be more than two hours of music before I needed to flip the reel. I sat down on the bed with her and we laid back. I lit a cigarette for us as we snuggled in. I wanted to appear as casual as possible about all this. After the smoke, I started kissing her in earnest. She was passionate till suddenly she stopped completely. She rolled over me without explanation. Her belt caught mine in the process so I joined her in a heap on the floor. I was half way through my "What the hell" when she grabbed her purse and beat it down the hall to the upstairs bathroom unmindful of her bra flapping loosely around inside her open shirt. Now, I would know exactly what was happening, but then, in my innocent state, I didn't have the vaguest idea. After about twenty minutes in which I went down the hall once, knocking to see if everything was alright, she returned. I had sat in bed wondering what the hell I did that was so wrong it deserved this sort of response.

"I'm sorry" she stammered, "I really am."

"What the hell happened, what did I do?"

She laughed, "you…you, didn't do anything…nature's working against us." and she continued to tell me that her "friend" had come. She was not on the pill or anything and she knew that it would come some time during the next few days. Just my luck. I chuckled, too. I told her that it didn't bother me (although it did) and it shouldn't stop anything we were planning. She said that SHE minded, but we could still have fun. As it turned out, she was right. We had fun, together and spent the night—till the truck-stop run with both passion and smiles.

Perhaps the absence of the possibility of our screwing made Saturday all the more enjoyable. The bunch of us, Bear, Greg, Campbell and even some of the "Earls" went up to the Blue Ridge Parkway for a picnic. While everyone else was stealing away to get laid, Beth and I sat on a rock cliff and talked about what we saw. I still remember that day as what love was supposed to feel like. It was not the hard urgency of sexual desire or a full prostate—no not even the relaxed and languid feeling of "afterwards." It was more like a natural and light "high" that made one feel unnaturally good and pleasant. I don't know how much of this I felt and how much I wanted to feel with and about Beth. We would kiss but never take it any farther. I imagined that our sexuality was so natural that we acted like we had been together forever.

The combo after dinner was great and after the last set we slept till the alarm went off five minutes before 3:00 am certain that there would be a giant Truck-stop run. This was going to be the last one for a whole year and we had a great time. The place was packed with W&L guys and their dates. There must have been twenty from our house alone. They couldn't keep up with us which meant we waited forever for our breakfasts; but the conversations, sights of truckers and other townies amused us sufficiently to keep us from our fantasy about retaliatory rioting.

Sunday morning's drive back to Lynchburg was quiet and very, very depressing. I had become convinced that I would not get to see, enjoy, or get close to making love to Beth in the weeks before we both departed for the summer. I couldn't keep from humming It's a long time till September or whatever the name of that old 50's movie theme-song is. To date on the weekend before her exams was courting disaster and, even if she did have time, I had two major papers due that week and my finals for which to study. It almost brought me to tears just thinking of being this near to completing the year and so far from completing Beth. Beth couldn't figure out why I was so sad till she finally got me up in her room and shut the door. Kissing me, she asked me "Why so glum?"

I almost cried, without having to try for its desired affect. I told her that this relationship excited me, fascinated me, intrigued me, and didn't want the end of the year to destroy any chances it might have. The summer is a long time—stuff happens and we wouldn't. I thought this pretty good because I was really thinking, mostly, "I didn't get to make love to you and won't till September, if then." She looked at me for what seemed to be forever and led me back to her bed. She sat me down and told me to "wait there" while she put a chair under the knob to slow down her roommate's possible entrance. Returning to her bed, she crawled up on top of me. She told me that if anything were real, it would and could wait. She was sorry about it too, but "don't get negative on me…and start to spoil it…with over-worry…Besides I kinda like your scrawny body." We became as passionate as possible and failed to contain ourselves at the end. I started to believe that she was watching and remembering—maybe even dreaming about the same movies I did. It was perfect as we just lay on her bed as we watched the sun set. We didn't say much because the next line had to be "bye."

I think that similar thoughts were going through the minds (no less the groins) of our whole Macon contingent. With their exams and then ours, there was no time in the next three weeks for us spend any time with our dates. There was one thought though; it must have been Mickey's, but its origin was never quite clear. What the Bear had in mind was a whirlwind post exam party for everyone just after their exams and right before ours. Their exams were all over by the Thursday of the week before ours began. Most of them were planning on leaving that Saturday or, at least, Friday evening. That left Thursday night. We had classes that Friday morning and then the pre-exam blitz. Bear thought of the idea of a pajama party at his apartment.

Sharon and he went up and down, throughout Wright hall to all the brothers who were with their Macon dates to spread the idea. They, Beth and I, Campbell and his date, Vicki and Greg, two pairs of Freshman made up the whole crew. They agreed to come up (we detailed a Freshman to drive a car down to pick them up) and cook dinner so that all we would lose of study time was the evening proper. They would all stay at Mickey's overnight and Campbell, whose first Friday class was at 11:00 this term, would take them back early. Their parents would never know, we wouldn't miss any—or much anyway—book time, and one more chance for Beth and I to be together. It was a great plan.

Thursday found us all looking at our watches throughout the day. We saw the frosh leave the house on time, and in due course, Bear came over to the house with the frosh complaining that the girls had kicked him out of the apartment. They had wanted him out so that they could fix dinner without interruption or commentary. Stan had been persuaded to stay the night at the house in the "Study Lounge" so that the party would not have a stray male to dampen things. Even then, and certainly not now, I couldn't determine if it were nerves about what was to come in terms of excitement or uncertainty that kept all of us on edge. At 6:00 sharp the six of us set out to the apartment to cap off what we saw was one of the year's greatest romantic adventures (although we wouldn't have called it such).

The dinner was everything an improvised college feast should have been or could be. We had cheap steaks, baked potatoes, green bean and mushroom soup-mix casserole, all washed down with liberal amounts of $3.00 a bottle champagne. None of the dishes or silverware matched and the candles were all different lengths and colors. None of those details mattered because the ambience was perfect. The music, conversation and sexual tension seemed to make the party vibrant but in a quiet, happy, pleasant way. Nobody really thought about the fact that, for us, May is the end of the year not the middle. After dinner the men quickly cleaned up and washed the dishes while the girls talked and drank more champagne in the living room. Desert was a "store bought" apple pie with ice cream. When the last of it was consumed, the girls accomplished the final cleaning chore and joined us in the living room.

To look at us we were way too respectable. Couples seated about an apartment all completely clothed and somewhat sober. It was right out of a "How to Date" movie they'd shown us in High School. Sharon looked around and asked us if we were feeling adventuresome. This peaked our curiosity and, of course, the guys all answered yes. She began to say that it would be interesting, since we were all such great friends, to try something new. I, for one, started getting some bizarre and exciting images of what she might be talking about. She continued to say that a "friend" of hers had left her some pot, since she could not safely take it home, and would we all like to try some? I knew that Bear and Greg got high; I had, of course, but did not know about the Freshmen, Campbell or the girls. The mood was so positive that we all nodded yes and Sharon got out the baggie filled with a small amount of the green herb. With great relish and ritual she rolled two fat joints with surprising skill. Bear put on an appropriate tape of <u>It's a beautiful Day</u>, <u>Abbey Road</u> and <u>In search of the Lost Cord</u>. Slowly, first one joint, then the other, were passed around the circle of friends. I noticed the guys, and Sharon were the most brazen in their attempts to ingest as much as politely possible. The others seemed just to sample it and not get too much of the smoke. Chokes, snorts and coughs were greeted with friendly help and giggling, but no scorn whatsoever. This was, indeed, an adventure for, to my knowledge, none of us with the probable exception of Greg and Bear had ever gotten stoned with girls before.

I don't think that any of us got very high from those Js that night. Mixed, however, with the dinner, the feeling of this being the last chance before September, the champagne and Lex's warm spring environment; it made us feel very mellow and good in no time at all. The conversation slowly died and we all just sat, snuggling with our ladies, enjoying the tunes. It's hard to imagine that now; after all this time. Just sitting and listening to the music, dreaming and floating in quiet caresses and murmured oblique kisses; so happy. It must have been almost two hours that we all just lay there enjoying ourselves and our dates drifting along the memories of what all of us there thought, then, to be a truly great year.

Dusk turned to completely dark outside and we turned on the black light. This new effect brought us all to life once again and we talked about the drug, feelings and our thoughts of the music. One of the Freshman's dates was wearing a thin blouse and the black light caught her bra beneath it. Though it embarrassed her, it brought all our thoughts to the sexual tension now literally raging within us. Vicki was the first to suggest that the girls all get ready for bed.

We knew from experience that girls planning to spend the night with company in the apartment brought night gowns. Sometimes they were traditional, sometimes just cotton slips, or maybe super large T-shirts. Vicki and the girls started going into Stan's sleeping area to change. After about five minutes there were six girls in an area, barely big enough for a bed and nightstand, changing clothes. They all made their trips to the bathroom but reassembled in Stan's room before coming back as a group. Vicki, Sharon, and, to my surprise, Beth, came out noticeably without bras under their gowns. This was a signal for a relaxation of the normal privacy between girls in regards to sex. Campbell's date and the Freshman wore theirs and all wore their panties. It was still, as we expected, very respectable. No one had yet figured just how we were going to arrange it, but we wanted to sleep with our dates, not just fool around like kids at a pajama party which, in many ways, of course, it really was.

The six of us had planned what we saw as a perfect lampoon of the situation. Guys usually sleep in underwear when in a group. Most of us even had special, dress boxer shorts for those occasions; to provide the most cover as practical for the coed environment. Tonight was different. We had all scoured the stores in Lex for pajamas large enough to fit us. Failing to find any, we had ended up in the Staunton Sears to find what we wanted. To complete the surprise we all silently got up at the moment of their entry and paraded to Stan's room. With loud bumps, groans, and the other various sounds of confused activity we changed into our new pajamas. Bear could only find a nightshirt to fit and modeled his "sleepy time tea" night shirt into the room first. It was an immediate hit especially since it had a sleeping bear on the back. The two frosh wore ones with cowboys and Indians on them. Greg had a set with short pants and some sort of design on the top that made it look like a suit coat complete with side pockets. I wore a red flannel nightshirt with an owl on the pocket. Campbell, however, stole the show with his Dr. Dentons stretched over his body. He even left the flap in the back (which Gladys had to make for him) open with only one button holding it all together. He was, of course, Dennis the Menace.

The girls were howling in laughter. When each of us would walk in, it would range higher and slowly, slowly diminish till the next appeared. We all started to talk and giggle as little boys and girls. Soon, the champagne and the music started to make the mood more quiet and serious again. We all realized that this was the end for the year. Bear asked Sharon to help him select a new tape. As before, the music reappeared, but they did not. It was a signal we all understood. One of the frosh girls got up to go to the bathroom. A moment later her date followed and they never returned after we heard Stan's bed creek. That left the four couples Campbell, Greg, the frosh and me nervously sitting with our dates. The girls had brought a couple of sleeping bags with them and Bear had two so I quickly distributed them one to a couple.

Each of us seemed to withdraw into our own cocoon with our date. The frosh and his date left the room for the comparative privacy of the floor beneath the dining room table. The three remaining couples slowly began to make-out, each in their own corner of the living room. One by one the sleeping bags were unrolled and unzipped with a couple under each. As the tape slipped into <u>Days of Future Passed</u> clothes started to be tossed aside and we all started to make love in earnest, if not a bit quieter than usual. I looked at Beth with my "longing and questioning" gaze as if to ask her for a decision. It would be not only the first time for us but, at least for me, the first time in public. She responded by rolling me on top of her and kissing me passionately. I did not ask for clarification, a repeat or anything in writing.

This was no loud, free ranging orgy. The six of us did our best to remain as quiet and reserved as possible. We all made a point of ignoring the couples in the same room with us. With the black light turned off there were only glimmering shadows barely discernible as couples. The music was loud enough to drown out everything but the most frantic cries. I don't know how long the others waited before changing from making-out to making love, but soon there were soft sounds of passion during the music's low areas. We all thought of this as quite brazen afterward, but at the time it all seemed and felt very natural. From time to time a couple would become uncovered in a position change and perform a quick shuffle to recover. As the night progressed, however, there was less and less concern for our own modesty. Each of us with our dates seemed consumed within ourselves—alone—and not with the others in the room. Each couple would make love, doze and then awake, whisper, make love again, in an ever more adventurous fashion, and then doze again. The music would die for a few minutes till Bear awoke or got to a convenient stopping place for him to put on a new tape, but, being an hour and a half per side, this was not too much to ask (besides—he had his own bed).

Dawn found us tired and silent rather than embarrassed. We knew that this would go down in house legend, not a loud and often repeated one, but a legend all the same. To us, the immediate tasks at hand demanded more thought and attention. Campbell had to take the girls back and we all had to say good-bye. Nobody's heart was in breakfast so we all just drank instant coffee and maybe nibbled on a piece of toast. The girls all washed up as best they could (there was not enough hot water for one long shower no less six—even short ones). Strangely no one was nervous or self conscious (that would wait till the next day). While no one was talkative about the whole thing, no one seemed upset or remorseful as we were all a bit depressed at this being the last day. The good-byes seemed to override everything. We had to leave for the house and class, they to

Lynchburg. We all said goodbye to each other and kissed—Sharon even cried. I would have wished for Beth's tears, but she promised to write and we all promised to be there at FHS the next year. Campbell pulled away from the apartment—his Mustang gliding down the street and around the corner toward 501. The year was over. We never talked about that night till well into the next year. We ate lunch, shrugged off questions from envious brothers and started studying.

Exams were almost a formality for me. I did well with an "A" in the Spanish Civil War and a "B" in Social Responsibility. It was strange, though. They didn't seem like the exams I had endured before. These were certainly tests, but my challenge was not IF I knew the answers, but HOW to present my knowledge at its best perspective as an answer to the question at hand. My blue books were brimming with information and ideas. For the first time in my life, these were almost fun. The day after the Spanish Civil War exam, I went over to Washington Hall to visit my professor. After confirming he had graded my exam, but not asking him the result, I began a discussion on the Anarchist Movement that lasted over three hours. Another of our class happened by about an hour into the conversation so we had to move it from the professor's office to the classroom. W&L, that year, was transcended for me from a "teaching" institution to one of higher learning.

After the last exam we had one more Sophomore party in the hall and made plans for next year. Since Stan was graduating, Bear was moving into the Spook House with three of the "Peer Group." Randy and I took his apartment and Campbell, Cal and one of the quieter brothers, Barry, took the apartment right behind it. Greg and Dimitri lived together with one of the Seniors in an apartment half way between ours and the house. Most of the "Earls" lived together over some dentist's office in town. We moved our stuff, said goodbye to the Seniors and headed home.

The Sophomore year is one of preparation. Mine, had allowed one to become a real student. I had done this. As I motored 81 north back home, I thought of the year, the romances, the "group sex"—even the drugs—the immersion into being a "true student" being lost in history and becoming aware of knowledge. It was wonderful and although I had three months in the summer to work my butt off to pay for the next installment, I was looking forward to September with no concerns whatsoever. Junior year was supposed to be the best of all. We, meaning my class in the house, Campbell and Greg most of all, were all looking forward to it. I more than most since I, at last, had a girl for whom to come back.

CHAPTER 7

The summer of 1971 settled very quickly into a steady monoto-
nous, almost boring rhythm. After the first day reunion, the job
at the factory quickly became old hat. Fred was there, as were the
entire crew from last year, but the newness wore off quickly. Fred and
I would, of course, still pass the time enjoyably talking about almost
everything and constantly redesigning my machine. He and our
change projects were enough to keep me from dying most nights,
but it became hard as the summer wore on. When not working I was
either sleeping, getting stoned with Dave or writing letters to Beth.

Dave had completely dropped out of his prior existence. He quit
his Aeronautical Engineering degree program and switched over to
being a Psychology major. Then, there were no two fields of study so
diametrically opposed as these. I don't know how his parents ever
survived the shock. They had been quite proud of their technologically advanced son and were convinced he had squandered his future
with the change. When we had seen each other over spring break, he
looked about the same as he had before—heck, the same as all the
way through High School, except his hair was bit longer—same as
me, but then he was planning to switch majors, not universes. Now,
everything was different. He exchanged his black plastic—Engineer
Friendly—frames for round wire rims (thank goodness he had
balked at the rose tint). His hair was well past his shoulders and,

more often than not, tied in a not-so-neat pony tail. The button down short sleeves and dark slacks were given up for faded t-shirts (the new, fancy, kind with the pocket on them) and tie-dyed bell bottom jeans. All this was the result of his Sophomore year's impact. Mine never even got close to what his must have been like. Up until then his college life, as all of ours, had been more or less an extension of our "High School" selves. Somehow for him more than others, the spring of 1971 became the turning point from which there was no return. It was the culmination of the entire year of changes since the Kent State killings and it consumed us totally, wiping all the surface traces of the past from our thinking and conscious identity. Dave was just a little more blatant about it; that's all.

Perhaps the reason for his tremendous change was that he had so far to go. Dave had always been consumed with cars, planes and electronics in High School. He was oblivious to anything else (girls, drugs, sports, anything) going on and, therefore, not aware of student trends or fashion. Since that day in the garage when we got stoned, his world changed. He had gone into drugs rather heavily and, what I found out later to be, at break-neck speed. Not that he did anything too dangerous, but from occasionally getting stoned he had developed into a regular "Starship Trooper." He began to see, understand and believe much of what the "counterculture" was all about. Mixed in with his rather typical social and political disillusionment, this new social peer group's ideas, philosophies and modes of behavior changed Dave dramatically. We would still tinker with cars, or go out on the weekends to plink with our .22s, but those activities took a second seat to stereo and getting stoned. When stoned, we would talk endlessly and sometimes actually listen to each other. Stoned, he would go to great lengths in explaining his change of major and new lifestyle. Most of the time we would wax on about some great truth that seemed especially relevant to us in our social or physical condition. Sometimes we would really get serious and talk about what we were going to do with our futures. Essentially, he would explain that he had moved because he saw "The challenge of the future is the alteration of human society through the development of the mind, rather than to extend the failures of the past through merely enhanced technology." This one sentence could keep us intensely occupied for hours.

Those were the days when everything was "relevant and concerned." We explored social situations and problems in the light of what we saw as the "new" thinking. Why not Walden II? We read (when we didn't have to!) several books by Aldous Huxley—<u>Heaven and Hell</u> and <u>Doors of Perception</u> among others—that summer. Dave was more idealistic than I (if that were possible) and, I think because of it, more upset by everything going on in the world around us. One of the advantages of being a History major was that it gave me a bit of perspective about how important things really were. Not that I considered all the world's problems with some sort of cool, stoic philosophy; but they didn't bother me the same way they would get to Dave. My parents didn't have to worry as much as they probably did about my time with Dave. I was not going to drop out just when things at school were coming together. My job at the factory made me keep some sort of realistic appearance going so I wasn't going to stop shaving or cutting my hair. I was not going to turn into a pot-head crispy critter just yet. It was just a cheap and enjoyable way to pass the summer.

When the conversations would turn to women I was light years apart from Dave. He had this "Love—Peace—Woodstock" thought-stream that prevented him from having romances, girl friends or being in love. He would say that he found time spent with certain women pleasurable in many facets of his life; not merely the emotional or physical. But, spending too much time with one denied him experience with all the other possibilities. What I roughly translated this to mean was that he would get laid from time to time but he couldn't keep or simply didn't have a steady date. It didn't matter to him, for in the crowd that he hung with at school, it probably *important*

wasn't that hard to find a casual relationship. He would discourse at great length about how "romances" were simply a matter of sociology, psychology and biology. I loved when he would go off with his: "how romance and dating was a continuation of the system; one which equated women with something to have and men as the things that owned other things" speech. To Dave, it all came down to power, money and subjugation. Romance, like family and love, were all part of the system keeping "them" in power by persuading "us" to sell out for convenience sake, if nothing else.

important

I maintained the purity and desirability for modern, spiritual love. I wanted romance; something above the sociology and biology texts. I wanted her and my "earth to move" for a lifetime. I rationally thought then, and to a certain extent still do now, that was possible. To make the sexes congruent if not politically equal would be more oppressive because then our own value would only be that of production. I wanted to love and be in love with a woman not just a person whose psychology and physiology was receptive to mine. If it came down to social forces or getting laid (although that would come in a close second) the relationships weren't enough pleasure or gain to justify the hassle or cost involved. There had to be something spiritual and mystic at the basis of the whole thing to make it stand above the empirical physical or social relationship—the stuff Dave talked about. I mean, that is what made it a romance, not just a good date! I was not looking for some young virgin stereotype of a beautiful Harriet Nelson—that would be the old school and certainly not sexy enough. I wanted a smart, passionate, assertive (yet properly infatuated), determined, equal helpmate (preferably double-jointed) to fall head over heels in love with me; for life. This was to be the new mixture of advanced politics, modern social forces and an almost medieval romanticism wrapped together. With this combination I was sure that one could conquer the grave problems and situations faced in the world as we were living it. Now, when I look back at what we said and how we said it; it amazes me that we didn't just dissolve into uncontrollable fits of laughter at most of this. But some-how, and maybe it's because there is still some innocence left; some of it still makes sense—even without the drugs.

Toned down, heavily clouded and made a bit more believable is what I would put down on paper to Beth about twice a week. We were still avoiding the word "love" but there seemed to be a bit of spiritual passion or life in our letters regardless. At least they kept coming regularly and did not degenerate into the old newspaper clipping style lists of happenings and weather I once feared. She was incredibly impressed that I had read some "heavy" books during the summer and vowed to read them as well. We discussed <u>Brave New World</u>, <u>Island</u>, and <u>Heaven and Hell</u> by overseas air mail. It was great fun making points and waiting till three letters crossed in the mail to find out her reaction. It kept me sane and, hopefully, us alive throughout the summer.

It seems funny to me, now, to think that I actually had to tell myself to think of her. I thought about her a great deal—almost all the time—or maybe it was really all the time. I don't know; it was different than with Becky. Surprisingly, I didn't center on the sexual. Oh, I recalled the slumber party and all the promise it held for the coming year. But, I found however, that I spent more time dwelling on the Saturday afternoon in the Blue Ridge. I had permanently etched in my mind exactly how she looked and acted, sitting under the birches in the late afternoon sun. I recalled the specks of shining gold in her hazel eyes; the way her hair would billow around her head and shoulders; and the way she folded her hands together around one knee. These were the images that kept me awake that summer. It was the smell of her hair and the taste of her kiss—the sharing of a cigarette that would be in my mind as I slept. I would write to her that I could "read (her) smiles among the words on the page and hear (her) soft and knowing laughter in the sentences." She countered by saying that often, while reading my letters, her "tea would grow quite cold." It was part of the same movie.

Intellectually, the drawbacks to a long range romance did not escape me—it's a story as old as writing. I knew that to a certain extent any girl is subject to the "out of sight, out of mind" syndrome. Also, I knew that the "we" which existed or the romance or relationship, whatever one would call it, was evolving in two different and individual frames of reference. Without constant communication and shared experiences, even the letters in which we were very specific were necessarily taken in two different frames of context—hers and mine. Two years at school had taught me this often led to massive disappointments once the realities and environments rejoined. I had seen it before with some of the guys' "home town honeys" (HTH). Letters and phone calls, no matter how often traded, would create situations, expectations and mental realities that could never be meshed together. The vacation reunion or weekend together on campus had often killed what once had been a thriving romance bulging with hope. All this, Dave and I would examine and clinically discuss if for no other reason than to keep my expectations in check.

By the end of the summer Fred and I had rebuilt the machine to the reward of $300 a piece in suggestion money. Also, in reward for my sterling grade improvement performance, Grandmother gave me a car. Though it was only a sub-compact Toyota; it was mine and with the extra money I had saved during the summer; I could afford the insurance and all the necessary items for school. R.O.T.C. would now be paying me $100 a month which would cover, nicely, my day to day expenses. The parents got to keep their car so they could lose it immediately to my brother and sister's new student licenses. Saying goodbye to Fred, family and Dave; I headed south on September 1st. Already, I knew that this was to be the best year yet.

Arriving too early to work on the house, the apartment was the first order of business. It really didn't take any time to fix up since the basic layout couldn't be changed. Once again Randy wasn't going to get into Lex till late, so I had the place to myself. As soon as I got posters on the wall it became a typical college apartment. You could sit on the john, draw a bath or take a shower (the shower-head only came up to my chest), shave and even open the fridge without moving. I think today the euphemism is a "galley kitchen." None of the silverware matched but I found more coffee mugs and spoons than two normal people could use in a week without washing—in other words, the necessities. Several pans, plates, bowls; a working gas stove and refrigerator—complete with ice tray; and a working heating system were ours for $100 a month—plus utilities. We added a good coffee pot, candle sticks, a second-hand blender and the tape deck to complete the necessities and create the aura desired. What we didn't know, but by the first cold day in October we found out, was that the heater was more for appearance than for function.

The apartment and its mate behind (with Campbell, Cal, and Barry living in it) had been fashioned from a loft above a very old store. The building with its present exterior configuration is in some of the Robert E. Lee funeral pictures. Sometime during the 1950s our landlady had found a great paying tenant in the Montgomery Ward Company for the first floor of the store. With the initial profits from this venture and in an unabashed lust for more money, she divided the loft above into two "student apartments" by putting up widely spaced 2X4s with painted sheet rock on either side. There was no sound or heat insulation in any interior wall. For some reason (known only to her and probably the city's building inspector) the rear apartment had never been occupied so none of us knew about the noise aspect. Moreover, since there was no insulation, once the outside brick walls got cold, the apartments were like self-insulating ice boxes. To fend off the cold, our landlady provided a gas space heater linked to an electronic thermostat. Once the room temperature would reach the desired level of chill, the heater would fire up and a fan would blow the heat at the thermostat which being only about 20 feet away shut it off almost immediately. The heat would then promptly escape up to the top foot or two of the fourteen foot high ceilings. It was too expensive to keep the place much above 60 during the day and 50 at night. Needless to say, we invested in wool socks and an electric blanket after the first frost. We never saw either a gas or a water meter or their readings, just the monthly additions to our rent. It was a rip-off, but what could one do? There were only a few dorm rooms for upperclassmen and those were for non-fraternity types. Since time in memorial it had been this way and was all part of the deal for student apartments in Lexington.

Over the summer, Randy had written to say he would not get to Lex until the first day of rush. He and Helen would be involved in some fascist training course for the Young Republican Bund or something. I had tried to tell him last year that he had met his match, but he wouldn't listen. Just as I had predicted, it was all coming true. Helen had put on the required brown-shirt as soon as she saw him. I didn't mind his absence since it would give me the first weekend of the year alone with Beth. Images of what I wanted to happen were making me tremble and break a sweat. These dreams were also, however, tempered by the fact that I knew and was certain that whatever the dreams were, I would have to build a new reality, as well. Best leave things to take their own time than expend lots of effort to make my images come true and ruin the dream.

The day after we all hit town, we returned to Macon for FHS—II. Like the year before, it worked wonders. This time, with the addition of the new Sophomores, we liberally blanketed both West and Wright's parking lots with helping hands. Vicki's parents were actually quite charmed by meeting all "her friends." They, since he had visited her over the summer, knew Greg well, but it was the first time they had met any of the other W&L boys. Luckily they had to leave that afternoon so Vicki could come back with us. I don't know what Sharon did with her folks but they were discarded quickly, as well. In fact, most of the afternoon we accused Bear of playing hooky on us and spending too much time with Sharon alone. I had picked up Beth at the Lynchburg airport. Greg, the Bear and I were kind of restricted from fully participating in FHS. We helped our girl friends move in, along with some of the new Freshmen on their hall, but couldn't really go out hunting. After Vicki had caught our wandering eyes, she told us to cool our jets. "None of them are going back to Lex either!"

We, the restricted ones, headed back before everyone else finished. Sharon lived in Bell so she and Mickey had departed separately early in the afternoon. Greg, Vicki, Beth and I piled into my new car and sped back to Lex. While the lively conversation about everyone's summer continued endlessly, we were all anxious to be alone with our dates. We had an entire summer to make up for and, except for a long passionate hello kiss and a couple of hurried hugs, we had not been able to re-establish the desired level of intimacy all day. Both couples knew why we really needed to be alone—adolescent hormones can only be kept in check so long. It was strange being so adult, so grown and yet feeling just like little kids who can't wait to open Christmas presents or take a bite of their Easter candy.

Beth loved the apartment. Not that it had changed that much, but it was now mine, that is to say hers; ours. It was a symbol of ours being a real college, hence adult, relationship. It was our place with no rules beyond what we might think, and no barriers to keep us from being us. Randy Mac had totally trashed any type of parietals or restricted weekend rules so we truly were free at last. Nothing was said to make a pronouncement that dramatic or stable, but I wanted to believe that she thought of the apartment at least as partially hers. She threw things in a couple of drawers I had left clean (empty anyway) and put stuff away I wasn't supposed to notice in the bathroom. She did this all quickly and without talking much. I made tea and handed a cup to her in an effort to stop her bustling activity and center her attention on me; or, better stated, us. She seemed nervous and I wanted to address that right away. It wasn't that I worried about anything; it was going exactly as I had expected, but I wanted to be sure and get things started right.

Once I handed her the tea; I took her by the back of the neck to the couch where I forced her to drink her tea and share a cigarette with me. We started talking about her family and her classes and almost everything about anything, except us. Finally, I couldn't take the tension anymore and lifted her off her seat into my arms and told her that it was good to hold her again.

"I've missed you…and I am happy just to be here…finally…alone…with you."

She smiled and said that she missed me as well. It wasn't as wordy as I had dreamed, nor as romantic or declarative, but it was said and, I believe, meant. We kissed and slowly sank into the bed and made love. I wanted and still, today, want to believe that she had not shared this with anyone over the vacation—I hadn't—but there were no questions; it was better not to know. We were a bit rusty but by the time dusk arrived we were in each other's arms, covered in sweat content to be drifting and dozing.

I was immensely relieved. I had envisioned all sorts of problems, declarations, and pronouncements about how the summer had changed things between us. I knew, intellectually, that it must have—it was certain to—but didn't want to face any of that, at least not right then. I had looked forward to this since the previous May. At least we could start the year as a couple. There were a lot of things going for us to make this a good romance. Foremost, we seemed to like each other in spite of our ever evolving personalities. We were in the beginning of what promised to be a compatible physical relationship or, with my then limited experience, considered compatible. On the social front all boded well, too. It seemed that all last year's Macon Contingent (minus Sharon) shared the same hall in West; so our dating relationships would be self-reinforcing. I was doing okay, or at least I thought I was, in my relationships in the house, and Junior year offered a lot about which I could look forward. Everyone always said that the Junior year was the best. By then you were who you were and didn't have too much to really be concerned about with one's fraternity brothers. On the negative, Beth and I had only three weekends together last year, 100 letters, and an afternoon in September to bind us, but it was a start. I, for one, was happy in that start.

We spent the evening in bed; talking mostly; funny during the whole ride back neither couple mentioned dinner plans. Finally, we got up, dressed and headed to one of the town's two student cafes for some burgers and a walk around the campus. She seemed happy and excited. She had not participated in Rush last year and Vicki had filled her in about all the different stuff—duties—strategies—general aspects of what had happened and needed to happen in the next few weeks. She seemed to enjoy the prospect of helping put the house together. It was almost as if she wanted to quickly become OTG (one of the guys) like Vicki had become last year. I, to be sure and especially in the glow of our recent tryst, hoped she would. It would bind her to me all the more; like in the movies. During the walk she had asked me if I had dated during the summer. I told her "No." I went on to explain that it wasn't because of any perceived restriction or anything, but working at night and my friendship with Dave kept me somewhat isolated. I purposefully did not ask her the expected follow-up. It wasn't because of all the liberal, freedom philosophy reasons; it was just that I did not want to know the answer. Things were going just fine without any search for truth or declaration of feelings. Maybe Junior year was different as, for once, I could control my emotions with my tactical good sense.

Beth was able to stay almost two full days before he needed to get back to Macon. In that time, at least during the day, I only saw her as our chores around the house happened to cross paths. She and Vicki spent a lot of time doing stuff for the Rush chairmen while I worked on the various house cleaning and restorative jobs. My specialty was re-saran-wrapping broken window panes; and over three days did at least 158 window panes (there were only four real glass ones surviving across the living room's back window wall.) Each night though, after dinner, it became our time. We would take a walk, sit on the lawn of the front campus to watch the colonnade slowly drift from focus and talk about History or books we had read in general. Both nights we seemed to sit for hours. Often we would just look at the beautiful mountains surrounding Lex or even at the town itself while discussing the beauty. It was, and we were, like it was supposed to be. Real relationships, real people, Real Love was supposed to be this way or at least so we thought. Quiet, contented, philosophic times together were peppered with periods of unabashed erotic passion. The only thing that was missing was our mutual declaration using the magic "L" word. She didn't, so trying to play it smart; I didn't and didn't press her. We were having too much fun together and I would just have to learn to be confident in her emotional and physical attraction for me.

Randy and Helen hit town the evening I took Beth back to Macon. The apartment which had been delightful for a couple was hell for three. After the initial telling of stories and filling in about summers, they were almost reserved toward me. While they were polite enough and kept their intimacies to themselves in Randy's room; I still felt like a third wheel. Helen developed an especially irritating habit of trying to convert or convince me to some sort of what I saw to be a right wing political stance. Every conversation took off in that direction. If there was no political talk, she practically ignored me. She would take forever in the bathroom. I could tell that it was going to be a long year. I could not figure out how four people were going to inhabit the place every weekend without killing each other.

The beginning of Rush ended our thoughts about anything but the essential tasks at hand. There was an incredible amount of work to do in terms of organizing, presenting, and just plain selling our house. We Juniors seemed to bear the brunt of it. The apartment was always crowded with at least four or five extra girls from Macon or Madison which gave Beth and I little chance to be alone—no less sexually intimate. But last year's success had spoiled us. The house was not doing well at all in getting Freshmen to join. Times had turned and this year's Freshmen were all too worldly for too much of the Fraternity stuff. It seems that most of the outside world considered Fraternities old-world and un-cool. W&L was different, to be sure, but the national trend was taking its toll on Rush all over campus, not just our house.

Actually, those we would ask generally said yes. The problem was getting some sort of consensus among the brothers to bid someone. The "Earls" would lobby heavily against any potential "Peer Grouper" and visa versa. The meetings that last year went till 2:00 A.M. this year didn't finish till dawn. Long hours of talking, and arguing left everybody in a combative mood, which was non-conducive to compromise about people or personalities. Every meeting seemed to go around in circles between the two factions. We in the middle were called upon to do yeoman work in gaining what compromise we could concerning potential pledges. By the end of what became an extremely long week, we had achieved a reasonable balance between future "Earls," "Peer Groupers" and us in the middle. We came up with ten pledges. While this number would have been a disaster two years ago, it turned out, in terms of the school as a whole that year, to be an average haul.

There were several houses that didn't even get five. For the first time ever, almost 50% of the Freshmen did not join any house at all. Times were changing and the fall of 1971 was not a good year for the Greek tradition; even at W&L. It wasn't that fraternities on this campus didn't have a function. There was still almost no place to eat or party as upperclassmen without them. It was that the very "form" of a fraternity was out of style with the times. Houses were seen as a throwback to less political and socially aware ages. The structure and rituals were seen as childish and weak—not relevant and not concerned. People didn't even party the way they had previously. Fraternities tried to adapt. There were no more displays or floats for Homecoming parades as before we were Freshmen. Those things had been left aside our Freshmen year. Heck we didn't even have Homecoming in anything more than a name for a Concert. People didn't wear house jackets as much. Every house took in "eating members" to help defray the kitchens' cost and "social members" to be able to afford combos. Two houses folded outright that September, several more hobbled on, barely keeping themselves open before dying at the end of the year. There seemed to be a crisis air about the whole fraternity life style that had survived for many previous decades. To combat the decline, a period of rapid, indeed revolutionary, change began.

First, the University dropped the requirements for Housemothers. Second, they again changed the parietals so that there were, essentially, none. The new "rule" was that "No opposite sex guest could now stay at a Fraternity house for more than two consecutive nights." This statute still did not make the houses into brothels, much to our general disappointment, but they were definitely at most times, co-ed. With two guys to a room, it still was a lot easier for all concerned to find an apartment floor to share, but with the low pledge count, most houses would provide single rooms for their Sophomores in the coming years. While girls in the houses were thought of as the most revolutionary, it was the Housemother rule that changed the nature and environment of the fraternities the most.

No one really loved Fazer. Up until now she had been a University requirement and thus not an issue. She was better than some and worse than others. The requirement made it useless to discuss any thoughts of dumping her because we knew our chances of improving on her were slim indeed. Her wishes were usually met and seldom complained about; besides she was a dynamite Bridge player. Our year living in the house with her had been without dramatic confrontation—more or less. Dimitri had put a mail order, inflatable sex doll in her bathroom once and we kept her up at night a couple of times; but that was about the entire atrocity list. With the change in rules, some of the brothers started finding excessive fault in her behavior and we all noticed that she was having increased trouble with us. The Bridge games were still great, but the weekends were becoming very troublesome for her and, therefore, for those of us who cared about what she thought said or did. Years later, when in the Army, I spoke to her again while she was Housemothering at a different school and she let some of the reasons slip, I think. She was from the old school where "nice girls" didn't even go upstairs in the house, (or appeared not to, anyway) no less stay there as much as dates had started to that year.

Then, she never said anything outright, but our dates and we could tell. Her comments at the Bridge table became increasingly caustic and less veiled. This year, the Sophomores were more blatant than ever in their use of marijuana and several times she was treated to green clouds wafting down the stairwell and into the living room. Even some of us were a tad blown out by this; but, universally, we felt what the Sophomores did in their rooms, the upstairs hall or anywhere not the living room or Fazer's apartment was their business. There was never a thought of restricting their behavior upstairs to satisfy Fazer. It would be like making the house non-smoking because someone objected to cigarettes. It is surprising today that nobody ever considered the fact that marijuana was still against the law and, therefore, we were all at risk. Even the brothers who never smoked dope didn't complain or complain much. It was simply considered part of being students. As long as those who did weren't too blatant (which was an every extending standard), everything was considered okay.

About a month into the semester the matter of keeping Fazer as housemother was formally brought up in a house meeting for a deciding vote. The matter was deftly tabled to allow the brothers more thought—and a whole lot more politicking—on the issue. The controversy raged for over a week. Most of the Juniors and Seniors wanted to keep her. Even Mickey, though Peer Group Leader, sided with keeping her though everyone knew it was because he was a Bridge player. The meeting where we made the final decision was a particularly bloody one. One argument made her out to be an expensive anachronism. We countered that she lent civility to the house and that she ran the kitchen, coordinated our servants and was, after all, a person we could count on to do parental things—like save us from horrible dates. In the end it was the faltering house finances and her discomfort with our new social mores that put her out. We gave her notice and asked if she could make the necessary arrangements by Christmas.

In a way, she seemed happier after the decision than at any time any of us could remember. While she continued with her normal duties as usual, she now played Bridge and spoke about certain brothers in a new, cutthroat manner which seemed to please her to no end. I, for one, was sorry to see her go. Housemothers were part of the required scenery for a Fraternity Movie. They were like the other fixtures I had grown to love; white pillars, red brick and wearing ties to class. Without them what would separate our fraternity house from a crude barracks with a mess hall? The house was never as clean, as happy or as organized after she left as before. Part of our house's essence went with her to the University of Arkansas where she had found a job as a sorority Housemother. She left early, right after Thanksgiving break. The only time I ever saw her again at W&L was at our graduation. She looked the same and said she was happier there than she would have been with us the "way things had gone."

Even the hill was different that year. While Juniors and Seniors typically wore coats and ties, few of the Sophomores and none of the Freshmen did. I would wear my jeans, pumas, oxford shirt with tie and blazer to every class. My classes were, again, exciting. I had more religion, a British Government course in political science, Russian history and a course on Britain's eastern empire. My Anglophilic tendencies went berserk. Every day was exciting and worthy of intense discussion. With Campbell right next door, our late night discussions were often lengthy and became quite animated. The intellectual world I had discovered the end of Sophomore year continued to expand for me. I was in love with all that being at W&L offered. Our job, it seemed, was to read, write and argue while on campus and date in between classes—what could be better?

That Campbell, Cal and I seemed to have steady dates made the year start off to be every bit as good as I had dreamed it would. Campbell was dating a Sophomore from Madison, Karen. She was cute, talkative (which was very unusual for Campbell) and very friendly. Beth did not get along with her very well because she gave off the aura of being both incredibly sexy and outstandingly stupid. I agreed with Beth that Karen was not exactly a rocket scientist but then again, Campbell wasn't looking for one. Karen was all for spending a lot of time in the small windowless bedroom that they kept furnished for "dating adventures" in the three boy's apartment. While I didn't think that Karen was coming on to me, she was noticeably friendlier to me alone than when I was with Beth. Campbell and I didn't let this friction get between us though, as our common love for History was more important than weekend women. History made things easier as I was spending more and more time in their apartment because of Randy and Helen.

Helen started coming down more and more often as I knew she would. Campbell was glad because it meant that Karen would come down also. This meant that Wednesday night Randy would be with Helen in the apartment and with Campbell seeing Karen in theirs, I was left either in our living room trying not to listen, in next door's living room with Cal or Barry trying not to listen, the library or giving up in frustration and heading down to Macon. Then, Helen started skipping her one class on Thursdays altogether. This meant that four days out of seven had Helen staying in Lex in our small apartment. I tried to tell Randy that this was the final phase of his freedom—that he might as well buy his and hers Sam-Browne belts, but he wouldn't listen. He was in love and was oblivious to his rapidly approaching entrapment. He probably mentioned something to Helen because starting in October or so, she was very cool when talking to me no matter what the circumstance. A date will never forgive even when a fraternity brother has forgotten some transgression long ago.

Thanksgiving was the final act to the drama. Over the vacation they decided they were too much in love to live separately anymore so they had to get married right away. Instead of going home, they went to North Carolina (where there is no waiting period, blood test or sanity requirement) and came back to Lex to find a new apartment. I came back from vacation to find myself living by myself above the Montgomery Ward store. Helen commuted to Madison three days a week and Randy dropped out of the house. This ended my problems with weekends being crowded, but it meant that I would be alone much of the time also. The weekend problem was solving itself by then anyway.

I continued to worry about Beth's avoidance of the magic and ultimate word. My tactical will prevailed so that I did not talk to her about it, although it constantly worried me. More and more she seemed to enjoy the outward aspect of our relationship more than our time alone. She was always inventing situations that brought us in with some group either at the house or at the apartment. While that was great with me, and for me; her actions led me to wonder about motivations. About that time Karen asked Campbell to bring me along for a Wednesday-nighter. All I knew was that she had a friend that "needed a date" who she thought would like me.

The date was nothing special, but I enjoyed the time spent with her. The next weekend Beth was busy and could not come to Lex so I invited the Madison girl. What started out as a simple date, turned into a major strategic debacle for my attempts at romance. My date and I had a normal time doing the normal things at the Apartment parties and the house. But, with the heavy Macon contingent present, it could not help making waves. What I knew about the girls being on the same hall making dating our house self-reinforcing works the same against you as well. All of them met and talked a great deal with her. I thought that they were making her feel welcome and, therefore, I thought nothing of it. But after Sunday, the stuff had hit the proverbial fan.

It was years before I could piece together most of this from conversations and anecdotes passed on by other brothers and some of the Macon girls. But, as it turned out, my date from Madison added immeasurably to some of Beth's political problems going on in West dorm. It seems that she had pissed off several of the girls on her hall. Now, I think that Vicki was reasonably neutral in that whole affair, but it was said, by she and others, that Beth was growing conceited and her opinion of her own importance and stature was much too high for those living around her. I don't know what started all this, or why it gained such importance, but my Madison date proved a great weapon in the hands of some of the Macon crew. My guess is that they knew that I wasn't interested in this girl the same way I was in Beth, but on their return to Lynchburg they all told Beth about her with enough graphic detail to make Beth upset—or at least that is the story that got back to me.

Beth knew that she had no real or legalistic right to feel jealous. We had never spoken of commitments or the "L" word and even never spoken of any real arrangement—and she, at least, knew that I had called her first. But, if she left this at what it was or appeared to be for most of the hall—hell, most of the dorm 20 minutes after the tale was told—a blatant two-timing or infidelity—she would lose much face among her peer group. Vickie, who probably could have helped her, didn't for some reason. Beth was in a corner. Now, over the years, I have seen what happens when a group decides that one of its number is not to be liked or tolerated for some reason. The pain and punishment of the antagonism is profuse. Then, I too, was in terror that this might happen to me someday at the house. From a distance, one can see it happening to people, but for the person involved, it is often a huge and tragic surprise. Besides, once a group sees you as negative there is little you can do to recover. Reputations take forever to build and are lost in a millisecond—never, never to be regained in the same way as they were before. The pressure of constant contact with those who, on the surface are friendly, but underneath are antagonistic or, at very least critical, can be very distressing. In the real world, once you're out, you're out. Banishment is better than the daily taunts and jabs, real, intended or simply perceived by the person, from people with which circumstance forces you to live. It's the same in Fraternities, Sororities or the second floor in West Hall at Randolph Macon Women's College. Worse, it was all done with smiles. Then, slowly, the smiles fell away.

In many ways Beth was caught. If she ignored this supposed snub from me the others would castigate her as playing "whipped" or dominated by her date—not at all the new woman she professed to be. Beth alone knew the price of dumping me. I think that she also had some real misgivings about our relationship. Though I don't know, she probably felt that I wanted it all—love, sex, romance, freedom and future. Not only did I push subtly for some rather blatant commitment (how could she not know this) but also, it seemed, now with my dating Madison and all, wanted to play the field. To her it must have seemed that I wanted not just to eat the cake, but add icing to the top. I don't' know, even then, nothing made much sense other than the truth. Neither of us wanted to lose face among our peers. As important as our dates were, they were only weekends. We had to live within our own group for five of the seven days; and for Beth and I, with the Macon crew dating our house, we were both immersed all seven days.

I, at the time, knew nothing of Beth's predicament and was feeling rather studly about the whole situation. I had always marveled at the guys like James, of Sweet Briar renown, that could date several girls at the same time and get away with, even prosper from it. Perhaps it was this sense of self confidence or maybe the desire to test my new capabilities on the social plane that led me to date the Madison girl in the first place. I said then that it was no big deal; but it turned out to be. An idiot could see that, whether or not I violated some unspoken contract between us, it would most probably lead to some sort of negative reaction on Beth's part. I think that I wanted, subconsciously of course, her to react in a jealous, possessive manner and run after me. While she had not dated any others that year, I knew that she had several acquaintances that would like to get the chance. This might have been the way to solve all that. To keep me, she would have to declare herself. I would win. I would prove to her that I was desirable by other women and that she had better keep "trying hard" to keep me. That's the way it worked in the movies. I must have lost that sense of awe in her understanding of my history and her warmth of emotion somewhere. It just might have been the oldest sin around: that of "hubris." I might have been trying to be someone studlier than I was in reality and lost. I don't know—now or then.

When I called Beth on Monday to invite her down to the Combo the next weekend, she was noticeably short for most of the conversation. The third time I tried to find out what the matter was; she told me. I don't know if she was in tears or anger or what, but she told me that the girls had told her about my Madison date and me. I tried to act cool and calm (but was nervous as hell) and told her that it had gone well, but I really had wanted to date her (Beth)—she knew that. After reminding her that I had asked her in the first place, I asked her if it bothered her. She told me that "of course it didn't" in such a way as I knew she was lying and since "we had never promised anything to each other; we were both free." With that out, she told me that she was busy for the weekend Combo. She was going to see a friend who attended University of North Carolina at Chapel Hill whom she had met last summer. (I knew that she was at least a little interested in that guy since she had spoken about him—but not too much—before.) I thought that she was just picking the time to say "two can play at that game." I said "fine, I guess that I can still get a date" adding "though I wish it were you" to make it sound softer if not better. I never realized that before the words had gone down the wire, our romance was then and there, maimed, bleeding never to stop, dead to all but us.

I had wanted her to run after me and she wanted me to apologize and declare, not too romantically for her—only her; or so I gather. I didn't realize what pressure she felt from her hall. Last fall, the Blue Ridge, the slumber party, letters of summer and Rush week, all were thrown out and all but over due to what we didn't say during a 15 minute phone call.

Afterward, I felt so bad that I almost picked up the phone to call her back. I would have said "do you realize what we just said to each other?" If I had said that, things might have recovered; but as I didn't, each of us parted thinking that the other was an arrogant ass. I thought then that we would date again, after she realized what she had lost. Both of us had taken for granted the peace we found together and emphasized the outward aspect and appearances of our relationship. I was trying to be cool and studly; a real college guy. She was trying to escape taunts and innuendoes from an antagonistic group of girls by running to UNC. By dating there, no criticism could be mounted; the girls on the hall would be totally ignorant of her whole social life.

I was in for a shock. My date from Madison for the combo date went well, not great, but well. The next weekend Campbell dumped his Madison honey which ended my prospects there as well. It seems my biggest supporter had been Karen and not my date. The weekend before Thanksgiving I tried to date Hollins but struck out. Returning from vacation, I settled into the apartment alone. I felt alone and lost; there was no victory in that ego crusade.

CHAPTER 8

Returning from vacation to an unexpectedly empty apartment was just the first blow to my attitude. My first reaction was to ask several of the brothers, who were living three to an apartment, if they wanted to move in with me. Since none wanted to change their living arrangements I quickly cleared a reduction in rent from my landlady in order to afford living alone. I could understand that no one wanted to change and tried not to take their decisions too personally. Obviously, some times I succeeded in this and sometimes not. In any case, at least then, I didn't think I would be alone for that long. That settled; I went about the job of trying to find a new date.

It did not look promising. I couldn't ask the "Earls" because even though we were fraternity brothers, we hadn't partied together for almost a year now and I had made my opinions clear about their underlying philosophy and their Semie dates. The "Peer Group" couldn't help because they didn't really "date" anymore, in the traditional sense of the word. They would hang around with women on Combo weekends, but more and more their dates were the new hippy type of women who didn't admit to "dating" at all. If I hung out at the pot parties, I probably could have met someone eventually but I wanted things to happen faster and, frankly, did not want to date the type of girl whose idea of a social life was to drift from one pot party to another. My short and long term objectives were much too traditional for those girls, anyway. Since I was friends with Mickey, I did ask Sharon. She said she had become so much of a loner at Macon that she didn't feel she could get me a date from Bell. She smiled and added that she didn't like any of the girls there enough to do that. Now, of course, I recognize that smile from the first glimpse. Then, I took it all at face value, and didn't know or think of the covering smile as anything but genuine. That left three options: try to get one of the old Macon crew to get me a date; wait till Campbell found someone new and get her to get me a date; or become a monk.

Obviously, the Campbell option was the best—though far from easiest. Unfortunately, Campbell was in one of his <u>Steppenwolf</u> moods. All of us had read Hesse's masterpiece, but Campbell thought that the book about a man comparing himself to a lone wolf ranging the sparsely inhabited steppes of Russia was written for him and him alone. He subscribed, no immersed himself, in such totality that all our own typical identification with Harry Haller faded into insignificance compared to his. Fran who was always quiet, became increasingly withdrawn and introspective. The only time he would talk was when he was castigating Cal over his continued failure to sleep, better stated have sex, with his steady date (one of the sexiest Macon girls we knew) or joking with Barry over his Vampirella comic books during the Witching Hour—a tradition that had made the journey from our Sophomore hall at the house to our two apartments without too much change. He would still, however, discuss History with me till late into the night. Long drawn-out discussions about some campaign or commander laced with numerous cigarettes and coffee were to become my personal highlights of the period but, about himself, he was silent.

That winter he began to go backpacking alone up in the Blue Ridge. He would go off into the snowy mountains to sit and contemplate on some frozen, deserted (rightfully so!) hilltop. Although he would take enough clothing and equipment for apparent safety, he would limit his matches to a bare minimum. "That's what makes the challenge…it's what gives the mountain a chance" he would say with a smile. I thought that he was trying to test death or maybe his will to defeat death. Cal and I thought him quite mad. Every other weekend or so, he would find a date from somewhere after a lone Wednesday night road trip, date her for a weekend or so, and then never mention her again. The girls were always strange, not that they didn't look good or sleep with him, but they were what we would call "lunch monsters." In some way, every one of them was out to lunch (and would never come back). They were not dumb like the typical Semie or freaky, like the "Peer Groupettes," but always, in some way, off their rockers. One never shaved her legs but wore skirts so we would be sure to notice. Another believed that she was a witch. We never figured out where he found them all but he seemed to produce an endless string of weird women. I remember the best or, better stated, the one that stayed more than two weekends as she probably was also the most significant.

She was a black haired beauty who stood a good 6'3" tall with hair down to her butt. She wore riding boots and leather shirts. From our first glance Cal, Barry and I made much of her S&M appearance. We thought maybe Campbell needed some taming or discipline until we discovered she believed that she, too, had been a wolf in a previous life and its soul was still within her. In the midst of a Friday conversation in their apartment she began talking about her past life on the steppes. We thought that Fran had met his match and anyone this crazy was a natural for Fran. Campbell dated her for a while and even took her into the hills for a weekend, something he never offered to us or, certainly, other women. After Campbell returned from that spring camping adventure with scratches and gouges all over his body, she, too, disappeared. Seeing him exit the shower on his return with bites, scratches and a few gouges deep enough to be seeping blood led Cal and I to secretly check the Roanoke and Lynchburg newspapers all week long.

After the second weekend in December, when I realized that
Campbell wouldn't be any help finding me a date; I broke down,
accepted the risk, and asked Vicki. I shouldn't have done it. I believe
that she honestly tried to find someone that would get along with
me, but the effort was doomed to failure. My romance and break
with Beth had been too big a topic of conversation in that dorm. Any
girl she would get would ask her friends about me which would trigger their stories and opinions. She found a nice, pretty Freshman girl
for the December Combo, but the date went miserably.

Friday, I met her in the living room among all the Sophomores
and Freshman. We both had a case of first date nerves. It took dinner
and most of the apartment party at the Spook House for us to be
able to talk much past one line observations. Even then I could not
seem to get any real conversation started. I sensed that she had
agreed to the date before she had talked to the Macon Crew. As I
would look around the room at them, I thought they enjoyed watching us in our nervousness. After an hour or so, the dancing and beer
took the edge off things enough for us to relax a bit. I took her back
to my apartment when the party broke up where she immediately
claimed tiredness and went to bed in Randy's room. I had not
planned any amorous moves, but sensed that I was being blatantly
shut down before any could develop.

The next morning, Cal's date was in and talking to her even before
I got out of bed. Instead of breakfast together as I had planned, the
six of us, Barry and his date along with us, went to the Truck-stop. It
was well after lunch till I could get her alone. My tactical sense said to
"assume that she knows everything or knows nothing…but don't ask
or talk about the past…try to be genuine and light with this one." I
tried starting conversations about everything; school, Freshman
year, parents, politics, philosophy, history: everything (and anything) that I could bring to mind. She just seemed to act nervous and
reserved; waiting for something to do that would put us together
with other people. Finally, I dropped into my chair across from the

couch where she sat, lit a cigarette and asked her what was the matter. Had I done something wrong? At this she stiffened on the couch, looked down at the floor and said "no."

"Then why are we having such a hard time of things...even talking?"

"I don't know...it's just that...I guess that...I feel that everyone is watching..."

"What do you mean?"

"Well...it's...just that...a couple of the girls...with Beth and all..." She never finished whatever sentence she had in mind. She didn't need to. She just kept looking out the living room window at the gray Lexington winter day. I probably should have asked her to finish, pushed her if necessary, but I didn't. Mentally, I finished it for her much more cruelly and mercilessly than was probably the truth. I was sure that they told all the old stories. The strange things I talked about; some of my more blatant social gaffes and maybe even some weird story (of which even I was unaware) about the slumber party would be twisted to be negative. Now, I am sure that they probably didn't do much at all and even meant no real harm, but probably got carried away. Now, I know that the same stories told in friendship from a person can be shaded with disdain to make any desired point. Then, I envisioned all the crew grinning in evil delight spinning story after story of some negative aspect of my personality. I must have had grandiose thoughts of my own importance to them. It probably never went past a couple of stories and "knowing" facial expressions. I thought at the time, however, that this Freshman probably felt as if she were dating some sort of weird, egotistical freak. Between her worried expectations and my paranoia we had accomplished the negative, expected objective. Here she was sitting on my couch with half the weekend and the Combo to go. Maybe I'd have been better off alone.

It started to rain. I got up to put on the tea pot and find my other pack of cigarettes. From the kitchen I called to her. She got up and came into the dining area, sat on a bar stool and leaned her elbows on the bar. I turned around from the stove and was, without plan or purpose, about a foot from her. She looked reluctant, not bored, but somehow wishing that it all was over. I looked at her worried face and caved in. "What would you like me to do?" The question had the effect of admitting that "they" were right or had the right to say the stuff "they" had. Moreover, I felt defeated, crushed and, helpless. Rather than point out my non-cloven feet, that I had not raped her the previous night when she was alone in my apartment, did not break mirrors with my appearance and that I was fairly fluent in the English language; I just lit a cigarette and let our mutual nervousness spawn defeatism. I was alone already with her still in the room.

She just sat there. She looked at me as if she wanted me to tell her what to say. What could I tell this eighteen year old that had only five months in college? I realized it was useless, turned back to the tea pot and asked her if she needed to study. She exhaled relief, said "yes" and settled down in the living room to do her Math. Math! A little later I followed her, gave her a cup of tea and settled down in my chair to do some work on Islamic philosophy. It had become a very long afternoon.

Even Sammy did not kid me about my date. He must have seen her face as she walked in from the sleet. I was none too happy either. The kitchen was silent as we worked, although I had fun chopping ice. I didn't have to focus too hard to motivate making small pieces out of one huge chunk with the ice pick. Gladys just looked at me every so often and wondered aloud what had happened to the boy who used to whistle just a few short weeks ago? I wondered, too.

The Combo was my final chance to clutch victory from the jaws of defeat. With the music and liquor, maybe she would loosen up enough to have a good time, freeing me from the past and maybe, if not a future, to construct at least a passable evening. It never had a chance; perhaps I tried too hard, perhaps not hard enough. She was surrounded by "Earls" with their Semies, "Peer Groupers and Groupettes" and the Macon Crew. No one she knew seemed interested in spending time with us though I didn't exactly act enthused about any frivolous conversations with the Crew. I was more interested in trying to get her to have a good time on her own, with me, rather than stick to the group. My own supporters were nowhere to be found; Campbell was in the hills and Mickey came late and only stayed a short time (he and Sharon were probably too stoned to provide much help to me, anyway). Instead of waiting till Sunday, I took her home that night. I had work to do and so did she. Driving back from Lynchburg that Sunday morning at 3:00 A.M. was perhaps the most depressing thing I had ever done. The whole time I constantly mulled over in my mind what they must have said and what they must have thought of me. The dream year was dead and I was busted flat in all the schools I knew. There was no where to go.

Parking my car at the house, I felt alone there, too. I walked through the wreckage of our first Fazerless Combo trying to find if someone, anyone, would be up for a Truck-stop run. I found only two drunk Freshman on the living room couch and a passed out, half dressed date snoring softly on the mattresses in the lounge. Everything was quiet. I just stood and looked at her wrapped in the blanket with her shoes still on. I lit a cigarette and dramatically, as if she were looking at me through closed eyes, made my anonymous exit. Upstairs was empty except for two closed doors with muffled groans coming from within and the dope den with its members floating within a green haze. Sunday brunch would be no fun at all. I was resolved, however, to go, if for no other reason than to face the Crew. Even though it was my house, there was no end to my masochism.

It was my turn to feel like everyone watched me. Now, I don't think that the brothers felt anything in particular or even noticed; I really don't. Then, I felt that everyone could see my abject failure. Perhaps all they saw was my self-rejected attitude and my sullen expression. I was sure that all the Macon Crew felt justified in their judgment of me. I saw it in their smiles and their glances toward me. I couldn't even keep the date the whole weekend. Finishing the meal, I left to study in my apartment without watching the <u>Lancelot Link</u> show which was traditional for us, especially me, after Sunday brunch.

I half expected someone to come over to the apartment to see what was wrong. I thought that Mickey, at least, would drop over after taking Sharon back to Lynchburg. No one came, so I ate dinner alone in the increasingly shadowed and darkening apartment. When I heard Campbell come up the stairs I walked over to his apartment to hear about his adventures and to share mine. He was too tired to tell much except that he had burned his lean-to down trying to keep warm and finally ran out of matches. He looked it, too, because most of what he was wearing was singed. Fran gave me his best fierce look, smiled so that his teeth showed and said that was the best part of the entire adventure. He was deep into his Viking or Barbarian Warrior role. I tried to relate what I had gone through but somehow he just wasn't interested or it didn't quite measure up to his struggle over death in the mountains. He listened politely enough and told me that the most I could ever get was "Maria." With that, he got up to eat some raw pancake dough and throw himself (literally) in his bed.

That was one of Campbell's favorite lines. "The most you can ever get from them (it could be women, professors, the government, parents or life itself) is Maria!" It seemed like the essence of social philosophy to him, and, maybe, us. He had internalized Hesse's <u>Steppenwolf</u> to the point of abstraction. It all stemmed from Harry Haller (the Steppenwolf) and his relationship with a girl named Maria. Harry, of course, loved with an intense, pure passion and self-consuming intellectual ardor the beautiful, but intangible, lesbian whore, Hermine. She, being kind to Harry, gave him her lover; the ample, giving and simple, Maria for his companion. Maria, though, did everything out of love and obedience to Hermine, not affection for Harry. Even making love with Harry was done out of her devotion to Hermine and not for Harry at all. The most she would give to Harry was the pronouncement that the time she spent with him was more pleasant than it could have been otherwise. That night, with Fran, his reference hit deeply and I understood perfectly. I lit a cigarette and silently watched him eat the white goo with ashes still clinging to his hair and sleeves. He attacked the goopy, raw dough with the wooden spoon he kept in his field-jacket's pocket. Before he finished, I silently went back to my cold apartment and to bed. For me, and I think for him, it completed the scene.

Being alone wasn't really so bad. I began to like it in a way which was much healthier than the masochistic depression the Macon crew had constructed, but of which I assumed complete ownership. It was quiet and I didn't argue. Things that were self-evident were true with no questions. I could go out and visit or stay home, but the choice of interaction was mine and stayed that way. Girls and love stayed pure because they were, for me then, simply matters of abstraction and imagination. I think I knew this was transitory. At least with the end of the school year it would pass and probably sooner given my luck so far. But, then, I wanted to believe that this was the way of life, the way of my, particular future—Hesse's novels and the Moody Blues' Melancholy Man forever to be my lot. But, thankfully, there was always something to read, some idea to argue—at least in class—and stuff I needed to do to keep my grades up. Being a student meant that no matter how depressed one was, there were always papers, tests and classroom discussions.

With the approaching end of semester, I had plenty of student work to keep me busy. The weekdays went well enough, or at least to say they were as before. The classes I had were alive with ideas, concepts and exciting interchanges among both students and professors. School, at least W&L, was like that. It was never dull or "work-like;" it was a series of passionate exercises in learning. The weekends, however, became murder. I avoided contact with the Macon Crew, who I believed were actively grouped against me, finding delight in my lonely torture. I sensed also that the brothers did not want me around either. Not that I could blame them. Who would want a depressed lone male around a party? I began to see myself more and more isolated in the house. I had never been a leader, but as a follower, I contented myself by believing that others wanted to include me. At the time, I felt that even that morsel of acceptance was lost to me. I tried to lose myself in my school work as all the old movies directed. I could, and did, spend a lot of time with my class work and papers. That still left the weekend evenings alone; thinking of all the other brothers partying and, later in the night, getting laid. I couldn't spend much time next door. Cal's perennial date, Susan, would be there almost constantly and she was one of the leading members of the Crew. I would feel so self-conscious talking to Barry or Campbell in her presence that not only did I probably come off as crazy, but also would add fuel to my already perceived raging fire of scorn from the girls.

To my great relief Christmas vacation finally came and I went home. Dave and I spent time together in what had become our tradition. In the midst of our green fog, I related to him how Beth and I had broken up. Every time I would relate a story about the Macon Crew's activities against me, he would shake his head and ask me if even I could believe myself. Nothing seemed to help my totally consuming depression. Dave would reply with, if I were more "Love-Peace-Woodstock" and less traditional about my relationships with girls; none of this would have happened. His efforts were totally lost on me. I was even more disposed to continue the quest for the total, pure romantic love that must be waiting somewhere for me.

There were positive effects of this period of loneliness. Upon my return to Lex, I spent more time concentrated on what my courses had to offer. More than just studying the material, I tried to internalize what I saw as the knowledge, which, in those days I would call "truth". I continued last semester's classes as I had attained a 3.1 average which put me on the Dean's List for the first time. I was, once again, happily lost in History and all the surrounding liberal arts. I became much more secure in my membership among the school's upper level Historites than in my membership in the house.

I thought that my friendship with Mickey would help me through this time. He was, though, going through reality shock himself and could take little notice of my problems. Mickey was a second semester Senior and, though winding down, the war and military were still a fact to be faced in a matter of a few months. His number was high but there was always a chance that some reversal from Nixon or a new Commie offensive would embroil us deeply in Vietnam once again. There was more to it than just a simple concern over Uncle Sam and the Army. Graduation from college brought with it all sorts of new environments, problems, concerns—most of all, reality. We all had been professional students since we could walk—that's all we'd been. Mickey had summer jobs like the rest of us, but hadn't exactly picked out a future, even thought of it that much or even seriously, till now. I would not ask Mickey, or anyone else for that matter, to pay attention to me or my problems; perhaps I should have. To me, then, any request for help, attention, or even a date after all the hassle I had been through, totally invalidated any response that could be given. What was the value of a requested gift? Mickey would be friendly and include me in his activities, but very quickly he became almost solely involved in Sharon and in the search for some graduate school. To him the future was real; he could see it and taste it—it was upon him only months away. To me the future was next weekend and attempts to return to the promise of fall.

I was, perhaps, the closest brother to Campbell, but this offered little solace to me. He was continuing to become increasingly weird—not that he started from a sane place to begin with. None of us, I in particular, was worried about him in the most ultimate sense, at all. He was Campbell; thus he was not only authorized but ordained to be weird. Friday afternoons and Saturdays, when he was in town, were spent bent over his military simulation war games with me. His date would study while we would replay some historical battle. If she stayed in his apartment, and we were playing there, rather than mine, we had to be careful to leave out the sound effects for fear of embarrassment. We had long since shrugged off any negative connotation about playing war games, but sound effects of tank attacks or furtive cries of the wounded would have put us over the edge with any of the more normal on-lookers. This was the stuff that needed to stay between us. It was the only activity that I could do in their apartment that allowed me to feel comfortable under the eyes of Susan or any of the Crew. Dinner and the parties would come and I would linger in the TV room at the house till I was alone and then retreat to my apartment to read or just stare out the window, thinking. As it became warmer, I would sit in the open window on Main Street and listen to the town below.

My mother had a friend with a daughter at Hollins. I asked her to come to the Valentine Combo. We had an okay time but did not mix with the brothers either at the various parties or at the Combo. There was usually a couple of dating couples (Freshmen or Sophomores) that were not "Peers," "Earls" or with the Macon Crew so we sort of bummed around with them. Mostly, we spent the time in my apartment talking and drinking sherry mixed with hot tea served in glass mugs. I thought this quite Russian and very romantic. I guess I dated her about three times that spring. I was never very enthusiastic about my experiences with her. She never excited me intellectually or physically, but she was a date. I could, once again, do things on the weekends at the house though I would make them become more painful then they needed to be with my paranoiac concern. Even our sex was more refuge for me than excitement. Her presence simply broke the deepening spell of my depression. I was not happy, but at least I had someone to call once in a while. But then, late some Sunday night while I still smelled of her, I would be reminded of what I wanted from college and what love and sex together could be and it would send me to the shower, depressed again that I had failed this year.

Spring's first breezes brought me renewed optimism, the Madison Mixer and a more philosophic attitude about me and my relationships with the house and women. I ran into Becky at the mixer and we chatted for a few minutes. She was dating a guy at Madison and said she was happy. She said that she really hadn't thought about me for a long time. Suddenly I realized that I wasn't the core of her existence or thought stream. I had been important once, to be sure, but was, now, a not very often visited memory. Far from being a slash, her comment was very liberating. The Macon Crew was probably the same way. Maybe it was my continuing paranoiac behavior that kept the aura alive rather than their thoughts or actions. Driving the bunch of Sophomores and Freshmen back, I resolved to myself that I was just going to be me and let the chips fall where they may. It sounds like it should have been obvious or a simple matter, but, then, it was a major breakthrough.

Saturday, after dinner, I dropped by for my one beer at the Spook House apartment party that was 90% Macon Crew. I was frightened to death on the inside, but put my tactical sense to work in order to appear calm and resolute on the exterior. It was the first time in months I had spent more than just a few nervous moments in the presence of the girls from West. I made eye contact for the first time in weeks and mostly asked school type questions which kept the conversation as light as possible. I stretched my beer as long as humanly possible attempting to talk to as many of the girls as I could. They asked after my Hollins date and all the rest of the surface questions to which I answered in as positive and surface manner as I could. It became a tactical game to match each question with the precisely "right" light answer and include within the reply a question which would lengthen the conversation. When the beer finished, I said goodbye to all, made the appropriate eye contact and left. The walk back to the apartment was, for the first time in a long time, a chance to smile. I had met the enemy and had not been defeated, maimed or destroyed. It felt great not to see myself all over the floor and, just maybe, I thought that I was on the beginning of an upwards roll.

Vicki came to see me in the apartment on Sunday morning. All I could think of was her visit the morning after Becky and I broke up. We just sat and talked while Greg was next door with the other guys. I was curious about what her motivation for this visit was. She said that it was good to see me back to my old self again. She had been worried about me during the long interlude. I quickly thought that "she was never worried enough to tell me before." As she talked, I began to get the feeling that we were avoiding some subject that was the real reason for her first visit to the apartment since the slumber party almost a year previous. I got her a glass of sherry hoping that the ambience or the liquor would help loosen the subject. My tactical sense was holding me true to a light and optimistic tone in all that I said. By the time Greg had come back to pick her up all that I could get from her is that she, "for one," missed my presence in the group and hoped that I could "rejoin as a regular real soon." Greg for his part was oblivious to anything said and, as always, just kept smiling and being himself.

I didn't have long to wait for the eventual outcome of her visit. The next Friday as I walked out of the kitchen to set the table, Beth was sitting there with Greg and Vicki. I just stood there, felt my knees dissolve, my bowels grow queasy and said "Hi." I quickly retreated back behind the swinging doors and stood there looking at Gladys. "Ya look as if ya'v seen a ghost" was her reaction when she looked up at my startled face. Sammy entered in a rush and jabbed my ribs grinning and laughing, thankfully in a low volume which, hopefully, could not be heard beyond the door. He started his banter about how he had told me so and all the rest as he explained to Gladys just who was outside. I still had not said anything during the hour and a half (maybe three minutes) that I had been in the kitchen. I picked up two more platters of food and headed out the door if for no other reason than to verify that I had not, indeed, seen a ghost.

I hadn't. There she was, sitting next to Greg and Vicki strategically next to my traditional seat. Greg never sat at my table especially since he, just after Christmas, had been elected the new president of the house. (We all called him "Sun King" to commemorate his modest appraisal of his own talents.) But here he was along with Vicki and Beth at my table. I knew that Vicki had more to do with this than Greg. She had been our class's mother hen too long to miss a chance of bringing one of the lost boys back to the fold. I smiled and said to her that I was "glad, more than glad" to see her again, but I had to continue my work. I thanked God for the activity since it gave me the time to evoke my tactical sense to try to determine what my objectives should be as well as how they would be accomplished. My largest concern was trying to figure out what my objectives were or what they should be or what was, really, happening. Dinner was nervous and the sparse conversation stilted. It took the combined efforts of Greg and Vicki to keep it from a disastrous silence. I was conscious that there were not a few surprised looks at seeing Beth sitting there and Greg away from his seat at the head table. (Appropriately however, his seat was left vacant.) Even the Crew seemed surprised. I gathered from their expressions that Vicki had done this without notifying or consulting the Crew. She hadn't needed to; she was above them in terms of Seniority and, at least in this house, more completely than any other girl, OTG. Dinner ended and the couples headed out to the various gatherings before the apartment party which, as a novelty, was not at the Spook House but at one of the "Earl's" apartments (word had circulated to wear disposable clothes).

We never made it to the apartment party. Since we were the only two people left in the dining room, I invited her back to the apartment. I was never so glad that I had decided to live alone. On the way, half way over the bridge, my curiosity got the better of my tactical timing, (which was telling me to wait till the second sherry) and asked her why she had come. "I just needed to get away from Macon" she said without looking at me. She continued on and told me the story of the ostracism and the intrigues against her from the girls in the Crew. She said that she would have split with me anyway since she had wanted to follow up her dating relationship with the Chapel Hill guy. They had become close over the summer. That relationship had run its course and was, now, she thought, in its final throws. She still loved him, but she didn't know if she could live with him and "relationships with no future are dead." She suddenly stopped, took my arm, turned me and very seriously said "You see…my tea doesn't get cold with him." There was no hint of a smile or any softening of her expression, but it was said with a seriousness that was far-reaching and strategic. It was as if she had been trying to work that phrase into a conversation with me for a long time. She said that she had moved out of her room in West this past week and into an empty room in Wright. She didn't know many of the girls there yet and Vicki had asked if she wanted to come to Lex with her. It had been the first nice thing coming from anyone in the Crew in a long time. She looked at me and wondered aloud if it were a smart idea. She said Vicki had told her that I would probably be free and glad to see me.

She still had a hold of my arm. I looked at her and was silent for a moment. My insides were shaking with fear. I was scared because I didn't know what I felt for her, about her, or even against her. I missed her, of course, and often thought of the happy or significant times we had shared. All of that, however, might have been the insecure longing for "golden times" past and not genuine emotion. I wasn't sure; I hadn't been prepared for this. "You're more than welcome…," putting my free hand under her chin, "…it's been much too long since I have seen your smile…heard your laugh." She smiled and swung around to put my arm around her waist as we walked on to my apartment. There she filled out the story of her problems at

Macon with its villains, arch-villains and, at least one, demon extraordinaire. She told me about her Chapel Hill honey and how they lacked the intellectual level of interchange or even the special friendship that we had shared. She looked at me all the while to see how I was taking all of this. I tried to look soft and understanding. I was falling again for this woman, knew it, and convinced myself not to declare anything till I was sure where and how it was going. Finally, she told me that she was going to transfer at the end of the year so that she could pursue her new found career goal of medicine and, more important, get away from Macon and Lynchburg. The school was too small to start a new life. So the end was in sight—being together was a way, a positive way—of passing the few weeks till the year would be over. I listened but couldn't help but wonder if I was a relationship with no future?

Being after 9:00 o'clock it was dark in the apartment since we had neglected to turn on any lights. The shadows seemed to fit our mood better, anyway. I had said maybe one or two sentences in the past two hours and had consumed only two glasses of sherry to her four. I asked her if she wanted to head out to the "Earl" Party. She looked at me and smilingly threw the question back to me. I told her that I would rather not go somewhere only to end up wearing beer. I reached over to her and held her hand. It was a quiet gesture, but a gesture all the same. I had always held her hand and it was an intimate test of what her intentions would be. A moment later, I pulled her to my lap where she sat, looked down on me with a smile and brushed the hair from my eyes with her hand. She smiled again and leaned down to kiss me, quietly, gently, without great passion, but with tremendous emotion. She paused, whispered a quiet "thank you" and went back to her kiss. We sat like that, talked quietly, kissed now and again for what seemed to be another several hours. We talked about courses and ideas; all the old stuff. Finally, after a bio break, we sat down at the table together and drank a cup of tea. I reached over for her hand and, without looking up, said quietly "What the hell are we gonna do?"

"About what?"

"About us?...I mean...you're still in love with Chapel Hill...you're leaving school in a couple of months...I mean why're we sitting here...like this...enjoying ourselves?...this is scary...I mean...I feel like you never left..."

"I didn't leave...you did" with a straight face that merged into and smile and then almost a giggle.

"No I didn't...ok...who cares...I mean it's like we never split..."

"Almost...yeah." She leaned over and placed her head on my shoulder. Obviously, my questions were to remain unanswered for the time being and she thought it best that way. I, too, was sort of glad. This was the first time I had felt whole and good and at peace in a long, long time. Why ruin it with reality, futures and decisions to make when you don't have to? We just sat there, at the table, her head on my shoulder, sipped tea and listened to our music. It was getting late, but neither of us were all that tired. I got up and threw her jacket to her.

"C'mon...lets walk around town." Instantly, she smiled, almost laughed, and raced me to the door. I grabbed my cigarettes and headed out after her. On the way down the stairs we passed Cal and his date coming up. We scampered by with short "Hi"s and "Bye"s too cheerful to be actually coming from people such as we had been a few hours before. I think both of us wanted to leave them confused. We walked hand in hand and talked about the buildings and homes we passed. It was, indeed, like old times. On campus, we stopped by the Chapel and looked up at the Colonnade—all lit up in the night. It was beautiful. I told her how, at quiet times such as these, I could feel the hundreds of years of history that seemed to live here. It was almost as if the place still echoed of all the boys since 1747.

"I...thought that these buildings weren't built...till the 1830s...it was the ruins back there that ..."

"Hush!" I smiled back in a whisper. We stood there, gazing at the white pillars glowing from the light above each door. Each building's brick faded from red into black as the light decreased into night's shadows. I could feel the happiness swelling up within us. We went farther down the walk and entered the Robert E. Lee Memorial Episcopal church. It was, and had always been, open all night. One small light, high above the alter was the sole source of illumination. The aura of a silent church in the middle of the night, with only faint glimmers reflecting off the windows, alter and walls was moving to both of us. We almost huddled together although we were both quite warm. After several silent minutes she squeezed my hand signaling that it was time to head back.

In the apartment we shared a last cigarette while I worked up the courage to ask her where she was going to sleep. I had my single bed, Randy's former bed and the couch. She chose Randy's bed. "How did I know that was where you were going to stay?" She had brought a small bag so she had all the stuff she needed and simply kissed me good night and left for the other room. I shut off the lights, left the tape on (it would shut off by itself) and fell into my own bed after throwing my jeans and shirt on the chair. Sometime early that morning (I thought I saw 2:30 A.M. as I turned over to find out what was happening) she slipped under my covers wearing one of my old t-shirts she had appropriated months before. "How can I stay in this place and not sleep here?" It is puzzling to me now, how, back then, a single bed had all the room we ever needed. I had rolled to face her and with her head even with mine, she leaned over and kissed my nose. "This is so nice…to be here…with you…" She closed her eyes again, but put her cold feet between mine for warmth. The streetlight shining through the window made her face glow as it peeked out under her dark hair. I softly kissed her eyes. I kissed her nose and moved to her mouth. There was no passion in all this; only some almost serene emotion that approached spiritual joy. I wanted to think that it was love. The kind of thing that I had remembered about the afternoon in the Blue Ridge so long ago or maybe a scene in some movie I'd watched too long ago to be specifically remembered. I continually had to remind myself that this relationship had a defined end point with her transfer (I would never go long distance again) and that she had a lover in Chapel Hill. How strange it was to me to look at her, here in my bed, and imagine her the same way in someone else's. I kissed her again and she opened one eye. She reached out with the arm she had free and, smiling, brought my head to hers, "commmere."

Being together again, like old times didn't change things or help clear them up, but it did make us feel better about each other. Making love made us feel more comfortable with the intimacy we seemed to share spiritually, to be again on the same plane physically. I knew that, if she had thought about it, she would have a hard time justifying having two lovers at once. She had told me that she still loved Chapel Hill, but the relationship was dying—whatever that meant. I had a hard time not falling head over heals for her again, forgetting the scheduled termination and her reluctance to commit to the "word" from before. It was like we were both suspended from the real world and stuck in one where the time of the moment was the only thing that existed. It wasn't the "love the one you're with" but more properly a love doomed can live if you create the exact environment for it to prosper—and we had. Luckily, neither of us spent much time pondering over such questions and we sure didn't ask about any of those feelings, decisions or plans.

We ate our traditional breakfast of eggs and grits (she had a way of making them with the eggs destroyed all mixed up with cheese that made them taste great). In order to cook it, Beth found that she had to get dressed and go out to buy provisions before I got up. I figured that was where she had gone off to and staggered to my shower. I was aware of her return when her hand reached into my shower to hand me my coffee. On my way out, I left my head wet and shook it as I started to kiss her in the kitchen. She shrieked, kissed me deeply and broke up laughing. This was fun and would continue until it wasn't. We both were on a kind of emotional and social pause.

The next weekend she went to Chapel Hill, but sent me a letter the morning she left. In it, she cautioned me from expecting too much but told me that "independently from our weekend together, but, in reality, because of it" (?) she was sure that she would "not be going to Chapel Hill again." I had not asked her for this or even hinted at it; frankly, it rather shocked me. It was what I had wanted months ago; now, it confused things. As long as we had been an "on the side", "just for fun" romance, strategic questions could be ignored and the tactics were simple. Both of us had wanted refuge in each other. With this new move, however, the tables had turned. If she were to do the same thing with her decision to transfer, the affair could turn out to be "big time." When I thought about it specifically, I knew that we would have real concerns in our Significant College Romance if it were resurrected. I knew that what I wanted and what she wanted were, essentially, the same in terms of life, career and all. I knew we could get along and were physically compatible. But her resistance to the romance and to the surrender needed to fulfill it, would always be a barrier.

I resolved never to talk to her directly about her decision to transfer as I wanted it to be her decision, without pressure. I was also never, really sure of which way I wanted her to make it. We were constantly together on weekends and we even found ways of getting back and forth throughout the week. I had lots of work to do and so did she. My semester finals were coming up and there were papers to write. While I still spent time with Campbell, my contact with the rest of the house became less of my life and was of secondary importance. During the week, there were the usual things; eating, the Co-op, and occasional movies in the Chapter Room, but my classes and Beth took up most of my energy. On the weekends we would go to the Combos and some of the larger apartment parties but we didn't feel comfortable partying if the Macon Crew were the only people

there. For us, there was none of the group camaraderie that had previously existed. We simply spent more time together, doing things as
a couple or with Greg and Vicki. I didn't care. School was fun again
and I had resolved never to let any group of people, even the house,
own my life as much as I had before. Surprisingly, none of the house
ever brought this up to me; never saw me as dissolving myself into
the date's life. I guess most who knew me just appreciated the fact
that I was again happy and things would work out the way they
would.

Mickey was constantly on edge and it was because he was becoming increasingly serious. Not simply with Sharon, but with life in
general. He had convinced a graduate school to accept him the following year and he was trying to put together plans for a new life in
College Park, Maryland. It was strange to see such a blatant change
come about so quickly. Before, he had been the Bear, a "Peer Group
Starship Commander" who didn't need to remain in that group or
remain hidden behind the green cloud as did so many of those
guys—but enjoyed being there. He had been solidly in Lexington, a
fixture at the house Bridge games (though they had all but disappeared since Fazer left), pinball and Senseless Roadtrips to anywhere.
All of a sudden he was involved with the future beyond W&L. I don't
know how many of the guys noticed it with him or any of the other
second semester Seniors. With Mickey, I noticed and felt the change
which was, to me, a loss. I couldn't say that we had been drifting
apart, but he was less interested in the house and the life in which I
was involved. Now, I know that he was growing up or maturing after
facing the specter of an uncertain future. Then, I noticed that he was
a friend who did not share in my life or care to as much as he once
had. From time to time, especially if Campbell were not around and
Beth not there, I would walk the two blocks over to the Spook House
to talk with Mickey as a long study break. I could almost always find
him in his room, sitting on the bed with his back against the wall,
reading a text or writing some paper. He was never in the basement

getting high with the boys anymore. I would walk in and sit down to his audible grumbling about being bothered again. As this was how he had always greeted me, I never paid much attention to it as a literal rebuke. We would light a cigarette and start to talk about whatever complaint we were in the midst of, some new atrocity of Dimitri's, relive a tale of the "old days" or simply philosophize.

It was during one of those late night discussions that I asked him why he had become so serious a student almost at the end of his tenure at W&L. I couldn't understand it, especially since he already was accepted into graduate school. He looked over and started to talk, but no words came out. He was to have a hard time telling me that everything had changed. He didn't mind getting a little crazy on the weekends, but he had more important things to do. He was not going to become one of those brothers that hung around the house, doing nothing beyond partying and existing after graduation now that they weren't being whisked off by the draft. We had both seen graduates make it back to "visit" during Rush, but never leaving till Thanksgiving. One had stayed this entire year, living on the couch at the "Earl" apartment. Mickey explained that he had his fun for three years, maybe too much at times, but now it was time to move on. He could escape reality maybe two more years in Maryland, but he would have to support himself someday and he wanted to marry Sharon.

All at once this realization hit me. I never thought of marriage as something real that I or any of us could or would do in the near term. Lovers and relationships, yes, but marriage—that was as far away as "kids." That was for grownups or adults—I didn't qualify. Randy had been different. He had been a social neophyte and had blindly walked into the trap. Planned marriage, like graduation, was out there in time somewhere, but continued to stay just over the horizon. The Bear actually wanted to marry the girl he had been dating for more than a year. Did graduation mean you're an adult? I looked at him. He wasn't a kid anymore and he didn't seem to want to remain one. He had to plan how he could make a living, not just to get by, but to prosper. He went on to say that he didn't think he would ever have a house in the suburbs, a wife, a dog and 2.2 children, but it could come to that. After all, that was how he had grown up. He went on to explain that the boys in the basement could party all they wanted to, but he couldn't be a part of that much anymore. He had places to go and he felt that he had to start now; in fact, he should have started earlier. I remember thinking that the next line was going to be about how he was going to cut his hair, shave and start to wear suits again. It was a strange thing to look at a guy who had for three years been a major part of your life growing out of it all. Distinctly, I remember thinking that I would be there myself someday and wondering if I would react and change the way that Mickey was in front of my eyes. In a way, I thought of it as being reborn as an adult, going over from the kid's world of school (and for me, the army afterward) into the world of work, of business, of marriages and of children. It was strange to think that I would want children because every month that qualified, I prayed, to a God I hardly knew anymore, that I not have any. It was a safety measure since I didn't care to put total trust in the Pill's infallibility. Adults had always been another word for parents or, now, maybe professors. I was 20 years old and not once had I seen myself as an adult—mature yes—heck, what college kid doesn't see himself as exceedingly mature—but adult, never.

I would leave Mickey, not even looking in on the boys in the basement and saunter back to the apartment or to the house for a snack. If I went to the house, more often than not, I would get involved in a bull session with one of the Sophomores or whoever was in the chapter room watching the tube. I still had time to savor being a student and was resolved to live it to the fullest. I did not even think of a world past graduation and the army. With my situation with Beth, I never put much effort looking past June. While one of these talks could motivate me to study for a week, it also made me appreciate the responsibility-less life I had at the time. Maybe that was what 1972 was all about. The war was winding down, politics were interesting but seemed more futile than anything else, but "studentness" had become an all consuming lifestyle. On the other side of all this was business, the professions and our Dads who had to make a living. It was worth it to escape that side, the dark side, for as long as possible. Maybe it all would change, who knew, being a student certainly had.

Exams came and went. Except for the break it demanded from Beth, they had been reasonably hassle-free. I did well with 3.5 GPA—quite a mark in those days before the great grade inflation. My parents greeted me home for Spring Break with applause when they received word on my grades. It had been an entire year (so far) on the Dean's List. Naturally, the subject of Beth came up, but my answers confused them as much as they did me. To them, it seemed that we had a very close relationship, but why did I consistently claim that it would end in June? If the relationship was that enjoyable why not carry it further? If it wasn't that strong, why continue it at all? I would counter with a line of reasoning that followed the general "it's just a fun thing and not too serious" course. I didn't know if I bought that or not. I did, however, put much thought, not to mention stoned conversation later, during the summer, with Dave, into that quandary. I thought that the deadline added something to the whole love affair. It kept me from examining every minute facet in the light of the future and allowed me to relax and enjoy the present. In a sense, it allowed me to let the minor hassles dissolve by themselves while concentrating on the enjoyable aspects of our time together. I determined that June was a hard deadline for me. I wanted a date, in Lex for the weekends, at the Combos, in my bed, not just letters and promises to get together once or twice a semester. Dating, successful dating, was too much of my college life to risk it on a long distance romance. Senior year was the last year and too important to sit on the sidelines at the post office. I had ruined the middle of my Junior year, I wanted all of my Senior year.

I would tell Dave that I loved Beth, but in an immediate way, not the "forever" type of love. Back then, these vocabulary differences were well understood among everyone our age. I remember girls telling me that they loved someone but weren't "In Love" with that person—kind of delineating which level of attachment they were admitting. I don't think that I believed that, but it helped justify my decision to let the romance live or die with her decision of whether or not to remain in Lynchburg. As much as I wanted to find the girl (the yet unknown and un-found double-jointed whore angel) I would eventually marry, she had to be part of the daily or at least weekly existence at W&L. That was the way it was supposed to happen and I would not miss it for the world, no less Beth. I never thought that I might be throwing away the future for one year of potential fun. Senior year was too important and was a barrier I could not see beyond.

I returned from my spring break just as Beth was supposed to leave on her's. Even she could not afford to fly back to Europe for every vacation, so she usually spent it with relatives. This year, I found her living in my apartment upon my return. She had told her parents that she was going to stay with a girl friend in Virginia for the week (so the phone number area code would square if they called) and decided to surprise me. It was a welcome surprise. Living together was one of those aspects of the new culture that was often talked about, but seldom, openly done. It was strange being together all the time for an entire week. In many ways we were playing house; playing adults. By Wednesday she would even answer the phone which is something she never did before when in Lex. What if it were my mom or someone else that might be upset if they thought she was staying over? I got up to go to class like I would go to work someday in the future. "Goodbye Dear" (?) We went to bed together, but unlike rumored married life, made love every night. We had not, however, lost our "studentness" completely. We ate lunch and dinner at the house and joined in the afternoon baseball or Bridge games. The most fun was working on dinner with Sammy and Gladys. Beth came down and talked with Gladys and joked with Sammy while I worked. To my knowledge, she was the only date ever to do that. She would ask Gladys questions and help her do things while listening to or goading Sammy into one of his tall stories. I don't know how she dealt with the language barrier, but she did.

She became, by the end of the week, OTG. It was something that I and, I think, she had always wanted. It wasn't the same as Vicki (considered a special part of the house over and above her relationship with Greg) but a kind of general acceptance that comes with familiarity. Other brothers would engage her in conversation independently of me. They would swear in her presence while watching the tube in the chapter room or at the pinball table; though, in general, swearing in front of girls was still not an accepted practice in those days. Nobody treated her as special or different from any other of the guys. It was a relaxed, comfortable feeling that being in Lex, at my apartment, a part of the house was natural. Sunday came and she returned to Macon, leaving my apartment that had been ours, together, for an entire week. When I returned that night, it seemed incredibly cold and dark; sleeping along again, was miserable and empty. I couldn't get over whether the week had been a taste of the life to come, or just a happy holiday before the end of our relationship.

My spring course was one on Historiography or the study of historians. Strangely, I had never considered historians as anything but purveyors of the truth. I thought that everything written was truth if it made it to the pages of a history book. It was in this class that I learned personal upbringing, philosophy, method, and political purpose all colored Historical writings and had to be considered when trying to interpret them in search of the truth. It became a very involved and demanding course. Not only did you have to read and know the subject matter of the period, but also the historian's biography. It was taught in a traditional seminar fashion. For the first two weeks Dr. Taylor and an ally from the Classics department lectured, but then each student had to present his paper, previously copied and distributed to the class, to the seminar and defend it against all comers. I found this atmosphere extremely thrilling and vibrant. It made not just the subject, but the experience live and the Seminar itself have an almost independent existence. It and history became a totally absorbing endeavor.

With Beth added to Historiography, there was little time for anything but an occasional war-game with Campbell. Beth and I were growing very close but the end was approaching quickly. Three weeks from the end of the year she heard from all her schools. She had made it into several of her top choices; notably University of Pennsylvania and Stanford. Those two schools' decisions sealed my decision about the romance. If she were to go, I would continue to write and everything, but not accept the relationship as a serious romance or in any manner have a future. Beth was slow in answering them with her decision. I knew that I would never give up W&L for a girl, nor would I even consider it—did I expect Beth to do something more or different?

During the following weekend the matter came to a head. On Saturday afternoon she asked me to take a study break and go for a walk with her. I looked up from my chair by the window and said "sure." She was silent on the way to the hill which I interpreted as a bad sign. While I guessed the subject matter, I didn't know what she was going to say and my tactical defenses were up. I was determined to stick to my decision no matter how much heartbreak it might cause. I had never lied to her or led her on. We had always spoken of the split in June, during our few, and short, comments on the matter. We didn't speak till we sat down in the meadow near the ruins.

"Ya know...I've never told...you...how much I...I have...grown to love you." Her voice was hardly above a whisper. Throughout the sentence she had been looking down at her knees held by her crossed arms. With the end she looked at me with a serious and intense gaze, almost a stare. It was the first time she had used the "L" word and the word "you"—meaning me—in the same sentence. Had it come in September, I knew we would not be in the condition we were, now. Had it come before our egos ran amuck, it might be different. But it hadn't and wouldn't.

"I know…" in my best soft and understanding voice. I let the sentence hang. It was important that she talk so that I could know if this were going to be the most important conversation of my life or the beginning of the realization that this romance would die in two weeks.

"I want…us…to continue…to last…" she was back looking at her knees. "But I…know we have always talked about us splitting…when I go away…" I instantly mentally pounced on the precise word "when" and saw what was coming. My heart was pounding to the point I couldn't really hear her words and wanted to make sure I did rather than merely believe what I knew was coming. She was crying; softly, but crying all the same. She was crying over and about me. Oh, how I had wanted her to cry over me last October or even just a couple of months ago. I was terrified that I would actually carry my intentions out and let her go. I knew I should or, better, that I must. "But as good as it is here…with you…I…can't take Randolph Macon any more…besides…I need to go to a bigger school…a place better suited to help me get into a good med-school…" Her mouth was tight and I thought I saw her start to shake as if she were about to not just cry, but to start sobbing. "I can't…can't sacrifice my whole life…all that I've worked for…" She started to gesture to no one in particular since she was still not looking at me. "all that Dad has paid for…everything I want to do with my life…to stay in a school that hates me…but when I think of doing that…I feel…like…I am sacrificing my life…because my life is here…with you…" She stopped and just looked at me, deeply, even her tears stopped mid-cheek. "am I making sense?"

She looked at me and I saw the tears well up and start to roll down her trembling cheeks again. We both had taken breaths and the world started again. The moment had passed. I was crying inside; dying inside, finally having heard those words that I had longed forever to hear about "love." It was as if she had written the entire scene for me from my dreams. But, I knew that she had to go away, and thus, split us. All of the things she talked about were all balled up into the giant and powerful concept called the "future." I was not there yet. I couldn't be. Here she was telling me that she loved me for the first time and also telling me that I not was her future; all at the same time. I had longed for the first and could not bring myself to deal with the latter. If she went, I knew that our love would die. It could never survive the time apart and would spoil both of our Senior years; the last year of freedom from being an adult that we would ever have. I reached out and pulled her to me.

I never had been much for hugging, but I did it now. Rubbing her back I began to speak softly and without passion. It was almost monotone as it was just a thought stream that I was sharing with her; not even sentences or thought out in any manner. "You must know that I love you…that will never…change…But I understand that you…you have to go." Now, I started crying. "You know that…and said that…you meant that." I held her out, away from my body and looked her square in the face. "But…you and I both know that long distance doesn't work, it can't work…being…that far apart…for that long…" I brought her back to my chest and squeezed her tightly. "We won't be a part of each other then…not a part of each other's life…" I stopped talking for a good minute that seemed to last a month. "You know next year's just the beginning…you'll have med-school while I traipse all over the world in the army, what then?…No…its better that we realize that we end all of this…here…now…so much in love. I can't…won't…go through the pain of splitting again…" I looked at her again. "It almost killed me last time…if it is going to last…let's let it make it on its own…" I leaned over and kissed her tears from her cheeks. That last part about letting our relationship make it on its own was a lie and I knew it. It never would because we didn't want it to. She grabbed the back of my head and pulled me down as she slowly fell on her back. She was kissing me passionately. She looked up at me and seemed to stop in mid kiss. Wondering what was wrong I leaned up and separated myself allowing her to speak.

"Come with me." She just said it and smiled. Evidently it was a new idea to her and her mind was rapidly flushing details out that might solve the problem of her future and of her heart. "Come with me…You'd love California. We'd be there together; your grades are good enough now to get in…I'll bet Daddy's company could even swing a scholarship." I could see her mind racing and her heart warming rapidly to this seemingly perfect resolution. "There's a great history department and a graduate school along with a Med. school. It'd be perfect." Slowly, with my silence, she sensed that the perfect solution was not going to be.

"Beth…I can't…won't leave W&L…Lex …" I was crying because it was admitting to her and to me that there were, indeed boundaries of our love affair and there were things I would not do. "Don't ya see…me following you there would be like you staying at Macon because of me. What would that be like? The hell you have at Macon for a whole year more? I didn't choose Stanford, you did. Its not my life there, its yours."

"But we could be together and stay together…this time, it'd work."

"Maybe…but Beth…did I ever ask you to stay because of me? She shook her head knowing I hadn't. "Beth…Stanford is where you've chosen and I can't go running after you…especially leaving Lex." I knew it had never been an option even if she could swing the money and acceptance and everything. "No Beth…W&L is where I live and where…in any real sense of the word, I was born…hell, we were born. It's something that has become a part of me now. For the first time in my life, I feel as if I am a part of something that is so different, so wonderful, and so alive that it transcends all that I've known before. I've got to finish it. It's not just a diploma to me…its being a part of Lee and the flags in the Chapel…its taking your exams under the trees on the lawn…its not locking your doors…it's the emblem on my blazer …" I pulled her up so that she could see the ruins. "Beth, I wanted you to stay with me…I did. But I never asked you…it had to be your decision…don't ask me to give up what I've become or what I have…on the bet we'd make it." Maybe it never dawned on me back then that men might follow women in their lives as I expected women to follow men. Maybe it was because, deep down, I knew that I didn't love her enough to leave W&L and Lex. Maybe it was because I was foolish and romantic and wanted the Significant College Romance to be perfect and not be some California relationship at Stanford. I didn't really know where Stanford was and didn't care—it wasn't Lex.

For the first time W&L became defined within me beyond the place where I took classes. I knew and never doubted that whatever it was that made it different; it was worth me finishing it out. Honor Code, class size, perhaps just the lingering presence of General Lee demanded that I finish. "I could hate myself for staying, but I must stay…do you understand…can you?" I didn't wait for an answer. "Do you realize that I love you and want it to last…but we can't make it last …at least not this way?"

We were both crying. She finally nodded. For the first time that I could remember my tactical sense left me and I was swallowed by the emotions and actions of the moment. We simply and quietly made love there in the long grass of the meadow, under one of the trees near the ruins. In those days, it was just a field with ruins and thus protected from the casual visitor. It was there that I learned that making love is as much a way of saying goodbye as it is a way of saying I am here with you or I love you.

As it became evening, we regained enough composure to readjust our trousers and shirts. We still didn't speak, except for our tears, as we lay there and thought of what had just been said and done. It was late and we had to get back to the house. In the kitchen, both Gladys and Sammy noticed our quietness, but pretended not to, in order to save our feelings or privacy. A couple of minutes before dinner was to start Gladys grabbed Beth and took her into the store room. I found out later that she pulled some leaves and pieces of grass from her hair. Finishing, she looked at Beth and asked if she were really going to leave. It's funny now, on recollection, that they both knew and yet I don't remember actually telling them. But they were part of the house, and I was to find out that the whole house had been watching and wondering which way things were going to go. When Beth nodded, Gladys just enveloped her in those big brown arms and hugged her. Neither said another word about the matter.

Dinner and the forced conversations at the table brought us back to a more normal plane of life. We stuck around for the news and then returned to the apartment to study. We never mentioned any of that again. It never came up although I, for one, thought about my decision almost constantly. She stayed in the apartment for the week after Macon closed down in order to attend Mickey's graduation, but more to have a last week together with me, as did most the Macon Crew with their dates. Two nights before graduation, which was the last night we students had as lords of the campus, the arriving parents taking over the celebrations on the next day, we had a graduation party for the Bear. No "Peer Groupers" or "Earls" were invited, it was all from the Macon Crew and he was the only Senior member. The dinner seemed to last forever and afterward we all told stories about the times together and house legends as we casually passed joints around. Finally, He stood up, banged his glass with his spoon and gave a speech. In it he called each of us by name and left us his will.

Dimitri got the crotch to his brown cords. Sharon immediately passed him a piece of brown corduroy that looked as if it had actually been cut out of his famous trousers. Greg, our Sun King got a gilt edged mirror. Campbell, who was the only dateless person invited, got a box of raisin bran. Mickey went around to all the people at the table, including the dates. Beth got a pair of sunglasses whose frames had the design of the American flag on them for her to wear at Stanford. I was the only one other than Sharon left. I got a new tape of Days of Future Passed with Nights in White Satin repeated 5 times and a comment that now I wouldn't have to constantly rewind it every time I wanted to hear that song over again. I almost cried, Beth hugged me and kissed my ear. The gift was so perfect. With that, Sharon started to clap which signaled the end of the affair and we all joined in. Mickey, who was still standing, banged on his glass once more and we all stopped. He cleared his throat and pulled at his collar. Greg and I looked at each other instantly guessing what he had in mind. He pulled a box out from his vest pocket and looked at Sharon. "And you, who has meant so very much to me this year, I give myself...forever...if you'll have me" whereupon he opened the box and held it out for her. There was a diamond ring in it. To this day I don't think that this scene had been rehearsed. While I am sure that they had talked about the future and maybe even marriage, I think that Mickey was seriously proposing to her at that moment. We all were quiet, each of us hearing only our own racing pulse. Sharon smiled and said "yes," rising to kiss Mickey and only after that was fully accomplished did she take the outstretched ring. We all cheered and clapped and broke open the rest of our cheap champagne.

Beth and I looked at each other but dared not to speak. We held each other's hand under the table and practically stopped our circulation with our squeezing. Two days later, I drove her to the airport after saying goodbye to Gladys and George and seeing Mickey and the rest of the Seniors from our house graduate. The ride and waiting for her flight found us almost totally silent. We both knew it was going to be. Anything that could be said might change everything; and neither of us wanted that—not really. After the flight's final call we kissed, cried and said our last "I love you"s. She ran to the boarding ladder, stopped and ran back, sobbing, to hand me an envelope. Without stopping to say or do anything she ran back to the ladder and boarded the plane. I never saw her again; not for real, but her eyes meeting mine when she reached the top of the boarding stairs have been in my dreams for years after and sometimes now.

Opening the envelope after her plane had taken off; I found some of the words from the Don Mclean song <u>Empty Chairs</u> written in her own hand.

And I wonder if you know—
That I never understood.
That although you said you'd go—
Until you did, I never thought you would.

Never thought the words you said were true.
Never thought you said just what you meant.
Never knew how much I needed you.
Never thought you'd leave—until you went

Yes, it was me that had left. I could have called her back; could have told her that her future was with me and told her she HAD to suffer through the year at Macon; could have told her to transfer to some other school in the valley; could have told her that I would go with her—but I didn't. No, I went even though it was she was getting on the airplane. She had finally said the "L" word and I had not taken it to mean she was mine. I still thought of her as a date and not the female part of "us." So it was and is that I left.

CHAPTER 9

❀

*F*or those of us in R.O.T.C., the summer between Junior and Senior years was reserved for 6 weeks of army training experience called "Summer Camp." Summer camp was an advertising euphemism for the condensed basic training—shorter, nastier and more humiliating than the real thing—given to all future officers. After a two week vacation at home, all the cadets east of the Rockies were either ordered to Indiantown Gap Military Reservation, Pennsylvania or Fort Riley, Kansas. Knowledgeable sources considered both to be only one step above the worst base in the entire free world; Fort Polk, Louisiana and thus could adequately and accurately be described as "Hell holes." Since I lived only about three hours driving distance from Indiantown Gap, I naturally received orders for Kansas. I had a strong inclination that this would happen figuring that, when all else would fail as a predictor, true military logic would win out. I didn't care; I was paid mileage both to and from the base and the going rate provided me with about half clear profit.

The two week period I got to use as vacation was spent mainly with Dave, the water pipe and the stereo. The Army left no time to do anything more than sleep, eat and party. Dave had purchased a motorcycle and we rode that quite a bit, but generally it was pretty boring since there was really no time to start a real summer only to pass the time. On the second weekend, I was anxious to go. I considered Lexington my home then and, though my family was around me in New York, it was no place to stay too long without something concrete to occupy one's time. I headed out to Kansas with enough time to take three days on the road and still spend the last night of freedom in the warmth and civilization of a motel bed. The drive out was uneventful. Long distance interstate driving was a constant fight against boredom. The only thing that saved me was watching out for girls and other interesting looking hitch-hikers along the way. I would slap in an 8-track, turn up the volume, and cruise at 75 to 80, not even watching for cops. On the second day I picked up a lone hitch-hiking girl which offered some hope of adventure, but struck out completely. She didn't offer me any dope, had no bizarre story to relate and, worst of all, was getting off the interstate to meet a friend at an exit that I would reach at about 4:00 P.M. that day. Once she found out I was traveling to join the Army, she was completely silent. To her and to most young people of the day, anyone in the Army was guilty of Mai Lie, killing babies and napalming undefended civilians in general. Based on what I know of our actions in Viet Nam, they weren't too far wrong. I didn't know or care, the Army was where I had chosen to be and I was going to make the most of it.

Mostly, I would watch the countryside change and think about school, my decision concerning Beth and plan the coming year. I did not regret my decision to end the relationship with Beth at all. I knew that I would never leave the Valley for California. It just wasn't an option. If our attraction proved to be so strong that it demanded attention in the future; so be it. Beth and I had promised to write each other, which meant that there could be contact and a method for communicating the necessary emotions if the need arose. I would not mortgage the future, though, on long distance feelings. Senior year promised many things, several of which were her former hall mates in Wright Dorm.

One was a moderately good looking, raven haired, rising Junior from Georgia, whose real name I did not know, but was called "Belle" by all who knew her since childhood. The other, also a rising Junior, was an absolutely erotic masterpiece named Alexandra whose friends, me included, were allowed to call "Alex." I had met both as a consequence of spending time at Randy Mac with Beth during the past spring. Without too much pressure, each had promised to write me during my tour in the army—each doing their part in keeping my morale high—"anything for our boys in green." Belle was dating some Veemie and some guy from U.Va. when not seeing the cadet. Alex dated very seldom and, then, mostly upperclassman at W&L. She never dated the same guy twice and Beth had confided that the practice was Alex's own iron clad rule. Beth said that Alex had some incredible home-town-honey (after seeing his picture once, I saw what she meant) who would come up and see her about once every other month. The only reason she would date between those visits was, as Beth would whisper and finding delight in the concept's naughtiness, "Alex would get so horny she couldn't walk straight." The very thought, concept, or idea of that girl, with such a tight butt, whose luscious figure seemed to flow in every direction as she walked, getting that horny made me shiver with anticipatory excitement. Several times I had spoken to Alex, alone, for long stretches of time while visiting Beth during the spring. Each time I believe that I scored major points by not running after her or steering the conversation towards sex. My tactical sense said that this girl had probably had passes made toward her since she was ten and by better men than me and the only way that I could make time was not to.

While Alex provided my day, and night dreams with plenty of acrobatic sexual fantasies; Belle intrigued me even more in a somewhat different way. She was only moderately good looking: 5'6" or 7"; about 125 pounds; and features and figure that were merely proportionate. Her best feature was her smile as it dominated a very refined face framed by long, long, straight, black hair. I think the whole refined atmosphere she exuded was the reason she seemed to excite my interest. She seemed to step out of one's mental picture of what a landed Georgia lady should be and yet also had a mischievous air about her which gave the impression that she would be a great deal of fun. If she wasn't out of <u>Gone with the Wind</u> she was definitely out of <u>Last of the Belles</u>. It was a perfect combination of a girl you would be proud to take home to your mother and the one you would sneak out into the bushes with, after that dinner. Besides nobody, in this century anyway, was called "Belle." I asked her how she got that name. She told me that her real name was something "dreadful" and that "ever since forever" she'd been called Belle. It had been her grand mother's nick-name and she liked it.

Even though we hadn't spent much time alone, we had talked at length several times. Each time I came away refreshed and fulfilled by her wit, charm and intelligence. What is more, she seemed to warm to me naturally. She always made me feel as if I, and only me, was the focal point of her total attention. Belle seemed to delight in getting me to talk about almost any subject, and then gently tease me about some of my more outlandish opinions. She didn't seem to be too serious about anything at all. She would joke that her "Daddy" had gone to W&L and therefore she "knew better" than to date there.

Both of these girls had been Beth's friends which made any advance on my part inconceivable while Beth was still at Macon. They had proven to be friends when it was important for Beth to have them. Neither had links to Vicky or any other girls in our Macon Crew; it was a small school, but like ours, Macon had its cliques. In a way, that was to my advantage since I knew both of them as "friends" before I would have to make any attempt to date them. FHS was prearranged with them; my only problem was that I could only ask one back to Lexington for Rush. I had resolved that I would make that decision in September based on their letters, attitudes and prospects apparent at the moment. There was no need to declare myself too early and perhaps guess wrong. With the proper planning and strategy, perhaps even Alexandra was available for long term involvement. Both of these girls served to keep my mind occupied for the entire trip to Kansas. Sometimes it was rough being alone in a strange motel at night. I would imagine all the erotic exploits taking place in the rooms around mine. Sometimes I could hear what was going on and that was worse. Thinking about girls or sex or just being with someone was enough to start the thoughts about Beth and I would write her a letter on the motel's stationery, working on it for several hours, vowing to read it over in the morning. I had promised myself that if, in the morning, I ever felt the way I had when I wrote the letter, I would send it. None of them ever got close to the mailbox.

About 3:00 P.M. on the third day I rolled into Fort Riley's camp town; Junction City, Kansas. I found the Econo-Lodge Motel where I had agreed to meet Greg for our last civilian night atrocity celebrating the end, at least for a while, of our freedom. We would find some barber shop in town to get our "basic training haircuts" and then proceed to drink till only one of us remained to hobble back to the motel. He came in at about 4:30. After a quick swim, we were ready to explore "JC" as we had already learned to call it. We found that we were not the only ones to plan that sort of activity. There seemed to be hordes of freshly shorn pairs and threesomes milling around "JC." The town itself was nothing to talk about. It was the usual assortment of small department stores, a town hall, and a shopping center on the exit from the interstate. What separated it from all the other small towns across America, and made it the same as all camp towns around the world; was that the remainder seemed to be mobile home parks, bars, massage parlors, and pawn shops. I had never seen a pawn shop before and had never been to a massage parlor. Lexington, having no bars hadn't trained me in "Bar Hopping" either, but it seemed to be the safest adventure available. Greg and I, bristling from our appointment with the barber, headed into the first joint that looked respectable enough to have had other college kids in it.

The future would make me become familiar with "Camp Town Bars." But then, for us, it was a new experience. Even on Sunday afternoon, it was smoky, dimly lit, filled with loud music, and well staffed with worn out, late-thirtyish waitresses wearing as close to nothing as Kansas State law would allow. Bottled beer was cheap which meant that it was practically all you could order, and the place made you buy the peanuts or any such sort of munchies. Strangely at least to my thoughts back then, there were more than a few girls around. We were to find out that they worked in the bar's back room or in some trashed out mobile-home that always seemed to be parked out back servicing troopers with cash.

My eyes slowly adjusted as we found an empty table, ordered a couple of Coors (having a great reputation and as yet unavailable in Lexington) and lit cigarettes. There were probably 30 guys in there, and 95% of them looked the same as us. Greg related how he had partied with Dimitri and Vicki the night before he left and was still feeling the effects. The conversation dragged as neither of us was fully "with it." Although we both maintained that it was all the days alone in the car, the truth was that we were nervous about this whole Basic Training experience. None of the expected individual events especially bothered us; I mean there was nothing specific of which we were scared. It was not that we thought we'd be hurt or end up dying or anything. Both of us realized that there would be physical challenges, but mostly, we knew that it was designed to be miserable; a royal pain in the ass and, in general, it was designed to humiliate and piss you off. Basic Training in the American Army had over 200 years of tradition behind it and had honed itself to its objectives perfectly. It would be session after boring session of combat training lectures, demonstrations, and labs interspaced with useless humiliation and physical punishment drills. Nobody ever died or even got hurt, but the tales about the experience didn't lead us to look forward to the next six weeks. If the Continentals hadn't enjoyed Valley Forge what made us think we should enjoy Fort Riley? There would be few smiles.

Greg had decided on a law career followed by running his dad's consulting business. Campbell and I thought that he had taken this "Sun King" thing a bit far with this dream of management by divine right. Even then, though, we realized that it was about all he was good for. No other field offered him as much status, power, money or glory for so little work. The amount of arduous effort was definitely a primal decision factor for Greg, who was not known to actually volunteer to do anything overtly—or even moderately—strenuous. This meant that this session was to be his last "military" experience already counting on performing his active duty with the Judge Advocates Corps. I, on the other hand, was more confused. I didn't know what I would do after graduation and had not given it any serious thought whatsoever. The army was my next job, and, as long as one finds oneself in the army, it might as well be doing something military. I had picked armor as being the right blend of high-tech and raw military excitement. I could stay warm and clean, yet feel like I was part of the central army rather than the postal service aura of the support branches. Viet Nam was almost over, so I didn't think that I could find myself in the jungle, but Israel was then a combat concern, and that was primarily tank warfare. The image of that made my choice not only adventurous but also relevant to the future.

We weren't talking about all that much except trivialities till our third beer. Then, a couple of tall, blonde, newly crew-cutted young guys loudly invited themselves to our table. Greg looked at me like it was time to leave. I picked up my cigarettes but was stopped short by a hand on my shoulder as they rattled off their respective introductions. They were from Nebraska and here for R.O.T.C. camp, as they loudly guessed we also were. Calling for another round, we were obliged to sit, drink their beers and listen to them talk about their school, exploits and plans. Soon we were introduced to a bottle-blonde young girl named "Cindy" rejoining them from the ladies' room. It seems that the boys had each just visited her in the back room and had enjoyed themselves immensely. They were giving testimonials to the power of her lung capacity and lack of gag reflex (using intended winks, hand motions and innuendo—or as much as two drunk guys from Nebraska could) as "Cindy" smiled and ran her tongue over her lips, silently looking through half closed eyes at Greg and I. She was not as drunk as they and seemed a bit annoyed at their continuing poor attempts to subtly describe the performance she had just given. To her it might have been par for the course. I, however, was disgusted. Looking over at them, I thought that it must have been their first. I could not, however, get over looking at "Cindy." The boys recommended her price of $25 as a good investment for "starting the camp off with a bang!" Both of them giggled at their high humor while Greg and I exchanged annoyed glances. She had not said a word through all this, except to order her beer. She looked at us with a coy, if not sheepish, smile. When she realized that neither Greg nor I would take her up on their offer, she relaxed into a bored expression and started sizing up the bar's other customers.

This was my first experience with a "pro" and I couldn't get over it. This was a real whore. She had taken money and provided sex to these two strangers not fifteen minutes before she was sitting next to me. "Cindy" was fairly attractive, and although a bit young, would pass as anybody's date when not made up so heavily or dressed in skin tight halter, miniskirt and boots. The reality of it all hit me like a ton of depressing bricks. She probably was or could be somebody's date either in the past or perhaps in the future. She was somebody's daughter, probably would someday be somebody's mom—if she lived that long. Catcher in the Rye's Holden Caulfield's discussion with his whore vividly returned and seemed to drown out the actual conversation. I felt the same things as he. Here she was; so real, so alive, not at all like the painted women who we had been led to expect, or the lost souls described in the sociology texts. So help me God, I felt like asking her how she got into that business, why she stayed and why, being such a nice girl...My tactical sense prevailed over the alcohol and curiosity so I continued to merely silently stare. I was intrigued with everything about her and thought about giving her the $25 to see how she approached her job. I wasn't scared of Greg reporting to the world that I had used a whore, but did not want him to think less of me because of it. He did not seem to be as bothered or blown out by her presence as by the behavior of our table mates. But then, we were both, Greg and I, trying to be invisible at the time.

We were within two swallows of being able to leave when our two guests saw someone they knew, called him over and repeated the entire advertisement to him. Not hesitating he rummaged through his jeans pocket to find a $20 bill and asked one of his buddies for a $5 loan. She got up, put out her cigarette, put her arm through his and led him through a door next to the bathrooms in the back. I had watched her as she made her transition, so obviously practiced a thousand (which made my stomach turn) times before. Her bored expression transformed instantly to a "saucy" smile. Before she led him away she, almost secretly, rubbed his crotch with her cupped palm and said "from the looks of things, I'm going to really enjoy this!" I was sitting not a foot away from the entire scene and was studying it intently. Though probably for his benefit alone or maybe an advertisement for me, this added bit of propaganda disturbed me no end. This was so blatantly an act, how could anyone be so drunk as to believe it or even begin to take anything about it seriously. The more I thought about it, the more my expression demanded that Greg and I finish our beers, cigarettes, and beg off saying that tomorrow would come early.

The night had cooled the air only slightly and the heat outside was more suffocating than the air-conditioned cigarette smoke we had experienced in the bar. We walked down the street towards my car saying nothing. As we reached the car I asked him if he wanted another beer or to go back to the motel. He paused, said "what the heck" and we entered another, identical, bar across the street. "Cindy" had put me in a somber, reflective mood. Greg, setting the beers he had brought from the bar down on the table said "cheer up...you'll get through camp." Looking at me again and probably knowing or thinking he knew what I was thinking said; "She's over 18...or...at least close anyway...nobody's beating or hurting her...what the hell...whatzamatter?"

"It just gets to me, that's all...she was pretty...I mean...to look at her...she could be a Freshman at Macon"

"And at Randy Mac you'd be busting your balls trying to get her in the sack rather than sitting around getting depressed about it..." He was right. But, I started out talking through Holden Caulfield's line of thinking in Salinger's <u>Catcher in the Rye</u>, anyway. Greg, spotted the source and footnoted it precisely. He ordered another beer and bummed my last cigarette. He was always doing that. We talked about "Cindy" and how philosophically we were disgusted; but he maintained "truly...we're probably more than a bit jealous of her...aren't we...I mean she's beat the system...as long as she doesn't let what she's doing get to her...the way its getting to you...she's got it made...Hell, she's probably a Freshman at Harvard...making more money than we'll see this summer and only needs some mouthwash and a shower to remove the evidence forever!" He got out a pencil and figured out income estimates on his napkin. "At...say $200 a night (already subtracting the $50 she would pay the bartender) and about 5 nights a week—she would pay for her college, a car and all the clothes she could wear with only some minor bruises and a sore body to show for her summer!...Hell...she could even marry some guy and never tell him...who would know...she's beat the system! She's winning while you and I work." Even then I knew he meant me, because he was sure that he, too, would figure a way to beat the system. Reality and the beer hit at the same time. He would not understand my romantic line of reasoning. She might be a golden-hearted whore like Donna Reed had played in <u>From Here to Eternity</u> or, more likely, just a lost high school dropout from a broken home. Whatever the case, it was a damn shame. I was ready to go back. Greg and I packed it in and went directly to sleep upon reaching the motel. Greg's final comment was right: he said I think too much about the wrong things.

We made it to the Post's front gate at 5:00 A.M. the next morning. Looking in my rear view mirror, I saw Greg for the last time for four weeks. From the moment we parked our car in the guarded lot, our time, and that of the other 5,000 arriving guys, was controlled to the extent that nothing was left for chance; merely overwhelming confusion and outright anarchy. We were bussed to barracks where we formed up in groups of twenty. From there, we were marched to medical huts, administrative huts, through equipment issuing huts, and back to our barracks dwarfed by the olive drab bundles we carried. By lunch, we were busily trying to put our foot lockers together as pictured on a poster pinned to the bulletin board at the end of our barrack's bay. I noticed that the copyright of the picture was at least 20 years before. Nothing had changed; Kent State hadn't affected Basic Training. I knew it was going to be a long six weeks. We bitched constantly and swore at everything. To my way of thinking it was our way, maybe every recruit's way of entering the Army; just like those who left for the Spanish American, First & Second World Wars, Korea and now our war, Viet Nam.

We had all introduced ourselves to each other several times. Nobody knew any last names and only a few first names, but the 36 guys on our ground floor of the WWII vintage twin level barracks knew pretty much what to expect from each other. Already we knew who were the military school "old hands" at this stuff, who were the future Green Berets (or wannabes) and the rest of us who could be trusted to keep an even perspective on all that would happen. I was definitely in the latter group, though I wanted to do well. I had the knowledge and acting ability to play the game like any war-mongering future baby killer, but, most of the time, tried to background myself. My father's last bit of advice for making it through basic training was "Never Volunteer." I learned and obeyed it well.

My bunk mate, on the lower bed, was a guy named Chieu. He was a third generation Chinese-American from Milwaukee, but everyone wanted to assume that he was Vietnamese, Thai or something equally exotic. He was an engineering student from Case Western and just wanted this thing to be over. Our lone mate to our left, next to the wall between the bay and the Sergeant's room was an Aggie. He was a member of the "Corps" at Texas A&M which made him of legendary stupidity, but also unrivaled in military ingenuity. He was the one who let us borrow his rubber cement to glue down all the articles on the upper shelf of our foot locker. That way, it was always ready for inspection. He told us that they would let us go to the PX sometime soon and we could then buy the stuff we would actually use. He was also the guy who had the clear floor wax for our boots so that we were almost instantly ready for inspection even though the plastic in the polish ruined the boots after a few months. Who cared? All we were counting down, one day at a time was six weeks, nothing beyond.

Once our foot lockers cleared inspection we were able to go to lunch. Because of the Aggie's help, Chieu and I decided, then and there, to take care of this boy. He was rumored not to be able to count or write (he was not to disappoint us on those counts) but he could make this experience a whole lot easier. The three of us were the first in the platoon to go to lunch. We raced down the gravel path, slowing to salute at least three times, and did our mandatory ten chin-ups before entering the mess hall. Until that moment, I didn't know I could do ten chin-ups, but I was hungry. Lunch was great. We were evidently famished and finished the enormous meal in about twelve minutes. It was to be the longest meal we would have in six weeks. When we were half finished with our cigarettes, we were interrupted and ordered out by one of the fascists from our bay wearing a blue helmet.

The Blue Helmet was the rotated badge of command allowing us to practice being squad leaders, platoon sergeants, platoon and company grade officers for the next six weeks. To most of us, having the Blue Helmet was a chore—to some it was destiny. Most of us looked at it as a challenging, but a generally bull-shit part of the basic training package and did what we could to minimize hassle and protect our friends. The crazed, however, saw it as real command authority and their job was to lead us as they would troops in combat. Maybe it was my R.O.T.C. ranger training, but all this smacked of military Chicken-shit. Any position could be done more than adequately by being able to answer two questions at any moment from any of the instructor officers or non-coms: Where are your troops (you had to know where everyone in your platoon, squad or section was) and where are you supposed to be at any given time. Not hard; not dramatic; and definitely not combat leadership training—though if you know those two things you'll always be in the upper echelon of military officers. That was all to come. At the first lunch our Blue Helmet Uber-grupen-furher (affectionately known as "Chicken-shit from that day forward) brusquely ordered us to "move our butts" back to start cleaning the latrine (which was on the end of the lower floor) so that it could be ready for our first barracks inspection that evening. We slowly complied, with plenty of gripes, but I noticed that the Aggie stepped on the Blue Helmet's shine while appearing to walk clumsily past. Chieu, the Aggie and I seemed to share a common opinion of power in the form of a peer cadet. We mentally made a note of where to put the shit tasks when we wore the helmet. For the next six weeks not only us, but almost all the other guys had the same opinion of that guy. His first day with the Blue Helmet destroyed any chance at camaraderie he had.

The whole bay survived the first week, including the overnight field exercise and the famed or infamous, depending on how one looked at it, obstacle course. We had no casualties other than to chiggers, poison ivy, and a couple of cases of heat exhaustion. By the end of the first week we could describe in minute detail the differences between "Bull-Shit" and "Chicken-shit" in military terms and denote the multitude of derivations of either. It was the American Army, just as my father had described; just as I knew it'd be.

The first and second squads (the first floor of our barracks) of the 3rd platoon of Bravo Company of Cadet Battalion 2 of the R.O.T.C. brigade training at Fort Riley slowly began to take its proper form. Most of us were regular guys from regular schools who, for a variety of reasons, had joined R.O.T.C. and were content to dutifully fulfill our commitments, nothing less; nothing more. Nobody wanted to die for their country, nobody wanted to be a general, and nobody wanted to do much other than eat in leisure, smoke a cigarette in peace and sleep—the rarest luxuries in This Man's Army. We would go through the motions and do everything asked of us as long as no one expected us to actually believe in or honestly get excited about the whole experience. There were one or two Junior John Waynes who took it all too seriously, but for the most part, we worked together to survive in as comfortable a fashion as was feasible. Aggie provided us with exemplary leadership in military tricks and all activities designed to short-cut or shirk arduous duty. Most of us had some talent that could be used to benefit the entire platoon. I excelled in writing operation plans (although my code names and check points were often labeled after British 18th Century or Spanish Civil War heroes) and field of fire design. Chieu could always be counted on to know military statistics and seemed a natural at map reading. We found the rest of what was needed amongst the line of nine bunk beds on either side of the barracks making up our bay. The guys on the top floor, though still part of our platoon were realistically in a world of their own and we never knew much about them past their names.

Both the floors were commanded by our platoon sergeant; Drill Sergeant Mike (we were specifically informed it was NOT Michael) Jones. He was tall, slim and definitely a Texan. He was about 25 or 26 and proud as hell of his recent graduation from Drill Sergeant's School and of being a two tour vet of 'Nam. After the first day full of bluster and barking, we began to catch a glimmer of humanity from him after our first trip through the obstacle course. Maybe this was part of his plan. Each platoon had attempted one pass before lunch. Almost everybody was bruised, sore or wounded in some way. The platoon's time stank. Sgt. Jones told us to sit away from the shade (which would put us separate from the rest of the company and battalion) as he wanted to speak to us while we ate. In silence we watched him take off his "Smokey" hat and start eating. Half way through his third mouthful he looked around, chuckled and told us we could eat as well. Quietly, without looking around, almost as if he did not want anyone to notice, he began to speak. He told us that we had to win the brigade platoon competition as he had money riding on the result and how, if we continued as we had that morning, we would never get close. "It's all a matter of thinking things through and working together." He asked the Aggie to explain the trick to each obstacle. Through mouthfuls of Korean War era "C" rations, Aggie dutifully explained the tricks of the wall climb, rope swing and all the rest. After Aggie had finished, Sgt. Mike told us that by interspacing the less fit or "fat boys" with the more physically able, we could help everyone through with a combined faster time for the platoon than any of our competition. With that, he got up and went over to the other sergeants to finish eating leaving us to consider and implement (or not) his suggestions. One of the Hitler-Jungend Blue-Helmet-For-The-Day started to tell people what to do during the afternoon attempt of the course. His opinion of Sergeant Mike's suggestions was that it smacked of "Socialism" and therefore should be avoided even if we didn't win. The rest of us, almost in unison told him to "screw off" (and other, less polite, suggestions) and when we finished our chastisement, the Aggie quietly told him the true learning point of the exercise; "winners get perks." Aggie just stood there and allowed the truism to sink in. There was no further discussion necessary. The rest of us talked among the squads to jointly, cooperatively, put Sgt. Jones' advice to work. Informally, those of us who had the "sensible attitudes" arranged the platoon properly, gained general consensus about the plan of action, and as a result, won that day's competition. With this honor the battalion commanding Blue Helmet announced that our platoon was allowed to sleep till six the next morning versus the usual five A.M. reveille. We were both proud and anxious to enjoy our extra hour as to us at the time it seemed worth its weight in socialist gold.

Some prize. We were all up at 4 A.M. trying to think of everything that needed to be done. While Sgt. Jones had appointed our Blue Helmet for the weekend, we all looked to the Aggie and our one Veemie upstairs to organize the inspection effort. We painted all the visible pipes with polyurethane to insure a disaster proof high gloss. We didn't allow showers after midnight so that we could wipe down the shower room with chamois "borrowed" from the mess tent during the field exercise. The Aggie also "borrowed" an immersion heater and a can of kerosene from the overnight in order to boil clean our M-16s. We all knew, of course, that dipping the actions of M-16s in boiling water made them shine in record time but destroyed their longevity. What officers didn't know wouldn't hurt them and this was neither theory, nor an exercise in following the rules, but one in passing our inspection. We used the shower room to clean the weapons but hid the heater under the outside stairs for future use. At the Aggie's suggestion, Chieu and I led a party of guys out to raid some barracks down the road (whose troopers were still out on maneuvers) to procure at least one, but never more than two, of the steel bed springs from their cots. Aggie taught us how to attach the springs to our blankets so that they would instantly snap tight enough to bounce a quarter. All we would have to do was punch the corners square and it was ready. Two guys did nothing but arrange every locker so that it was perfect. While some of the other platoons were naming their units "War-Hawks" or "Thor's Hammer" on their platoon banner, our motto became "Winners get Perks." One of the dead language majors upstairs even translated it to Greek, in order to hide its real meaning so we could display it proudly on our blue banner.

Everything was perfect; except that we had left some lint in the trap of our dryer. It was, itself, clean, but there was about a 1/8 inch piece stuck to the trap holder. We flunked. In front of the officers, Sgt. Jones yelled at us about how disappointed in us he was. As soon as they left, he shared that every barracks failed the first week and it had taken the inspection team an incredibly long time to find our error. He, for one, was going to get a couple of beers at the NCO club and would never be able to know if we obeyed the "Restricted to Company Area" punishment prescribed for platoons who failed the inspection. As long as we didn't get caught we could do anything that we wanted. Most of us caught a base bus, from a stop a suitably safe distance from the barracks, to one of the enlisted men's movies theaters. We really didn't care what movie was running. That wasn't the point. Happily, we returned at dusk having enjoyed several hours of sleep in air-conditioned buildings. Not only could we sleep, but we luxuriated by sitting in chairs with backs and drinking a soda with ice for the first time in a week—one that had seemed to us like several months. Its funny how those small pleasures; all of which we take now for granted, seemed so wonderful.

That night, relaxed enough to become regular guys again; some guys took the time to comb their hair, play cards and talk. The pressure of the week had not allowed such trivialities. Survival had allowed us to relax and become human. We wore jeans, wrote letters, listened to rock music and talked about stuff other than the army. We were civilized; for a couple of hours, anyway.

Many of us became religious in the army. Not for any God-fearing reason, but for one of personal comfort and survival. The first Sunday, seeing Aggie get dressed for church brought forth the obvious question from Chieu and me. He explained that since church was air-conditioned and exempted you from duty, therefore it should become almost a required activity. Everyone in our squad followed his lead yielding a couple of additional hours of air-conditioned relaxation and peace for the price of a couple of hymns and a buck in the plate. One of the guys from the University of Tennessee taught us a great trick. He related that the army is almost fanatic about respecting a soldier's religious beliefs. Before we could get lost in some philosophic analysis of this tendency, he told us that he carried a pocket New Testament with him, wherever he went. He was not some hard core Baptist, just smart. He said that Sgt. Jones had passed him three times looking for volunteers while he was "reading" his bible. Chieu and I even bought one for the Aggie (large print and he never let on as if he got our joke) and the four of us started our own little bible study group at every halt. I don't know if Sgt. Jones ever caught on, or merely rewarded us with freedom from details for our ingenuity. Winners get perks.

The platoon was doing great. That weekend of humanity sealed our camaraderie and, except for a few Green Beret wannabies, we all got along. By Monday we had even manufactured a guidon, complete with military insignia and a motto in Greek (supplied by our Ancient Languages major from Brown). Over the Platoon numbers, mirroring the "Winners get Perks" was another inscription in Greek which, roughly translated, read "Always protect oneself with a condom before getting fucked." The joke would only work if we all kept silent, which was surprisingly accomplished. It just went to show that there weren't many classics majors among the officers or enlisted ranks in the army.

The next two weeks were survived with similar spirit and in a thoroughly professional manner to boot. We aimed at being always second in every event except the obstacle course where, as a matter of pride, we would actually try to win. We figured that by being second, consistently, we would win in the general platoon competition. Not only would we not attract attention, but also we would not have to exert any herculean effort in military performance (the very thought of which would probably make us all sick to our stomachs). In any military marching song that called for "Airborne Cavalry" or some similar bloodthirsty phrase, we would substitute "Airmail Finance" or some such indicator of our philosophic tenor. It drove the Hitler-Jungend crazy, but it became our signature and even Sgt. Jones didn't yell at us for it (when out of sight of officers). Screwing the barracks inspection became a matter of pride, so we would leave a sock in the dryer for the officers to find and be otherwise perfect. It seemed to make us more human, in our own eyes, if none other. More, we were beating the army at its own game—something we did for our fathers, brothers and all the males who had worn green before us. Sgt. Jones seemed to be proud of us and even joined in one of our evening games of splatter hockey.

While there was a general feeling we invented this sport, I can't imagine that our thought process was unique or ahead of its time. It was just a way to have some fun with the materials at hand. At either end of the bay a boy would kneel and use a shoe brush to bat a tin of "K"-ration jelly down the length of the bay to a likewise armed companion. During its trips back and forth the tin would become more and more deformed till one hit would make it splatter all over the losing player. It was great fun. Since we flunked inspection we had to stay on base, though Sgt. Jones let us steal out on Saturday afternoon as long as we were all back by taps.

One of those Saturday afternoons Aggie, Chieu and I "borrowed" a floor buffing machine from the base hospital having "borrowed" Sgt. Mike's jeep to get there and back. I was never so scared in my life, but the Aggie brought good luck. That buffer bought our way out of every duty roster chore for the duration. We hid it in Sgt.

Jones' locked storage closet which was opposite from his room. Chieu had simply popped the exposed hinge bolts to gain entry. Had Jones ever looked, or looked in such a way that people had known that he looked, under the old army blanket covering our find, we probably would have caught hell. There was no other place to put it as the immersion heater took up all the room in the more customary hiding place beneath the outside stairs

The end of the Week Three marked our halfway point and our first two day (overnight) pass. We were lined up and paid, like any other group of soldiers, with crisp new, visibly marked, $20 bills. Though the army wanted to know where we spent our money; we were, from noon on Saturday till 9:00 P.M. on Sunday free. More, we were to be paid that Friday. Like every other soldier since before the time of Hannibal, we had cash and would be, hell, we demanded to be separated from our money in the most hedonistic way possible. I tried to find Greg but couldn't. Chieu, Aggie and I went into town along with about 10,000 freshly paid cadets and soldiers. Everybody wanted a cold beer and, in their dreams, a hot girl. As we piled into my car, I felt that we had the same thoughts and desires as any other group of soldiers since time in memorial; it was just different technology.

All I really wanted was to eat a good dinner in a leisurely fashion, sit and talk afterward, smoke a cigarette without field stripping it immediately afterwards, enjoy several cold beers, take a shower by myself and then sleep till noon the next day. Chieu had similar thoughts and the Aggie just didn't want to be left behind. Sooner or later, Chieu and I were determined to get a real conversation out of him, but his smile, cunning, and idiotic observations made him indispensable none the less. We settled for being taken to the cleaners by one of the two "good" restaurants in town. Townies knew when payday was, and never ventured into town that night. The restaurant probably raised their prices for that day and let all the trained staff off for the night. They knew their business; we didn't care. It was enough to be out in civilization again. Still being early after our meal was devoured, we went back into town. The place was crawling with cadets, troopers, MPs, and girls adorned in Fredericks of Hollywood attire walking around alone or in pairs. At first glance, they might have been college or high school girls strolling around town merely dressed a bit provocatively. As we past two, they smiled and asked if we wanted dates that night. I looked at their tube tops and miniskirts with an almost salivating relish. Almost instantly, the thought of who and what they were; turned the sexual desire into intellectual depression. The three of us were a decidedly clean cut looking crew, nervously rejected their offer and dived into the first decent looking bar we found. We were in there for five minutes, having been asked by three girls if we wanted a "good time," before a fight broke out among several troopers and cadets who took life much too seriously. Even the Aggie suggested that we leave. It was too much.

In the car, we decided to head up the road to Manhattan, Kansas, home of KSU. Perhaps there we could meet and talk to some college people—by which we meant girls. Two seconds in our first bar reminded us of our hair cuts (we had gotten used to them) and how unpopular the army was even among these Middle-America Americans. We figured that they thought we were troopers and once they found out that we were college kids also, everything would be okay. After almost fifteen minutes at the bar without service, we got the hint. This town was off limits to those such as us. In the end, we found a motel outside of "JC" and settled in for the night; each in his own room so that we could wallow in the luxury of privacy for the first time in three weeks.

We made it back to post in time for Sunday lunch and spent the rest of the day to ourselves. I read and wrote letters. I tried to describe our exploits to both Alexandra and Belle. After the first week, they had, true to their word, both been steady in their letters. The letters from both were newsy, cheerful descriptions of their jobs and home life; nothing special. My replies were much the same, but I tried to introduce, in each successive letter, a bit of philosophic analysis or insight about what was happening around me. It was my way of deepening the relationship. I was, hopefully, breaking through, subtly, the barriers of friendship into the arena of date or prospective lover. Alex's letters did not respond much to this effort at all. I figured she spent all her emotional energy with her "fabulous" HTH. Belle, on the other hand, was coming along nicely. Her letters were still mostly news and bits of light family gossip, but somewhere in the middle was usually a paragraph or two discussing my last philosophic observation or idea. She made no initiative into deep thought herself, but she did respond, and did so in a way that gave me the distinct impression that she enjoyed it. Her letters were written with such emotional sincerity that I began to believe that she was becoming interested in me. She began to write as if not merely passing the time or filling the letter in order to help a "friend" in the army. Her Veemie was to attend next year. With the army tedium inspired by the "hurry-up-and-wait" style of life, I had plenty of time to study the letters intensely. I would underline significant phrases and circle words that suggested personal, emotional input. It beat the boredom and allowed me to spend my time thinking and planning the coming year. That was better than analyzing the trajectory, terrain and tactics needed to effectively use a flame-thrower—especially since we all knew, nobody used them much anymore.

The second half of Summer Camp was mainly field exercises and physical competitions interspaced with appropriate humiliation drills. I don't know if they expected us to take any of it, especially the field exercises seriously—like it was real training for us to use in Viet Nam or some such place, but we didn't. To us, it was most like playing "army" with really cool stuff. It was an experience to get through, something we couldn't escape. The real world of the military with people dying and the shells being truly high explosive versus smoke was somewhere else—this was being a student, a kid—and that world, the world of real death, power and the army was that of adults. Monday morning we would head out to some prairie tract five or six thousand meters square on post in either buses or converted (hardly) cattle trucks like one might have seen on the highway. Our sleeping gear would be delivered to some encampment area so that, in the evening, the platoons would reassemble, and put up their pup-tents. One or two companies would use this as the home base for the ensuing week. Several nights each week would be spent "tactical" by each platoon allowing the other platoons of the companies to actually sleep in their tents. The tactical platoons would do a field problem overnight which meant digging fox holes, eating "C"-rations, night patrols and being ever ready for an "aggressor" attack which always came and we always reacted as we should. If there was supposed to be a connection to this and real life we missed it. Most of the time, we saw it as the Army's way of making sure everything we owned was dirty beyond belief so they could expect us to have it spotless by Friday evening or be punished.

Philosophically, I didn't let it get to me. The problems were always constructed so that we were defending ourselves against the bad guys. We all played the game well enough; everybody was smart enough to know that a "bad attitude" would bring themselves and their mates a load of grief. The one time I faltered was on the rifle range. In the forth week we actually got to fire live ammunition through our weapons. Until then, all we had been doing was firing blanks which while having the same noise and recoil as the real bullet merely made the weapons incredibly dirty; thus meeting the military's primary objective. But on the live fire range it was different. We each got about 200 rounds to sight in our weapon on the practice range. Many of the guys had never shot a rifle before and to them it was all confusing and their scores were very poor. Having been around rifles since I was ten, this was not hard for me at all. I was one of the first to go across the street to the "fire for record" range to qualify.

During a "fire for record" exercise an enlisted man sat behind you as you would take firing positions either in a foxhole, sitting, kneeling and standing, each in succession at his direction. Targets would appear, at random ranges, from 25 meters to 400, for fifteen seconds and fall if not hit by your fire. This should have been very easy for me to score well. I was in the foxhole and the first target popped up about 50 meters away; no sweat. Except, as the target turned and I realized it was comprised of a man's silhouette, what we were really doing all came home to me. The black silhouette was done to show you that people were the targets. From the first time I had ever picked up a gun as a boy, I had been told about pointing my weapon (as I had begun to call it) at people. Looking down the sights, I could not bring myself to squeeze the trigger. The rather bored trooper behind me seemed to realize my frustration and quietly assured "only a target sir, only a target." His words soothed me immediately and I spattered 47 of the next 49 silhouettes earning me an "expert" badge. At the end of the session I went back to pick up my score card from him and asked him why he had said what he did. He replied that he had done this enough to spot someone at home with rifles and that many guys didn't like the silhouettes their first time. I offered him one of my square C-ration cigarettes as a "thank you" and walked down the burm to hand in my score to the Officer in Charge. "Only a target" continued to burn in my mind, but I knew that even with this little bit of work, the military was making it easier for me to actually fire weapons at people; real people—yellow, brown or white—didn't matter. Hear the order and kill the people. Is that what I had gone to W&L to become?

Week Four seemed to speed by after that. We would just drift through the week's exercises not looking ahead to anything past the cigarette break or, at most, the next meal. Most of us shunned the opportunity to "command" as often as possible. Wearing the blue helmet was always a pain in the ass. Chieu, the Aggie and I stuck together. Two of us would always be in a good enough mood to keep the other going if they were in some momentary depression after going through a particularly bad exercise. Now, I wonder if it is the property of all such groups of men, but then, I felt that our platoon was very finely tuned on personalities and skills. After four weeks of living together, we were a well oiled group—working effectively as a team almost unconsciously.

On Friday of Week Four we were treated to the first really dirty exercise. I believe that these were purposely scheduled on Friday knowing that you would have to spend the day dirty, wet, uncomfortable and, worse, go back to the barracks that way. Coming into a clean barracks after a week in the field could have been a joyous occasion, but to do so in a filthy condition made it horribly frustrating. Five minutes after our return our barracks would be so messy and dirty that it mandated a night long effort to prepare it for Saturday morning inspection. None of this was immediately apparent to us riding home, covered with the drying mud, from the morning's rope bridge building exercises, in sullen silence on Friday #4. Only our Aggie had seen the officer's subtle deviousness. He quickly passed around a suggestion that after we were excused from formation two guys would strip naked outside, surrounded by the others at the door, race in to get into new clothes and return. All the dirty clothes and gear would stay outside and be cleaned there so that the barracks could be left as pristine as when we had left. Dust the barracks and dip clean the weapons and bed by Eight! Sgt. Jones foiled this brilliant attempt soon after we started it.

Noticing that we were all still outside shaking off our gear and such while all the other platoons were collapsing inside their barracks, he walked over to investigate. Waiting till two of the guys were completely naked he called the platoon to attention and ordered us to formation. There he scolded us for our brazen attempt to desecrate the army's morals by public nakedness as the two naked guys were in formation along with the rest of us. Finishing, he ordered us inside, with all our gear. On the way through to his room, he laughingly told us that it had been a "nice try" and to "keep it up." We, of course, did not pass inspection as our platoon tradition dictated but, as we were the lead platoon in the brigade contest, we got passes anyway. This was the weekend that Vicki was coming to see Greg and the three of us had planned to spend the evening together. Although it would be good to see her and Greg again, I knew that I would end the night depressed at being alone and a third wheel. Chieu and the Aggie had made plans to spend the overnight with a bunch of guys from the platoon who were making a road trip to one of their fraternity houses in Kansas City. I could have gone and probably had a good time with all the guys, but I had already committed to Greg before camp began.

I beat Greg to the Econo-lodge prearranged rendezvous by a good half an hour. Vicki and I sat and waited for him by the pool talking of the previous spring and my adventures at camp. She couldn't keep from remarking about my haircut and the peculiar tan lines I had developed. Soldiers had tans half way up their nose from wearing helmets in the sun and on their arms from the elbows down from rolled fatigue sleeves. Her non-military manner of speech, her delicious college innocence (although an incredibly erotic young lady) contrasted the army's harsh reality. Her knowledge of the "me" from college seemed to make me intensely aware of how different from the outside our life with Sam had become. Greg finally arrived, having been held up with some sort of hassle with his platoon's inspection. He sat down to spend the afternoon drinking beer and enjoying the pool. Like before, most of the time was spent in discussions about school and the adventures we were having at camp. Once in a while some talk about the future would creep in. Vicki was thinking of graduate school and Greg, of course, law school. I figured that my future was already decided by Uncle Sam. It was in this vein that the subject of Beth came up. Vicki had heard from her once, early in the summer, and wondered if I was still in contact with her. I, who had received only one, rather impersonal, letter from her a short while before, said "yes—sort of." I went on to relate that we had decided to let things "find their own level" rather than push anything for fear of some "artificial pressure making a long term romance where there was none." I asked if she knew Alexandra or Belle. Vicki quickly answered that Belle was a rather typical southern girl at Macon, out for her MRS degree but, arching an eyebrow, asked me how I knew Alex.

As Vicki began to relate the gossip about Alexandra, I started to put my own information into perspective. It seemed that Alexandra's reputation was that of a rather eccentric, if not a tad slutty, egotist. Alex's high opinion of her HTH was well known as were her sorties to W&L, but being so far from the normal lifestyle, they were looked upon negatively. To all social criticism or scorn Alex presented a level of contempt rare to people of her age. Alex would have no criticism of her decisions about her life and simply told all who might give judgment that they should "go screw themselves." Vicki closed the conversation by stating that she knew neither very well and it, perhaps, was not fair for her to speak of them since I was "so obviously interested in them" as dates. Did it show that much?

This was the signal for us to move on to dinner at the restaurant that I had visited the previous weekend. Afterward, we gave Vicki a rolling tour of Fort Riley, even stopping at Greg's barracks, about a half mile down from mine. She found everything fascinating and foreign. Whether or not this was the case or it was just her attempt to say something that would seem so, I don't know. If I had been in Greg's shoes, I would have done the tour the next day in one of the short lulls between trysts. The guys, seeing a girl looking like Vicki walking around with two of their number made quite a commotion. Vicki loved it; we loved it. For her it was tourism, for us it a respite from thinking about two more weeks of crap. We finished the evening at one of the nicer bars in Junction City. The three of us sat and drank beer listening to a live band. Each of us danced with Vicki several times. After one dance with Greg, Vicki came back to the table and asked why I didn't ask one of the unattached girls to dance. Greg and I just looked at her, and almost laughed simultaneously.

"Because…a dance would cost me…that's why." I looked at her, watching her expression change from one of casual conversation to one of general confusion.

"What do you mean?"

"I mean that they rent their time…Vicki…They're personal recreation relationship specialists…they're prostitutes…whores."

She looked at me with a hushed, bewildered expression with obvious interest; "No…really?!" I went on to relate Greg's and my first evening's experience to her. She was almost giggling in her fascination. Greg, to my chagrin, duly reported my reactions to the girl in question in his recounting of the story for Vicki. I didn't know whether to be embarrassed or try to appear sensitive and thoughtful in order to hide my apparent naiveté. Vicki responded with a girlish laughter that bordered on a little girl when caught doing something naughty. She started asking all sorts of questions about them and how they did their job. Since neither Greg nor I knew first hand (well, at least I knew that I didn't) all we could relate was what we'd heard.

We spent the next several hours dancing and talking about school and people we all knew. Vicki would touch my or Greg's arm and smilingly nod in the direction of any of the girls when they led their customer out into the parking lot. By the 9:30, true to expectations, I was feeling alone and useless. I told Greg that I could not make it any further since I had KP duty at 4:30 A.M. the next day. I lied but Greg's expression at the news told me that he was glad. I couldn't blame him. It had been a long time since Greg had seen his beautiful girl friend and he wanted to have some time alone with her. I knew that I could always find something to do; even sleep if nothing else came up.

I walked the mile to the motel and, rather than going to my room just drove around and stopped into one more bar for a "night cap."

Really just wasting time before I headed back, I thought the people watching entertainment might take my mind off Greg and Vicki. Twenty minutes into my first bar, I did run into someone I knew; "Cindy" who was now named "Brandy." She came over to the table where I was sitting alone and asked me for a light. I gave her one and asked if she could sit down so that I could buy her a beer. The line had come natural enough, but I even surprised myself in its delivery since my heart was racing and I was nervous as hell. I had never spoken to a whore before. I knew that I shouldn't be nervous since it was impossible to impress her and it shouldn't matter at all what a whore thought of me. It was her job to make me feel important. "Hello again…my—you're ravishing tonight—and I am hungry!" She looked at me like I had three eyes. Well, I had tried to make some sort of opening line but bungled it badly—where to go from here? It was a situation that was completely foreign to me and I did not know into which tactical self to put myself. She smiled at my stumbling line. After ordering her beer from the waitress who had swooped down as soon as "Cindy" or, now, "Brandy" took a chair, she looked at me, smiled and said "Wasn't that supposed to be my line?"

She laughed at my hurt expression, patted my thigh and told me her name was "Brandy." I asked what had happened to "Cindy" to which she answered in a laugh that I must have met her before on a Monday evening because she always used that name on Mondays. To this she asked if I had enjoyed myself that night. Frowning, I put a couple of bucks on the table, put my cigarette in my mouth, picked up my keys and started to get up to leave. Not letting me straighten, she pulled my arm down and asked me to stay as she had not meant any harm by her remarks. I did as she asked, not sure if it was the best of decisions. I did, in truth, want to talk to her. I probably also wanted to have sex with her, but was lost in some neophyte's romantic confusion about what to feel. Should I be sorry for her; intellectually talk to her about the sociological and psychological questions I had for a girl with her vocation; or just plain lust after her body like every red-blooded American soldier should.

She had seen this before because she took a sip from her beer and told me that it was "nice" just to talk for a while as she stared blankly at the glass. I realized that I was relating to someone who was a complete lie, maybe not just to her customers, but also to herself as well. I figured that as long as I kept track of my wallet there could be no harm. I drank from my beer frantically thinking of the first question I could ask her without losing too much face. "Why Brandy or Cindy…what's your real name?"

She said that she picked new names because it helped business since "who would feel sexy with a girl named Ruth?" With that she laughed and asked how old I thought she was. I guessed 19, but thought 16, to which she said that I was close as she had just turned 18. I don't know if that was to excite me further or to rest my fears about her being underage. I lifted my beer to toast her birthday which, being my first statement that was not a disaster seemed to set both of us at ease. I watched her eyes. As long as she looked at me, I would stay and talk. If she started to look around the room for customers, I would leave. I didn't want to keep her against her will or have others think that I would lose a prostitute's attention. She looked at me and with a knowing smile took my hand and started asking me what I studied in school, where it was, what my girlfriend was like and stuff like that. In that vain, I probably talked for almost a half hour without noticing. I felt relaxed and enjoyed holding her hand. When the waitress took our order for another beer Brandy / Cindy / Ruth looked at me, without her smile and I returned the gaze with a serious, depressed sort of expression. She could see it. I squeezed her hand trying to snap her out of it. We had lost consciousness of where, who and what we were. She just looked down and stared at the empty glass. All at once she looked up and asked if I wanted to know how she got into this business since almost every boy (she used that exact word) who acted like me had wanted to hear "her story."

She began to relate, and continued through another beer as well, a teenage mother who didn't want her, an enlisted, drunk father who beat her when he wasn't "handling her," bad marks in school, and finding out that she was pregnant from some high school jerk. True or not she would have made my sociology professor proud. "Luckily," she said that she had a miscarriage and only faced getting thrown out of the house (or mobile home as was probably the case), rather than becoming a mother. She found a job in a bar pushing beer, but kept on getting propositioned and became disappointed at the little money she made. A friend asked her and her roommate if they wanted to try working at a massage parlor. There the money was good and the work easy but the boss kept most of the money and demanded "freebees" for himself and his friends. She added that he also kept trying to get her hooked on drugs. Not that she minded getting a little stoned once in a while—probably too often—but the hard stuff was too dangerous. She started working parties and the bars when her boss forced her to do some "really perverted stuff" with a couple of his friends. Here, as long as she paid the bartender and the cops, she was free and more or less safe. She wanted to be a dancer or a designer some day and was saving for school. Someday she said she wanted to be "normal...a mom and all that."

All the time she had been talking I was watching her. She told the story haltingly, staring at the glass, like it was the truth or an extremely well practiced lie, anyway. At least it made sense or made the sense I wanted it to make. I didn't feel sorry for her because I didn't sense that she wanted me to. Like the factory in the summer, this was sociology in the raw. It was a view of society that I had never seen and from which my life had protected me. While my brain was absorbed in what she said, my spirit was looking for a way to ease the pain I thought she must have felt. At the pause she looked at me, pleading that I start talking again and returned her gaze to the half empty glass. I took the cue and told her I didn't know what I wanted to be when I grew up or after school, which ever came first. I started talking about what I wanted as a future; meaningful employment, making life better for people, something intellectually honest and creative. She started looking at me again and I smiled. I must have sounded as if I was planning on being a cross between the Chairman of the Board of GM and Albert Schweitzer. She must have been very good at her job because she stayed glued to me as if she hung on every word. We were still holding hands.

Squeezing my hand, she sat up straight and asked if we could take a walk, just to get out of the noise and smoke. I was puzzled and suspicious. Where was this leading to? Outside we were available to muggers, drunken soldiers or MPs. I suddenly worried about if she had the clap or anything. She patted my hand and told me that we'd be okay and could come back if I wanted to. Why was this woman, a whore, chasing me? If she were out for money she would have left me an hour ago.

Outside we walked down to the center of town where, in front of the town hall, they had a small park. She said we could sit there safely for a while. Biting my tongue, I asked her if she read much. She replied that she did, some, but what type of book did I have in mind. What I had in mind was a mixture of James Jone's <u>From Here to Eternity</u> and Leon Uris's <u>Battle Cry</u> (but I hadn't read them yet). I was groping for an answer though my muddled thoughts made fuzzy by beer, horniness and an ardent, romantic desire to find a heart of gold inside this whore. I told her that the book I was thinking of was Salinger's <u>Catcher in the Rye</u>. I half expected her to chime in on cue with the footnoted reference and the entire scene, thinking it must have been as popular as the "how did a girl like you" line. Maybe for my sake she didn't, and she asked me to tell her about it. That did it. I stopped and looked at her. At first, I thought I was going to kiss her, but was suddenly angry. "What the hell is…going on…I mean here we are walking…hand in hand…like a couple of kids…20 more meters (mentally footnoting my military use of the term "meters") and we…would be sitting on a park bench…necking…like a couple of God-damn love birds…. Just what is this?" I was speaking in a low level, but with a hostility and harshness that made the words feel like I was almost yelling.

She jerked me along with her while she quickly resumed walking. "Do you wanna get busted?" she hissed through clenched teeth, "Well if you do…jes keep talking out loud like that…you're working up to yellin…this place is crawling with MPs with a quota…I don't wanna go to jail again…an you probably don't either." That cooled me off. We walked in a depressed and angry silence, but, curiously, our hands had not let go. I was still mad. I wanted to pick her up, kiss her and make mad passionate love to this girl—the Ruth, not the Cindy or the Brandy. I knew that those actions were not part of the deal and that the action itself was foolish since the girl was a whore and making love was not what they do. I also realized that I was being too romantic and was, in fact, very foolish. I wanted her to be just a plain girl, but knew that she wasn't. I hated myself for caring what she was or the images that realization brought forth in my imagination. I felt like she was mocking my innocence or something. "Here…sit…shut up." She almost spit the words. I responded with military efficiency. I had not even tried to speak but she was now clearly upset. "Ya know I could be back at that Silver Dollar makin money but…noooo…no…I spent the last hour an a half with you…God damn you…I figure that you don't want just sex or nothin…you just looked lonely 'an nice…an maybe…maybe lookin at you…I need to be with someone…just ONE time without him thinking he was in me, any part of me…I know how you guys look at me…What is this? I'll tell ya what it is…its a Goddamned camp town on a Saturday night at about 1:30 in the morning an I'm givin up a lot money bein her with you, asshole…this is freakin prime time…" She started to get up to leave. But, this time it was me who hung onto her hand as she got up and physically yanked her back.

"Sit down!" I reached into my back pocket to get my wallet to take out a couple of $20s to throw at her. I stopped about half way through the gesture and just looked at her. She was just looking at me; kind of angry, kind of sad. All of a sudden she seemed so small and young; and I became aware that she really was pretty. She was genuinely as upset as I was. I reached around instead to cup her head with my hand and bring her over to my face to kiss. I gave her a peck on the cheek thinking it more gentle and kind and not at all passionate or erotic. She just exhaled and shivered; all at once relaxing. She slumped against my shoulder and we sat that way for a short while that seemed like hours. "Let's go for a drive." I looked at her and she was questioning me with her eyes. "Just a drive...okay?" The last words were really a question; one from a boy to a girl. We got up and started walking back to the strip where my car was parked. "ya gotta understand...I'm not used to all this..." She squeezed my hand, and we were silent all the way to the car.

There's not much to see in Kansas in the daytime and less to look at driving around at night. I was going nowhere in particular and got on the Interstate. The conversation picked up where it had left off; with <u>Catcher in the Rye</u>. I tried to reconstruct the story as best I could. The book's plot, however; was never as vibrant as the intensely personal experience of reading it. We talked, or better stated, I lectured in a wandering way about the books I had read that had been significant to me. It had been an hour since we had gotten in the car. She sat, looking at me, smoking and asking little questions about this or that. I pulled off the highway, circled over and started back. She sensed what I was doing and after about two or three exits of silence she asked me quietly if I wanted to spend the night somewhere. "Won't your roommate worry?"

"No...she moved out a couple of months ago."

"How 'bout your boyfriend?" I asked, with my voice almost hushed as if I were trying to cover the concern in my voice. The tension of her job, her life, came back into the aura of the night. For a while, we had forgotten about it, but now it was unavoidable.

"No...I don't...have one...if you don't want to...or if it would bother you..."

I reached out and held her hand as I drove. We were both silent for a while as I thought. I was very confused. I wanted this girl for the base physical reasons of her beauty and my testosterone; that I knew that I and she were lonely; and for the very real emotion I felt for her. But, after all, would I be just another guy within in her? Was it merely her way of saying "thanks" for a night away from a more crude level of soldier sex? Was it safe or would I get the clap or something? Would I be one more oppressor in the long line of men, in her past and, regrettably, in her future, damning her into an existence where she was nothing more than a collection of wet orifices?

I stopped at the first decent looking motel we came to; no need to go back to the Econo-lodge. It was only about twenty miles outside "JC" so the clerk was well accustomed to short haired young men signing in, without luggage, late at night with a female companion and paying with new $20s. We shared the nervous silence as we walked up the stairs to our room. I worried about my decision to do this and what I had gotten myself into. Only our joined hands kept my mind and body on track. Once within the room all aspects of the past and future vanished as I held her in my arms; just to hug. Her smile welcomed my silent kisses and we both felt at home this close to each other. To me, at least, she seemed to say she was relaxing and not working. She was just a girl with which I had spent the evening and to which I had enjoyed talking. She was almost hesitant and shy as we slowly undressed each other on the bed. Deep in an embracing kiss she pulled back and excused herself to the shower where I joined her. Much like the movies, there was nothing said; nothing needed to be said. We slept very little in what was left of the night.

Our joy lasted all the way through our joint shower the next morning. It was strange just to play, almost as a child, with this girl whose name I still did not really know. We finally hit breakfast about 11:00 in the plaza outside of "JC." There, during coffee, the reality of what was happening started to intrude into our minds. Both of us drifted into silence, withdrawing into our thoughts, wishes and fears. I didn't know what to do; what to say; what to feel. Looking at her sitting there in one of my college t-shirts (I had not permitted her to wear the tube top in which she had started the previous night). I wanted to see a cute, young girl, anticipating life like any other 18 year old; a Freshman at a reasonable school somewhere, with her life, career, husband, and family ahead of her. No matter how much I wanted it; I knew that this dream was too romantic to be true. She was a whore with whom I had spent the night both us sharing a refuge from loneliness. It all could have been some kind of elaborate joke. Maybe it was some kind of charity from a girl who had merely wanted a night off from the crude reality in which she lived. Maybe I was the small price she had to pay for the time as a date, a girl versus her life as a whore. I don't know. She wouldn't look at me for more than a moment. I got up and told her to wait there. I made a point of having her notice that I had left my car keys on the table but walked past the men's room. I walked into the neighboring jewelry store and quickly purchased a jade pendant with the money I had left from payday. I had never spent $100 on a girl before. I had them wrap it but left the receipt in the bag (in case she wanted to return it) as I came back, paid the bill and got her into the car.

There, I gave her the bag. She smiled and almost giggled as she held it up and shook it. She told me that I "shouldn't have" and dutifully kissed me in happy anticipation before she opened it. Seemingly overjoyed, she had me immediately help her put it on just like girls do in the movies. She kept fingering it as she gave directions for me to drive her home. I parked in front of a block of pre-fab apartments in what seemed to be a reasonably clean lower-middle class part of town. It surprised her when I got out of the car to walk her to her door. She unlocked it, then turned and looked up at me, her face tense and sad. I leaned down and kissed her. She asked me in, but I refused and finished the kiss. As she walked in she turned and asked me to write. I told her I would, but we both knew that I wouldn't. I still had no idea of to whom I should address it. Driving back to base, I couldn't help but think that it was all a romantic dream, some sort of movie playing in my mind of what I wanted to happen. I started the night alone and here I was in the morning alone. Maybe I would always wonder; but she had been real, I think. Her cigarettes were in the ashtray, and the bag from the jewelry store was in the back seat—she had been real.

I spent the rest of the day reading or working, with some level of guilt, on letters to both Alex and Belle. My mind refused to concentrate on them and constantly wandered back to "Cindy." From time to time throughout the training I worried that I might have picked up something besides a guilty conscience from the encounter. It wasn't quite guilt, but more of a sadness and resolve about the reality of it all. It had been an interesting moment and not the basis for anything in the future except an anonymous memory.

The next two weeks were the climax to the whole Summer Camp experience. We climbed a cliff that had been blasted out of the Kansas prairie, repelled out of helicopters, trained in tanks, fired howitzers, and even used flame-throwers we had ignored during training lectures. It was real army stuff. We had the joy of going through the confidence course which Sgt. Jones described as the obstacle course's bigger brother. Each squad would rotate being first through each challenge. With my fear of heights I was, of course, third behind the head of the line for the pole climbing.

This was a structure consisting of two 85 foot telephone poles placed eight feet apart with 2X4s attached on each side, between the poles, at increasingly wide intervals. For the first 20 feet or so they were only 3 feet apart. You could easily climb on each, reach up and grab the next—without letting go of the first. By the top however, the stringers were almost seven feet apart. That meant you had to climb on one, balance carefully as you straightened up to jump to the next. The guy in front got half way up then came down without completing the event as did the next. I stayed close to the pole as an emergency measure but I kept my eyes on the next stringer; concentrating on not looking down. I made it to the top and was very proud. I felt like yelling in victory but Sgt. Jones merely told me (through a bullhorn) to get my ass down as fast as I could since we didn't have all day. More than any other in the camp, maybe for years to follow, it was the most memorable moment from the entire camp experience; never dying from my memory. My face in the sun—it was the first piece of graphic courage that I had ever displayed. Not every guy made it to the top that day. Being there made me feel very good—getting down was hell.

The final week sporadically became very quiet. The entire platoon had made it through with no wash-outs and we were happy that it was almost over. Increasingly often, however; we would realize that, in all probability, we would never see each other again. Cameras were purchased and hundreds of pictures were taken. Many of the exercises were only perfunctory in nature and were understood as such. We coasted. The night before the end, we cleaned the barracks one more time. It was accomplished easily and completed very early in the evening. Sgt. Jones brought us a couple of cases of smuggled beer and eight huge pizzas. We presented him with a plaque we had purchased and inscribed with our platoon motto. He sat and joked with us for a while, but then left so that we would be freer to be ourselves, among ourselves.

The 36 guys on our floor must have looked like a picture out of Life magazine or the subject of a Saturday Evening Post magazine cover. We sat around, joking and talking in our underwear, white, yellow, black, all young, muscular men (some more so than others) from every part of the country. We had different majors, plans for the future and attitudes towards the army. We, then, belonged to the strong fraternity of platoon mates who had made it through basic training together. The stories ranged from those of first day jitters to hysterical night patrol mishaps. We laughed late into the night. Unlike previous years when one had to think about whether the guys you knew were going to be alive in another year after their tour in Viet Nam, this was merely a sense of graduation; of leaving, never to return. But, it was hard in another sense as well. Graduation, the real graduation was just one school-year away for all of us. This was dress rehearsal. If we felt this way about guys we'd known for six weeks or so, what would we feel about guys we'd known for four years?

At the closing ceremony we were named the honor platoon of the brigade. But, the only real pride we felt was for having Sgt. Jones as a Platoon Sergeant. Afterward, we stopped back at the barracks to change and pick up our stuff. There were a lot of hands being shaken and addresses exchanged. Chieu, myself and the Aggie promised to stay close and each had a signed copy of the same photo showing the three of us armed to the teeth, out on patrol, as our souvenir. Everyone was anxious to leave but hated saying goodbye, but, after lunch, we started to move off. I stopped down and told Greg, who was about to leave himself, that I would see him in about a week and a half.

As I headed out of "JC", I contemplated visiting "Cindy / Brandy / Ruth." It could have been horns, or just a sense of emotional unfinished business. Maybe I wanted the movie to have a happy ending. I actually drove up to her house and stopped the car. I could see her curtained windows from the road. Since it was the afternoon, I felt sure that she would be up, but I hesitated as to whether I should stop in. I decided not, there was no telling what I might find in there. I was, however, certain it would not be a future.

CHAPTER 10

*T*he time home was good, but short. I had time to show off my new physique and tan-lines to the family, tell stories to my Dad and get stoned a few times with Dave. But in less than two weeks, it was time to go to my real home, to Lex. Driving down, I knew that it was to be the last time I would drive to Lexington at the beginning of a school year. The entire drive was, to me, the last glimmer of final transition before some climatic scene of a movie. For this reason and those of the expectations I held for the next few days in Lexington and Lynchburg, I became especially aware of everything around me. Everything had to be, and was, significant. The weather was brilliant, cloudless and the hills on both sides of me as I drove down the valley were greener than I remembered them ever to be. September was, for me, the best month in which to view the countryside both in the Pennsylvania mountains and the Shenandoah. While many might think that fall would highlight the mountains and allow the valley towns to look their best, I preferred the robust optimism of summer's growth. These colors were not dying gasps, but vibrant roars of life. It was all optimism and strength.

Smiling, driving almost on auto-pilot, I was lost within my daydreams as I planned the first few weeks in Lex. There would be little to do with the apartment since it was already arranged precisely the way I wanted. Campbell would hit town at the same time as I, and

the same with Cal and Greg. The four of us would invariably tell stories and compare notes on the summer till well into the night. The
next day, the important one, we would get the underclassmen
together for the FHS III sortie, our class' last, to set the house up
with dates for Rush. By now, I knew that Rush almost ran itself. As a
Senior, even as an assistant Rush Manager, I could sit back, and
watch the show rather than worry incessantly about how it was running. Only my hair bothered me. After R.O.T.C. camp, it was growing as fast as it could, but still was way too short to be even close to
stylish. Only the fact that there would be many like me kept me from
real disappointment or worry about its looks.

The classes I had registered for last fall were interesting without
being destructively laborious. Most of them even promised to be
fun. I had planned on taking a couple of history classes, Freshman
psychology (pass / fail no less!), some religion, and, if this particular
macro class lived up to its reputation, maybe a "light" economics
class. I hoped that I would be on the list for the History Honor Seminar or asked to do an Honors project. The History Department
reserved the projects for the top two History majors and the Honor
Seminar for the next ten. I felt that I qualified, but the History professors chose among themselves who was invited, so we were held in
suspense till we saw the list or got our class sheet upon matriculation. On the academic scene, things looked very bright. Ten hours of
driving didn't even put a dent in my enthusiasm or excitement; I
could taste the success I knew this year would bring.

Campbell beat me to the apartment by about an hour. As I parked
and unloaded the car I heard his stereo blasting out Jethro Tull's
Aqualung, announcing to the townies that we had arrived and
within a few hours we'd be taking over for another year. I simply
dumped my stuff in my apartment before flying from my door to
his. It had been too long. Without looking up, he threw me a beer
from the refrigerator door. I caught it effortlessly and dropped onto
his couch with a smile. We related to each other, with appropriate

flourish, color, detail and exaggerations, all the summer's adventures. Each story was interrupted time and again with remarks, questions, and jokes. He was anxious to hear all about the Fort Riley experience and my military exploits. Telling each, trying to keep them in context, I took pride in that these tales didn't grow inordinately under the fertilizer of elapsed time and alcohol. "Cindy's" Saturday night was not mentioned as it was still too romantically foolish to really be an exploit; besides there were moments when it still bothered me; hardly the material for adventure tales.

"Cindy's" evening with me and its following morning had consumed many hours of thought. I would replay all the scenes over and over, hoping for some insight into her motivation, words and deeds. If I gained that, some insight into mine might also come forth. Sometimes, I thought that she was, in her own way, mocking my innocence in some kind of personal contrived joke. Other times, I thought that the episode was merely a safe and comfortable vacation for her—occasionally needed by someone in her line of work. Maybe I was a small, insignificant act of pity from a girl who could offer some physical soothing (a trifle) to someone who radiated loneliness as I had at the time. Why me? Most of the time I thought that I had projected a kind of romantic innocence to which she had been drawn by some sharpened professional instinct. Maybe she was attracted to, and enamored with, my efforts to talk to the "girl" in her rather than simply relate to her as the whore she and I knew she was. Perhaps this became for her a fantasized island of youthful tenderness and, at least, pretended affection. I was afraid that all these thoughts were just another one of my overly romantic dreams. I was mad at myself for not being mature enough to understand that she was a whore; treat her like one, and let her be a mere financial and physical transaction. Instead, I was ensnared by her beauty, youth and sensuality; all of which made me lose perspective. Moreover, I was not sensitive enough to forget her lifestyle and deal with her as a person, the girl that she really was. The more time I spent with this episode, the more I knew that I couldn't win my own battle. Rather than resolve the ambivalence, I packaged it off into a tightly contained and sealed memory. I was certain that this year would make this episode, and all the proceeding romances, meaningless in terms of importance and intensity.

Campbell had spent the summer working on the ranch. From his appearance he looked like he had worked outdoors every day of the summer. He was still, more or less, his same scrawny self, but there was a bright blonde shine to his shoulder length hair. Even his moustache, the corners of which had grown down well past his smile, was bright yellow. I told him he looked like some under-nourished Viking; a comment he greatly appreciated. His deep, sun-baked tan coloring, his leathery skin and slender body displayed new muscles and made him look the part beyond the coloring of his hair. In his own way, he looked quite dashing, almost dangerous, dressed, as always, in boots, jeans and horizontally striped t-shirt.

Cal came in with a packaged dinner from his home sometime around 4:00 P.M. His mom had asked him to invite us over, as she did from time to time, but he was anxious to join us, leave his home and become a student again. Alone among the three of us, he had kept in touch with his Macon Crew date, Susan, over the summer. Cal told us right off, almost the first words out of his mouth, "Alas…your inspiration and words of strategy have failed me…I am still pure…" He stood there, staring at the floor with his hands outstretched in a forlorn Christ-like fashion while Campbell and I immediately picked up couch pillows and beat him severely; chastising him for his foolish "fiddle—faddling" when there was serious sex to be had. Somehow the term of "faddling" stuck and, from then on, was applied to almost all his amorous or other inane activities. Being two beers behind, he uncrated dinner and drank quickly to catch up.

By the time the sun set on our first day in Lex, we were fairly swacked, playing loud music and enjoying our reunion to the fullest. By the time Greg found us at 10:00 P.M, we were practically out of commission. We found enough life within us to relate Cal's news and begin the chastisement anew with Greg adding color commentary to our jibes at Cal. Somewhere around midnight we set 10:00 A.M. as the rendezvous time for the FHS III foray to Macon. Cal, Campbell and I knew that if we said 10:00, Greg would get there by 11:00; the actual time we wanted to leave.

Alone in my apartment and sobering fast, I sat in my living room chair and tried to decide which one of the girls I would attempt to date the next day. This was important; this decision would determine the tenor for the year and, possibly, provide the foundation of my future. I just sat, smoked cigarettes and looked out the open window over the sleeping town. The warm night refreshed me as it billowed in. All I could feel was that it was good to be back in Lex. It was home and the family that mattered most to me was together, around me again. Even then, at the start, I knew—hell, I could feel—that my life would never be this way again and that I should savor every moment. The girls, however, presented the most immediate challenge.

Alexandra offered the promise of incredible, beyond-my-imagi-nation sex. I knew a girl like her could keep me interested, if not exhausted, for a lifetime. She didn't look like she would get fat or anything by age 30 and she was smart enough not to embarrass me in whatever environment I found myself throughout my future. Negatives for her included an incredible ego, strength of will that was way beyond stubbornness and that she traveled with a very fast crowd in which it would be troublesome for me to join. No, in my dreams, I wanted a girl to join my life and not look at this as any drop in status, excitement or promise. I didn't know if that could be true with Alexandra. Moreover, I didn't think that I could hold her interest for long without a major miracle. I had seen the picture of the HTH and knew the type of guys she dated on her solo weekends at W&L. They were jocks and facemen—and all of them rich; against which all I had was my wits, a scrawny body and tactical sense to compete. One true advantage I had was, unlike almost every other male since she had turned thirteen; my history with her was that of relating to her as a friend, a person, for a period of time (soon to end, maybe) rather than just a frictional opportunity. Her letters had been punctual and full, but not as personal as I desired. I had the feeling that she thought of me as a friend still, not a prospective lover. I had doubts if I could overcome that obstacle in the next few days. If I chose her to come to Lex, not only would Belle be out of the question forever, but I would also have to become completely victorious on the first date. I was sure that I would get no second chances to keep her from reverting to her old way of life.

Belle, on the other hand, was also very interesting, almost intriguing, but in a completely different way. By every judgment, she was not my type of girl, or, better stated, I was not her type of guy. She was not overly intellectual, but could be considered reasonably smart. She was not gorgeous or erotic, but was charmingly pretty and had a sensuality about her that defied traditional "Southern Lady" description. It was a "happy" beauty, almost mischievous, that subtly told you that she could be free with the right guy. The major negative was the difference of her lifestyle from mine. She had a social heritage that testified to the best of country clubs, horses, land, gentility, distinguished grandparents and hordes of cousins; all of whom she knew well. She was accustomed to maids, other house servants and the like taking care of her family since she was born. All this made her seem unattainable to me. But, contrary to these barriers, she had written; and wrote directly, personally, to me more often than had been necessary. She wrote to me of deep, personal subjects. It was much more than I had expected. Her letters would start out with news and family, but end with thoughts about "reality," about what is "true" and about "freedom." She would add historical incidents to illustrate her points. While I didn't know if those were specifically for my benefit or were her, genuine ideas; they were in the letters. Either way it signified not only an interest in me, but some inner depth that I might be able to touch. She had even responded to a stolen poem of Shelley's I had sent her with one of her own. A relationship with her offered hope that I could figure out the way to her heart, if not her body, early in the fall.

I fell asleep in the chair till dawn's morning noise (yes, Lexington still had roosters back then) convinced me to crawl to my bed. Even after my shower, I had not made any decisions regarding Alex or Belle. By ten, I had come to the conclusion that I should merely judge each girl by their initial reactions as I met them later in the day. There was a lot riding on that decision and I didn't have a clue as to any real criteria drawn from observed fact rather than merely the analysis of letters. Somehow I thought, more like wished, that it would be the most important choice of my life. Senior year seemed to depend on it. I knew that it would prove to be interesting to say the least. My gut and tactical sense would just have to carry it off.

We left most of the Sophomores to work preparing the house for Rush. Our Sun King had proclaimed the first Rush meeting for the next day which left us morally and legally absolved from any further work till then. While being the originators of FHS gave us some real priority, I noted to Campbell that it helped things when the president wanted to go down the road himself. We had at least seven or eight cars that year as more and more of us went down with two in a car rather than four. September optimism was such that we all knew, or better stated, hoped they would be coming back full.

In our car, Campbell and I fell into a discussion of the 1939–40 Finnish—Soviet war with long, judgmental lectures on tactics, weaponry, command competence and results. With the mountains as backdrop along 501, the warmth of the day, and both of us smoking Lucky Strike cigarettes—for the sheer symbolic nature of the brand name—the day was perfect. It was good to be back; as it was the way it should be. Conversational history taken seriously, but treated lightly, the prospect of Significant College Romance ahead and a winding road through the Virginia mountains; what more could we want? On the outskirts of Lynchburg, I told him why I would go to Wright dorm first and of what I was trying to decide. He had never met either girl and kept asking me leading questions about their motives for writing me, what they looked like, what their major was, and all the other important aspects so he could, as he put it, "help me in my judgment." My reply was a question as to what he had eaten for breakfast. Knowing that if he had eaten Raisin Bran, I would maneuver my actions so as not to introduce him to either girl till I made my choice.

As it turned out, I shouldn't have wasted my breath; it was over before I started. When we pulled into the back lot, behind both Wright and West, there were already lots of cars full of girls and their families. I parked in a shady spot, out of the way and walked with Campbell to Wright to see if my girls had already arrived. The last car we came upon was that of Alexandra and her dad. She smiled, hugged me and introduced me to her father. As soon as she finished she looked back at me, probably to say something, and looked over my shoulder at Campbell; who was just walking up. It was as if I had just turned to vapor and disappeared. I had never seen anything like it in my life; there seemed to be stars in her eyes and her body trembled, even tempered by her father's presence next to her. If this had been the movies there would have been a lot of violins playing. It was something akin to the expression I had seen watching South Pacific's <u>Some Enchanted Evening</u> on the late show or maybe something out of <u>Love, American Style</u>. I knew my surrender didn't mean much, because there had been no real battle—I was never there. Looking at Campbell, I saw him straighten up, quietly smile his cunning smile, and subtly pull his shoulders back. He had seen Alex's expression, as well. His eyes darted to mine as if to say that it was his "just due being a Viking God and all." I quickly looked back at her dad to judge his reaction to this spectacle, but he was oblivious to it all being totally consumed in unloading the trunk and all her associated stuff. Alex had, in a moment's glance, obviously taken the decision out of my hands. After quickly introducing the already infatuated Alex to the intensely interested (but calm and quiet) Campbell, I grabbed the free end of the foot locker and, with Alex's father, started up the stairs. Campbell stayed back to "help" her, I guess, with some of the other stuff. As I passed him I mouthed the word "Asshole" to which he replied the smile of anticipated victory. He mumbled to my ears only that he had lied about breakfast.

It took about an hour to finish the job with Alex's stuff since Campbell hardly did anything at all. He walked next to Alex, always talking while carrying a box or something, and quickly gained the tactical initiative. Afterward, Alex and Campbell went to get a soda at the Skeller. Like hell. Watching her fawn over him made me laugh with self-conscious disappointment. There was no telling what those two's hormones were capable of—even in restricted circumstances and timeframes. Campbell had some sort of invincible charm that no one had been able to explain. Better here, before I saw Belle, than back in Lex during some party. I went back to work with a bunch of the Juniors who were moving some of the old Macon Crew into West.

The Macon Crew had started to arrive and they dutifully said their "hello"s to me' but didn't fall over themselves to make me feel wanted or welcome. It was as if I had been banished along with Beth to Wright dorm. When they were at Lexington, at our house, they would be polite enough, but in Lynchburg, on their turf, I was just another guy they knew. Vicki was the only one of their number whom I considered a friend and shouldn't have cared, but their coolness still brought my attitude down. It wasn't a hurt or emotional pain, but maybe the loss of face to my own optimism and desire for a perfect year. It was strange for Marion's parents to be genuinely friendlier than she.

I had just finished a job moving a new Freshman into the third floor of West when I looked out and saw Belle standing next to her family's Oldsmobile station wagon (I was relieved that it wasn't a

Bently or some such symbol of abundant wealth) apparently looking around for someone. I bounded down the front stairs and headed in her direction, consciously slowing my pace at the foot of the stairs so that I could hide my exuberance. Anticipation was straining every nerve when I saw her face explode into that gracious, Southern Lady's Smile-of-Happiness when our eyes met. She walked to meet me and hugged me when we were within reach. She whispered in my ear that she was "ever so glad to see me" before she pecked my cheek and pulled back to introduce me to her family. Southern hospitality and graciousness or sincere happiness; I couldn't tell which was being displayed. Compared to the other guys in the house, I must have looked reasonably clean-cut and respectable. I was in my jeans and Pumas, of course, and some of us had worn ties, but with my army hair cut not yet grown out, I looked downright center-stream. Since she had become my choice; I now had to pull off a favorable showing for her parents if I were to capitalize upon her blatantly positive attitude. For the Nth time at Macon, this situation would call for circumspect tactics.

I stepped forward and firmly shook hands with the graying-at-the-temples-but-still-vigorous dad whom I knew to be a W&L alumnus. He looked like a Playboy magazine dress shirt advertisement down to his cuff links and creased trousers. I looked him straight in the eye and made a point of always calling him "Sir." Mom was also dressed to kill. She had on some earth tone suit that, if she had been wearing a hat, would have made her appear as if she was going to church. She exuded charm and grace, and told me how pleased she was to meet me. Smiling, she started asking tactful questions about my time in the army while dad was stretching his legs after the drive. What is more likely than any genuine interest was that mom had seen the all the letters come in and she wanted to know as much as possible about the boy she could now connect to the envelopes. Between answers I even said "hello" to Belle's sister, Kelly, a high school Senior, who seemed to be aching to get to college, herself.

Dad broke into the conversation by asking what the "deal" was about having all these W&L boys here.

As we worked on getting Belle's trunk out of the back of the station wagon, I related the origin of the house tradition and its ostensive objective: meeting girls before the onslaught of Rush took up all our time. He seemed impressed and asked to which house I belonged. My answer didn't seem to faze him, but he followed with the natural and unassuming statement that he had been an SAE. It figured. I should have guessed it by looking at him. The house had probably not changed in the 25 or 30 years since he had been a member. Most of those guys in that house didn't have to worry about jobs or careers; they would simply fill the shoes of their fathers. They were the kind of guys who brought Tuxedos to school and were so cool, confident and self-assured that they didn't have to act that way. Right then I knew that Belle's mom had to be named "Babs" or "Missy" or maybe she, too, was called "Belle." I wondered what my house had been like back when her Dad had been a student. From some of the old composites we had found in the attic, it was probably best for my confidence that I not know many of his specific impressions.

Belle was in jeans (but they were the sort of clean and neat variety which met the approval of one's mother), a stripped long sleeve blouse, and had worn her hair down, loose, over her shoulders. She looked great. She grabbed her sister and told her that she would show her around. Dad and I took our cue and finished unloading the car. As in the previous years, it never ceased to amaze me how much junk girls brought to school and yet they still did not have many of the essentials items; stereos, records and books. It took a good 45 minutes for us to get all the boxes and trunks up the four flights of stairs to her room. Her room was right next to Alex's and down the hall from where Beth had been last year. Looking at Beth's door left me a bit silent for a moment. When I saw a new Freshman come out of it with one of our Sophomores in tow, however; I knew it was a new year and the remembrance of Beth quickly passed.

Alex's dad had long since gone and all seven of us were in Belle's room talking the polite chatter that passed for conversation when parents were either present or momentarily expected. Belle offered to get some drinks and I volunteered to help her. Campbell, who was wishing everyone would go away, smiled and nodded as he put his arm around Alex, thus relating to me that things were going well. I suggested Kelly stay here and smiled which signaled Campbell he owed me this, at least. Once one flight of stairs was safely behind us, Belle put her arm around me and gave me a kind of moving hug with her head on my shoulders. I looked at her and she smiled. I stopped and she kissed me, this time properly, hello, but immediately kept moving as if her mom would lean out over the stairs and check on her at any moment. I asked her back to Lex for the weekend and she said "yes," but her parents were going to take her out to dinner so I would have to wait till seven or so. I figured that I could bum around with Campbell and Alex for a while, pleasant at the fact that it would keep them disjointed, or maybe go to dinner with Greg and Vicki. Either way, I wouldn't feel too out of place and the time would pass quickly. She looked at me strangely and told me that all that was "nonsense" as I was going to dinner with them. She had already planned it. Whose tactics were winning was impossible to tell. All this made me very nervous.

A bottle of pop tasted good back in Belle's room, but there was more to do. It was only 3:00 and there were more girls to move in. We figured that we should help the Juniors and the Sophomores find dates as best we could. It would give Belle some family time (and get me free of Mom and Dad's examination for a while) and let Alex cool her hormones a little. On our way down the stairs out to the parking lot, I asked Campbell if he were properly thankful. He mumbled something about Vikings and their occupation of Normandy and some rot about "Right of Conquest." It was then that I noticed the large bruise beginning to darken on the side of his neck. He had already gotten laid! I chased him down the walk telling him that he was ridiculous in his "alley cat morals and would end up getting shot one of these days!" He just laughed and told me I should have had some Raison Bran, as well.

After another Freshman apiece we both found refuge in Vicki's room with Greg. Hidden behind the closed door, the four of us, six when Cal and Susan entered, just sat, smoked and told summer stories amongst each other. Both the room and the company was warm and close. This ease and familiarity made us different, in our minds, than all the other guys chasing women. I felt as if we were somehow a lot older than the kids who were just like we had been only a year before. I knew that I felt almost immoral lusting after some of the Freshman. They looked at me somewhat differently, too. Their expressions said to me that I was not, to them, a college kid, but at my age more of a college man. It was something I noticed almost universally in their mothers, as well. It frightened me. It meant that I or we were growing up. I looked at my watch and asked Vicki if she would stand at the door of the bathroom while I took a shower before I left to meet Belle's parents for dinner. It felt weird being in a shower room with no urinals and tiled in pink. Ten minutes later I was on my way to Wright, and to eat with Belle's parents.

I don't remember too much about the meal at all. Somehow I was too busy analyzing everyone and every thing around me to relax and let any of my observations sink in. Luckily, most of the talk centered on school and my army summer, so there was not much thought needed to keep things positive. Just before coffee, her dad asked me what I was going to do after school. The stock answer of the army didn't stand up to his retort of "and after that?" I knew that he was a lawyer and owned land. Almost anything else would have been a step down, but I didn't have any line of thought prepared for the projected line of questions he was likely to ask. I resorted to the risky practice of the truth.

I told him I didn't know. "Two years in the army should give me the insight and time I needed to formulate some tactical idea of how to proceed on a career, I guess." The sentence simply flowed from my thoughtful and serious pose. Continuing, I stated that I wanted to "do something with and for people." I was on a roll and, after the appropriate eye contact with both adults, I knew their eyes were on me. "I have…been blessed in terms of resources…intellect…of heritage…and ability…I think that it is up to me to put some of that to work…for the good of us all…the country…I guess maybe…the world…I don't know…but maybe teach…maybe work in public health…maybe even law…" All I left out was the Love-Peace-Woodstock line, but I had planned the last phrase as a lead to him, hoping he would bite and take the conversation from me. He didn't. There must have been a century of silence between my last words and his comment about how my ideas were "interesting," spoken more to his coffee than to me. I sensed that I had blown it and started to think of how to recover. Her mother saved my nerves by telling me how "noble" my thoughts were and how one of the cousins had followed the same lead and so forth and so on. I looked at Belle when it was safe and asked her with my eyes if I had screwed up. Surprisingly, she looked at me with a proud smile and sneaked her hand down under the table to touch the side of mine, telling me it was all right. Dinner ended, and I hung around and said goodbye to all them. One advantage of having her dad be an ex-Mink (as the older generations called W&L guys) was that he understood girls coming to help with Rush. No long explanations of why she was spending the first several days of her school year at my school were needed. He, of course, most probably did not know of the new rules or absence thereof.

We scooped Alex and Campbell out of her bedroom through a series of loud knocks and an announcement that we were going to leave in ten minutes whether they were ready or not. The four of us drove back to Lex in a quiet and tired car. Alex and Belle carried on a sporadic conversation about their summers; mostly we listened to clear channel, high power AM stations available only at night—WOWO out of Fort Wayne, Indiana and to WABC in NYC when that faded out. It was interesting to listen to disc jockeys talk about local news in cities hundreds of miles a way. Campbell was asleep, and the girls almost so, as I came out of the mountains on 501, through BV and into Lex. It was only 10:00, but it seemed very late. I was happy. Despite the loss of Alex, the day was going better than I had planned. I was sure that the year was going to be all that I thought it would. I remember reaching back to wake Campbell and Alex when I parked the car in front of the apartment and told them we were "home." I knew then that it was, indeed, the right word.

Everybody was up for some coffee and sherry. We all settled in the living room of my apartment while Campbell went next door to see if Cal or Barry wanted to come in. Barry didn't party or date much. He hardly ever joined in the weekend activities so it didn't bother any of us when he declined. Cal and Susan did, however, join us. Alex and Belle had never seen my (or Campbell's) apartment before and were investigating everything. They had heard Beth talk about it, but had fun comparing those tales to what they saw before them. After about fifteen minutes, Belle had the coffee water on and was treating the place like another part of her dorm. Just looking at her, seemingly at home, made me feel like the summer's letters had been a wise investment. We talked through two pots of coffee and several tapes of music, but by midnight, our guests left us to be alone themselves. It was the first time for Belle and me. I pulled my chair in front of the window and turned out all the lights. Asking her to sit on my lap, we sipped coffee laced with sherry and just looked out the window. Quiet and alone, we whispered comments to each other about the letters we had exchanged during the summer. I told her how important all the "meaningful" parts had been to me and how they had kept me going. She answered all my comments with short phrases and just continued to sit and gaze out on my town as it slept. I could feel her getting closer to me by the minute. I looked up and kissed her. She made it a long and passionate kiss. I picked her up and carried her to my bed.

Still standing next to my bed and holding her in my arms I asked her to stay here that night. "Its up to you how close we get…physically…tonight…but I feel…this close…to you now…" She smiled, kissed me and snuggled her head into my shoulder. She got down and went to the bathroom while I changed the tape. We slept together that night, but I made no move to make love. I knew that I didn't have to work for something I felt confident would come on its own. Once again, I found that there is something about a college single bed that allows two young people enough room to sleep and dream unencumbered.

The next day started early with Belle's attempt at making breakfast. She had never developed the knack for cooking, especially under my apartment's primitive conditions with hardly any pots, pans or utensils. Half way through I took over to avoid the utter destruction of the remaining edible portion. We walked over to begin our Rush work on the house. Lunch would be the official start of house meals, so Belle and I helped Gladys open the kitchen for the year. With Gladys' smiles and Sammy's rib attack five minutes after meeting her; I knew that they liked her. It was a beautiful day and the house took shape quickly with the efforts of the members and their dates.

After dinner and the Rush Meeting, we would have one or another apartment party with everyone, couples and stag, invited. It was in these gatherings that all the new dates picked up both the house mythology and knowledge about the various house characters. Dimitri could often be heard spouting off about Communist politics and trying to recreate the atmosphere of the 18th Century French salon. Maybe the "Earls" would put on a Motown Blowout Preview or a thirty minute version of a night full of beer and dancing. These were just the preliminaries of the main event—Rush. Both Alex and Belle warmed and excelled in Rush work. Belle was at home in the mass reception, swirling groups of conversation and behind-the-scenes political intrigue. She was a marvel of being able to keep two separate conversations going; one of which she was trying to get a prospective Freshman to give us a House Date and the other merely occupying some DNAB. "Charming" was the precise adjective. Assisting Vicki, she became the consummate hostess. All the brothers, and quite a few of the Freshmen, were impressed and their expressions were those of appreciation if not admiration. It was obvious she was on her way to quickly becoming OTG.

Alex was considered to be a knock-out weapon for political offensives. In all the activities she would hold court in a corner chair with a complete ring of men standing around her as if they were her personal attendants. From time to time she would be asked to go over and talk to some Freshman in order to get their total, focused attention or, maybe, influence their decision in some manner. It was comical. She would go over and talk to some eighteen year-old who thought of himself as a stud—a couple flutters of her eyelashes and some direct eye contact during the conversation and he became a blithering kid; putty in her hands. Her smoldering sexuality, her self esteem and her quiet, almost moody disposition made Campbell an object of house adulation. Thoughts of those two together in bed would, and did, shake the foundations of many of the brothers' imaginations. I knew first-hand; their muffled sounds coming through the thin walls separating our two apartments the previous night had shaken mine. No one could quite understand the basis of their attraction. But, for me, it seemed easy to understand. Campbell was the true "Steppenwolf;" the loner who camped in the mountains during winter with only a few matches. He was the uncivilized warrior trapped in the wrong time, who refused to surrender to modernity. There was a level of pretense about living in the present world, but all who knew him saw it was merely a facade. He was deep and dangerous unlike most of the college student crowd. Women never stood a chance if he chose to center his attention on them. He was, and even in my present life, unique. I am sure Alex had never had one like him before and thus, even to this very popular girl, the attraction. Unlike me, he did not demand a future, only the present and that was only on his terms.

Belle and I had settled into an almost taken for granted type of love affair. After two days we were a "couple." By the third day she had moved out of her suitcase and into the empty drawers. Alex and Campbell were the next door neighbors and did much with us. It was close, easy and happy. After the third night Belle started to open herself a lot to me. Of course she felt obliged to catalog her previous serious love affairs, a subject that I dutifully listened to and instantly discarded from my thoughts. I didn't care or mind that she told me; "good" girls did that back then when they were becoming emotionally involved. She would ask me about what I thought about or felt about a situation or idea and we could, and would, carry the discussion for hours. She seemed to enjoy getting me started about the college or the town, maybe the mountains and listen to me go out of control with an emotional, if not an overly scholarly, soliloquy on History. If I tried to get her going, she would quickly turn the situation around and in minutes have me talking again. Campbell and Alexandra provided the needed social context for our relationship. With them we could be close and sociable as a couple. Since they, and we, didn't fit into the rest of the Macon Crew and having adjacent apartments we had the advantage of proximity; the four of us had already developed into a self-contained unit of college life with all its expected appearances. After Saturday's long post-Rush Date meeting, they had met us at the door of the apartment with coffee and brandy, ready to talk about the impact of the evening rather than the details. All of us talked—listening in between phrases as if all four of us could finish each other's sentences. Somehow college made us pack months of familiarity into a few days. Relationships would grow in hours where, on the outside, the same development would take weeks, months or years. After about a half hour, Alex took Campbell by the hand back to his apartment after telling us good night.

When we went back to Macon on Sunday it was as a new couple; as lovers. The year had started precisely as I had wanted, hoped and dreamed. Belle played to all my strong suits. She seemed to relish and enjoy my strain of emotional intellectualism, my anti-athleticism and even my anglophile tendencies. When I had told her my thoughts and feelings about the camp girls (though I never told her of my time with "Cindy") she was genuinely empathetic and snuggled me soothingly. Though it had been a tremendous start, I knew that Belle was a many faceted girl from a world in which I had no experience. She and "we" would demand more than one good weekend before I could count on her emotional commitment, not to mention devotion.

Rush week and the following Combo were great opening events of the year. As a Senior, I didn't get too involved in the Freshman once they pledged our house. We Seniors, though, enjoyed a new-found sense of community or fellowship among ourselves. Dimitri had suggested that we make the first Combo an "Earl" Review or a "50s Party," which met with general acclaim. It may have started out as a mocking gesture or joke, but almost immediately everyone got into the spirit and had a good time. It was great to see us together, having fun, almost as it had been at the start of our Sophomore year. Over the ensuing two years, the three groups had grown almost into entirely separate cliques. The middle was by far the least defined as it was the guys who didn't fit, to differing degrees, with the "Peer Group" or "Earls." As such, we were just groups of two and three guys each who spent most of their time together. Campbell and I were tight, with Cal as the loner who ranged between the "Earls" and us. Greg and Dimitri were comfortable with us, but tended to spend more time with the "Peer Group." There were several other Seniors, Juniors and Sophomores who sat in the middle with us, but it was an amorphous bunch of guys.

The "Earl" Review provided an interesting chance for me to survey the differences that had grown over two years. The "Earls," "Peer

Group" and those of us in the middle dressed and acted only a bit differently at the party, but the most apparent difference was our dates. If someone had put us in a room and asked if we belonged together, I think the answer would have been generally "yes." But, if someone had put our dates in a room and asked the same question; the result would have been a resounding "no!" The "Earls" had their painted, floozettes from Sem, the "Peer group" had their proto-hippies from various schools and we had our girls in the middle, mostly from Macon and Hollins. Beyond appearances, the personalities of the girls seemed to accentuate the differences all the more. It didn't matter much to us, for it was not for them to get along, but us. Our new Senior unity and party spirit made the evening work. Belle drank too much beer and started a "Earl" Line with Dan, while Alex lost her haughty, reserved exterior and started letting loose on the dance floor during the 50's numbers. The night ended with everyone doing a mass rendition of the Four Top's <u>Reach Out and I'll be there</u> and a memorable expedition to the old Lee-Hi truck-stop for fried cheese and onion sandwiches.

Belle and I were an established couple as far as the house went. Alone, we became as close as I could imagine a boy and a girl ever being. Even so, I knew there were limits. She was still intending to date the Veemie. She had explained late one night that he was still a part of her life, "not as intense...or as deep as you...but...just the same...a real part of my life." She had been dating him off and on since her Senior year in High School and throughout her years at Macon. He had taken her to her Senior prom when he had been a cadet at a boy's military school near to her home. I suspected that it was he to which she had surrendered her virginity during the summer after high school. His father was a business partner with her dad. Luckily for my sanity, and for us, she didn't dwell on him or their relationship at all. The only reason the subject had come up was my offhand question about what had become of the guy she dated last year. Her pronouncement bothered me, but did not take an overwhelmingly important position in our relationship. This was a girl who knew over 50 cousins and had friends galore. She was not going to hole up and become the social property of me, a loner, overnight; probably, (hopefully) never at all. Besides, I assumed that with her genteel background, our physical relationship was proof of, as yet unspoken, a very real romantic declaration.

Her social skills and her pre-eminence in that world were some of the reasons she attracted me. I was always on the sidelines of a group and she in the center. She opened the door to all those things to me. She was completely at ease among people, whether they were parents, teachers, "Earls," "Peer Groupers," Semies, or even the people we started meeting in our Sunday morning trips to services at Robert E. Lee Memorial Episcopal Church. Her management of the friendships between Alex and Campbell and, to a lesser extent, Cal and Susan brought a longed for sense of fullness to my social life in Lexington. Yet, she seemed always to return, and smilingly so, to just her and me, alone. Sitting in my apartment in our chair or in our bed late at night, she seemed to radiate a quiet enjoyment in what we did, said, and with whatever concerned us at the moment. We talked or, more accurately, I would talk for hours about people, books, feelings and philosophy. It was the "us" that she used to call "our Poet's Corner." Maybe it was her phrase or just the hard felt emotions of being a Senior, because I did, indeed, start to write poetry. Late at night during the week, when I would feel especially alone or just spiritually restless; I would open the living room window, grab my clipboard and start to put words to paper. Often I would write when I woke up early on a Saturday morning allowing Belle to sleep-in a bit. The results were embarrassing, but I enjoyed the attempts and reveled in the role. It was the finishing intellectual and emotional touch of the student existence that I enjoyed to no end.

School had developed into a tremendous, enlightening experience. I took the History Honors Seminar (I was proud to be invited), Napoleonic Era, Psych., Macro Economics, and a comparative Religion course. It was a life of reading, writing, thinking and arguing. Was there more to school? Could there be? My schedule was full mornings Monday through Friday and Thursday afternoon spent with R.O.T.C. Rangers. Most afternoons would find me reading till I worked in the kitchen for dinner. The Bridge games had died with Mickey's graduation; the table—once the center of the house, now used as a book drop or simply a place to lay jackets. After dinner I would study and, in accordance with tradition, break only at midnight for some time next door. Grades were not entirely outstanding, but I would get enough "A"s to be considered respectable by those in my major. Campbell was part of both History courses so the immersion was complete. It was hard to believe that there would be anything better than this; ever.

Belle balanced her time in our relationship well. She saw her Veemie on several of our off weekends; always letting me know well in advance when she would be "busy." She would not lie or try to cover, but it was so transparent to our relationship that I lost sight that she was seeing anyone else at all. It seemed our Wednesday night date before those weekends would always end up in her room for a stolen, passionate hour. I thought that it was her way of giving something for me to remember her by or to tide me over till the next weekend. Maybe it was to keep her mind settled as well. He became a kind of ghost—a presence that was known and could be reacted to, but seemed to have little to do with our reality.

Campbell and I didn't intend to go down the road every Wednesday, but it started to work out that way. Men were not allowed past the dating parlors during the week and only between 11:00 A.M. and 7:00 P.M. on the weekends. At first, we thought the dating parlors would suffice. After one close call where Alex (thank God it was her) barged in, through the chair not properly braced against the door, we were forced to find a better place to be alone. At Alex's intrusion, Belle had vainly struggled to pull her pants up past her knees while simultaneously attempting to pull her t-shirt down while her bra dangled out of one sleeve. I had dived behind the couch to find my shirt with my pants around my ankles. Alex's only comment was a laughing "I'm sorry…was I disturbing something?…oohh…this IS interesting…should I invite the others in as well?" The four of us put our minds to the problem and resolved to gain safety through utter audacity.

The rain gutter downspout in the rear corner of Wright Hall ran down the wall several inches from the frosted windows of the shower room on each floor. That corner was somewhat sheltered from full view by a couple of tall pines. Beth or Alex would open the window while the other stood guard at the door while we would use the downspout to walk up the wall four floors and into the window. As long as we were quiet and climbed quickly, no one would notice. It wasn't the sort of thing for which people would look. Once inside, it was easy to smuggle us down the hall to the appropriate rooms. Luckily for the entire enterprise, Alex and Belle both had singles. It was great fun for all involved to have some clandestine escapades which provided meaningful thrills to her knowledgeable, but not involved enough to be indicted, hall-mates. There were always some touchy moments when we would be discovered by some Freshman whose silence was not assured. For the most part, however; the girls accepted us as part of the hall. It was OTG in reverse.

We actually broke tradition several times by going to spend the weekend at Macon rather than bringing the girls up to Lexington. It was strange being on a deserted campus with maybe only a hundred or so of its usual 900 inhabitants around. Campbell and I had great fun as we became the communal hall "secrets" and thus, I think, added to both Alex and Belle's status and maybe spawned a dorm legend or two. No one doubted for a moment that Alex could have had a hand in these escapades, but it ran counter to the popular perception of Belle. She seemed to enjoy this new level and reputation for mischief and rebelliousness. We became honorary members of 4th floor of Wright to the extent that they put a label on an empty mirror and cabinet in the bathroom for us. I wonder how they explained the razor, shaving cream and the other noticeably male items to any of the non-initiates' questions.

Sometime in November before Thanksgiving the four of us were in someone else's room talking, as usual, on the edge of decency, along some ribald topic. Alex asserted that girls certainly outdid men for "personal sexuality" which was her term for masturbation. Campbell and I howled while Belle and the rest nervously joined in our laughter and series of comments. Alex continued that if the truth be known most of the girls probably had vibrators and used them regularly; which prompted Campbell to start humming. This was becoming quite brazen, even for us, to be conversing among eight or nine other girls. I suggested a contest. I thought I saw Campbell blush and Belle almost fainted. "No…I mean vibrator races…it works like this…Fran and I will go out…and be back in about…a half hour…you people…in the strictest of anonymity of course…come up with the vibrators…we'll race them…it'll be out-tasight!" With that, Campbell and I scampered down the spout for a run to the convenience store in the small shopping center close to the campus. When we returned, there were about five or six vibrators sitting on Alex's bed. While we made jokes about the probable owners and uses (one was about 10 inches long and black) we took the axles and wheels off the toy cars we had purchased. I attached them to the vibe's body using rubber bands around the axles. To this we added stickers with numbers that had come with the toy cars. Since the wheels were simply pressed on, they rotated freely on the stationary axles. When turned on, the vibrations propelled the newly manufactured "moto-vibes" down the hall. We all laughed as we had several races and obstacle events. I did the "play by play" commentary while Campbell judged results and determined competition classes. Between the uproar and the buzzing, we must have piqued the 3rd floor girls' curiosity. Suddenly we heard several girls raucously rushing up the stairs. Fran and I had just enough time to dive in one of the rooms behind a cover of girls rapidly trying to hide the vibes. We made it, but the girls didn't. What could any of them say with the numbered vibrators still on their way down the hall? Belle and Alex were left attempting to explain the spectacle to the outsiders. We spent a good hour under a bed in some Freshman's room till the coast was remotely clear. From then on, 4th floor Wright had a very peculiar reputation among the students of Randy Mac. (Months later we heard a more interesting version of the incident, told unknowingly to us, by one of the Macon Crew from West. The story was much more interesting than the reality, but such is the nature of legends.)

I had become serious as I found myself more than simply socially attached to Belle. I knew that I was in love. It was a "relationship" love, very close to that I thought I had with Beth, but more intense. This love was tied to a future. We had not talked of futures together or even had spoken the magic "L" word to each other, but I was sure about how I felt. The Wednesday before Thanksgiving I gave her a couple of poems I had been working on in secret for weeks.

Spirit's Quest

> Drifting veils of smoke soften music and words, as they caress our skin and minds.
>
> Together we strive, reaching for the night sky. Soaring with our senses we find climactic peace. Motionless in our velour explosion, we are lost within soft infinity.
>
> Wrapped in music's cloak, we return, bonded by sleep, bounded by reality.
>
> Rest to take the quest once more; only to take the quest once more.

and

Night

Darkness—save one low wicked glimmer.

Darkness—enveloping all but the ivory glow of lovers.

Cloaked in grey-black warmth we see, instead of look, behind our eyes and below our skin.

Touches, soft as loving words, search for our womb of peace together.

Communion, bounded by arms and infinity, leads gently to our goal.

Darkness within Darkness.

Darkness shrouds the blazing world till all there is—is us

Reading them, now, is painful. Both in respect to their form or content, but, most of all, for the almost silly youthful intensity they contain. But to me, then, they expressed to me, and hopefully to her, what our weekends were about. I realized that these were hardly the kind that she could put on her wall or show to her mother. Now, they embarrass me, but then, they were powerful statements of the emotional force she kindled within me. I had put them in a small binder I bought along with some pressed wild flower we had picked once during a walk near the ruins. I wrapped it all with a white hair ribbon. I will never know if she expected that sort of gift from me or not. I gave it to her about an hour before Campbell and I had to leave down the spout. She opened it slowly, saving the ribbon as she knew that I would want her to. She opened the folder, picked up the flower and softly touched it to her lips as she read. Slowly, she put the flower back and closed the poems. She just looked at me and said my name, almost as a plea. I leaned close and kissed her. As she returned my kiss, I picked her up and told her that I loved her. Looking straight into her eyes I repeated my statement, but in a kind of questioning, wondrous expression. I was getting into the scene. She melted and pulled me down upon her. The love we made was simple, direct and quiet. For the first time I thought that she was making love not just for fun or enjoying the naughtiness. No matter how involved she became she never slipped and said the words. I read them in her eyes, her touch, our love-making and her smile, but never did "I love you" pass from her lips.

Afterward, when I started thinking about how ominous the absence of her declaration was, I considered asking her. Seeing how much she smiled and how she never stopped touching me, I could not. It would break whatever magic the moment had brought us. This too, could be some kind of beginning. Campbell's soft double knock on the wall signaled the time to go. As we pulled on our gloves in the shower room, still steamy from some girl's shower, we got our goodbye kisses. It must have been a special night for both of us. Alex took forever to break her embrace with Fran; Belle seemed not to want to let go either. Finally, as Fran disappeared down the gutter, and it was my turn to go, I told her that I would be back in a week. She smiled, gave me one more kiss, and said "I know…and…I will miss you till then…" For her, this was as blatant as she had ever been in public. I thought that it was her way of saying what I wanted her to say.

Campbell's car "the muskrat" was cold for at least twenty minutes as we headed back to Lex. We talked of the coming vacation. We had decided not to go home for the holiday, but stay and eat Thanksgiving dinner with Cal. He was having Susan stay to meet the folks and we both figured that he wanted covering reinforcements. We had already planned to spend the four free days playing a war-game simulating WWII's entire Eastern Front on an eight foot square map of European Russia with separate counters for units as small as divisions. Thus, we would be immersed in History and battle, endless cigarettes and coffee; and the boy/man joy of workless, womanless play for 96 straight hours. While our parents might be a bit upset at our desire to stay in Lex; for us it was finally and probably the first vacation spent entirely for ourselves. I guess that both Fran and I suspected that it was probably the last time our lives would allow it to be that way.

The Thanksgiving feast at Cal's house was an experience. Both Campbell and I were welcome guests of about three times a year, so we were not strangers. Cal's father would hold court for the guys in the living room making sure that no one's glass would get empty as he talked about politics, hunting and, of course, the "modern state of affairs." He was no reactionary, but as the booze would get to him; he would become more and more philosophical. Campbell and I would merely talk along with his points and resist the temptation to be drawn into arguments whenever we could. Usually, Cal would be one of us, loud, lively and fully within the occasion. This time, however, Cal was useless. He was so nervous that all he could do was "Faddle" around. His tie was crooked, his shoes came untied and his hair wouldn't stay behind his ears. Susan was making points and becoming part of the family by helping his mom in the kitchen. Cal tried to divide his time between us and them with the result that neither effort was successful. His mom, never too organized, had dinner evolving from the kitchen and had carried on a multi-level conversation with Cal, Susan and the men in the front room. Cal's younger brothers wouldn't budge from the TV till dinner was called and on the table. All the disasters were small or at least still edible, and the meal tasted wonderful to Fran and me, who had been living on coffee, cigarettes and raw pancake batter for several days. It was a great night till the youngest brother, about seven years old, asked if Susan was going to be Cal's wife. Cal, "faddler" that he was, answered "well…I don't know…I guess…it depends on her…"

Fran almost died then and there. I practically jumped up to break any possible continuation of the conversation. Both he and I understood that Cal had inadvertently asked Susan to marry him. Fran and I quickly exchanged glances and he kicked Cal under the table so hard that he cried out in pain and looked at Fran. Both Fran and I used our fingers across our necks to tell Cal to cut it out. His mother and father were still confused, but staring at Susan, with his mother, almost frantically asking Cal what he meant. Cal started talking to her again and I, in desperation, started to speak in a squeaky falsetto voice "Oh Cal…I do, I do, I do. Just name the date." Fran and I would never be asked to the ceremony after this. Cal's father quieted everything down by getting up and asking if anyone needed another drink. He skipped Cal in his request. Susan just looked at Cal, with a loving smile and then with disgust at me and Fran. She never forgave us—ever.

On the way home we both beat Cal with our gloves (Susan was staying with his family, of course) telling him that he owed us his life. He was not to get married to anyone with whom he had not had sex—especially not one of the Macon Crew. Just because he was "faddling" around in love didn't give him the right to risk marriage without plenty of thought, sweat and real consideration of what the term "married" meant. Not that we did, of course, but at least we were sleeping with our girlfriends. He was properly thankful and bemoaned his innocence. If he only knew that both Alex and Belle had told Fran and me, individually, that they considered him very desirable and if they were dating him—they'd be in his bed—he would have died. There was something incredibly erotic about a 21 year old virgin that drew both of them undeniably. Maybe it was the knowledge that he would never use this attraction against them.

The time between Thanksgiving and Christmas break is a mad dash of papers, finals, parties and Senior Christmas Plans. Some of the rich guys took dates and went skiing in the Rockies or to fish and drink at Key West. Others would travel to parties in NYC for New Years or just bring a couple of friends and dates home. Campbell took Alex home to the ranch. I think that he would have asked us to come along, but I found out that his parents were in Europe and he wanted the ranch for himself and Alex alone. He was getting a bit strange when it came to Alex. She had lasted longer than anyone else and she even talked about going into the hills with him. He didn't stop her talking about that as he had done with other women. He didn't take us there! In his own way, I think he was in love. For Alex not to go home to her HTH, it was a blatant statement of her own emotions. Both Belle and I were happy to see them that way.

Belle asked me home to Christmas, but made it very clear that it would be full of friends and family which meant that we'd have very little time together. She explained that it was her job to help her mother take care of things and it would be one non-stop set of family functions. They always had a large family Christmas celebration and then hordes of people throughout the week till one big New Year's bash at the country club. All this frightened me a great deal. I told her that I wanted to spend some time with her, the girl I love. Once the ice had broken, I had lost no opportunity to tell her of my emotions though she had still resisted any answering declaration to my statement. She said being alone with her was not in the holiday cards, though she was hoping I would get some time to talk to her father. He had not been too pleased with me in September, and while she told me his opinion didn't bother her too much, it would be better if "he liked me more."

Great; a vacation of testing by lots of people I didn't know. When my mother asked me if I were coming home, I answered yes. Everything I could feel told me it was the wrong decision even though I had not been home for Thanksgiving and thus had a great excuse to head north. I just couldn't go to Georgia and weather the promised storms without some support from Belle and she had blatantly given me none. We got some time to talk about it the last weekend before finals, but not as much as we had hoped. Her sister Kelly had come up to visit her and we double-dated with one of the Freshman. There is nothing less romantic than an older sister mother-henning a younger sister at her first weekend Combo at W&L. Everything worked out fine except that Belle lived out of her suitcase, ignoring her clothes and personal items already in the drawers and slept with her sister in Randy's old bed. She had even put her "personal" stuff in a bag in the bathroom closet so that Kelly would not find it if she perchance opened the medicine cabinet over the sink. Belle did find time for a snuggle and snooze with me on Saturday afternoon while Kelly was out with her date, but it was bothersome to me for her to renounce our relationship in front of her sister. It wasn't like it was her whole family.

When I brought it up to her she reacted sharply. "What am I supposed to do? Just tell her I sleep with you?…"

"Well…yes…I mean…are you ashamed…Hell we're 20 and 21…I mean…do you really think she thinks we don't?"

"Of course she thinks we don't!" She continued to explain that her sister would die if she thought we were having sex (she never called it making love). I think that girls of that period put mothers and younger sisters into the "she still thinks I'm a good girl" group and thus needed to act the part. I had other ideas and thought Kelly was a lot more in tune to what was happening than she thought. Belle told me that I didn't understand her family, how they thought, or what they expected of her and her sister. It wasn't the same as with Alex or the other girls who could be more honest and open with their parents. Her's still lived in the world where she was a "virgin till marriage and would get properly married to a proper young man." These were ominous words causing me no end of worrisome thoughts.

I recognized that one could never be totally honest with your parents. They expected at least a nominal effort at appearing to live by society's rules. I remember my mom's reaction to me talking to Belle who was in my apartment when my mother called me on my 21st birthday. Luckily, I could say that Belle was there for a birthday party and that was the reason she was there on a week-night. It was almost the truth. But, there was something more important in all this, which intensely bothered me. Slowly it began to take shape that I was not the "proper young man" her heritage expected. I started to sense that my visit to her house for Christmas was somewhat of a test to see if I fit in, if I could make it in her world; with her family. When I asked her if she wanted me to come and tell my family that I wouldn't be home; that I could do it if she wanted me to; that I would if it would make a difference to her; she said "no…It isn't all that big a deal…and we wouldn't get any time together alone…and I know…how…grumpy that makes you feel." My thoughts brightened when I saw her face when I gave her my Christmas gift of a carved white ivory rose on a gold chain. She gave me a leather bound set of Freeman's Life of Robert E Lee.

It wasn't a completely relaxing drive home through the snow. Somewhere in Pennsylvania there is always a blizzard, or at least the threat of one, making the drive home miserable. That time, the ten hour drive became fourteen and my nerves were shot. I had kept myself awake, if not focused, by considering the various options and decisions I made or could have made with Belle. I knew that it was an act of supreme foolishness, maybe of cowardice, to let her go home without me. Maybe I thought that it would be a test that she had to have me pass. If so, I had refused and tested her commitment, albeit a silent one, to the love we made. On Christmas day I called her and at the end of the conversation I told her that I loved her and she answered "I know and it makes me glad." That was as blatant as she ever got, maybe I was winning.

The Wednesday we returned, Campbell, Greg and I headed down to Macon and found our dates up for an adventure. There was a legend that there was a statue at Sweet Briar College, hidden in the woods, which screamed on nights with a full moon. We had all heard the story about the daughter of the man who had founded the school who had been raped by Negroes. After the child's birth, the girl had done the honorable thing by killing the child before committing suicide. He had founded the school as her memorial and erected a statue to her in some secluded glade. The statue was a shrine to the local Klan and was said to scream (as she had during the attack) when the full moon shone on her face. Now, I know both the legend and the statue are myth, but, then, none of us could resist. We thought it a proper legend; the moon was full and we had to find the statue. Six people in Greg's Mercury were a tight fit, but better than my Toyota or Campbell's Muskrat. I had wanted some time alone with Belle, but settled for this group activity instead. She seemed to be treating me fine, almost better than before, so I grew comfortable that our relationship had survived the holidays apart. On the way to Amherst, Virginia, Vicki told ever increasingly bizarre aspects of the tale we had only known glimmers of before. It seems that Vicki had wanted to find this statue and had been asking around.

Back behind the main group of yellow buildings at Sweet Briar, there is a road that leads to the stables. We could think of no more sacred place at that school than the stables, so we headed down toward the long, low barns nestled in the dark Virginia woods. Behind the last, there was a bridle path that looked fairly well traveled leading off into the woods in a completely different direction from all the others. We could smell adventure as we crawled down the path in the car. It had started to rain hard and we could hardly see. All at once the path ran down an embankment almost off a cliff. The car started to skid down the mud in ever widening circles. The girls screamed and I wondered if this were going to make the papers. We heard a bang, felt a thud and then the car suddenly stopped.

When Vicki opened her front door there was no ground under it. The car had slid sideways, knocked over a post, and was balanced precariously on the edge of a stream. A bridge held the front bumper and the post we had knocked over was holding the rear wheel. There was three feet of air, water and mud beneath the rest. Greg volunteered to stay with the girls, of course, while Fran and I would go off to find help. The walk back was spooky, wet and cold. Between us we had only three cigarettes, two matches, two quarters and a dime. Hopefully, there was a pay phone at the stables and an all night tow truck that wouldn't mind coming all the way out to wherever we were, to get us out of the jam. It took us more than half an hour to make the stables. They seemed to be deserted, but we figured with all the valuable horseflesh quartered there, it was a safe bet that there was a security rent-a-cop around somewhere. Sure enough as soon as we got under the awning and lit our cigarettes a voice boomed out of the darkness "Can I help you boys?"

Startled we just stood there nervously looking around. Finally, I answered "Yes. Yes, actually you can." We still did not see where the voice had come from. With the storm wind and rain, it was an incredibly eerie feeling of being watched by some unseen man. But the fact that we'd answered probably startled him as much as us.

"I'll bet you're in that car that headed down the ol' path a while back. Shooot, what're ya'll lookin for…the statue?"

Campbell just looked at me and then in the direction of the unseen voice. "Well…I guess…yeah"

Suddenly a man stepped out of the shadows about ten feet from where we were huddled. He was laughing and started to relate how every so often students come up here looking for the "Screaming Statue" and get lost or stuck or both. We just looked sheepish and agreed. Campbell told him that we wanted to use a phone to get a tow truck. The man howled and asked us if we thought we could get a truck out here on a night like this one. Both of us looked at each other feeling dejected and lost; the man was right. We would just have to hike out and do the best we could till morning. We turned to walk back to the car. "Ya know, I could probably help you with the tractor…if it were worth my while." I pulled out my wallet where I had stashed the $20 dollars that my mother had sent me for spending money. Campbell got his out and emptied the two $10s and a $5. "That'll do…wait a minute." The man took our money, put on a rain coat and grabbed some keys from the wall. All this was accomplished in the semidarkness and we still had not seen the man with whom we had been speaking. In the darkness we heard an engine turn over which spared us from the dual embarrassment of being not only stuck, but also taken by some invisible con-man. He loaded a length of chain on the old fashioned farm tractor and started down the path. We ran along side almost falling several times in the mud. He stopped and told us to ride on the rear and hold on to the seat. At the car he asked the girls to get out and, still talking and laughing to himself, fastened one end of the chain to the rear of the car. With the tractor slowly churning in the mud, he pulled the car back to the edge of the ditch and to safety. He showed us where we could safely cross the path to the other side and followed us to make sure we got on it safely. Once back to the road I jumped out to tell the man we would leave and to thank him. All he said was to check with him next time and he would show us where the statue was. I didn't think that we would return but assured him that, if we did, we would take his advice.

Wet, muddy and tired, we returned to Macon very late at night. It was too late to go back to Lex so we stole into the dorms with the girls. It was very strange to spend the night with Belle in her bed in the midst of hundreds of girls. It felt somewhat foreign and eerie. Belle softly kissed me as she left for class. I had watched her dress through slit eyes. Watching her without her knowledge made me feel incredibly close. By nine, Campbell and I were the only ones left in the hall. We headed to the shower, washed and shaved. We figured that we had to be out by ten or so before the cleaning crew arrived. Dressed, we both left notes and got down the drain figuring we would meet Greg in the Skeller. Sure enough, Greg was there with his own tale of how he had to sneak down the stairs past the dorm matron because the shower window had been painted shut. Unanimously, we agreed that the adventure was worth our missed classes.

The following weekend was one of my weekends off from Belle; although not by choice. There was a concert at VMI, so I figured she was there. I walked past their field house while the concert was on hoping to catch a glimpse of her and her Veemie date. More than ever, I knew that I wanted Belle for a future. I didn't know how I could make her past fit well into my future, as much of it as I could then determine, but I would try. The army was a start and after it we would have been on our own long enough, with enough "us" experiences to compete with her heritage. Hell, there was law school, or business school, something would turn up from which I could make a living. But, how would I get that far? That night, walking past the field house with music rolling out, I felt far from confident about Belle and me. I would press her for an answer; the best defense was the audacious offense. With all that we were together, how could she resist? Being alone without her on a weekend was miserable. I walked alone that night for hours trying to plan the assault on her noncommittal position.

I was doubly alone that weekend for Campbell had taken Alex up on her offer to go into the mountains with him. Cal and I had dropped them off at one of the exits off the closed Blue-Ridge Parkway and watched them slowly walk through the snow into the mountain forest. It would be no picnic. Cal and I discussed what would happen. Alex was too strong to whine or bitch, but could she face the stoic competition with death that Campbell had told us about upon each return? We hoped that the weather stayed clear and did not snow or, worse, rain. More important, we both knew that Alex was invading the inner sanctuary of Campbell's world. He must have loved her to a degree of which we had not known him capable. To let her accompany him after the thoroughly negative experience the year before must have been an act of love. Could she stay there with him and not destroy whatever emotional tie they had? Neither of us thought this had been the best idea for either Fran or Alex. Campbell was strange about his mountains and Cal worried that when we came back up on Sunday night there would be bad news waiting for us.

As it turned out, we had to wait an hour past the agreed upon time. Cal and I had stopped honking the horn and started idly talking through emergency plans of action when Campbell and Alex trotted down the path toward the car. Campbell was just ahead of Alex and neither was smiling. Campbell walked past us and announced "Rupert Peen returns to civilization—and a bath—bringing news of wondrous discoveries and unheard of adventures from the lost worlds." Neither Cal nor I were sure what he meant by what was surely a parody of a 30s newsreel broadcast. Alex looked okay, frozen, but had a smile for us as we shuffled her into the car. Cal and I started talking at once about why they were late, asking what happened and "how was it?" Alex answered that they had left camp late and had to push the pace to make it as soon as they had. We headed directly to Lynchburg taking Alex back to school. She was all talkative about how they had camped on a mountain top under only a tarp and watched their small fire till dawn. She was excited and told of the animals they had seen, the silence of a winter forest and the stark beauty of dawn on the frozen Blue Ridge. Campbell was silent except for monosyllable grunts he used to answer our direct questions. He fell asleep on the way back to Lex.

It was not unusual for Campbell to be quiet about his backpacking adventures, but we were sure that we would hear stories of Alex. There were none and he declined to go down the road on Wednesday. As I left the dorm with Belle heading toward the Library, Alex asked me about Campbell. Campbell had not called her since she had been dropped off from the mountain trip. I told her that I didn't know, but I would try to find out. He never did tell any of us what happened in the mountains or at the ranch over Christmas vacation. He never talked to her or even about her again. I knew that it was over when he didn't invite her down to the Combo the next weekend. He was strange with girls and though Alex was hurt, I knew that something in him had snapped and something about her had ended any capability for the relationship to exist. He never told me and, as far as I know, he never told Cal or Barry why he dumped her or what had happened. Such is the manner of Immortal Viking Gods. He spent the weekend bent over a map of the Austerlitz battlefield wiping out regiment after regiment of ill led Austrians and Russians besting Napoleon's record of victory.

That was, of course, all secondary to the weekend's purpose. I was out to ask Belle where she stood. I smiled on the way down to Lynchburg for I had planned and thought through things as far as anyone reasonably could. Orchestration was one of my long suits. Friday, I cooked dinner for her alone in the apartment with cheap champagne, mushrooms and everything. I even tried to subdue my "I love you"s to put her at ease. We made love till late in the night and then watched the town through the frost glazed window above my bed wrapped in my electric blanket in our dark apartment. I gave her one of my new poems when we were about to drift to sleep.

Before Dreams

The night is still and our breath has slowed. I smile and ponder, lying here by your side, feeling your heart upon mine.
Before my eyes close in a satiated sleep, the communion of our souls warms my mind. Together, in sweat, purpose and goal, we shared passion, words and life.

The dawn will rise soon and color the sky. We, too, shall rise to meet the world, to pay its price—to follow its paths. Alone, separate, in my sunlit existence,
Your smile will remain, warm in my heart. The velvet of your soft caresses will yet soothe my skin and nourish my soul.

Neither time nor miles will be distance. There is no space—for you and I—are us.

It probably could have used a couple of weeks more work, but it did its duty. After reading it, she let it slip from her hands as she embraced me to make love, again; not acts of erotic passion, but ones of intense feeling. We spent Saturday studying, laughing at Sammy in the kitchen and at a "Peer Group" pre-Combo party at the Spook House. The Combo was great, but both of us missed our next door neighbors and remarked to one another that we had to try to get them back together again, soon. The night ended with us exhausted after a Truck-stop run, falling into bed, in each other's arms, but not having the strength to make love even one more time. Somehow it was closer without it, just to touch and drift to sleep.

After church and lunch at the house, but before we had to head toward Lynchburg, we sat in the apartment and read the paper. It was then that I started the planned conversation with a smile, and an "I love you, you know." She looked up, smiled and reached for my hand to give it a squeeze. "How come you have not said the dreaded L word?" I tried to make this light enough for her to ease into the statement without much soul wrenching thought. She continued to hold my hand, but looked at me as if to see if I were joking. I switched into a fervent, ardent manner and continued "I can't stand how much I love you…I want this weekend…with you…forever…(I was getting carried away with my hormones)…you are my dreams…my <u>Nights in White Satin</u>…"

She let my hand go and slowly reached to touch the side of my face. "You know that I…DO…love you…" I smiled and exhaled and was about to wrap my arms around her when she went on. "But…you know…it's not a forever…thing…I mean…here…with you…it's so special…so real…but not forever…no…I can't…never have been able to explain it…to me or to you." Her face was soft and hurt, like she had just been forced to say something painful or ugly.

"Why…what have I done…how am I…or do I…fail…how do I not measure up?"

"It's not that…you've done nothing wrong!" She sat up, away from me and looked serious; her face losing the tenderness that it had contained a moment before. "Its just that you and I…we're for right now…I mean…do you…or me, when I am with you here…think that it fits with my family…with what I am going to be…with what I have to be…have always wanted to be…" She was not letting me answer, but was not mad or angry just serious and urgent. "It's beautiful here with you and I love it here, but it's not for next year or graduation or life…or…marriage…or children…"

"Those things are all for your past…your future…your Vee-mie…right?…Someone like dad…at the firm and the club…maybe even votes liberal as long as it is not generally known!…What about us?…What about the love we make?…How can you say this when…I know how you look when we are making love…how can you be with me and…" My face had hardened and was moving toward anger.

She touched the side of my face with a tenderness I had grown to love. "You make it sound so…harsh and…wrong. Like I am some sort of shrew or gold digger…or socialite queen." She was almost crying now. She quickly reached back to my face after wiping away one large tear drop coming down her cheek, its predecessor having fallen to her jeans. I had watched that tear throughout length of its entire journey. It was as if the tear-drop was me and the chances for our life together in love. I knew that it was over, but it hurt so badly inside of me—I didn't want to let us go. I wanted this girl, who had allowed me such happiness; who inspired such bad poetry; who could captivate me physically; and could be moved by me into incredible feats of passion herself. She saw all this in my eyes and spoke in small whispering sobs. "You…you…will always be inside of me…you'll be the smile in my eye when I listen to our songs…you'll be the romance…that I'll never tell my daughter about…but hopes she has…" Hearing the orchestration of those words assured me I wasn't the only one who had planned a conversation.

"But I'll never be her father…is that it?…No, I'll never fit the way you were supposed to be…never an adult with you.…But look how you are…how you feel…now. Think of the look in your eyes when we make love…you know that you love me." I was playing desperation hard-ball now. I knew that to attack the Veemie was to lose instantly. He was dad and home, past and future. He was the planned orderly life that was what she had been raised to have, in which to believe and of which to dream. She had to want to leave. I thought that she did, but now understood that she wouldn't let herself leave him, and all that he was, real or imagined, to join me.

"No…I DO love you…but I wish to god I could be IN love with you (there was that dreaded ambivalent verbiage again)…the way I know that you love me…It rips me apart when you say it….You and I…we…are something I don't understand and wouldn't give up for a million dollars, but its not forever…it's not a life I could live…could love…and I know that….I…can't feel for you what you want me to feel…what you say you feel for me…it's just…not IN me….Please don't hate me…" She was crying now, but completely in control and serious. I wanted her to collapse in my arms. Instead, I admitted the effort's failure (and thus the year's) and brought her to me in my arms. Her head was on my shoulder. Perhaps it was better that she not see the defeat, the hurt in my face. Then and there I told myself that I had known this all along. Inside, I chuckled that I had the same conversation a year ago with Beth, only with reversed roles.

"What goes around…comes around." She looked up at my muttering comment and asked what I had said. "Nothing…but…this doesn't mean that I love you any less…" The scene ended well with our lying together, for at least an hour, her crying till we made silent love again, both thinking that it was for the last time. When she left with me for the trip back to Lynchburg I knew that she was moving out. She didn't take all her things, but most of them, the important stuff anyway. She didn't think I had noticed. How could I not? It would never be the same if I did bring her back; if she'd come back.

When I kissed her at the dorm door and turned, I walked past my car and up to Main hall. From there I looked back at the whole residential side of the campus. There was West and Wright; behind them the dell and the Pines; all important parts of my college life or at least those not at W&L. I lit a cigarette and looked at it never thinking that I would see the campus again. I would finish out the year, but it would not be the same as I had planned or dreamed. I looked up at 4th floor Wright and saw a girl standing in the hall window. It was dark and I could not tell if it was Belle, but I hoped it was. I took a drag off my cigarette, dropped it and snuffed it out with my shoe. I walked quickly to my car hoping that she had not seen all the same movies I had and she would think my exit was original; at least it felt genuine.

Getting home, I found Campbell starting to set up a recreation of Fontenoy. With me the British and he the Frogs, we played till dawn and in a miracle (he was a god at these games) I managed a draw. The Brits had put up a spirited attack, the Guards and Scots had never taken so many Frogs down with them in such a glorious defeat. Their valor and bravery, along with my audacity and unconcern at taking perilous casualties kept the Frogs from winning. I don't think that we traded ten words in five hours, but we both knew that the British gamble had not paid off—not with victory, anyway.

CHAPTER 11

*T*he Shenandoah January seemed the perfect backdrop to my mood after the split with Belle. Constant overcast, drizzle most every day and a cold, damp wind dominated Lexington and my thoughts. To lose the battle for her heart was the closing argument on the year which was only half finished. I thought, at first, I would throw myself into my work. Although the idea was romantic enough, I could still study and get things accomplished without the scholastic efforts diminishing my thoughts of her. I tried writing; but the poems did not improve in quality and did nothing to lift my spirits or bring me back to any level of optimism. After the first several days, the guys next door asked me what was wrong. When I told them that I had broken with Belle, they commiserated, but left it at that. From their prospective there was little else to be done. This happened from time to time and they figured I could find another date from some other school to round out the year.

It was impossible to communicate all of what Belle had meant to me. She was more than physically exciting; she was "wife-able," yet still an interesting date. She had not been merely a girl or a date at all; because she embodied all the physical, emotional and intellectual aspects for which I searched. Belle became almost a concept rather than a person. Being the Significant College Romance of one's Senior Year had evolved her into a kind of pinnacle of romantic dating endeavor. To lose and to lose to a Veemie combined with some image of respectability was an almost unthinkable fate.

I continued my depression. In many ways, the role of the tragic, romantic casualty fit well into my thoughts and fantasies. I took night walks around Lexington in my black riding cloak (It was a dyed VMI uniform cloak that a friend of Beth's had given to me after her romance with a Veemie had died). Belle was right and had done the proper thing. More often than not I would spend the last half hour in the darkened sanctuary of the Robert E. Lee Memorial Episcopal Church before returning to my empty apartment. There I would sit, consider my plight, and brood about the deep sense of failure that pervaded my social life. But to be sitting in the darkened sanctuary of a huge Episcopal church, a church that had been our church, was a great scene and fit my sense of the theatric. I was careful, however, to keep these private actions hidden from almost the entire public, including the house. I went about my school and house duties as usual, but with a somewhat dispirited air about me.

Campbell never talked about women and, having summarily dumped Alex at almost the same time, he probably didn't have much sympathy for my situation. I think that he tried to be a true friend to me by spending more time than usual talking about history during our study breaks. Very late at night he would knock on my door (it had been almost always the reverse), ostensibly come in to get a cup of coffee and stay for a couple of hours talking about or playing the simulation of the Korean War, one of Napoleon's campaigns, or one of Wellington's battles. This was his way of trying to help me with the hurt. Thank god the Robert E. Lee Hotel was open all night when our supplies of Camels or Lucky Strikes would run out. It would take this two-block walk, late at night, to bring us back around to reality.

Maybe it was just our house, or just the guys I hung out with, but we seldom talked intimately about our dates or the emotions we went through. Appearances were one thing, but the reality of what was happening inside a relationship was quite another. It was all very private. During the course of a conversation, one might theorize about someone else, but never about yourself. Belle became my constant internal topic of conversation while I played a rather subdued, but altogether coherent, college kid to the rest of the world. The biggest clue to my condition was my reluctance to date after the break and my increasingly frequent stops by the dope den, now a tradition on the Sophomore hall at the house.

After Fazer had left the house, there was little reason to keep those who wanted to "party" from partying in their rooms, provided they not get completely out of hand. None of the Sophomores studied in the house anymore. The only guys who would stay on the top floor between the news and midnight were those who wanted to listen to music, throw the bull and smoke dope in the den. The den was our name for one of the Sophomore's rooms where partying was the constant event. The guy living in the place made most of his spending money selling marijuana and spent most of his time consuming it. We never thought of him as a pusher or a dope-fiend however, just a guy with good connections. When you sold small amounts to friends and fraternity brothers and didn't cheat on weight or gouge the price, the consensus was you weren't an actual pusher; frankly, we considered it a service. Most of his business was from brothers who felt obligated to buy some dope after smoking his for free. If he could stay in school wrapped within his green fog, so much the better for him. Most of the non-"Peer Group" thought of him as reasonably unbalanced, but not overtly negative or dangerous in any way.

All that had to be done was; walk into the den, sit down and listen to some of his Santana or Pink Floyd albums played at an incredibly high volume. After about fifteen minutes, he couldn't stand being straight and would offer to roll a J for the both of you. This meant that by 10:00 P.M. there were usually three to five stoned brothers (the hard core members of the "Peer Group") in the corner room on the Sophomore floor of the house. The first time I had stopped in, earlier in the year, I had only taken a couple of hits and gone down stairs to watch TV. Everybody knew that I was the kitchen steward and carried a set of keys for the pantry. Usually I put out a loaf of bread, a jar of peanut butter and one of jelly to provide after dinner snacks for the brothers. Everyone knew, however, the keys would unlock the rumored and, mostly mythical, treasures of cookies, graham crackers and the like supposedly stored in the pantry. The brothers in the den had probably been talking about some food foray for a while after I had left. Finally, they must have worked up the emotional courage and physical coordination necessary to find the top of the stairs and begin their chant of "Freaks want FOOD…FREAKS WANT FOOOOOD!"

It took the crispy critters a good ten minutes to make it to the bottom of the stairs and the door to the Chapter Room. All through the process they had kept their chant the same except for increasing its volume and tempo. All at once they burst into the room, picked me up bodily and carried me off to the kitchen. I could have successfully resisted their rather inept and uncoordinated attack, but I was having too much fun and laughing too hard. They grabbed the keys and stole about four bags of "Chips Ahoy" that I had stashed in the back of the pantry. From then on, if I came over to the house at night, the freaks could be counted on to begin their stoned food chant. I did, however, devise a suitable type of vengeance. Instead of cookies, I bought individually wrapped cream filled sugar wafers. While these tasted great, it took a level of manual dexterity that was hard to attain for the blitzed brothers. To me, frustrated freaks were funnier than hungry ones.

After Belle, I would find myself there Wednesday, Friday and dateless Saturdays. Finishing my studying early, I came and soared with the music. Between the tunes and the drugs, I found a refuge from thoughts of Belle. A couple of hours there, late at night, could make it easier to sleep and was my best relief from the sense of loss and failure. It became one additional facet of the tragic hero facade. In reality, I knew that I was just having fun and did not consider it at all dangerous to lose the pain once in a while. I was hardly the type to become a "DCY" in the second semester of my Senior year.

It was Saturday night of the third week from our parting, an off weekend. I had spent a little time with the "Peer Group" in the den and had walked home in the night's bitterly cold mist. I wasn't really stoned, but pleasantly buzzed as I carefully climbed the apartment's stairs, eventually got the door open to my apartment, turned on the tape, and proceeded to make my self some tea. The streetlights provided enough light to see my way around the apartment and I didn't want to disturb the aura of the emptiness by switching any lights on. Waiting for the kettle to whistle, in that condition, can be excruciatingly frustrating. It seemed to take hours. I sat down in my observation chair, now placed permanently facing the window, to watch and smoke till the water was ready. This was one of my favorite pastimes, especially when stoned. It gave me the sensation of observing people's lives unawares; as Jimmy Stewart did in Alfred Hitchcock's <u>Rear Window</u>.

That night I noticed a girl coming down the street alone (which was strange). Presently, she stopped in front of the "Pit" (the lyric theater) across the street from the apartment to find some shelter under its overhang. While I had thought, or guessed, it might have been Belle by her silhouette and the way she walked; it was only under the "Pit's" lights that I became sure. My pulse started to pound and my breath came in gasps. She stood there for a moment and looked at my dark windows. Quickly, I got up, raced to the kitchen and turned the light on. I bounded to the bed in order to peer out of the side of the curtain so I could observe and not be seen. She must have been watching for some sign of life because she immediately crossed the street and started up the stairs. She knocked at the door just as the kettle whistled. My heart started to do somersaults and I prayed that, even in my slightly altered state, I could carry off whatever would be expected of me. I ran to the stove, grabbed the kettle and rushed into the living room. I opened the door only to find her, hand raised in mid-knock, looking at me with a startled expression. We stood that way and stared at each other for what seemed to me to be at least a decade, but was probably three to five seconds. My throat was dry from fear and my mind cloudy from the activities of the den. All I could manage was a week "Tea?"

"Whaa (?)...oh...yes...I mean...I'd love some." Her face thawed into a smile, then a giggle as she came into the living room behind my still steaming teapot and shed her coat on the couch. I turned and continued full speed to the kitchen with the kettle still trailing steam behind me. There, I rinsed out two mugs (I hadn't done dishes since she left), fixed the tea, and looked for some sherry with which to spike it. During all this activity, I frantically thought of what I could say that would make this girl mine again. But nothing came. Hell, I didn't even know what this was all about, no less what should I say? I knew that she wanted me to say something first to relieve the pressure on her. Returning, I took the noncommittal approach. I handed her the tea and asked her what she wanted to listen to. The tactical me (a bit groggy—but sobering fast) thought highly of that question. It would indicate precisely what mood she was in.

"Oh, anything." Foiled again. I put on Mary Travers' <u>Mary</u> which fit my mood; sensitive, romantic and hopeful, but sung with a bit of a mournful voice. After all, if she were merely returning for her things, she would have come during the day or sent word through someone on the Macon Crew. There was something else in her visit and it might work out to be good; maybe all was not lost after all. I tried to not let my hope race ahead of my tactical sense. I sat down in a chair facing her on the couch. She was beautiful. Perfect, in her jeans and her button down shirt, unwrapped from her London Fog. Conservative, yes, but beautiful all the same. A moment of two of silence and I couldn't take it anymore. "Ok...I...'ll bite...why did you...come tonight.... I thought..."

"I wanted to see you…" Though she had cut into my sentence, she left hers open for a long, thoughtful pause. "…I…missed…you…and our talks and stuff. I wanted to make sure you were okay and…" Throughout her words, she had started to smile; that soft wondrous smile that I believed, then, was reserved for me alone.

I wasn't buying it. "And what?" I had lost all the philosophically soft romanticism in my voice. I had not yet attained anger, but could have done so quickly. I tried to keep my face as neutral as possible. If she were here to gloat in sham concern or to bring a happy face to my pity party, she had another thing coming.

"and missed YOU that's what!…You know…what I said…was true don't you?…you know that we have no future…that we could never have had…don't you?" She looked away as she uttered the last phrase and was almost argumentative in her tone. She was making a point and wanted to be sure I understood it.

From the weeks of mulling everything over and, yes, really, from the clues I had before that, I knew she was right. I didn't ride: I didn't play golf: I didn't have a big southern family and the heritage or money or country clubs or anything about me that really would have made me fit in. I didn't even have an overwhelming ambition to be a great, successful attorney or businessman which would have soothed much of this over. Heck I didn't know what I wanted to do. I would have been the poor guy married into the moneyed family—not exactly any girls dream. I softened, not just my eyes and face, but my voice as well. "I know that I…I love you…I know that if that love…means anything…it means that I must…acknowledge and…understand…even if you…don't…include me in your life…" There, I had said it. It was tactically sound, romantically tragic and all that, but it also happened to be true. Rationally, I knew that you could not trap or force fit someone into a future with any hope of finding happiness. I knew, perhaps had always known, that she would have to change her whole life's plan and outlook if we took our chance at a future. Emotionally, it had all the makings for a splendid, romantic martyrdom, but not a solid future. Maybe that was why my love for her was so strong: tragedy seemed to breed ardor. She looked at me with an unflinching, stony expression as if she were trying to figure out if what I said were true and, if so, make some decision. I sipped my tea. She put her's down.

She stood. Quickly crossing the step to my chair, she dropped to her knees so that she could put her head in my lap. "I missed you…so…so very much…" She looked up at me as I put my tea down. "We can't change what we are…but…we can…we can have this…time…together." Two things hit me immediately. First, was that if I didn't push the forever stuff and lived within some set of guidelines, which I expected would be explained later, but in reality were pretty self-evident, she was back here to be my lover. Second, I was proud of her preparation, in a sense, her staging. This whole thing had taken a lot of thought on her part. She had probably practiced that line as much as the daughter piece at the end of our last scene. Probably closer to the truth, she came to most of what she said spontaneously, from genuine emotion and didn't have to engineer her conversations as I found necessary for mine. She was better than me at this stuff. There was really never any decision to be made. I loved her and wanted her and she would be gone if I held myself to a more honest relationship. Maybe there was still a chance. I looked down, put on my "healing, tragic lover" expression and kissed her lightly on the lips and both eyes. She started to murmur things I could not, and did not, want to understand and rose to kiss me in return. The night was one in which, though wordless, I tried to communicate the depth of my hope and love for her.

My alarm clock woke me from my state of semi-unconsciousness at 8:00 A.M. I couldn't understand it since it was Sunday, which meant that I didn't have to get up and I knew that Belle always slept late. This morning of all mornings, I knew that she had cause, incredibly just cause, to be tired. I would not have been surprised if she had not been able to walk, no less wake up. We wouldn't be going to church, that's for sure. But up she was and had rushed to the bathroom where I heard the shower start almost as soon as she closed the door.

I started the coffee and, while she showered, started to talk to her trying to determine what the conditions were bounding our new found relationship. First, I asked her if she wanted breakfast and then if she at least wanted coffee. She peeked out of the curtain, smiled widely, said that coffee sounded heavenly, kissed me wetly and went back to washing her hair. Well, at least she was happy. As she stepped out of the shower she blew me a kiss and started hurriedly to dress. I loved to watch her dress; it made me feel so much at home in the relationship. She told me that she was in a hurry. Handing her the coffee, I inquired about the rush. She drank the coffee and stepped into the kitchen to where I was standing. Putting the cup down, she seemed to gird herself for some coming pronouncement. Whatever it was, the joy and truth we had shared last night had been worth it and made me feel, whatever the price, would be worth it again. She forced out that she was meeting the Veemie at Church. I was expecting something like that, so there was no change in the emotion shown on my face. She said that she didn't know why or what was going on inside her, or why she would act the way she did last night, or if she would in the future—but I was too big a part of her to let drop as we had a few weeks prior. Her face hardened to a scared look—not of me, but more of herself or her words—almost a stony stare. There was no hint of a smile or anything happy. "You realize that I am going to marry him."

"Yes" I lied. I hadn't realized that their romance had gone that far or that she had made that level of decision about him. I kept myself neutral, totally blank waiting for her to show me where she was going with this line of thought.

"I love him…I really do…but…there's…a part of me that wants to come here, too…to find some sort of sanity and to share…what we have and what we do…with you." She walked past me into the bathroom and started brushing her hair in the mirror. "Here is where I am…here is the us I enjoy" She looked at me and smiled because she knew I was staring at her and listening to every word. "Here is where you are and where we…are just us." She went back to brushing. "So, I'd like to come back…if you will have me…don't think that its…anything…but…anything but the time together it is…for some damn reason (she never swore) I want to be here with you…but I can't leave him either…can you understand that?…"

Coffee cup held against my chest, just my jeans on, I was still staring, knowing her words were saying we were having something adults would call an affair—something I'd never even considered possible in my stage of life. "I guess…I'll…have to." My response had been little more than a whisper for we didn't even need the words; she had known the answer before she uttered her question. My eyes had been locked on her since the beginning of her speech. What she had told me was that I could be her secret lover; her egotistical, romantic and utterly naughty fling; as long as I lived within the bounds of her rules. I guessed then, that the rules would be that after the Veemie dropped her off at wherever she was staying, she would walk over to my apartment, then simply meet him wherever they had arranged the next day. (It wasn't all that different than picking up the girls at VMI's gate at 11:00) Though the sexes were switched, this was right out of the 19th Century. I looked at my watch and knew that we had another five minutes. I simply stepped forward and kissed her lightly on the lips while she stayed perfectly silent and still, brush in mid-stroke. Then she smiled and kissed me passionately in return. By the light smile that returned to her face, as in the old days, I could see that the battle was over within her.

Campbell sauntered over just as I heard the street door slam shut behind her. As he handed me a cigarette and used the coffee pot, he looked over his shoulder and smirked. He asked if I wanted to explain what he thought he had seen walking down the stairs or should he assume that it was a figment of my over horny mind destroyed by too many drugs and self-abuse?

These interludes went on almost every weekend for almost six weeks. I didn't date, but spent time with Campbell sprawled over some battle map or at the dope den overdoing Santana. Belle and I ate early breakfasts or very late dinners, laughed, listened to music, but mostly just made love and talked. I was careful to tell her I loved her only once per session, avoided any mention of the Veemie and never said anything that suggested that I expected her the next weekend, for which I was grateful. Most of the time Belle made it to me on both Friday and Saturday nights of the weekend. To this was added a couple of mysterious weeknight visits and one weekend that she did not show at all. I found out, on her next visit, that the Veemie had signed out to his parent's residence and they had simply spent the weekend together in a hotel in DC. To this news I asked if the Veemie was sleeping with her also and how she felt about having two lovers at once. What would he do if he knew about me as I knew about him? I realized that questions like this were rude and destructive, but I found that, romantic or not, the situation was becoming intolerable. It was destroying me that she would walk out of here with part of me still inside her only to smile when meeting him with a loving fiancée's kiss. She would spend the day with him, laugh with him, build a future with him; while she would sleep and dream with me that night. I had visions of crashing the Ring Dance to be a kind of Dustin Hoffman character out of <u>The Graduate</u>. While I could be very sane and rational during the day, I was still very much in love with Belle and the time we spent at night was furiously passionate and very intense.

My life at school had picked up. I could totally dive into my classwork without any competition from a social life. Weekends were still spent at the house or with Campbell. I would not date, of course, but would range around any of the normal activities talking and being friendly till about 10:30 or so when I would return to my apartment.

The guys next door knew of course and Greg probably guessed, which meant that Vicki was in on it. Everyone observed a sense of oblivious denial concerning Belle and I, at least around me. It seemed that the affair was a strict secret from most of the outside world. Since this was an illicit romance, I guess it stayed the subject of gossip, not discussion, among the brothers and certainly nobody talked of it to me. I think that it gave me a kind of wounded, but gallant trooper status among the house brothers. I imagined that some probably thought that I was stupid or weak to put up with that treatment from a girl, but they didn't know what it was like after she would knock on my door.

It was getting hard to keep up the pretense that I didn't expect a future. I knew things could not continue this way for long. Playing by the rules allowed her to have and eat her own cake, but it was destroying me. Part of me wanted to re-establish my pride by "taming the shrew" or win the girl for the movie's happy ending. Part of me realized that my love would mean nothing if I destroyed myself (whatever that was) in the process of loving her. I would win her or lose her; but I'd had enough of the life in the middle, especially this middle of shadows.

It was the first week of April and spring was in high gear with foliage, warmth and optimism—all racing for May and the summer beyond. I called Belle and told her that I wanted to see her that night, a Monday. She sounded surprised on the phone, but agreed. The whole hour drive I planned my moves and words carefully. I wasn't sure of whether I wanted to win or lose, but it had to end that night, one way or another. I was not convinced that I would lose out of hand. She had risked a lot to continue seeing me, both in terms of her relationship with the Veemie, her peer group at Macon and her own internal sanity. This had to be eating her up as well. I sat in Wright's smallest dating parlor and smoked while I waited for her to make it down. It was funny sitting there as a guest after being almost a resident of the dorm just a few months prior. Belle walked in trying to be her happy, gracious self. I stood and held her at arms length. After a suitably meaningful pause, I kissed her lightly and continued to look in her eyes. She had doubt in her expression. I knew at that exact second that I would lose. She, on the other hand, probably just wondered what was up. I started talking to her softly and steadily without taking my eyes from her. I was shaking but knew that I had to get the words out.

"You know that I love you…don't you?"

"Yes" almost inaudible as she whispered, and knew not to break the spell.

"You know that I want you not just at night…but in the day…every day…or…at least…to try for every day…?"

"Yes."

"I want you to come home—to Lex—with me now…I'll get you back for class in the morning…but come with me now…" With that she started to smile as if the price I was asking was payable and would not disrupt the arrangement. "and this weekend…and the next…and home with me for Spring break." She exhaled and looked as if she had folded from the inside. She knew in an instant, before an instant, what I was now asking just as I knew what her answer was to be.

She frowned and pulled slightly away. "No…no…I…can't…." the words were coming so softly, but so clearly that I could have sworn we were using telepathy to communicate. "…I am so very sorry…but I know you know that…please trust me enough to know that…" I did. It didn't help the hurt, but I did. I was crying silently as I looked at her. The tears would not stop going down my cheeks. I fought the sobs, but felt better now that it was over, again.

I touched her cheek. "Bye" and with that, I opened the parlor door and simply walked out of the dorm without looking back. Safe in the car, I started to breathe again, wiped my eyes, lit a cigarette and drove back to Lex.

Campbell followed me into my apartment and just listened. I carried on for almost an hour. I was pissed at her for ruining my Senior year, pissed at the Veemie for living, but, by the end, mostly relieved that it was over. It was not going to destroy the spring as it had the first two semesters of Senior year. He knew that I was profoundly hurt and, late at night, I would bring Belle and our relationship up, in the quietest of conversations for years to come. He knew, and I did too, there was spring break to patch up the wounds then half of April, and all May to spend in the fun of our History Honors Seminar. It was to be in those activities rather than parties, dates and plans of social futures, that we would savor the last moments of our life at W&L. He didn't say all that. All he did was ask me along for a Hilton Head adventure (he used the word "Atrocity") for the week of Spring Break. He continued to talk about my paper for the seminar which was a sure winner even though he was always probing for holes in my defenses. We ended the night with a four hour discussion over 18th century tactics and whether the Brits were fit adversaries for the Frogs or had the Prussians carried the brunt of the War of Austrian Succession as most historians seemed to feel. Dawn found us exhausted, out of cigarettes, but with the night's decision and its associated pain purged for the time being.

The next day, I put on my R.O.T.C. Ranger uniform and delivered the last, remaining bag of Belle's stuff to the dorm at VMI. On the way over, I daydreamed of emptying it with her frilly underwear, spare birth control pills and the like spilling out over the desk while all the cadets were at attention (after all, I was an officer) and thus humiliating her and her Veemie forever. Instead, I just told the guard to get it to the Veemie and left no other message. It was enough for me that he know—not only that it was over, but that it had been in the first place.

The campus, especially the front campus, with its long sloping lawn and trees was exploding with early summer flowers. Leaves and buds, even the warm breeze seemed to welcome my return as I walked back toward W&L from the main VMI barracks. In the afternoons, especially warm sunny afternoons, the campus was an informal place. Groups of students sat on the lawn, drank soda on the steps of the co-op and guys could always be found tossing baseballs or playing lacrosse in the quad. While the girls had always occupied the more colorful of the three and a half years' operations, the school, the atmosphere, its aura had provided a gentle layer of protective foundation. Without the college being the institution it was, nothing beyond grades, exams and papers would have happened. W&L, with its white pillars and red brick not only looked like the idyllic college, but was. Lectures, debates, books to be read and papers to be written, had provided the sustenance—the body of the life for which the romantic concerns had only been the skin. It all became very clear to me that day as I walked back to my apartment, to change back into my jeans and to study for my final.

CHAPTER 12

*H*ilton Head promised to be, and was, a legendary adventure and a chance to put the year's romantic disappointments behind me. Campbell and I went down with two other brothers. One of them had "borrowed" his parent's condo on the island for Spring Break. While this was a true beach resort, being almost totally private and nestled near the sleepy town of Savannah, Georgia, it did not compete with the raucous popularity of Fort Lauderdale among college kids. This was a resort where kids came to visit their wealthy grandparents, the rich gave wedding receptions, and where the local girls came to work at hotels and restaurants. One of the benefits of these jobs must have been the chance to meet affluent young men. It was quiet and low key, but the beaches and the girls we found there were beautiful. This was precisely the environment for which we had been looking.

The four of us spent the week doing only what came to mind and, often, not much of that. It was an easy life of sleeping late, dozing on the beach and attempting to form a group to meet the shrimp boats returning from a day on the Atlantic. Pounds of shrimp could be purchased for a pittance. We would find a bunch of college age kids (or close to that age—if they were girls), to clean and shell them whereupon I would produce pounds of scampi from the condo's kitchen to be washed down with gallons of cheap, very cheap champagne. Our advertising term for these nightly events was "Shrimp Orgies." Almost every night we each found ourselves paired with some reasonably presentable date who would at least claim to be above 18. All four of us tried for waitresses, though, as they seemed to have few qualms about sleeping with mere acquaintances if there was a chance of an advantageous romance or opulent fun. Doze, talk, read or just wander around looking for fellow partiers during the day and Shrimp Orgies at night—a true student existence.

Both Saturdays we crashed wedding receptions at the best hotel on the island. Dressed in blazers and slacks, we became whatever we needed to be to get in and through the event. We were the fraternity brothers of the groom to the bride's family, or friends of the brother of the bride to the groom's. With our W&L polish and experience hob-nobing with rich people, we had the intellectual resources to bring it off; or at least thought we did, which is more than half the battle. To us, it was a challenge to see ourselves successfully play this game of nerves and wit. It was the closest we ever came to fictional adventure as we manufactured personalities and pasts to go with our assumed identities at the receptions. In the eight days we were on the island those two nights provided us the best company and entertainment. Campbell and I shared the drive back to Lex. It was quiet in the car most of the time as the realization hit that these times and the ability to have these times, was fast drawing to a close.

The final six week semester at school was the completely consuming college experience. It was a good precursor for the graduate school life to come, but compared to the college life before, it was one of incredible intellectual intensity. For me, without a date, but with the almost constant company of Campbell, it became a great final act. Twice a week we would spend three or four hours in History Seminar and about that much time in its daily preparation. The rest was reserved for us to gorge ourselves on our life's last totally free era. Since both Campbell and I had finished our papers before the spring, there was absolutely no pressure but that of graduation; or better stated, preparing oneself for the process of graduation.

The History Seminar Room on the top floor in Washington Hall was about twenty-five feet long encasing an ancient oval oak table. Arranged around the table were large, green leather "wing-back" chairs. The backs of the chairs were high and large enough that one could hide himself from the seminar leader to avoid questioning or to daydream about whatever was to become the evening's activity. There were portraits on the wall of long forgotten deans and prints of the Virginia countryside out of some colorful 19th century publication. The windows were high on the walls and light shone through always cutting visible beams in the smoke filled air. Like many of the row chairs found in the classrooms, the edge of the table showed the carved signatures of class members almost a century old. We added ours in hidden moments. The room could have been a transplanted study from some British club in it furnishings and aura. At 12:30 on Tuesdays and Thursdays ten students and one of the History professors would meet in the room armed with notebooks, coffee and cigarettes. Each student was prepared to "discuss" one of the other students' papers. This work was to be not more than fifty pages in length, but had to be a significant piece of "Historical Study" which the department would copy and distribute to the other seminar members a week in advance of the discussion date. Most of us had been in the same classes for over three years, so we knew a lot about the other guys' frames of reference, interests, weaknesses and strengths. This came in handy, for after the initial commentary from the professor and the student presenting the paper, it was a free-for-all, a donnybrook of scholastic debate.

This seminar became, for me, the ultimate class. Being my last class, it occupied the correct place in my career at W&L. No other experience compared with this demonstration of what W&L trained a boy to do or to be. To be successful here, one had to be very good at all four of the essential elements of the liberal arts: reading; writing;

thinking and speaking. Moreover, the thinking and speaking elements were under the pressure of a fast flowing and wide ranging
argument. Leaving the seminar room we would find ourselves totally
exhausted after what was scheduled to be a three hour, but often
lasted four or more, argument. It was so intense that we all lost perspective; that it was only a history grade and not our lives on the line.
As we became increasingly veteran, we realized that this was what
college or studying was all about and found it wonderful. Our problem was, of course, it was the end of college and life was not about
this, but about jobs, graduate school, the army or whatever—not
these hours twice a week on top of Washington Hall. That, too,
became increasing apparent.

I volunteered for the second presentation. I never liked to be first,
but always wanted to be as close to it as possible, thereafter. I did well
and, more important, had the best time ever during my stay in Lex in
or out of bed. Out of the ten guys, I gained three allies and since I
had been living my subject; "The 1904 British Army Reforms of R. B.
Haldane" for the better part of a year, I was prepared for any attack. I
was no subtle artist of the debating ambush. I met every attack
straight on: bearing facts to beat those who would argue and well
phrased retorts for those who would try to make subjective ground.
Campbell was always, and expected to be, on both sides. He, being a
true anarchist, seemed to delight in jumping to the aid of whoever
seemed to need it the most. Thank God, it was he and not Dimitri,
who had been chosen for this class. Campbell at least retained some
sense of loyalty and decorum—Dimitri who was writing a History
Honors Project, would have just worked as an ally of whoever promised to spill the most blood.

I began to excel, or felt that I did, in the art of speaking effectively
on a subject or in explaining some line of thought. While others
would question or merely point out an error; I could not only illus-
trate, but capitalize on it. Good sounding and properly chosen words
flowed from me almost thoughtlessly. It was not only a gift of gab in

terms of aesthetics, but I became increasingly effective with it as well. I tried to tie my points into a framework of defense or objection that the others seemed unable to do in the context of a many sided argument. I was, fortunately, political enough not to step on any of the points the professor put forth in his opening remarks; however; past these, there were no sacred cows. While I did not prevail all the time, I was in the lead often and felt that I had finally found my place.

Other than preparation and attendance at the seminar, our time was totally free. Often, we organized expeditions to ride inner-tubes down through the nearby Goshen Pass rapids on the Maury River. While not quite the Colorado, it was an exciting, if not a bit dangerous, way to spend a hot summer afternoon. In the quiet pools between each series of rapids one could drink ice cold beer that was tied to the tube. If one worked parking the cars properly, four trips could be made in about three hours which made for a great afternoon in the sun. There was intramural softball or the back yard games of baseball for traditional team athletics. When it rained we restarted the house Bridge games though they paled in comparison to those of the past. It made me think of and miss Mickey. After dinner there were war games with Campbell or a visit to the den for some Santana, Pink Floyd or maybe some Deep Purple to cap off the day.

Through April and May we were enjoyably distracted by outdoor sports, study and other pastimes, all of us sensed, though, it was fast coming to a close. Many times we would wander into each other's apartments, ones we hadn't visited in months, just to talk with no real purpose, point or subject in mind. Often we would fantasize aloud about how great it would be if we could do this whole thing one more time. The idea of going through four more years, knowing what we knew then, was fraught with exciting possibilities. We would go for true "Senseless Roadtrips" to White Sulpher Springs just to do so, or go to the Truck-stop, or up to Staunton just to be together one more time. While we did not consciously exclude any of the underclassmen, they lost much of their importance in our consideration of what was said and done. They had slowly become shadows to our lives; we knew they wouldn't really exist for us in a few months. It was then that I realized how Mickey and all before him must have felt about us as second semester Seniors. It was no longer months or even weeks, but the end (or the future) was near enough to be expressed in days. College ceased to be real; it took on a dreamlike quality into which W&L and Lexington fit well.

Campbell and I would sit up till dawn, maybe with Cal or just by ourselves, to philosophize about our world, what we would do in it and about our past at W&L. Much of it was just sentimental, adolescent reasoning or lines of thought brought to an oral state by exhaustion, being a bit stoned or simply the nervous concern for the future. He was never as talkative as I. He would often speak only several sentences to my paragraph upon paragraph, slowly spun out in the night like some long story. More often than not, I would talk about how this part of our lives was at once our zenith and yet only its beginning. We would never again be this free and thus be able to have this much fun.

We were free to be childish or adult; frivolous or mature, without thought about its implications on our life on a grander scale. We could wear what we want, have our hair the way we desired, associate with whom we chose and be who we wanted to be with very little pressure from the "real" world. We could, furthermore, change as many of those things as often as our whim dictated. Never would we date girls with such thoughtlessness as to the consequences of our romances. We had lived when it was best to be a student; during the height of student status in terms of lifestyle and absence of control. We had been able to play like children, wander aimlessly through several years like adolescents and yet taste the joys, sorrows and emotions of life as an adult. We knew that we were lucky to have this and were amply thankful for our freedom throughout this endeavor. As long as we produced the grades expected of us, found the money from parents, loans, scholarships or the army; we were free from parental control, legal scrutiny—even censure for the most outlandish of activities. It had been great, but it was over for we had to start our real lives that June. We were days away from awakening from this beautiful dream and not one of us wanted to awaken.

Graduation would start the decades of career, family and purpose that the education had shielded us from and for which it had prepared us. Somehow or another I knew that we would all gain some level of success in the world. It was our birthright. We had earned a measure of it by performing, at some level of proficiency, the necessary acts at W&L. A few of us, perhaps, would gain the level of some of the fathers; rich and powerful men; but almost all would ride in the upper cushion of comfort that America promised boys such as us. Vietnam had ended that Christmas, so the army was just another two year experience before we all started the grind of job—which even we were beginning to think of as careers—marriage and kids. During the last few days of school the future didn't look as bleak as it looked boring and traditional. We all knew that we could extend it a couple of years; the army, graduate or law school; but sooner or later we would cut our hair and, like it or not, become successful.

The night before our parents arrived, the Seniors had one last blowout at the house. It was beer, dope and music. Except for the dope and that it was mostly Seniors (almost all the underclassmen having gone home), it could have passed for the first night of rush from the old days. We were not "Earls," "Peer Groupers" or in the middle, but Seniors whose parents were expected in a few hours and wanted to get in one more bash before we became children again (and even that for the last time). We were survivors and looked back at the casualties—those who left or flunked out or just disappeared. The boys around the Chapter Room that night were both victors of their lives so far, but yet, with that victory, merely uninitiated beginners in real life. Greg and I took a breather from the dope, booze and music by walking "one last time" to the hill. There we sat on the front steps of Lee Chapel and looked at the Colonnade. It was beauti-ful, the pillars and red brick glowing in the circles of light cast by the hanging lamps, with just a hint of breeze rustling the trees and grass. Such a sight, especially on one's last night, had to be significant.

As we smoked our second cigarette in silence, I finally asked him what he thought would happen to us all. He and I listed them off, one by one, each with some either dire or desirous end or the simple and expected dissolution into upper-middle class society. Each was primarily labeled by the career—Lawyer, CPA, businessmen, what-ever. We agreed that Campbell would never grow up. He might get married, even spawn children, but in reality he would always be up in the hills alone or bent over some terrain map replaying one of his-tory's military feats. Maturity would merely require him to hide it all a bit better. I told Greg that he would marry Vicki (at which he laughed), run his dad's business reasonably well, become over-paid, too important, be prone to drive expensive sports cars and chase women by the time he was 40. He looked at me, chuckled, shook his head and crushed out his cigarette. It was as if my words had caused him and me to picture a common image that was both plausible and, we both knew too well, probable. After a suitable pause, I told him that I would marry, have a kid or so, and feel guilty about my future success because I wouldn't, didn't or couldn't change the world. Greg paused and looked at me as if to say that we already know precisely what was to be. Success as seen from the outside would come to almost all of us; but success by what we saw was possible within us, or what we really wanted from ourselves would come rarely. W&L had educated us to see and understand these possibilities and our potential; it had given us the basic tools to realize it among ourselves, but it was us that had to, now, construct our lives. We, who knew we were self-centered and cynical yet innocent and optimistic, would find our place in the world's machine. I am sure, we were thinking the same things—trying to figure out the biggest questions we had yet faced—What now? Soon he smiled and pulled a long "J" from his shirt pocket. "Here, let's smoke this on the way back to the house."

This is where the credits started rolling for the movie of my years in Lex. These were the slowly moving variety playing over the final moments of the movie. From the major stars to the assistant key grips and even the buildings, everyone and thing was mentioned and thanked. But, it, meaning my years in Lex, the college life of a life-time—IT—was, indeed, over.

Our parents came into town the next day and assumed total con-trol without a moment's thought for the instantaneous revolution or better stated, the exact same assumptions they held when they dropped us off four years previous. Except for our being a touch green around the gills, we were ready to meet them. There was the Army R.O.T.C. commissioning ceremony, the non-religiously affili-ated church service, and our Senior dinner held in the Freshman dining hall after which we were asked for money by the Alumni Association for the first time.

The morning of graduation was warm and sunny. As we waited in line I snapped the picture of Campbell and Cal that still sits on my desk. One by one the 253 names were read off and we got our real sheepskin diploma (another of the school's deals of the cen-tury—being purchased in bulk around 1905), handshake and made our entrance, by walking across a makeshift stage, into adult life. After the ceremony there were quick conversations and introduc-tions of parents to faculty and friends. By an hour after, we were all on our way to the future. Though we might visit Lexington many times hence it would never be the "Lex" of our home as it had been. After three hard years of striving, and one year of complete domin-ion, it took us only moments to surrender Lex to the rising class.

I gave my parents a letter that night. This was my final gesture of thanks for all the work they had accomplished to get me there, keep me there and, frankly, deal with me while I was there. In it I tried to explain to them what I thought my four years at W&L had meant to me. I didn't know it wouldn't mean as much then as it would after 30 years. Albeit, written on the evening of graduation, it was written too close to provide very good perspective, I tried to give them a flavor of what I knew then.

∾

1 June 1973

Dear Mother and Father,

Having to write about the meaning of my four collegiate years in Lexington is a little like writing about one's summer vacation. How can you list or explain what has been learned in this short, but probably most important, span of years. Perhaps it is enough to say that I have learned. I use the word "learned" meaning more than the knowledge of History that I have amassed—it is much more than that. It probably means gaining a conception of life and of living—of gathering data on myself and others in my world; maybe the world itself.

These four years have seen me go through a lot. I have been in love and learned how to love. It has been a maturing (bad word) experience of seeing people as more than just "other persons." It has been a growth of my mind in order to become a man, a person, a human. I have felt the touch of a woman and walked with her hand in hand, only to find myself, once more, alone. These four years have become my life's foundation. The thoughts, actions and passions involved have been instructive. I believe; No, I hope that this has given me insight.

This insight, when combined with the other skills gained here; that of thought, perspective and feeling; is what my stay in Lex, at Washington and Lee, has been all about. College doesn't really prepare you for the future—it provides you with a past. A past I know that I can draw upon during the years ahead. I know that it has been hard for you, because for the first time in your lives, you have not been the central figures in my life these last four years. In fact, the people that have helped shape it have been apart and unknown to you. Know that you have been there nonetheless.

I find myself here today not being able to understand where I've been or where I am going. W&L has been the final process in of making me—me. I don't know what to say other than "thanks" for the help and support. Both you and this school have provided the foundation

for a life I can not yet foresee. College has not left me happy or satis-
fied, but provided me the capability to go on from here.

Thank you, both of you, again.

Yours,

As we drove from the valley I knew that the credits had stopped,
the movie had ended and only the trailing bit of the theme music
remained. It had been one of those "modern" endings. I saw it to be
a bit like <u>Shane</u> except no one was calling after him.

Epilogue

If one is expecting a list of who was who or what happened to each character—there is none, there can be none—because this is fiction. The 25th reunion, some years back, gave us more insight as to what happened as we drove out of Lex that day in May so many years ago—but there were no stories ended. What I found interesting during the reunion is the real kernel of character I knew of my classmates and house brothers was, essentially, still true and real. There were many refinements, but few real changes. At that reunion, a previous manuscript of this book was circulated and seemingly much enjoyed although some one related that a few people from Macon were a bit concerned. They needn't be—for with all the years, the tragic marriages, the jobs, the money spent, children sired, the Cinelli, and Colnago, the races won and lost, the wonderful love I finally share with the wonderful woman (the true girl of my dreams) with whom I now live—it's all been for the best—at least for me—because it has produced a journey that has always been interesting and isn't yet over.

About the Author

Andrew G. Hollinger graduated from Washington and Lee University in 1973 and, after a stint as an armor officer in the Army, earned his Masters from Emory University in 1976. He has held a variety of positions in Information Technology management and consulting organizations beginning with 17 years with IBM. His latest was as a Partner with an internet consulting firm. He has written and spoken widely on Business Technology and Business Strategy issues. He lives in Bedford, Texas with the woman of his dreams, his 20-year-old son and his 3-year-old daughter. He is an avid road bicycle racer and is an officer and life member of Team Bicycles, Inc. He is Webmaster of several internet website sites among them; www.aghollinger.org and www.teambicyclesinc.org. When not at work, with his family or in front of the computer, he is pedaling across the prairie atop his beloved Cinelli or his magnificent Colnago C40. At 51, his soul keeps writing checks his mind and body have trouble cashing.

0-595-22236-6

F
234
.L5
H65 00
2002

CPSIA information can be obtained at www.ICGtesting.com
Printed in the USA
LVOW051542120912

298510LV00003B/4/A